RED HAZE

Scott Smith

Independently Published in Houston, TX for Ambassadors United, a 501c3 non-profit organziation dedicated to rescuing souls and ending human trafficking. Visit ambassadorsunited.org for more details.

Cover and Interior Design: Scott Smith

Red Haze

Printed in the United States of America

AUTHOR'S NOTE

The plot and characters of this book are fictional; however, the information regarding human trafficking is factual. I drew upon my background in anti-human trafficking operations to provide readers with accurate and purposeful information in this regard. Readers will encounter some darker elements which may be deemed offensive by some readers. Because I wanted my teenage children to be able to read and enjoy my book, I refined some of the content to make it suitable for a wider audience.

PROLOGUE

Chief backed out of the front door of the old farmhouse, the porch creaking under his black, snakeskin cowboy boots, Mrs. Eden on his heels. "Ma'am, my team and I will do our absolute best to find your daughter. As I said, we specialize in high-risk operations," he restated in his twangy West Texas drawl.

"Promise me you'll bring our Samantha back home to us!" Momma's bloodshot and swollen eyes gave way to an aggressive resolve—almost like a wounded momma bear unable to protect her cub, but still with a bit of fight left.

"Ma'am, in all honesty, I can't make that prom—"

"Promise me!" She raised her voice and closed her eyes tight, unable to keep the tears from escaping.

He hesitated, grabbing the back of his neck, but seeing no way of avoiding her, finally relented.

"Yes, ma'am…I…I promise," he mumbled, removing his black, sweat-soaked cowboy hat, exposing a full head of sandy-brown hair mixed with tinges of gray.

With a defeated look, he tucked the envelope of cash into his back pocket and spun away, hurrying to escape the imminent eruption of raw emotion.

Come on, Chief. You know better than to make that promise? The girl has been missing for several days in a third world country—you don't even know if she's alive, he thought, silently scolding himself as he reached his pickup truck, his gait slightly unsteady from the emotionally draining meeting.

He climbed inside and felt the truck's warm vinyl bench seat, looking over his once perfectly pressed polo shirt, now wrinkled and saturated from Mrs. Eden's tight embraces and uncontrolled sobbing, remnants of her shattered soul.

He rested his forehead on the steering wheel and closed his eyes, recalling the conversation, wondering if he said the right words. He had wanted to tell Mrs. Eden and her husband that their daughter was likely gone forever, but they wouldn't have been able to handle it; that message was best delivered by someone who understood death on a different level anyway—a pastor or priest maybe—not a mercenary contractor who had sent scores of people to their grave.

He placed the girl's two-year-old senior portrait on the dashboard, glancing at it as he drove the lonely highway from Oklahoma back to West Texas. She had won the Homecoming crown that year, and anyone could see why. As the sun's early morning rays danced across the photo, it highlighted her light blonde hair, emerald-colored eyes, and a smile that could brighten even the most miserable soul.

Chief wanted more than anything to deliver on his reluctant promise, but there was an unnerving darkness overshadowing him as he considered what needed to occur for the rescue operation to be successful. Unbeknownst to him, that darkness wasn't even a glimpse of the danger he and his special operations team were about to encounter.

ONE
THE RESORT

Days Earlier

The Myanmar Air Dragon 747 airliner came to a screeching halt on Mandalay International's runway and the passengers stood to stretch their legs from the long flight, impatiently waiting to disembark. Standing out from the Burmese passengers were Mike Carpenter and Sam Eden, 20-year-old sweethearts from rural America, eager to begin the backpacking vacation of their dreams and erase their pasty white skin from the long winter season.

"Phew. That was a long flight," Mike suggested as he opened the overhead compartment to retrieve their backpacks, revealing his short physique. Sam was five-foot-eight and he was a good three inches shorter, two if he spiked up his sandy brown hair.

"Great things take time, Mikey," she smiled.

"I still don't understand why we had to come all the way to Burma," he grumbled, his board shorts, flip-flops and patchy facial hair a dead giveaway of his youthful status. "We could have gone to France or Italy and saved at least ten hours—and I'm still not convinced Burma is safe."

Sam looked at him and smiled from the corner of her mouth. "They call it Myanmar now, Mike, and we already had this discussion. TJ said it's perfectly safe...you know how the news hypes everything up. "

"Right. TJ. The tour guide you found on social media, but with no website. He barely spoke English when I called him."

"Don't you think it's a little too late for this, Mike? Besides, he was so nice on the phone, and the pictures he sent...oh so amazing! Everyone goes to France and Italy—and it's not like we had the money for Europe. Just wait till we see the Burmese villages and beaches in person. We'll be the talk of Elk City!"

"Sure, and they'll also be talking about how they think we're having...you know..."

As they spoke, an older Asian woman gawked at them as though she understood their conversation.

"So what, we're not," Sam retorted somewhat loudly. "Let the people talk; that's what they do in small towns. You're acting like we're still teenagers. We're 20 now, and we can do whatever we want," she smiled widely, clutching his hands in hers. "C'mon, we're already here. Let's make the most of it!"

"You know what, you're right; we're gonna have a blast!" he replied, trying to change his attitude, but his words didn't match his unshakable apprehension.

"Yes! That's the spirit!" Her face lit up. "Now, I need to let TJ know we're here. He said he's not far from the airport...oh, and I need to let my mom know we landed safely. She's such a worrywart; she actually wants me to text twice a day...ugh!"

"Same with mine. She's just being a mom."

"I guess you're right," she suggested, lifting off her retro sunglasses and trying to flatten the wrinkles on her white tank top and tan cargo shorts from sitting so long. Moments later the door on the fuselage opened and they exited onto the jet bridge.

Sam nearly skipped through the airport terminal, her pack hoisted over her shoulder, contemplating the adventure awaiting them. She was grinning in anticipation, but Mike moseyed several steps behind, trying to ignore his sense of dread while scores of mostly Asian travelers toting luggage and briefcases hurried about.

They neared the terminal's exit when Mike caught a glimpse of dark storm clouds through one of the large plate-glass windows.

He stopped and stared, fascinated by their swirling. They were like a dragon ready to release its fury on the earth, the shadow of its wings swallowing up the mid-afternoon sunlight.

"Hey, I thought the captain announced it was mostly sunny out?" Mike called out to Sam who was a few paces ahead of him.

"It's the start of the monsoon season. It's probably like Florida—wait an hour and it's sunny again," she suggested as the automatic sliding door in front of her opened up, prompting her to walk through.

"Mike, you've got to see—" the automatic door slid closed, severing her sentence like a guillotine. He couldn't hear her, but he could see her excitement, and he rushed out and looked up.

"What is it? What are you looking at?"

"Don't you see it?"

"See what? What am I looking for?" He wasn't sure if he was supposed to be looking at a plane or something in the clouds.

"The gold…the idols…the culture!"

"Umm, nope, I don't see it…but I feel the hellish humidity."

"Stop it!" she punched him in his arm. "You see that the airport is made to look like an Asian temple. This is a sign of all the amazing things we'll see. Here, look at this…" she replied, hooking her arm through his and pulling a magazine from her back pocket.

"Look at these beautiful beaches!" she exclaimed, flipping through the pages.

"Honestly, they do look amazing."

"You know what? We should go snorkeling. What do you think?" she asked giddily.

"Umm…you do know the waters surrounding the Burma coastline have the highest concentration of sharks on the earth, right?"

She abruptly unhooked her arm and faced him, her lips tightly pinched together and placing her pointer finger over his partially-opened mouth.

"Nope. No more Debby Downer attitude."

Mike coolly pulled her hand away. "I just mean there are a lot of unknowns about this place."

"That's exactly why it's going to be perfect for us! Wait and see!"

They stood under the airport's covered concourse for a few minutes when a faded yellow motorcycle taxi rumbled up and stopped in front of them. It was a crude vehicle, a small motorcycle with what looked like a wheelbarrow bed attached at the back and a blue canopy extending over it.

"Oh, Mikey, look at that taxi! Isn't it the cutest thing ever?"

"Um, no. Not really," he replied, studying at the Asian driver who appeared to be in his mid-30s. He wore a black, lightweight leather jacket, tight-fitting jeans rolled up slightly at the ends and a pair of round, Jon Lennon-style sunglasses, which were a good match for his oval face and center-parted black hair.

"Hello, nice meet you. My name TJ. I be you guide," he stated enthusiastically, but they could barely hear him over the motor's rumble.

Sam nearly yelled as she held her hand out to greet him. "Hello, TJ. Nice to finally meet you in person. I'm Sam, and this is my boyfriend, Mike."

TJ turned the engine off and stood up from the motorcycle and that's when Sam noticed two large scars under TJ's left eye extending down to his chin—that and the fact that he and Mike were the same height, which made her snicker under her breath.

"You see scar, yes?" TJ asked.

She was embarrassed that she had been caught staring. "No, I...well...yes, I did."

"Tiger," TJ replied, running his hand along the scar down to his sparse, black goatee beard.

Her eyes were wide open. "You got clawed by a tiger?"

Seeing her uneasiness, he spoke fast. "No worry. Many year ago. Tiger no problem here...So, I no sure you serious come here," he stated, changing the subject. "You so young. What about parent?"

9

"That was a bit of an obstacle, but we're adults now," she replied and continued. "Honestly, we would have gone elsewhere had you not been so personable. You made me feel like I've known you forever. Oh, and the video ad you put up of how safe it is and your years of guide experience made it an easy decision. Speaking of that, when do you want your guide fee?"

"No worry about fee. I get later. Make sure you best stay ever," he smiled. "By the way, I love American. Beautiful and nice people...plus, Michael Jackson."

Mike spoke up to not appear rude. "So, TJ, you enjoy Michael Jackson's music?"

"Yes, look," he beamed as he removed his jacket, revealing a graphic T-shirt with a print of the late pop singer. "My favorite shirt. I wear when meet American. I went to Jackson Thailand concert '96 when I was kid. So radical!"

When TJ removed his jacket, Mike caught a glimpse of a faded tattoo; something that looked like an Asian symbol, partially hidden under his shirt sleeve.

"Oh, yes, very nice shirt," he suggested, nodding in agreement, still eyeing the tattoo.

"Where you want start? You want check-in motel?"

Sam beamed, excited to begin their adventure. "Yes, let's check into our hotel, and we can talk about the best place to snorkel," she finished, batting her eyelashes at Mike.

"Really, Sam? You still want to go snorkeling after what I told you?" he asked firmly, ignoring her attempts to soften him up but finding it difficult to do.

"Look, let's go to the beach and we can go from there. We don't have to go snorkeling if you don't want to, but we can at least check it out. If it doesn't look safe, we won't even get in the water. Let's just enjoy an amazing view and get a nice dinner. Sound good?"

"Sound great!" TJ excitedly interjected, "I know best spot. Beach and fun cafe next to motel. You love. Hop in back. Short ride."

"That...umm...does sound great. I'm guess I'm up for it," Mike replied, helping Sam into the back of the motorcycle taxi.

"Okay, we here!" TJ yelled back as he drove off the highway and sped down a two-tracked dirt path. Surrounding them on every side were giant pine trees and thick, dark green, subtropical vegetation.

"I don't see anything but endless forest," Mike stated as the trees blurred by.

"There's probably a nice resort back here," Sam suggested as the sun became blocked out by the dark clouds that had caught up with them. She no sooner made the statement when they heard sporadic raindrops dancing along the canvas roof. She stuck her hand out and the cool droplets disintegrated on her warm skin. Within seconds, the drops assembled into a torrential downpour, so heavy they couldn't see but a few feet around them. Then, almost as quickly as it started, the rain stuttered back to a sprinkle and the overcast clouds cleared away, leaving behind a fresh, earthly aroma, a few puddles, and a stifling humidity.

"Man, it feels like I'm being smothered in a moist blanket," Mike complained, reaching in his pack for a small towel to wipe away the sweat.

"Seriously, Mike? It's summer. We'd have the same heat if we went to any other beach destination."

He glanced at her from the corner of his eye. She was right, but he wasn't about to let her know it.

TJ pulled into a clearing in the trees and up to a dilapidated building at the edge of a mostly dried up lake. The exterior looked like something from a horror movie, a combination of several single-story, Asian-style shacks joined together, about 70 feet long and propped up a few feet on thick stilts. The white paint on the wooden exterior had all but peeled away, the tin roof was speckled with rusty holes, and the windows were covered with plywood like the place was condemned or being prepped for a hurricane.

"I hope this isn't TJ's idea of the best spot," Mike criticized as he surveyed the rundown building with its crooked neon open sign and the handful of pecking hens near the entrance.

"Let's give it a chance," Sam whispered as she grabbed his hand. "Maybe it's more authentic. Plus, TJ said the rooms are free. We only have to pay a day fee, like a resort fee, I guess."

"Resort fee?" he muttered. "I know I didn't come half a world to resort to this."

"It's already getting dark and we don't want to offend TJ on our first day. Let's get through the night and if we don't like it, we'll get something else tomorrow," she stated, doing her best to ease his apprehension and convince herself at the same time.

"Hopefully we're backpacking tomorrow night because the open stars would be better than this place," he grumbled, rocking the motorcycle taxi as he jumped out.

Getting a closer look at the building, Mike spotted the same Asian symbol he had seen tattooed on TJ's arm, somewhat faded and peeling away. He studied it for a moment but didn't make much of it.

"Okay. Follow me!" TJ stated enthusiastically. "I show you around joint." He grabbed their packs, climbed a few steps to a solid metal door with a tiny tavern-like window and rang the doorbell with his foot.

Creaaaaaak! The door swung open into a small foyer area that looked as rundown as the exterior. A single red lamp sat on an end table, giving the entire room a ruddy glow and a peculiar burnt cherry-like odor rushed into their face.

"Come in," TJ smiled widely, motioning for them to step inside. They were both waiting at the door's threshold, clearly uneasy but trying not to show it.

"It get better. I show you best part...cabana area. Very nice. Mike, you pay fee, Okay?" TJ instructed as he sat their bags down and pointed to the front desk where an older, bald Burmese man was seated behind a front desk, watching six security monitors.

Mike reached inside his bag for his wallet and approached the desk, staring at the clerk's grungy V-neck shirt and too short pants. He was getting ready to ask about the price when the clerk stood up and yanked some of the money from his hand and sat back down in his chair.

"TJ…um…is this a real motel?" Mike asked as he placed his wallet back into his bag.

"Very real. You see. Leave pack and follow," he replied, grabbing a beer from an ice bucket behind the counter, his smile painted on his face.

TJ led the kids through an adjacent bar area where a handful of Burmese men relaxed in restaurant-style booths, the white smoke from their cigarettes appearing pink as it swirled under the dimly lit red lights. Soft music played in the background as the men sipped their alcoholic drinks and gawked at a young lady wearing a skimpy outfit. She was slow dancing alone on a small, wooden dance floor in the middle of the bar.

Sam walked in behind TJ and the men's attention quickly shifted to her. They ogled and grinned in a seductive manner, but she continued on despite her discomfort, figuring it to be a typical Burmese bar.

Just get through the day, Sam. It's going to get better, she thought as she continued following TJ.

"This is sing area. How you say it…carekey?" TJ did his best to say the word karaoke as he unlocked the metal door at the exterior of the bar area. He opened it up and stepped down on a dilapidated wooden deck that led to a sandy area with two tiki-style cabanas.

Taung the Man Lake was 50 feet past the cabanas, a large body of mostly stagnant water only a few inches deep due to the fact that they were coming out of the dry season.

"Please tell me this isn't the beach. There's hardly any water," Sam spoke aloud, no longer able to bridle her dissatisfaction. She gazed across the lake at the nearly dark sky, spotting the faint glow of the Mandalay city lights, wondering if Mike had been right about vacationing someplace else.

"Lake dry now. Great place though. Come alive at night. Dance. Sing. Build fire. Much sand. Build castle maybe," he smooth talked.

"Yes, there's certainly lots of sand out here," Mike stated sarcastically as he and Sam both looked at each other, their body language expressing their displeasure.

"I take you to room. You ask for two room, right?"

Neither of them responded, still overcome with disappointment.

Mike finally responded a few seconds later. "Oh, yes, right, two rooms."

TJ stepped back inside and ushered them through the bar area that had come alive. The music was louder, two additional young women were dancing, and it was now full of men of various ages.

"You see...much action," TJ stated, almost yelling to be heard over the loud Asian discotheque-style music. "Every Thursday, they play Michael Jackson set. Fun time," he replied, turning around to make sure they were behind him. He moved past the bar area and picked up their packs from the foyer, leading them down a long, red-lighted hallway that was lined with red shag fabric from the floor halfway up the wall.

"Here room. Other across hall," TJ indicated as he unlocked a padlock from one of the six guest rooms and opened the solid wood door. "Why not leave pack and join on dance floor?"

"We might do that," Mike replied, guardedly entering the room and quickly closing the door behind them.

"No make wait too long," TJ raised his voice to be heard through the door.

"Something's not right here," Mike whispered with his back to the door. As he scanned the room, he noticed a surveillance camera facing the bed. "There's no way a legit place is going to have padlocks on the outside of the doors and cameras in the rooms. And why is everything red? I'm about to go crazy because that's all I'm seeing—and I don't think this is a honeymoon spot."

14

"I know, Mike. I'm trying to stay positive, but this is looking worse by the second."

"Look at this," Mike plopped down on the bed, his face showing deep concern. "If this was a real motel, the bed would at least be made up and actually have pillows. And what's with the hard liquor on the end table here and that weird smell?"

"I...I don't know what to say," she stuttered. "I hoped it would get better, but it's super creepy...and I can't stand how those guys in the bar were gawking at me. There's no way I can sleep here."

"We can't just leave though. We don't know where we're at and it's already dark."

"Good point. I'm going to use the bathroom down the hall and then we can ask TJ if there's another place close by that we can stay at for the night."

"Sounds like a plan."

TWO
SPECIAL OPERATORS

Days Later

C hief pulled his truck off the barren highway onto a dirt path that extended through a sagebrush prairie and dead-ended at a quaint, 1870's Spanish mission church, complete with white stucco exterior, a red clay roof, and the original stained glass windows. A tiny cemetery was adjoined, sprinkled with a couple dozen cracked tombstones and deteriorating wooden crosses, ghostly relics of the families that once called the church home. But although the exterior of this building looked religious, its heart was fully black. Black drapes, black guns, and black ops. The church's soul had been converted into an office for Chief's private contractor team.

Chief parked his truck and stared out the window, captivated by the rhythmic swaying of the drought-parched wheatgrass in the warm breeze, lost in the thought of how he would introduce the volatile mission to his team—especially since it was irrational to him. Moments later, he stood inside the church, unable to recall his last few steps, his body operating on autopilot.

Still in a slight daze, Chief walked past the small kitchen and closet-sized armory, stopping inside the sanctuary area. He leaned against one of the bunkbed's frames, scanning the interior and settling on Mack, the oldest and most erratic operator on the team. Mack sat at a card table next to one of the windows, cleaning his new sniper rifle and suffusing the air with the gun bore cleaner's distinct rotten banana-like odor.

"You gonna come all the way in, or just stand back there creepin' 'round," Mack asked in his raspy, redneck-accented voice.

With his cover blown, Chief sauntered over, still mulling over the right words to present the mission. Mack had pinned back the blackout drape and the sun's late afternoon rays penetrated through the yellowish stained glass, outlining Chief's square jaw and causing his steely cobalt eyes to appear a limey shade of green.

"Mack, we've got a new op!" Chief announced excitedly, trying his best to hide his uneasiness, but his voice cracked slightly as though he was entering puberty.

"Where to this time?" Mack asked, still focused on his rifle cleaning, but not missing Chief's obvious nervousness.

"We're searching for a missing 20-year-old girl."

"Sounds easy enough. Where we spinning up to this time? Here in Texas or—"

"No, um, overseas." A single bead of sweat formed on Chief's temple, rolling down his beardless cheek for a plunge to the floor, eventually exploding on top of his boot.

"Well, that narrows it down," Mack's sarcasm was obvious. Chief drew in a long breath and held it for a few seconds. Unable to hold out any longer, he finally relented.

"Mack, the uh, the girl went missing in Myanmar."

Mack jerked around and locked his partially bloodshot and puffy hazel-colored eyes with Chief's. "Myanmar? You mean Burma! And you can't be serious!"

"One hundred percent serious, Mack. I've already deposited the family's payment. I just need to make sure you and the team are on board."

"I know you Delta Force boys like challenges and all, but this is madness. Did you forget about the brutal Burmese Military? We ain't ready for this type of contract. Protecting cargo ships from Somali skinnies and watchin' over some Iraqi oil fields is one thing, but this is crazy."

"Look, I'm not thrilled about it either, believe me, but the State Department gave that momma the runaround, and if we don't go, there's no chance she'll see her little girl again."

"That's your reasoning? Take a look around, Chief. Johnny's been hungover for the past month, Switch's brain is mush from all his gaming, and your new hire don't even believe in carryin' guns, much less killin' nobo—"

"Hey, I heard that…" Switch interrupted from several feet away, seated in front of three computer monitors, playing a first-person shooter video game.

"Chief, seriously brother, we'd need six months and at least a dozen more specialists to get ready for this type of op. I just ain't seein' how we pull this off," he reasoned.

"Look, here's the truth. We haven't had a solid contract in three months. This op will get us back current on the mortgage, plus give us some padding."

"Chief, speaking of money," Switch spoke up again, "some thrift shop pickers came by early this morning and wanted to buy the church's old steeple bell. I guess it's an antique."

"What?! Absolutely not! That's what gives this place its character," Chief argued.

"That and the fact that a bunch of former military guys live here and shoot scary guns out the windows," Switch responded, glancing at Mack who had reassembled his gun and opened the window for some target practice.

"Er…yeah…and don't forget about our resident ex-con," Mack reminded them both.

"Right, how could we forget about Bling," Chief somewhat mumbled, smiling from the corner of his mouth. "So, out of curiosity, how much were they offering for the old gonger?"

"Chief," Mack redirected, trying to stay focused on the main issue. "I ain't tryin' to step on your toes here, brother. I just wanna make sure you know what we could be dealing with. Burma is only a few hundred miles from Nam and it ain't nothin' like what you seen in Afghanistan. I still have nightmares of them POW camps."

"I get it, but no matter how hard I try to shake it, there's something inside me that says we're supposed to take this op."

Mack stayed quiet for a few seconds and finally responded. "Then we'll take it, but before I pack my gear bag, I need to know one thing."

"Sure, what is it?"

"Did you tell that girl's momma we ain't never done no search and rescue op? I know you advertise that and all, but—" he paused mid-sentence to align the scope's crosshairs on a practice target several hundred yards away.

Chief didn't answer, but he didn't have to.

"Hey, and speaking of full confessions," Mack spoke up again, "did you tell them what may have happened to her—especially since Burma is known for traffickin'?"

"Of course, but they said no one contacted them about a ransom."

"That ain't what I'm referrin' to, Chief."

"Look, if you're asking if I had the brass to suggest she might be held up somewhere being forced to provide favors to vile men—of course not!"

"Woah, there, brother, I'm only askin'. I know I couldn't tell no momma that, but last week I seen a show about how them Burmese gangs be forcing young girls into a life of slavery. Sick monsters…somebody outta kill all of them pieces of—"

"Boss, not to be all insensitive," Johnny spoke up, lying on his bunk, his hands behind his head and his words muffled through the black baseball cap covering his face, "but what's the bag on this gig anyway? Sounds risky."

"Risky?" Mack exclaimed as he chambered a bullet into his rifle. "I thought Rangers were always down for a good fight. Unless you're planning on skipping out to get married again— how many times has it been now? Five? And you're barely into your 40s," Mack let out a good laugh, his rotund stomach bouncing vigorously. Johnny sat up and glared at Mack while adjusting his dog tags over his military-green T-shirt, but Mack ignored him.

"Mack, I'm gonna get you a red suit to go with your long, white beard and jiggly belly. That way you can pass out presents at the old folk's home. You'll fit right—"

Boom! Mack squeezed the gun's trigger and the deafening sound filled the old sanctuary, followed by the distinct, firework-like smell of burnt gun powder.

Mack checked his shot through his scope. "What?! I'm way off target! Missed the zombie's head by a full meter! Someone must've messed with my rifle."

"You're just going blind from diabeetus and all your junk food eating," Johnny joshed, taking his typical jab at Mack who was a couple decades older than everyone else on the team and didn't look the part.

Switch spoke up, taking a break from his gaming. "Not to interrupt the family feud here but what are the chances this will be more than a body recovery? Parts of Burma are stuck in a perpetual civil war…the place is a mess."

"I'll be filling everyone in with a full briefing when Bling arrives. Y'all just get your minds right," Chief stated as he pulled up a map of Burma on his phone and jotted down some notes.

A half-hour later, the church's large wooden front doors swung open, making a loud creaking sound. For a few seconds, the sun's rays sliced through the opening, illuminating the dust and backlighting a dark silhouette figure like a scene from a western movie, only this wasn't a saloon, and the person was no gunslinger.

"Yo, I'm here!" Bling exclaimed, strolling inside in his typical swagger, decked out in a bright, sky blue jogging suit and perfectly matching Jordan shoes.

"Good thing you're so flashy, Bling. We might have missed you come in," Johnny heckled, poking fun at Bling's short stature. He was nearly five-foot-five with his patent leather-tipped Jordan shoes on.

"You always got them jokes, Johnny."

"Nah, I heard him bumpin' that lame gospel music from the highway," Mack stated. "What do you call them things in your trunk again?—woofers? If you ain't careful, you're gonna bump that old crucifix off that there wall and be on Heyzeus' naughty list," he jeered.

"Theys solid beats, Mack—stuff my mom's played when I was a kid. Good 90's Gospel. Yo, you should listen. Might smoove some of them stress lines on yo forehead."

"Wisdom lines, Bling," Mack retorted as Bling continued his stroll into the sanctuary.

"Yo, Chief, so what did I miss while I was gone?" Bling inquired. "I see y'all got the geek to take a recess from his videogame. Must be sorta serious."

Switch stayed silent, glaring at Bling beneath his high-powered, black-rimmed eyeglasses, trying to replicate a menacing eye squint, but his small frame and black, combed-over hair made him less than intimidating.

"Would you look at this? The Lollipop Kids are gonna have a rumble in Munchkin Land," Johnny laughed, moving over to the weight bench for a better view of the imminent fight.

"Guys, come on. Knock it off," Chief ordered. "Save your energy. Believe me, where we're going, you're gonna need it. Besides, this is the house of God."

"I was just flippin' Switch's switch," Bling remarked. "Ain't got no beef. Just my flesh axin' up. And this ain't no house of God...this here is a run-down buildin' contructioned by sinners...but peoples on the other hand, even y'all, are temples constuctioned by holy God for a pacific purpose."

"Here we go, again," Johnny protested. "Boss, why you gotta go and hire a holy-rollin', jailhouse preacher?"

"Wait, hold up, Johnny," Mack chimed in. "What Bling said is sorta deep. Makes me think a little."

"Yeah, we saw the smoke, Mack," Johnny scoffed. "Just do me a favor, Bling. Drop the made-up religion—and your made-up words."

"Ain't no made-up religion," Bling countered. "Tink 'bout it. If religious buildings were dat big a deal, da Devil be destroyin' 'em on the daily. Naw, son, ain't no one fightin' over these here buildin's. Dat's why Chief picked up dis old west, Tombstone-looking church for next to nothin'. Value increase when everyone after it. How much you tink human souls is worth when both God and da Devil battlin' over 'em—think about it, yo."

"Alright, enough guys," Chief interrupted. "Everyone take a seat. I need to fill y'all in on our new contract."

The team moved to the front of the sanctuary near Chief's personal office and spread out on the two remaining wooden church pews.

"Hey, Chief, I like this new look," Mack uttered with a grin. "It's like you're the priest and we're gettin' ready for your sermon."

"Yeah, except we're gonna do more than just talk…and I won't be taking your money. I'm actually gonna pay you for your time," Chief gave an exaggerated smile as he flipped over a whiteboard and wrote down two names.

"Several days ago, two 20-year-old kids, Samantha Eden and her boyfriend, Mike Carpenter, left rural Oklahoma for a backpacking adventure in Myanmar—aka Burma. No one has heard from them since arriving at Mandalay International."

Switch cut in. "Chief, so let me get this straight. That girl's parents just up and let her go with her boyfriend to an unstable foreign country?"

"From what I gathered, her parents did all they could to convince her not to travel to Burma, but the kids told them they were leaving with a larger group of friends. I suppose there wasn't much they could do to stop them because they are of age. However, her mom did share with me that they didn't leave in a group—it was just her and her boyfriend."

"Ah, we know what that's about," Johnny giggled. "Sounds like something I did as a youngster, but I wasn't as dumb as to do it in a third-world country."

"Yo, Chief, I don't know 'bout goin' to no Burma," Bling interjected, his voice somewhat shaky. "Ain't dat where them Burmese Pythons is?"

Switch laughed. "Oh, look, he's scared of a little snake. Don't worry, Bling, they're only attracted to glittery things."

Bling blinked rapidly and gulped hard.

"Serpents will be the least of our concerns, Bling," Chief responded and continued. "Here's the deal: I personally met with the parents, and as you can imagine, they're devastated, but they operate a small farm and they don't have much money, so I—"

"Well, there it is. We know what that means—free work," Johnny sarcastically interrupted.

"This isn't a pro bono op, Johnny, but we aren't getting rich either. Each of you is looking at ten grand for up to two weeks of work. If we bring the girl home, we'll get another small bonus. Obviously, that's a lot less than our usual take, and there's quite a risk, but I just feel that we need to help this family." He held out the picture of Sam for everyone to see, hoping it would motivate them to take the job.

Johnny piped up. "Well, my feelings say otherwise. I've heard horror stories about that place…but I suppose I'm good to go if it's only a couple week op."

"I second that. Let's give it a shot," Switch tagged in.

"Yo, I'm down."

"Eye!" Mack snarled as he used his knife to open a can of smelly sardines, "And enough talk…let's get to fightin'."

"Soon enough, Mack," Chief resolved and continued. "Listen up. I know y'all like the M4s for all your gadgets, but we'll be taking the MP5s this time. 9mm will be easier to obtain in-country if we need more. Make sure they're fitted with suppressors and have your tactical vest outfitted with flashbangs, smoke, and several extra mags. Mack, I know you'll have a few frag grenades, so we're good there."

Mack grinned. "Roger that."

Switch stood up. "Chief, Burma's slightly smaller than Texas. How are we narrowing down such a large search area?"

"I've got a contact in Thailand who has good intelligence on the region; he'll help us narrow our search. We'll fly into Thailand, meet with him, and form our plan for Burma."

Bling raised his hand as though he was in school. "Chief, I got one more question yo….we ain't gonna just bust a cap in e'erybody is we?"

"Bling, look, we all know you found God in prison and that you're against guns, but we have a job to do. That being said, we'll only use what's necessary to complete the contract."

Johnny clenched his jaw and snorted. "Boss, I don't get why you hired this guy. What's he gonna do to the bad guys—tie their shoelaces together and bite their ankles?"

Everyone laughed except Chief, and when they saw he wasn't amused, they straightened up.

"Hold up, Johnny," Chief replied rather sternly. "We may not all agree here, but we're gonna respect Bling's convictions and my decisions."

"Yes, sir," Johnny sarcastically responded while saluting.

Chief ignored him and turned to Bling. "You don't need to fire a gun, but you still need a vest. There's a stun gun in the weapons locker that will fit perfectly in the holster and you can fill the ammo pouches with extra MP5 mags in case we need them. That'll keep our bags lighter."

"You got it, dawg…uh, I mean, Chief. And thanks, yo…"

"Men, get to packing. Wheel's up in an hour. You can get your rest on the long flight."

THREE
TRAPPED

Days Earlier

O h, sorry, I knocked. Didn't know you were in here," Sam embarrassingly backed out of the tiny shared bathroom at the end of the swanky red hallway.

"It's okay, you can come in. I'm just redoing my makeup," the young lady in her early 20s replied, propping the door open with her foot, her voice flat and face expressionless.

"Hey, you're American!" Sam stated enthusiastically, trying not to stare at the young lady's tiny, nearly see-through nightgown, bare feet, and extremely pale skin.

"Yeah, you figured it out. Well, I was American," she paused, looking down. "Now, I'm just a—I guess I'm just a nothing."

Sam furrowed her brow, trying to put everything together. Something was definitely off about everything she had seen in the motel, but she wasn't sure how to say it—or if she wanted to say it.

"So, why are you here?" the young lady asked as she layered on some makeup to hide her black eye. Sam didn't respond. A whirlwind of emotions consumed her as she tried to wrap her mind around what she was seeing and hoping her dark thoughts weren't true.

"Oh, uh, sorry—" Sam broke her gaze and continued. "My boyfriend and me, we came from Oklahoma to see the Burmese culture and everything," she replied, still with a bit of enthusiasm in her voice.

"That's how I got here, too. I originally came to see the islands, but that never happened. I've been trapped here the entire time like most of the other girls out there."

"What do you mean, you got trapped here?" Sam's voice quivered.

"That Asian guy you came in with—"

"TJ?"

"His name is Tuan. Let me guess, you saw a video and called up a number to a nice man who introduced himself as one of the top Burmese tour guides...Made you feel like you knew him forever, right?"

"Yeah, umm, how did you know—?"

"Because that's what he does. He gets paid for every girl he brings in. This isn't a motel, it's a brothel—one of several Tuan and his goons operate in Mandalay and in other countries."

"No, no...This can't be right," Sam swallowed excessively, unwilling to accept what she heard. "So all of these girls here were...were kidnapped?"

"Shhh...hold your voice down...No, not kidnapped like you think," she whispered. "More like an elaborate deception. But only a few come in this way. Tuan's especially proud when he can get girls to fly in from another country like you and I did—especially American because we bring him more money. He calls us the *luu htones* or the dummies," she sighed. Sam listened in horror, wanting to run out, but something held her back.

"I...I'm...how could this...I don't under...understand," Sam stammered, overcome by the nauseating smell from the nearby squat toilet, a jagged hole cut out of the bathroom's hardwood floor and the stagnant bucket of water sitting next to it, a swarm of gnats hovering over both.

"Hey, don't be too hard on yourself. When I first got here, Tuan made himself out to be our...my...long lost Asian friend. Then before I realized it, he trapped me and took all of my personal belongings," she replied, angrily gripping the sink and staring into the mirror without blinking, terrified by her own words.

"How...how long...have you—" Sam struggled to get the words out.

"How long have I been here? At least a year. I stopped counting after that because I lost hope of ever escaping," she replied, locking her dark, hollow eyes with Sam's for the first time. "Listen, you and your friend have to get out of here. Promise me you'll try," she insisted. Sam couldn't stop focusing on her black eye that connected with the light brown freckles on her cheek. She was saddened for her, but it soon hit her that she wasn't far behind.

"Wha...what is...is your name?" Sam asked, still reeling in confusion, finally able to complete a full sentence.

"My real name...or the name these creeps call me? My real name is Kylee—but they all call me Jin, which means Ginger in Burmese; it's because of my red hair."

"My name is Sam—"

"Sam," Kylee interrupted, her eyes intense, "you can still get out of here. I can help. Go back to your room and tell your friend what's going on—and whatever you do, don't drink the alcohol in your room. Give me five minutes and when you hear all the hollering and whistling from the men in the karaoke room, that'll be your sign to slip out. I'll try and draw the lobby bouncer away as well."

"I...I'm...will this work?"

"You have to try. If you don't go now, you'll get trapped like me...and believe me when I say that they'll get rid of your friend for good."

"No, I want to help you get out of here, too! You've got to go with us!"

Unaffected, Kylee blotted her tears with some tissue.

"Hey, don't be a hero. Save yourself. There's no hope for me. I tried escaping once before. Did you see that scar on Tuan's face?"

"From the tiger?"

27

"That's what he tells everyone. I did that to him trying to escape, but it was no use. He beat me within an inch of my life. I woke up three days later strapped to a bed and several men were..." she faded off, choking back tears. She tilted her head back and blotted her eyes again. "...they said if I ever tried escaping again, they would kill me and that they had connections in the US who would hurt my family." Her eyes were red and puffy, but she shook it off, staring into the mirror again, attempting to get control over her emotions.

"No, they're lying—keeping you in fear. It's got to be worth the risk to get out of here. This place is horrible. Let's leave together."

"Look, even if I could escape from here, where would I go? They would find me again. Tuan is connected to the corrupt Burmese Military and the authorities—and they're everywhere. They even have people at the consulate. When you get back home, if you could just look up my parents for me, I would appreciate it. I know they must be so distraught...not knowing what happened to me. Tell them I'm still alive. Would you mind?"

Bam! Bam! Bam! Someone pounded on the bathroom door, interrupting their conversation. Sam and Kylee stood quiet, staring forward, their eyes wide open.

"Jin! You too long!" A man yelled in broken English.

"Be right out," Kylee replied in a forced pleasantness as she hustled to fix herself up and cover the water lines created by her tears.

"I've got to get back out there now or they will suspect something...five minutes...get out!" Kylee whispered, bolting out the door.

As the bathroom door swung open, Sam looked down the hallway and saw TJ. He gazed at her, still holding his beer, his feet spread apart as though he needed more balance. He smiled deviously and winked at her as the door slowly closed on its own.

Get yourself together, Sam. Act normal. Don't let on that you know anything. Smile at him and calmly walk back to the room, she thought.

Sam waited in the bathroom for a couple more minutes as she gathered herself together. She wanted to cry, but she had to be strong. She splashed some water on her face and gradually opened the door, peeking down the long hallway, but this time there was no sign of TJ. She rushed back to the room, slamming the door closed behind her.

"Mike, we've got to get out of here, now! This is a brothel!"

"Wait…what? A broth—" He wasn't putting it together as he tinkered with the window, trying to see why it had been boarded up.

"Just trust me. In five minu—"

Bam! Bam! Bam! As Sam attempted to explain their grave situation, someone knocked hard on their door.

"Who…who is it?" Mike asked as he looked at Sam, still contemplating what she had told him.

"It's TJ. Come join. It will be blast."

"Don't open the door," Sam whispered.

"Okay, sure," Mike raised his voice, trying to sound congenial. "We'll…umm…we'll be out soon. Give us a few minutes."

"Ahhh…I see…save energy for dance," he slurred and finished with a sadistic laugh.

"Sam, what's going on? Start from the beginning."

"I met a girl in the bathroom who came as a tourist like us, but they're forcing her to work here and service the men. Pimps, Mike! Human trafficking! We don't have a lot of time. I'll explain more when we leave. She's going to give us a distraction so we can slip out the front."

"That explains the windows. Oh, God. This…this can't be happening. I knew something was off about this place," he spoke aloud as he placed both of his hands on his head, anxiously pacing back and forth, unable to come to terms that people could be so evil.

"I'm gonna text my parents in case something happens to us…that way they know," she stated, unzipping her pack to retrieve her phone.

"Yeah, good idea."

Mike paced the room, his mind reeling from the new revelation as Sam rummaged through her pack, but she couldn't locate her phone. Frustrated, she dumped everything out on the floor and sifted through the pile of clothes, small water bottles, and food bars.

"It's not here, Mike! Everything...everything is gone! My passport, money, phone...it's...it's all gone...just like she said happened to her."

Sam dropped to her knees and her face wrinkled as though she were about to break down and sob uncontrollably.

"Sam," Mike gently placed his hand on her shoulder. "We gotta stay strong," he encouraged her as he checked his backpack for his phone, but it too was missing, along with his wallet and passport.

"No! No! No! This isn't happening." He was now as frustrated as she was and the shock and anger were setting in for both of them. "TJ must've grabbed our things when we weren't looking. This is serious."

"What are we going to do?"

"I don't know, but we need to get out of here."

As he finished his sentence, they heard whistling and hollering coming from the bar area.

"That's the sign—the distraction. We gotta go now!" Sam exclaimed.

They grabbed their backpacks and cautiously opened the door, inspecting the hallway for TJ. They watched for several seconds and saw no movement, so they moved as stealthily as they could down the hallway until they stood behind a thin wall separating them from the bar area.

Sam inched as close as she could to the wall's edge and peered around it, spotting TJ. He sat in a booth facing away from her, sipping on his drink, his eyes closed and swaying back and forth to the rhythm of the music. She scanned the room until her eyes settled on Kylee. She was dancing in an alluring manner and the male customers had encircled her like animals around fresh meat, each one vying for a dance. Sam desperately wanted to run in and help her escape, but it would have doomed them all.

"Sam, get to the door and run to the wooded area," Mike whispered. "Wait there for me…I'll be right behind you."

Sam turned to him, hugging him tight. "You better," she replied and then darted into the foyer. The desk clerk was gone, so she continued on, reaching the front door and grabbing the metal lever to open it, but it was locked tight, latched at the top, out of her reach.

"C'mon, Sam," Mike muttered as he watched her struggle with the lock. There was no way she could reach it, so he rushed across the foyer and boosted her up so she could unlatch it.

Click! The bolt slid over and the door opened slightly. Mike pushed it open to let her out, but when he did, the door made a slight creaking noise. He hurried Sam out, but before the door could close one of the men spotted him.

"Raut! Raut!" The man shouted in Burmese, pointing in their direction as the door slammed closed. TJ jumped from the booth, stumbling as he entered the foyer. He was so drunk he could barely stand up, but he managed to reach the door and put his weight on the handle, propping it open enough to get a glimpse of Mike and Sam as they ran down the dimly lit path.

TJ braced himself with one hand on the door's lever and pulled his Makarov 9mm pistol from his waistband, fumbling it and dropping it. His eyes were seeing double when he finally picked it up and pointed it into the air.

Pow! Pow! TJ fired two shots above Mike and Sam's head and they dropped directly into a mud puddle. Mike looked back and saw TJ hanging on the door to keep his balance.

"Sam, we have to keep going or they'll kill us…Roll into the weeds."

Sam went first and Mike followed, rolling into some nearby overgrowth. They crawled on their hands and knees until they were about 30 feet into the waist-high vegetation, their hearts pounding, hoping they wouldn't be seen.

"Stay still," Mike whispered. The smell of the freshly disturbed peat soil ascended into their nostrils as they lay in the middle of a cluster of leafy palm bushes and reeds. "Let's hope he's too drunk to find us."

They huddled together, staying as still as possible, trying to ignore the strange creature noises coming from the nearby weeds.

"I can hear someone coming!" Mike whispered as a motorbike approached with several flashlight beams waving in every direction.

"Raut!" One of TJ's men spotted Mike's bright colored backpack and yelled for the driver to stop. He jumped out of the back and rushed into the weeds with TJ following.

"Keep crawling! I think they saw us," Mike insisted, but it was too late; the goon was already standing over them, holding a pointy butterfly knife in his hand, daring them to move.

Mike and Sam held their breath as they scrutinized the sharp knife. Moments later, TJ staggered up to the matted down area of weeds, getting a clear view of the kids. He lifted his pistol and aimed it right at Mike's head.

"Don move or I kill," TJ stated heatedly.

"We have to give up or we'll die," Sam whispered.

Seeing no other way, they slowly stood up with their hands raised in surrender.

"Why you leave?" TJ barked and lunged forward, striking Mike across the cheek with his gun, gashing it open, his blood oozing down onto his shirt.

"I should kill you now boy!...No, that too easy. I make you suffer. Make you watch us have our way with you girl first," TJ growled, grabbing Mike by his neck and yanking him back to the path.

"Start walk," TJ stood behind the kids, holding his pistol to the small of Mike's back. They hesitated at first until TJ kicked Mike in the back of his thigh, prodding him to walk faster.

Ominous thoughts ran through their minds as they trudged closer to the brothel. They tried to stave them off, but hope dwindled by the second.

As they got closer, Mike considered ways to escape, but all he could think of was something no one in their right mind would attempt—but it was all he could come up with.

"Sam, remember Krav class?"

"No talk! Keep walk!" TJ snapped, jabbing the pistol's barrel into the small of Mike's back.

"Agh! Mike cried out, doubling over and glancing at Sam to see whether she agreed with his unspoken plan, but she wasn't giving him any indication. In truth, she knew what he was planning, but she wasn't sure it would work. If he messed up, he would be six feet under by morning.

She remained silent for a few more seconds and finally nodded, a few tears dropping onto her now sweaty and muddy tank top.

This was it, their short life had come down to one untested martial art technique—a technique Mike hadn't practiced in years and was never really skilled in.

FOUR
HUMAN TRAFFICKING

Days Later

T he team exited out of a small, white Learjet and moved across the tarmac to a nearby steel-gray hangar, their bodies still adjusting after the long flight. Everyone was dressed in their street clothes except Mack. He had on his usual camo tank top, desert-colored cargo shorts and black military boots. A bundle of various keys were clipped to his belt loop and they jangled with his every step.

"Man, it's muggy here," Mack protested, taking a whiff of the heavy air as he dropped his duffle bag full of weapons inside the hangar. "Smells like a mixture of wet cat and dirty socks; gives me flashbacks of Nam."

"Stop being so cantankerous, old man," Johnny replied under his breath, dropping his bag next to Mack's. As they spoke, Chief stepped behind a long rectangular table and shook hands with a short Asian man outfitted in a black T-shirt and tan cargo pants.

"Men, welcome to Thailand. My name is Randall. I'm a narcotics task force operator with the Royal Thai Police department and I'm your support contact while you're here," the man stated, his right hand casually resting atop the grip of his police-issued Glock pistol that was clipped to his belt in a black holster. Mack glanced at Johnny to see if he was aware that they were working with the police, but it was clear by the look on his face that he wasn't aware of it either.

"Chief and I go back several years, and if you're wondering, I'm doing this off the books, so if there's anything you need, don't hesitate to ask. You can stash your gear in the Range Rover, and we'll take off to Pattaya City at 1600 hours."

"Thank you, Randall. We appreciate your hospitality," Chief stated as he turned to address the team. "Hopefully everyone has studied the paper with the pictures of the kids that I passed out to you on the flight. As you may have noticed, on the back, there is a map of Pattaya City...As Randall said, we'll be heading there shortly. If you didn't already know, Pattaya is a tourist trap off Thailand's gulf coast, unofficially known as Asia's murder, suicide and prostitution capital."

"Uh, quick question, Chief," Mack cut in.

"Go."

"Why Pattaya? I thought we was coming here and hitchin' a ride to Burma."

"I know you'd like nothing more than to head straight into Burma, Mack, but we're initiating operations in Pattaya because it's a hotbed for human trafficking."

Bling tipped his head to the side and rubbed his goatee, his black and gold, flat-brimmed hat nearly falling off. "Chief, human traffickin'? So they are like them um—what do they call 'em?— them coyotes in Mexico? They sneakin' people in from one country to the next?"

"Nope," Switch interjected. "That's human smuggling—and it's pronounced ky-oh-teh, not ky-oh-tee," he advised, tapping into his part Hispanic heritage.

Johnny stepped up, bobbing his head in agreement. "That's right. Human trafficking, human smuggling, and even kidnapping are all very different. Human trafficking is forcing or tricking someone into performing work, sex, or special favors to gain a profit from them. Many people think it's about snatching someone off the street and throwing them into a van, but it's not the same as kidnapping. Human trafficking usually involves someone taking the time to build a relationship with another person, whether in person or online, and then taking advantage of them in some way…and many times the victim is so deceived that they don't even know what is happening until it's too late."

"Couldn't have said it better," Randall affirmed, adjusting the two-way radio on his belt and placing the headset over his dark, flattop-style haircut.

"Sorry, I ain't know da fancy definition," Bling submitted, removing the outer jacket of his all-black wind suit to get more comfortable. "On da streets we calls it pimpin'."

"That's correct, Bling." Chief agreed. "And more than likely, we'll encounter both pimps and smugglers on this operation. We have confirmation that the kids' flight landed in Burma, but we also have an attractive girl from America; she would be a huge score for sex traffickers."

"Exactly," Randall spoke up. "Burma is a top supplier of trafficking victims to Thailand. If she's been forced into prostitution, chances are she will be in Pattaya or Bangkok's tourist areas."

"Good info, Randall." Chief replied and turned to instruct the team. "Men, make sure you're carrying low profile. Many of the brothels, bars, and hotels we're heading to have tight security and they do body searches. I'm hoping we can blend in as tourists. Mack, that means you'll need to drop the camo outfit and that Rambo knife on your hip."

Mack let out a long sigh and reluctantly removed the large knife from his belt.

"Don't worry, Mack. I've got a nice Hawaiian shirt and a Polaroid camera for you," Chief stated as everyone chuckled.

"Boss," Johnny interjected, "Pattaya is the bottom of the gutter, but it's a big gutter. The girl could be anywhere."

"I won't lie to y'all. This is a process of elimination, but the one thing working for us is that she'll stand out. She'll also bring in a lot of money, which means we can rule out the lower end joints. Randall, do you want to fill us in a little more?"

"Sure, Chief," Randall stepped up, ready to take charge. "I've got good intel on all the major trafficking pimps in Pattaya—and guys, by pimps I mean seriously organized criminals, not the top hat and cane stereotype who have a couple girls in their stable. If your girl is here, they'll have her, or they'll know who does."

"Did you just say stable? Like the kind for horses?" Switch asked, his gaze focused and sincere.

"Man, Switch, you such a nerd," Bling smirked. "A stable is street talk; it's a term for a group of girls turnin' tricks for they daddies—for da pimps."

"Unfortunately, you're right, Bling," Randall replied and repeated to the team as though he were translating for him. "The pimps, also known as daddies—and sometimes even as mommas—often refer to the group of girls or sometimes boys under their control as their stable."

Switch pursed his mouth, disgusted by what he heard. "They use an animal term? That's pretty stinking low."

"Sho is," Bling agreed, uncrossing his arms.

"Thanks for the info, Randall," Chief jumped in. "It'll be useful. Alright team, let's tread lightly here. We don't want to set off any unnecessary alarms," Chief glanced at Mack as he finished.

"Why you eyin' me? Johnny is the twitchy one," Mack rattled off.

"One more thing guys," Randall interrupted, looking at Chief for permission to speak. Chief nodded and Randall took a wide stance, "Listen closely. Absolutely do not trust the authorities here. Corruption is rampant. Many of the beat officers are paid off by the mafia. If we get into a jam with any of the cops, let me do the talking."

"Yeah, roger that," Johnny affirmed.

"Chief, can I axe a question?" Bling inquired.

"Chop away," Johnny replied, laughing through his nose as he made fun of Bling's mispronunciation.

"What's up Bling?" Chief asked, giving Johnny a look that told him to back off.

"You ain't mention dat boy. What's da deal wit' him?"

"Look, if we can get the boy, we'd all like that, but there's a high probability he's already out of the picture. The girl's family paid us, so she is our primary focus."

Bling tilted his head and narrowed his eyes, looking away from Chief, trying to determine if they were only there for the money.

"One last thing, everyone," Chief stated. "Johnny will be number two for this operation. We all know his vice stories. His experience will be helpful. Everyone understand?"

Mack grinned. "Yeah, we know the stories…is he gonna show us how to rough up the prisoners and get fired from our job? That is why you got kicked off the force, right John boy?"

The vein in Johnny's neck throbbed and he glared at Mack. "What did you say, old man?"

"Guys, calm down!" Chief exclaimed. "Get your heads right. We've got a long night. You can aggravate each other later."

"Amen," Mack blurted out as Johnny continued eyeing him.

"Johnny, are we gonna have a problem?"

"No, I'm good," he groaned.

"Good. Y'all need to get your gear into the Rover and grab some grub. We're hitting the streets in fifteen."

***

"Man, dis here traffic is whack—remindin' me of LA!" Bling exclaimed as he drove the blacked-out Range Rover down the three-lane, one-way beach street toward Pattaya. Chief sat next to him, riding shotgun, and Randall and the rest of the team were in the seats behind them.

"All these tourists lookin' for some flesh," Mack suggested from the rear seat.

"Chief, the drone's almost ready," Switch called up.

"Good. We're about a quarter klick from Pattaya. Bling, pull over here."

Bling pulled into a parking spot a few feet from the gulf waters where dozens of ships dotted the horizon, their navigation lights flickering on as the blueish-gray dusk sky turned darker by the second.

"Got it. We're linked up. Now the Rover's display screens will show exactly what I'm seeing."

"Great, launch it out."

Switch let down the Rover's darkly tinted rear window and a rush of tangy saltwater and a fishy smell infiltrated the cabin. The calming sound of waves rolling onto the sandy beach and the chirp of seagulls gave everyone a temporary feeling of tranquility amid a sea of unknowns ahead of them.

Switch launched the small drone and navigated it down Beach Street using an electronic tablet device, flying it into Pattaya City and hovering over the neon-saturated entrance to Walking Street, the city's main tourist strip.

"Check it out," Johnny spoke up as he stared at the Rover's drop-down video screen. "That jumbotron screen in the middle of the street reminds me of Times Square in New York, only a bit smaller. What's written on it; I can't quite make it out."

Switch zoomed in on the entry gate. "Looks like it says, Passion of Colorful Paradise," he replied.

"It's certainly colorful," Chief responded.

"Yo, it's a rainbow of colors," "Bling proposed as he looked on. "But it ain't no paradise...dis here da Devil's lair."

"What we're looking at right now is Pattaya's beachside entry area," Randall indicated. "If you'll notice, the gap between the pillars is only wide enough for people, motorcycles and maybe food carts to go through...all the other vehicles have to divert."

"Lookin' like da entrance to Beelzebub's temple to me," Bling surmised.

"That's pretty accurate. Lots of crime and horrible things happen behind that gate," Randall confirmed as the drone hovered over the street, supplying video surveillance. Crowding the street were dozens of scantily clad young ladies standing outside rows of shady businesses, holding signs indicating their availability by the hour.

"As you all can see by all the skimpy-clothed women and the intense reddish-orange neon glow, we're now in the heart of Pattaya's Walking Street; it's basically one big red-light district," Randall stated as the team watched the screens. "Pattaya is the equivalent to your Las Vegas, but instead of tourists hoping to win big money gambling, they spend big money for women to fulfill their fantasies."

"A one-night negotiation—no commitments or promises beyond that," Johnny piped up.

"That's one way to put it," Randall replied. "There are hundreds of go-go bars, karaoke and disco clubs, massage brothels and seedy motels on this small strip that's less than a klick long—and all of them offer prostitution. There's also something similar to this a few hours up the road in Bangkok."

"I had heard about this place, but seeing it is unreal. The brothels and clubs are basically stacked on top of each other," Johnny stated.

Bling looked confused. "Yo, what's a klick?"

Johnny shook his head. "Really, boss? Do we have to teach him everything?"

"A klick is short for kilometer," Chief replied without acknowledging Johnny.

"Why ain't y'all just use miles?"

Johnny shook his head. "Because we're ex-military and they drilled it into us. The military switched to kilometers so they could coordinate easier with allies from foreign countries."

"Makes sense, I suppose," Bling replied.

As they continued watching the drone's footage, Randall took an opportunity to provide the team with more intel on the city. "Guys, before you all head in, you need to know that Pattaya is controlled by four organized gangs, one of which has ties to the Burmese Military. Considering that the girl arrived in Burma and may have been trafficked here, I've narrowed your search to the Burmese connected clubs and brothels, but I also need to warn you, some are associated with the Russian Mob."

"Seriously?" Switch asked, momentarily averting his eyes from the tablet's screen to look at Randall seated next to him.

"The Russian and Asian gangs basically run this place behind the scenes."

"I ain't suprised by dat one," Bling interjected. "When I ran wit' da homeboy's gang back in da day, we did this same stuff. My homeboy found out dat pimpin' was easier and more profitable than runnin' drugs. A couple years later, we made over half a mill from runnin' only a handful of ladies."

"That's true, Bling," Johnny affirmed. "Working on the force, I learned many drug dealers switched to trafficking ladies because drugs need to be resupplied, but girls can be reused again and again."

"Man, that's horrible," Switch replied.

"You ain't know da half of it," Bling responded. "Seein' all these clubs out here reminds me how we recruited most of da girls back in da day. We'd find 'em at da strip clubs or bars."

"I can't believe you used to be involved in this stuff," Johnny replied with a reproving look.

"Them boys I ran wit' took care of da pimpin', but I profited from it. I ain't proud of it, but God delivered me from all dat."

"Man, there sure are a lot of school-aged girls out here," Switch cringed as he zoomed in on the streets from the drone.

"Fo' sho'. Most of the girls we ran was young, too. We'd find da teen girls at da high schools and local colleges—'cuz dat's when they brain still formin' and ain't so street savvy. My homeboy used to call 'em da young and dumbs, 'cuz they easy to trick…Dawg was whack."

"How did y'all pull that off?" Chief asked inquisitively.

"We posted locations of hoppin' parties online and got as much juice—or what y'all white boys call alcohol—as them kids could drink. Being they underage, they couldn't get it, but we could. Once they came to our parties, we'd get 'em hooked into da life by offerin' 'em bottomless juice, drugs, and Benjis. Before they knew it, they strung out on dope and turnin' tricks, givin' us all da profits."

Switch looked puzzled.

"What is a Benji?" he asked.

"Come on, Switch, you can't be that street dense," Johnny suggested. "Benjamins...as in Benjamin Franklin..."

Switch wasn't getting it.

"Oh, Lord. Benjamin Franklin is on the hundred dollar bill. He's talking about money, nerd."

"Oh, righ...right! I knew that."

"Uh-huh."

"Guys, notice anything unusual about these places?" Chief asked as the drone provided close up surveillance of the buildings.

"Yeah, they have cameras angled in every direction," Switch noted.

"That's one of the ways we were able to spot illegal brothels stateside," Johnny replied. "On every raid, we would see surveillance cameras in every corner of the building, watching the girls and watching for us cops."

"They got these stateside?" Switch asked innocently.

"You gotta be kidding, right?" Johnny asked. "They are literally in every state and every large city. At one point, I worked a joint operation in Houston where they had more massage brothels than Mickey D's and Starbucks combined."

"That's gotta be a lot of massage parlors," Switch submitted.

"Right, over 500 at one point—and many of them were full of trafficked women from Asia—young ladies living inside a small strip center building, locked behind a caged door 24/7, 365, some of them not even knowing what city they were in. When I did my awareness meetings, I would always start by telling the crowd that if they knew someone who patronized Mcdonald's or Starbucks, they knew twice as many who frequented a brothel, they just didn't know it. It shocked them because most don't think it happens where they live."

"You sure do know a lot about this prostitutin' stuff, Johnny," Mack interjected with a snarky laugh. "I guess that's why they call you John, huh?"

"I guess they call you Mack because you have the personality of a dump truck!" Johnny countered sarcastically. Surprisingly, Mack let out a slight laugh and the rest of the team followed, easing the tension.

"Look, I'll be honest with you guys," Johnny replied. "I'm not innocent in this stuff either. There were a couple times I actually patronized a brothel...back when I was young and dumb as well, like Bling said. Honestly, I thought the women wanted to be there, wanted to be prostitutes, but when I got on the force and saw how men would treat them—chaining them up, hitting, cutting and biting them, even urinating on them—it changed my mind forever."

"Man, that's horrible," Switch cringed.

"Nearly every lady we helped out of the lifestyle said they were raped and beaten multiple times by both the pimps and the johns. There were several times I had to call in homicide to investigate the murder of a naked woman with no ID except a tattoo that her pimp branded on her to show ownership."

"I seen dat stuff first hand," Bling stated, shaking his head in disgust.

"I can imagine. The movies and media glamorize prostitution, but the reality is that it's horrific—and the sad thing is that most people don't want to know the truth. They want to keep on doing life oblivious to the reality that girls are enslaved down the street from their suburban homes."

"Johnny, thanks for sharing your heart brother...it took guts—and you're absolutely right about people not wanting the truth," Chief replied. "I think there are many factors—the main one being that people are involved in it on some level. I know I'm not innocent. Back in the day, I visited my fair share of strip clubs and dabbled in pornography—and both are closely linked to trafficking."

"True," Randall spoke up. "We've seen busts here where the girls are secretly recorded in the brothels and the content later sold online as porn; it's one big revolving door all built around money."

"Very true," Switch replied. "When I discovered that porn fuels sex trafficking and that every mouse click on a raunchy website helps support it, I didn't want to be involved in that anymore—plus, I always felt shame from porn, so I left it behind."

"Computer nerd," Mack snickered. "We know you was into porn, but are you sure you ain't still in it?"

Switch gave him an evil look, but Mack replied before he could respond. "Look, I'm just messin' with ya. We've all been there. I messed around with some ladies of the night back in Nam."

"Now that we're done confessin' our sins, maybe we can continue with the mission," Chief replied rather firmly. "We've got a lot of work ahead of us."

"Right," Johnny agreed.

Switch converted the drone to night-vision, zooming in on several girls hidden in the dark alleys. "Man, I don't think I've ever seen so many prostitutes in one place. I still don't get why girls choose to sell their bodies to strange men."

"There are nearly 30,000 prostitutes here," Randall replied.

"30,000?!" Mack muttered. "That's the size of a small city!"

"It's the world's largest red-light district, but as Johnny said, these girls don't choose to be out here. They enter prostitution because it's the lesser of two evils. I mean, what little girl fantasizes about growing up to be a prostitute?"

"Hmm…good point. I don't think I've ever considered that," Switch tilted his head, glancing at Randall.

"Many of these girls are here because their family is extremely poor or because they're forced into it to pay off a debt. Some are tricked by those they thought were boyfriends. Some are runaways. But the most common factor is that nearly all of them have a history of extreme abuse. The short of it is that these girls trade their bodies for the hope of a better life…and many of them get into the lifestyle as young as 12 years old."

"12?! I honestly had no idea; that's awful," Switch eyes bugged out. "They should be playing dress-up with Barbie, not walking the streets for some monster's Barbie fantasy."

"It's horrendous—and the tendency is to think these men are monsters, and in a way they are, but they didn't start that way; they grew into it. Just like most of us, many of these guys dabbled in pornography at a young age and it twisted their thinking to view women only as objects for their pleasure, pushing them into a downward spiral until they sought out what they had seen on screen…and the only way to fulfill their unrealistic fantasies and the high they get from it is on the streets with these girls."

"Ef'n, men," Bling muttered under his breath.

"Woah! What did you say, Bling?" Johnny asked. "I didn't expect that from you, but I guess I knew deep down you were like the rest of us."

"EF'N is a reminder to myself dat these types of men need extra forgiveness. E-F-N, Extra Forgiveness Needed."

Johnny threw up his hands and crossed his arms.

"More like extra bullets needed," Mack snarled.

"Alright, team, listen up," Chief stated, bringing everyone back to the task at hand. It's time to put in work. Bling's gonna drive us to the Walking Street entrance and me, Johnny, and Mack will go in on foot while everyone else stays in the Rover with Randall. Randall, if you can provide translation when needed that would be great."

"You got it, Chief," Randall confirmed.

"Good. Let's move in."

FIVE
ESCAPING

Days Earlier

Mike replayed the martial art gun disarm technique over in his mind, contemplating every detail, but things were different from when he had done it in the dojo. The dojo was well-lit, the gun was rubber, and the sensei wanted to rank him up to his yellow belt, not kill him.

Is it move in first and trap or trap and move in? Mike thought as he trudged along, sweat dripping from his forehead, deliberating his escape plan. With TJ holding the gun to his back, it was nearly an impossible feat, but they were in an impossible situation, so there was nothing to lose.

"Move faster!" TJ bellowed, his voice echoing into the clear night sky. TJ stood behind him, a bit off-center, erratically waving the gun while staggering back to the brothel.

TJ is super drunk. I can do this. I just have to make sure Sam isn't in the way of the gun. I'll turn into his body to redirect the line of fire, gain control of the weapon, and attack until he can't fight back, Mike thought as they plodded forward, eventually stopping near the brothel's steps.

"Girl go in. Boy stay out," TJ angrily commanded as they stood in front of the steps, but neither of them moved; their bodies were frozen in place.

"I love you, Mike!" Sam screamed and it caught TJ by surprise. Without thinking, Mike whipped around, closing the gap between him and TJ until his body was outside of the gun's line of fire. He trapped the gun with his arm, kicked the front of his knee and then struck his neck with the edge of his hand, incapacitating him long enough to break the gun free from his grip.

"Arghhhh!" TJ doubled over, holding his neck with one hand and grasping his knee with the other, groaning in agony. Mike aimed the gun, whipping it back and forth between TJ and the other men, amazed that he had been successful at gaining control of the weapon, and yet, he was far from celebrating.

"Get back or I'll shoot!" he shouted, pulling Sam behind him.

TJ got his bearings and stood upright, still reeling in pain and spewing curse words. Saliva dripped from his mouth and murderous intent was in his eyes.

"Get them!" TJ shouted through gritted teeth, but the other men didn't move. Mike had the gun trained on them and they could see in his eyes that he wouldn't hesitate to shoot.

The men held their hands up as Mike and Sam backed away, their faces glowing red from the neon sign and eventually disappearing into the darkness.

They darted down the path and when they reached the edge of the weeds where they had been hiding, Mike scooped up his backpack and they continued on, running as fast as they could.

"Mike, wait, we forgot my pack!" she exclaimed, slowing down and gasping for a decent breath.

"We can't go back!" he yelled as he reached out for her hand, pulling her along to get back to the highway.

They ran for a few minutes when Mike heard a motor start up. He turned to see headlights coming from near the brothel and they quickly diverted off the path into a wooded area, hiding behind some trees and taking a moment to rest.

"If we go to the highway, they'll find us," Mike panted, the rust-colored pine needles somewhat slippery beneath his cheap sandals. "We'll have a better chance if we cut through the forest."

"But what about the wild animals? We don't know what's out here!" she asserted, her eyes showing her apprehension as they moved from one tree to the next.

"You're right. But we know the animals searching for us if we walk the highway. This is our best chance," he indicated as they moved deeper into the endless rows of lofty pine trees. Sam nodded. He was right. Meeting a wild animal was a better option.

They crossed through the woods for another hundred yards or so when they came to the edge of the lake—the same one they had seen earlier at the brothel.

"Mike, look, the city lights! We can follow them and get help."

"Yeah, and look over there," he pointed in the opposite direction at a partial view of the brothel about 500 yards away. All they could see was its faint red neon sign, but it was enough to provoke a wave of menacing thoughts for them both.

"We can follow the shoreline out of here," he proposed, staring at the sand beneath his feet and the frothy, cappuccino-colored water glimmering several feet away, the dim sliver of moonlight barely illuminating it.

They journeyed along the mostly sandy shoreline, maneuvering through waist-high reeds and sporadic bamboo shoots until they came to a small inlet canal about 15 feet across. The canal connected the lake to a nearby river, but the drought had all but dried it up, leaving behind a muddy bayou full of dead fish, crab carcasses, and the smell of something like decaying roadkill.

"This looks like the driest section; we'll cross over here," Mike pointed out as he inspected the canal and then slid feet first down a slight embankment. When he reached the edge, he touched the mud with his foot to test it and it swallowed his leg almost to the middle of his calf.

"Sam, be careful," he called out as he held out his hand to help her down. "It's not as dry as I thought."

"Oh, this is disgusting," she replied, stepping down after him, the mud overtaking her boots.

"I think we'll do better if we crawl—that way we can disperse our weight and get through quicker."

"That means I have to put my face near the mud!"

"Right. I know, it's disgusting, but—" Before he could finish she had already dropped down on all fours and started crawling, her tank top lifted over her nose—determined to get as far away from the brothel as possible.

They crawled a few feet when Mike's sandal got stuck in the muck. He stopped to dig it out, but Sam pushed on ahead. She got a few feet from him when something soft and scaly brushed up against her arm.

"Mike!" she nearly yelled, staring at what she first thought was a stick, until the yellow and black bands coiled up near her hand. Overcome with panic, she stared at the snake's swaying movements, its metallic-like scales reflecting in the moonlight.

Mike remained still, his eyes pinned open, watching as it slithered along her body and stopped at her foot, its forked tongue flickering in and out, curiously inspecting her.

"Sam, don't move. Stay still," he whispered. "It's more scared of you than you are of it," he did his best to calm her, but the alarming look in his eyes indicated to her that this wasn't a harmless, garden-variety type snake.

Sam didn't even blink until the snake finally slithered away to investigate a decaying fish several feet away. Afterward, she released a breath she didn't know she had been holding and continued on.

"I told you we needed to get my pack!" she scolded him. "At least I could've used my flashlight to see what's lurking in these weeds."

He recognized her fear and frustration and tried redirecting.

"Sam, the lights are closer now. That village has to be less than a few hundred yards away," he suggested as he climbed up out of the muddy canal onto solid ground, holding out his hand to assist her back up the bank.

"Good. Hopefully we can get some water. I'm parched," she responded rather sharply, refusing his hand and swapping attitudes with him.

Continuing on to the outskirts of the village, they observed several long-tail boats beached on the sand, each filled with fishing poles and conical-shaped crab nets. The wooden boats were basically the same shape as a canoe, except three times longer and crudely outfitted with an automotive-type engine with a long driveshaft and small propeller. Sam crouched behind the first boat they came across, locking her eyes on it, slowly rubbing its rough panels as though she were charmed by it.

"What is it?" Mike asked, but she didn't respond.

"Sam? Are you okay?" he asked in a stronger tone, curious as to what she was doing. Finally, she snapped out of her gaze.

"I...I'm fine," she stuttered. "It's just that I remember seeing one of these boats in an advertisement and I was so excited to see one in person...and now...now I am hiding behind one in a fight for my life."

Mike knelt down next to her and reached out to hold her hand. She felt the touch of his warm skin and quickly jerked away. She wasn't upset with him, she wanted to be done with it all, and his sympathy wasn't going to help her get home.

"What do you say we move behind that last boat and get a closer look at the village?" he asked, changing the subject.

"Only if there are no reptiles," she responded curtly, crossing her arms and pursing her lips together tightly.

"We'll be careful."

Mike moved up the beach, not waiting for her response. Sam continued sulking, wanting to stay behind to prove a point, but she also wanted to keep going, so she gave in and followed, crouching behind him as they maneuvered to the boat about 50 feet from the village, being careful not to be seen.

The boat provided perfect cover where they could lay low and still have a view of the tiny village. A few feet beyond the shoreline they surveyed two rows of about a dozen bamboo huts with rusty, sheet metal roofs. Each hut was connected to another and was suspended about 15 feet above the sand on telephone pole-sized stilts. Breaking up the dreariness were colorful clothes hang drying on the hut's doors and railings, along with the smell of freshly cooked rice that suffused the sultry air with its semi-sweet aroma.

"We need to wait until morning to see if we can get some help," Mike advocated.

"My thoughts exactly. I can only imagine how they would respond to two white kids knocking on their doors late at night, frantically asking for help—especially with all that blood on your shirt."

"Oh…right," he replied, pulling his shirt away from him at the bottom to get a look at a long streak of dried blood from the gash TJ had given him; it looked as though he had murdered someone. He hurried to remove it, turning it inside out, and then put it back on.

"Think we could get a little closer and find something to drink?" she asked. "The only thing keeping me from being totally parched is this thick humidity."

"Yeah, but we need to be careful. We'll look for some water and we'll come back and rest in one of the boats until sunrise."

They followed a sandy path leading from the beach to the village, being careful to stay below the weeds and long grass, eventually reaching a fork in the path. One path led directly to the village and the other smaller path veered off in the opposite direction. Mike popped his head above the weeds, inspecting the path, noticing that it led to an old water well pump.

"I think I see a well," he whispered as he crouched back down. "Maybe twenty feet down the path."

"Oh, thank God!" she whispered with a glimmer of positivity.

Mike checked the huts, making sure it was still clear and then they squatted behind the weeds, traversing the winding path as Sam searched for anything that remotely looked like it was slithering.

"This looks really old," he indicated as they reached the well pump that was situated in the middle of a small clearing.

"Sam, cup your hands below the spout," he instructed, lifting the rusty handle.

Creaaaaaak! The handle made a horrible screeching sound as Mike brought it down, startling Sam and waking some dogs in the village.

"Mike, shhh! We need to be quiet."

"Don't you think I know that? We already woke the dogs up; might as well keep trying."

Creaaaak! The ear-piercing sound continued, but with each pump it faded, along with the barking dogs. He pumped several more times until they heard a faint gurgling sound and saw the trickle of glistening water falling from the spigot. Sam knelt down, collecting some of the water into her hands, slurping it like it was her favorite soft drink.

"Oh, this is so good right now!" she exclaimed as she lapped up the water. After she had her fill, she switched places with Mike, operating the well pump's lever until he couldn't drink anymore. Then they slumped down next to it, too exhausted to even think about swatting the huge mosquitoes buzzing around them.

Tears formed in Sam's eyes as she processed the day's events and their situation.

"Mike?

"Yeah, Sam,"

"What are we going to do?"

"I…I don't know," he whispered, trying to think of something encouraging, but coming up short, "We just have to keep moving. At least we're together."

"At least…at least we're togeth—" she nearly got all the words out, but could no longer fight the fatigue and nodded off to sleep. He brushed her hair back and surveyed the glittery stars set against the night sky's dark canvas, his eyes also becoming heavy. Unable to fight the drowsiness any longer, he drifted off to sleep, his head resting on Sam's.

***

Sam's eyes were still closed but she had been stirred by the monotone ensemble of mosquitoes relentlessly buzzing around her ears. She struggled to raise her eyelids as she peeked through her lashes, noticing it was still dark. She opened them a little more, unable to recall the last time she had seen so many stars. Then she felt something. An itch. Several itches. She was itching so severely that her body felt as though it were on fire. She looked down at her arms and they were nearly black as the night. The mini vampires had congregated on her sanctuary of flesh for their own personal communion. She jumped up, frantically brushing them away.

"Mike! Get up! Get up!" She nearly yelled as she stood to her feet, swatting the bloodsuckers off his arms and face.

Mike jumped up, still half awake.

"Huh. What? What's wrong!" His words gradually got louder as though he had been awakened by a nightmare.

"Shhhh! Mike, open your pack. Do you still have your mosquito spray?" she asked, waving her arms around, still swatting at the bugs.

"You nearly gave me a heart attack! I thought TJ was on to us...Let me look. I think so." He opened his backpack and felt around for the spray.

"Here it is."

"We need to make sure we ration this," she suggested, spraying a little repellent on her hands, rubbing them together and patting her exposed skin.

"Good thinking. It would be horrible if we escaped only to get malaria," he surmised, scratching the top of one of his feet.

"I really wished I would have brought my hiking boots like you. My plan to pick up a cheaper pair here didn't work out so well," he fussed a little as he removed his sandals to rub some repellent on his legs and feet.

As they talked, Sam's face suddenly turned pale. She grabbed her stomach and doubled over on her knees, groaning loudly.

"Mike, I…I don't feel…don't feel so well."

"Aughhhhhhh…"

"You don't look well," he replied, helping her sit down, and feeling her clammy skin. "Here, lay down on your back for a little while."

She rested on the sand and within seconds her stomach muscles cramped and she vomited what little food and water she had in her system. Mike grabbed a face towel from his bag and wiped her mouth as she dry heaved.

"Maybe it's the stress," he suggested, caressing her hair and pulling it away from her face.

He rubbed her back to calm her nerves, but then the squeamishness hit him, but he brushed it off.

"Try to get some more rest. It'll be daylight soon, and we need to leave before then," he urged, not knowing they had only been resting for about a half hour. As soon as he finished talking, his squeamishness became a full-on assault on his stomach.

"Arghhhh!" The stabbing pain caused his eyes to water.

"Are you okay?" Sam turned to him, barely able to get the words out through her own pain.

"My stomach…I need to lay do—" Before he could finish his sentence, he projectile vomited all over the well pump's handle and collapsed in front of it. He stared at the handle in agonizing pain, and that's when he finally figured it out.

"Sam, argh, don't…don't drink any more water. Our bodies aren't handling it. We need to…arghhh…get going while we still have the cover of dark…darkness," he stammered through the piercing pain.

"No…I…I can't right now. I'm too tired…can't we rest here a little longer?" she barely got the words out as she spoke with her eyes closed, nearly already asleep again.

"For an hour, but then we have to go," he stated, noticing the pain was easing a bit. He rested his head against Sam's and they both drifted off to sleep, their bodies completely exhausted.

SIX
NEON CITY

Days Later

The three one-way street lanes leading to Pattaya's Walking Street entrance were bumper-to-bumper with truck taxis and other vehicles driving toward the neon jungle, each filled with enthusiastic tourists who were eager for their personal parties to begin for the evening.

Bling herded the team through the stop-and-go traffic as motorbikes and mopeds impatiently split the lanes around them, weaving in and out of traffic, their horns honking incessantly. Chief, Johnny, and Mack each inserted a small, intra-ear, hearing aid-like earpiece and placed microphones around their collars, connecting them to their two-way radios. Moments later, Bling saw the pillared entrance gate and pulled over to the side of the road.

"Delta Team, let's go," Chief glanced back at Johnny and Mack as they stepped out of the Rover, congregating on the sidewalk. Chief had ditched his cowboy hat and boots, looking quite uncomfortable in his tennis shoes, slightly too short stone-washed jeans, and white, T-shirt. He did his best to stay loose and mimic the movements of a tourist, but it was an act easier said than done for a military man.

"I still ain't understand why I gotta wear this flowery shirt," Mack nagged, unbuttoning it until only the last few buttons were fastened, his gray chest hair curling out.

"Flowers look good on you, Mack. You need a little touch of the feminine side," Johnny suggested.

Mack lifted his chin and grunted loudly. "The girly shirt looks better on you," he countered.

"Listen up," Chief announced, "First on our list is Darkhouse Club; it shouldn't be too far down on the west side," Chief instructed, raising his voice over the loud music blaring into the street. Everyone nodded and strolled toward the pillared entrance, but before they could pass through three young, half-clothed Thai ladies solicited them.

"Hi boy! You want fun time?" One of the ladies asked Chief, rubbing his shirt collar in an alluring manner. The other two stood next to Mack and Johnny, flipping their long hair, each vying for the men's attention. One of the girls put her arm around Mack and his cheeks blushed red.

"Not today ladies," Chief replied in a gentle but firm tone, twisting away from the young lady and giving Mack an exaggerated smile, motioning with his head to break away from them.

"Delta Team," Switch spoke into his mic as he watched from the drone, "Darkhouse should be about 25 meters down from your location...I'm still only seeing one bouncer at the entrance, over."

"Copy, Echo Team. We're on the move, over," Chief replied into his hidden microphone as they advanced down the street, walking under the inundation of neon billboards and a crowd of mostly men from every walk of life, ranging in age from teenager to senior citizen.

"Man, what is that smell? It's like a combination of sewer, rotten fish, and Thai noodles," Johnny cringed as they sauntered past a shadowy karaoke bar that spilled into the street.

"Man, this place is a trip," Mack called out. "It's like a big party scene."

"Reminds me of Spring Break on steroids," Johnny responded as they continued past tourist vendor outlets of all kinds, from tattoo parlors to sunglass peddlers and even huts selling edible bugs and grub worms.

"Chief, check it out," Johnny announced, pointing to the neon Darkhouse Club sign; it featured a champagne glass and the outlines of female bodies, flickering rapidly to get the tourist's attention.

Chief stood on the still sweltering pavement, surveying the exterior of the club. As Switch had indicated, only one bouncer stood in front of a shiny, stainless steel door. Silhouetted women provocatively danced behind glowing red window screens on both sides of it, living billboards of what they were offering inside.

"Okay guys, let's spend some money. We'll drop some cash and see if the girls know something," Chief instructed as he sauntered up to the short, stocky Asian bouncer and stuck up a conversation. "We heard this is the place for a good time," he announced flippantly, studying every detail of the bouncer who looked like he enjoyed donuts more than he did the weight bench.

"Turn around. I search," the bouncer sternly replied in broken English, motioning for the men to all raise their arms for a body frisk.

"Okay, everyone good," the bouncer conveyed after checking Chief and Johnny, but as they were about to walk through, he felt something on Mack's ankle. "Stop! What this?"

"Oh, that's my ankle brace. No biggie," Mack explained trying to play it cool as the bouncer lifted his pant legs for a closer inspection.

"Okay, you good. Go inside," the bouncer stated, finally assured they weren't carrying any weapons.

"Phew, close call," Johnny submitted as they walked into the dark hallway that led to the club.

Mack chuckled. "Yeah, and I don't even have a gun on me...just my boot knife behind my brace."

"Delta Team," Switch spoke into his mic. "I've still got your audio, but we've lost visual. You guys are on your own."

"That's a good copy," Chief replied.

"What the—" Johnny scanned the inside of the club and his eyebrows raised a notch.

"Everything okay in there? What are you guys seeing?" Switch nervously questioned as he continued surveilling the streets for potential issues.

"A big ol' buffet of flesh is what we're seeing," Mack replied as they stood at the threshold of the club's grand room, spying out a red linen stage where more than a dozen young Asian ladies in skimpy red dresses were seated on long, black couches, their legs crossed and sitting proper. They ranged in age from what teenagers to early 30s, each of them with round numbers pinned to their dresses. An older Asian woman hovered over them, walking back and forth, clearly in charge.

Delta Team strolled in and took a seat on one of a dozen red, felt-covered, round boudoir sofa chairs in the middle of the room, making sure to steer clear of the four dazed male customers, each examining the girls closely to see who they would spend their money and their next hour with.

"This is definitely a brothel," Johnny whispered, as Switch, Randall and Bling listened in. "Reminds me of the cantina bars in the States: several young ladies on stage for men to pick from— all of them with dull eyes and flat smiles. So far we see five subjects, a bartender and four male patrons."

"Don't forget about that rank smell," Mack muttered.

"Believe me when I say that I'm glad I can't smell it," Switch radioed.

"You've smelled it before. Smells like a nasty strip club…a mixture of old man's cologne, body odor and spilled beer."

"Guys, split up and choose one of the girls," Chief whispered. "Try to get some info from them. They'll know if an American girl is in town," he finished, taking a seat on one of the boudoir sofas and nodding at the girls on stage. Mack and Johnny followed, plopping down on one of the empty sofas on the opposite side of the room.

"Hey, bartender fella, I'll sttake snumber sneven," Mack raised his voice, slurring his words and acting as though he had a little too much to drink.

"Sir, may I help you?" a short, Asian man in his late 30s asked, popping out from behind a dark bar area with a small paper tablet and pen. As he stepped into the dim light, everyone could see his shiny, black, slicked-back hair and full tuxedo.

"Yeah, I want snumber sev—sneven!" Mack belched.

"Sir, seven no here for you. Pick new number or come back later."

"If Mack keeps this up, he's gonna get them kicked out," Switch spoke into his mic, forgetting that everyone could hear.

"I want snumber sneven!" Mack raised his voice belligerently. The other male customers nervously stared at him and got up to leave, anticipating a problem.

The bartender pressed a button on his side and the bouncer from the entrance came rushing in. Two other guards entered from the rear of the room, surrounding Mack.

"Please ask friend to calm down," the bouncer asserted, taking a defensive stance as he hovered over Mack and glanced at Chief who was about 15 feet away.

"Don't look at me. I don't know who he is right now!" Chief raised his hands to absolve any relationship they thought he may have had with Mack and returned his attention to the young ladies on stage.

"Mack is trippin'," Bling stated, listening in from the driver's seat of the Rover.

"Why swon't y'all just gives sme snumber sneven?" Mack yelled even louder, this time raising up from the sofa and slamming his fists on a nearby table. The guards seized him by his arms and pulled him back to the entrance and, surprisingly, he didn't resist.

"Come back when not drunk. You scare off customer," the guards shouted as they led him down the hallway and pushed him out into the street.

Mack stumbled, nearly falling and staggered away to an alley at the side of the building.

"Mack, what's with the drunk act? I can see you in the alley next to the club, over," Switch spoke into the mic as Chief and Johnny listened in.

"Yep, 3, 22 and 28 seconds crazy."

"I'm not following, over," Switch replied as everyone awaited Mack's explanation.

"They got three guards. Took the bouncer 22 seconds to get to me and 28 for the goons in back," he advised as he checked out the gloomy alley.

"Great, Mack, just great. We're not knocking off a bank here," Chief whispered. "Just hang out and try not to look suspicious, alright?"

"Roger roger, Chief," he replied, making a saluting motion, playing his drunk role a little too well.

***

Back in the club, Chief called the bartender over and provided him with a number corresponding to one of the girls on stage.

"You got cash?" the waiter asked sharply, now suspicious of him and Johnny.

Chief flashed a roll of cash to the bartender and he jerked it out of his hand, thumbing through it. Satisfied by what he saw, he pointed at the girl and she gradually rose to her feet, forced out a fake smile, and moved behind the curtain.

"Go behind curtain. She wait. Pay girl," the bartender stated, throwing the cash back at Chief.

Johnny watched as Chief got up and cautiously moved behind the red curtain that was about 20 feet high and extended the length of the stage.

Once in the back, Chief saw the girl he had requested standing near several smaller rooms the size of a walk-in closet, all of them partitioned off by more, smaller red curtains.

The girl invited him into one of the rooms and Chief stepped inside. Seconds later she pulled the curtain closed.

***

Back in the grand room, Johnny picked one of the girls and met her in one of the rooms.

The girl approached Johnny, trying to walk seductively, but she was unaccustomed to moving in her red stiletto high heels. "Whatever you like, I do," the girl told him, wobbling a bit. She removed her shoes and lifted the edge of the mattress to reveal a small baggy of white powder, a mirror, and part of a straw.

"This only little extra," the girl suggested with an insincere smile.

"Listen, all I want to do is talk," Johnny held up both of his hands to make sure she understood.

"Talk not free, okay? You want talk. Still pay," she insisted, still maintaining her flat smile.

"Yeah, sure. I get it. No problem. Here you go." He unrolled several Thai bills and sat them on the bed.

"This lot money. What going on? No one pay this for talk," she responded, taking out a comb and brushing her hair.

"Look, I'll make it plain. I need to know if you've seen this girl?" he asked, pulling up Sam's picture on his cell phone. "She's lost and we're trying to find her."

"I...I no understan'. English no good." She diverted her eyes from the screen and turned away, her body tensing up.

"Listen, I'm not here to get you in trouble," he spoke calmly to her. "I only need information to find my friend. There's probably enough money here for you to get a new start. Just tell me if you've seen her around. That's all I need to know...and maybe where you last saw her."

"No...I...I no understan'," the girl stuttered, standing up as though to walk away. Johnny stood up, blocking her from leaving, and held the phone in front of her face.

"Look at this picture...have you seen her!" he spoke through his teeth, showing his impatience.

"Echo Team, my girl didn't talk...got spooked and ran out as soon as I asked her," Chief whispered into his mic, still seated where the girl had left him. "Johnny, keep your eyes out. Chances are they will alert the guards."

Before he could complete the sentence, the guards had rushed in and pulled back the curtains, confronting both Chief and Johnny.

"You no here for good time," one of the guards angrily yanked back the curtain and reached behind his waistband for his gun.

Chief rose to his feet and held out his hands. "You don't need that...we'll leave peacefully," he spoke fast. "Johnny, let's go."

Johnny popped out from behind the curtain as the guards ushered him and Chief back through the grand room and down the hallway to the exit. The guards grabbed them by the backs of their shirts and Johnny perked up, ready to fight, but Chief signaled to him to stand down.

"No come back...," one guard shouted as they pushed them into the street. "Be big trouble for you."

As they stood in the middle of the road fixing their clothes, Switch and Bling ran up to them, the tourists going out of their way to avoid them.

"Chief, we came when we heard the guards kicking you out. We wanted to make sure you didn't need backup," Switch stated. "Randall is still with the Rover."

"Yeah, I'm still here listening in," Randall spoke into his mic.

"We're fine, but we need to hit the next spot on the list," Chief indicated. "Hopefully our cover isn't blown already...speaking of blown cover, Mack, where are you at, over?"

Everyone listened intently, waiting for him to reply, but he didn't respond.

"Mack, we don't have time for this. You better be dead or jammed up," Chief's face turned red as he scanned the crowd of tourists, searching for any sign of him.

"I'm here…y'all meet me in the alley," Mack finally chimed in as Chief pressed his hand to his forehead in frustration.

"Boss, that brothel is definitely illegal," Johnny suggested as they walked to the shadowy alley. "That girl was willing to do anything I asked of her. She even offered drugs."

"Mine too. It's a sad situation in there."

"What are we going to do about it?" Switch asked curiously. "I mean, you indicated that several are teens—and there's no way a teenager wants to be with old men. Someone needs to help them."

Chief stopped walking and looked him in the eye. "Listen, there's not much we can do. Even if we went in guns blazing, we'd be kicking them out into the streets into possibly an even worse situation. We need to get Mack and proceed with the mission."

"Unfortunately, Chief's right," Randall interjected as he listened in on the radio. "But while you all were inside, I contacted the captain from the sex crimes division to set up a raid. When they do, I know a great outreach organization that will come in after the bust and make contact with the girls. They'll offer them a way out and a new life."

"That's good news," Switch replied.

"Unfortunately, there are hundreds more of these brothels on on this strip and hardly anyone cares enough to do anything about it," Randall spoke again into his mic. "If the entire community got involved, we could shut this stuff down for good, but that's another problem altogether."

"Like we talked 'bout earlier, da community part of da problem," Bling interjected. "Can't rescue a drownin' person if you drownin' yourself."

"Man, you're right about that, Bling," Randall affirmed.

As they spoke, Mack nonchalantly popped out of the dark alley, stroking his long, white beard.

"Mack, what's up with you? Why did you leave like that?" Chief asked rather harshly. "Did you forget our motto? Individuals fail in battle, but—"

"Teams survive." Mack over talked him. "Of course I know our motto. I live that out every day, but I had a gut feeling."

"You can't just go by your gut. You could have gotten us into a bigger issue."

"Right. The last time we went by your gut we were led into that nasty Mexican buffet in Amarillo," Johnny teased.

"Yeah, well, if I stayed inside clubbing with you two, I wouldn't have met this nice gal right here," he remarked as everyone's eyes grew large, their curiosity clearly piqued.

"Yo, are you still trippin', Mack? I ain't seein' nobody," Bling suggested, the glow of Pattaya's red neon lighting glimmering off his gold tooth.

"It's okay, sweetheart, come on out," Mack called out in an uncharacteristically graceful tone as a young lady in her mid-20s stepped out of the dim alley. She wore a form-fitting white skirt and black, patent leather knee-high boots, her eyes showing uncertainty about what they wanted.

"She says she saw an American girl come into town a few days ago, and she knows her location," Mack stated, smiling about as wide as he could.

SEVEN
INCOMPLETE CALL

Days Earlier

The first rays of sunlight hit Mike's eyelids and a warm breeze brushed over his cheeks, waking him from a light sleep. He gradually opened his eyes to see a light mist on the tall reeds and the nearby well pump handle.

"Sam, wake up, we have to go now!" he insisted. They had slept longer than planned and the sun was already inching over the top of the hut's roofs.

Mike knelt on one knee, collecting items that had fallen out of his pack while Sam rubbed her eyes until they were no longer blurry. He popped his head up over the weeds, checking the village, his stomach still aching slightly.

"I can see a few villagers. They'll be here at any moment. How are you feeling? Can you move?" he asked.

"I feel better. Not a hundred percent, but I think I can move." Are we going to ask them for help?"

"Not here," he whispered, crouching behind the weeds and feeling for the gun to be sure it was still in his waistband. "The city should only be a mile or so away. I think we'll have better luck there. We can blend in as tourists and hopefully find someone who speaks English, but we need to be cautious. We don't know who we can trust."

"I agree. I'll follow your lead."

They stayed low behind the weeds, nearly crawling down the winding path until they were only a few yards from the village. Mike knelt in the sand where the paths intersected, pointing to the outlying row of stilted huts, silently indicating to take cover under them. Sam nodded and they held hands, darting across the path until they were directly under the hut's dilapidated flooring, stopping for a moment to rest against one of the stilts.

"What's that strange smell?" she asked, turning up her nose.

"Smells something like soap and noodles," he proposed, bending over and resting his hands on his knees, wheezing a bit. "I thought I was in better shape than this."

"It's the stress."

"Right. Let's see if we can change that today."

"I'm with you," she forced out a smile as they hustled through the loose sand, reaching the opposite side of the village where they maneuvered up a sandy knoll through a section of thick bamboo trees, eventually coming to a small side road.

They walked the road for several minutes until they came to an intersection at the highway. Taking cover behind a few trees near the road, they watched as various vehicles from motorcycles to taxicabs and even large commercial trucks carted people and products to their destinations, ready for the start of a new workday.

"It's got to be 100 degrees out here," Mike huffed out, pulling back and forth on his shirt to create a little personal breeze. Sam felt it as well but stayed silent, remembering how she had tried to tactfully rebuke him when he had complained about the temperature the day before.

Following the highway toward the city, they weaved in and out of the trees, staying out of sight. Mike kept an eye on the highway, making sure no one could spot them while Sam scrutinized the leaves and pine needles, watching for any movement, still leery of creeping creatures.

They cautiously trekked for what about a mile until their path was cut off by a wide, muddy river. They stood at the riverbank and peered across, able to see a small portion of the city and what appeared to be a farmer's market with several street vendors opening up for the day.

"Mike, look! Maybe there's a phone we can use!" she stated eagerly, a flicker of hope flashing across her eyes.

"We'll have to cross the bridge," he indicated, still watching the roadway as the cars were almost bumper-to-bumper. He hesitated to leave the cover of the trees, but it was the only way.

Sam agreed, and they cautiously stepped out, following the embankment up to the two-lane concrete bridge. As they got closer, they saw a group of Burmese women approaching the bridge, their jet black hair shimmering in the early-morning sun, each one carrying straw baskets filled with colorful fruits and vegetables.

The women were dressed in traditional Burmese attire—dark-colored, baggy, capri-style pants and striped ankle-length skirts tied at the waist in a large knot. Above the waist, they wore bland buttoned-up shirts and bowl-like straw hats that came to a triangular point at the top, each nearly the same diameter as the women's thin, square-framed bodies. The only similarities between them and the kids were their thong sandals that closely resembled the ones Mike had on—only theirs weren't caked in mud.

Mike and Sam reached the bridge at nearly the same time, pausing at the grassy edge to allow the women to pass first. Sam tried to see their faces, but their hats created a shadow that hid them well. Of those she could see, they appeared determined, almost as though they were on a mission. Sam struggled out a slight smile and waved, but soon gave up when they refused to acknowledge them.

That was rude...or maybe it's just their culture...or maybe something worse—maybe they're being abused, she thought as she stepped up on the sidewalk leading across the bridge. Mike followed closely behind until they were standing at the entrance of the sprawling market not far from the busy highway.

The street market was lined with mostly female vendors, their blankets spread out on the sidewalk to offer their products to customers. Several wooden lean-tos and umbrella-covered carts dotted the street where merchants sold items ranging from farm produce to flowers and even freshly cooked noodles.

Entering the market, they noticed a tiny convenience store tucked into the middle of a couple lean-tos. The store had less than ten feet of frontage space with an umbrella canopy jutting out over it. The large windows were full of posters advertising all sorts of items from phone calling cards to bubble teas and multiple rolling racks of snacks and knickknacks nearly blocking the partially opened door.

"That convenience store might have a phone," Sam stated eagerly.

"Let's check," Mike replied as they approached a short, older Burmese man squatting in front of the store and silently watching everyone opening up their vendor spaces for the day.

"Hello, sir," Mike stated as kindly as possible, but the man didn't respond.

"Sir, excuse me!" This time Mike raised his voice several octaves higher and the man finally acknowledged him.

"Do you have a phone?" he asked. Sam raised her hand by her head, extending her thumb to her ear and pinky to her mouth, figuring at least he could understand the universal sign of a telephone.

The man sat still for a moment and eventually stood up, motioning for them to enter his shop.

"300 Kyat," the man spoke for the first time, his back turned to them as he shuffled around a counter stacked with snacks and fruits.

"I'm sorry. We don't have any money...no kyat," Sam uttered.

"300 Kyat...or go," the man bluntly waved them off.

Mike rubbed his head, looking down at the floor, pondering how he could persuade the man to allow them to use the phone. They were so close. They could see the phone and even reach out and touch it, but they needed some leverage.

"What are we going to do," Sam looked at Mike but his eyes were glazed over. He reached his hand behind his back and placed his hand on the gun, feeling the warm metal between his fingers. He closed his eyes, ready to make the pull, but Sam reached around him and stayed his hand with hers.

"Mike, no…not like this," she insisted, tilting her head and staring into his dimmed eyes. He thought for a moment and eventually relented, bringing his hand back around to the front. The old man locked eyes with Mike and gradually backed away from the counter to get a little distance from him, unsure of his intentions.

Desperate to use the phone, Sam broke down and sobbed, hoping the man would see her emotional appeal and have compassion. When he heard her crying, he stood on his tiptoes to peer over the counter and saw her kneeling down on the grimy floor, her hands cupped to her face as the salty tears fell from between her fingers. Mike's spirits fell as he watched her break down.

With nearly no expression, the old man shuffled to the phone and picked it up, holding it out to them. Mike stared at the old man and then the phone, reaching out for it, but before he could grab it, the old man placed it on the counter and moved away.

"Sam!" Mike excitedly called out as he picked up the handset of the all-black, vintage rotary-style telephone. It was so archaic; so simple, and yet it was the lifeline that would secure their freedom.

Sam looked up through red, swollen eyes to see what he was holding, desperately hoping it was a phone.

"Oh, thank God!" she mumbled, wiping her tears and snotty nose with the edge of her tank up, getting a clear view of the phone.

"Here, you call your parents first," he insisted, holding the phone's spiral-corded handset out to her.

She stood up, cupping her hand over her mouth, her eyes locked on the phone. They could see the end of their nightmare for the first time. She held the phone to her ear, checking for a dial tone and placed her finger into the number five on the circular dial, moving it clockwise to the finger stop, letting it click back. It took only about a minute to enter all the numbers, but to her, it was taking an eternity.

She pressed the handset tightly to her ear, contemplating what she would say to her parents. They had been adamant about them not leaving for Burma and here she was calling for help. Her pride nearly caused her to hang up…almost, but her pride also wanted to live.

Uuuuur Errrrrrr Eee. Sam didn't understand the words that followed, but she was familiar with the sound. The call couldn't be completed. With her optimism dashed, she placed the phone back on the receiver and tried the number again, hoping for a better outcome, but the result was the same.

"No, we're so close!" Sam's eyes welled up again. Mike grabbed the phone, holding it up to his ear, listening to the sound of the phone company's intercept message.

"Don't panic, Sam. Let me try my parents."

Mike did his best to remain calm, but after entering their number twice and getting the same result, he too was getting worried.

"They must not have international calling," he stated, pacing with his hands interlocked on his head, attempting to stave off the encroaching anxiety. "Maybe we can call an 800-number."

"Sam?" he called out to her, but she didn't respond. She was fully enveloped in debilitating fear.

"Mike, what if…what if we're…we're stuck here," she stuttered.

"No! Stop it. We're too close. I'm trying another number," he insisted, picking up the phone and dialing a random 800 number. He held the phone to his ear, tapping the floor with his foot, impatiently waiting for it to connect him with someone, anyone who might help them, but seconds later he got the same unnerving results.

Frustrated, he slammed the phone down and grabbed Sam's hand, rushing out of the store, nearly pulling her behind him.

"We've got to find another phone, a cell phone maybe. Someone has to have service to the States."

With intensity in his eyes, he studied every detail of the market, looking for anyone who might have a cell phone.

Several yards away, he spied out a group of three younger men seated at a round table in front of a small café. The men were in their mid- to upper 20s, dressed casually in T-shirts and shorts, and playing what looked like a dice game.

"Maybe one of those guys will let us use their phone," he spoke fast as they walked through the street, but then abruptly stopped.

Athletic build, military-style haircuts…wait, what is that on their arm? he thought as his legs became weak.

"What's wrong?" Sam asked, seeing his rigidness and sensing a problem.

As they stood in the street, one of the men spotted them. He leaned in and whispered something to the other men at the table and they all watched them from the corner of their eyes, trying to play it cool, but Mike noticed.

"Sam, turn around slowly and go to the next shop."

"Mike, why, what's wron—"

"Trust me…keep walking…act interested in something at the shop," he whispered under his breath.

They turned into one of a nearby street vendor's lean-to and hid behind a T-shirt display, acting as though they were shopping.

"What is it? You're scaring me."

He didn't respond as he peered back out into the street and saw that the men were strolling in their direction, one of them using a cell phone to make a call.

Mike grabbed Sam's hand and moved to the side of the shop, slipping in-between another lean-to.

"Why won't you tell me what's going on?" she insisted.

"Look, their working for TJ!"

Sam listened in horror and her hands went numb.

"Oh my God…what are we going to do?" her eyes widened, too worried to even think of asking how Mike knew that.

"Just follow my lead. We'll get out of this."

71

Mike strapped his pack tightly to his back and grabbed Sam's hand, darting through the back of the shops and weaving through the workers who were still setting up for the day.

"We're gonna...get back to the bridge...hide under it," Mike could barely get the words out as they sprinted back to the bridge, his sandals breaking and falling off his feet in the process.

They reached the bridge soon after, but the men had given chase and were only seconds behind. Seeing no way to outrun them, Mike stopped in the middle of the bridge and faced off with them.

"Why are you stopping?!" Sam shouted as cars rolled by, the passengers gawking at them.

"It's...it's no use," he spoke, gasping for breath. "We'll make our...stand here," he finished, moving her behind him to protect her.

The men slowed to a saunter, grinning and heckling. There was no place for the kids to run. One of the men reached into his pocket and pulled out a switchblade knife. He held the small, rectangular chunk of metal in his hand and pressed a button on its side, causing the six-inch-long, spike-like blade to spring out. He waved the menacing knife back and forth, the sun reflecting off the polished blade, which prompted the kids to reflect on their short lives, wondering if this would be their end.

As the men pushed closer to the kids, a faded yellow motorbike with three men in the back stopped on the opposite side of the bridge, blocking traffic. Mike and Sam looked back and saw TJ and two of his goons, each holding wooden axe handles. They were trapped with no place to go.

"Why run? We always catch," TJ smacked his lips, approaching them in a cool manner.

Mike reached behind him and put his hand on the gun's grip.

"TJ—or Tuan—or whoever you are—don't come any closer. I've got your gun and I will shoot!" Mike shouted as he pulled the gun from his waistband, aiming it at TJ.

TJ laughed sinisterly. "You got gun, but I got bullet."

Mike examined the gun for the first time, not realizing when he had gained control of it the magazine had dropped out. He had only one round in the chamber.

"You no take us all," TJ grinned widely, all but assured of his victory.

"But at least I can take you out," Mike snapped back, aiming even more intently at TJ.

TJ's smirk instantly turned to a violent frown.

"You shoot me. You better kill. I come for you…forever," TJ cracked his neck as he motioned for the men behind them to advance.

Mike glanced over the edge of the bridge at the swirling river below, calculating the distance and their chances of survival if they jumped. It was at least a 20-foot drop. He wanted to shoot TJ and take his chances with the other goons, but that was senseless; there was no way he could take all of them on with only one bullet. Sam saw him contemplating the jump and whispered to him.

"I don't want to die in that brothel, Mike. Whatever you decide, I'm with you."

That's all he needed to hear.

As TJ's goons rushed in, he grabbed her hand and stepped up onto the guardrail, both of them leaping off and plunging into the river below, instantly disappearing beneath the murky waters.

EIGHT
RED HAZE

Days Later

What's your name, darlin'?" Chief asked, his voice abnormally calm and gentle. The dark-skinned young lady considered his question as the colorful neon street signs reflected off her silky skin. Her shiny nose ring, bright green high heels and matching waist-long wig stood out in the gloomy alley like a hunter wearing orange.

"My...my...my name—you want to know my name?" she eventually answered in a thick, West African accent. She glanced at the team member's kindhearted eyes and noted how they were connecting with hers. They weren't like her typical customers; they were unmoved by her tight-fitting dress and partially exposed body—and her guard was gradually falling.

"Is everything okay?" Chief asked.

"Everytang fine, but men here usually only want to know price."

"Well, we want to know your name—your real name. We're trying to help another young lady like you and you could very well change her fate tonight."

She looked down as though this was the first time a man had told her she had a purpose beyond what she could do to please him with her body.

"My real name? I haven't...haven't told anyone in years, but my real name is Adaeze," she responded delicately.

"Nice to meet you, Adaeze. Everyone calls me Chief, but my real name is Eric. Where are you from?"

"From Ghana. I'm what everyone calls a freelancer, but, I, um..." She abruptly paused and fear overtook her eyes.

Mack turned and looked across the road to see what had caught her attention. On the opposite side of the road, an older Asian man in a black suit and gangster-style hat was smoking a cigarette and glaring at her. When he saw Mack, he puffed out a plume of smoke and casually disappeared into the crowd.

"Look, I know you're probably afraid," Chief stated, "But you will be helping—"

Before Chief could finish, Mack whispered into his ear, "Chief, she got spooked by dude in the street. He looks like he's mob."

Chief listened intently, considering the situation, and finally addressed her. "Okay, darlin', I understand. Here's what I want you to do for us..." he leaned in close and whispered. She whispered something back and nodded as though to signal an agreement.

"Alright, let's go," Chief stated sternly, placing her hands behind her back and zip tying them together.

"Chief?" Switch was confused by his actions.

"Everyone follow my lead," Chief stated, grabbing Adaeze by her cuffed hands and leading her into the street.

They walked a couple minutes when Chief stopped to look at a street map. While he was preoccupied, Adaeze kicked him in his midsection. He doubled over and she ducked into a nearby bar.

"Get her!" Johnny cried out, helping Chief to his feet as several tourists ogled in their direction.

"Y'all never mind her," Chief groaned.

"Boss, are you crazy?" Johnny asked, "She knows where the girl is."

"I know."

"Then let's get her."

"Johnny," Chief whispered, "She already told me. We were role playing. I'm just doing this so she doesn't get any heat."

"Oh…that's…that's brilliant, boss, brilliant. Got it," he replied as everyone smiled at Chief's wisdom in getting the info and still managing to protect the girl.

"Let's get back to the Rover and I'll fill everyone in."

***

The team loaded into the Rover and Chief pulled out his phone, opening a map of Pattaya.

"Guys, listen up. Adaeze told me the word around town is there's an American girl at a massage parlor at the opposite end of Walking Street, apparently across from a large pier. She couldn't recall the name, but she said we couldn't miss it."

"Chief, I know the place; it's called Bengal Massage," Randall advised. "It's located opposite of Bali Hai Pier, which is where the ferries drop off the boys they pick up off the US Naval ships in the bay—an American girl would bring in big bucks there."

"So, wait, the US military is part of this stuff?" Switch asked.

"Not by design," Randall advised. "The Navy uses the bay because it's a safe place to anchor and the beaches are a beautiful place for shore leave, but it wasn't long before the sailors discovered that Pattaya has more than just pretty beaches."

"Alright guys, pay close attention," Chief instructed. "We're going in super soft on this place. I don't want us to spook them."

"I have an idea, boss," Johnny spoke up.

"Let's hear it."

"I know these Asian massage joints well. Let me and Switch dress up in Navy fatigues and you can drop us off at the pier area. We'll play it off like Navy boys fresh off the boat and get one the girls to invite us inside."

"That might work," Chief suggested.

"There's a military supply store about two klicks from the brothel where you can get fatigues," Randall indicated.

"Okay, that's the plan then. While you guys are doing your thing, we'll stay close, listening in on the radios. The map shows a parking area adjacent to the lot near the brothel. We'll provide surveillance from there," Chief pointed at the map as everyone affirmed the plan.

***

Johnny and Switch jumped out of the Rover near the pier and fixed their blue and white camouflage hats, doing their best to appear like sailors who had come to Pattaya looking for a fun time. On the same side as the brothel was a long strip center and directly across the street was a bar connected to a dance club.

"Echo Team, we've got a visual on Bengal Massage," Chief indicated as Bling drove the Rover past the front entrance and pulled around the rear of the building, parking behind the adjacent strip center. "It's a skinny two-story building down on the north side—about 20 meters, over."

"That's a good copy, Delta. We're leaving the pier area now, over," Johnny replied.

"Chief, while we're waiting around, do you think I can change out of these flowery civies?" Mack asked as he listened in, searching around for his pack in the back of the Rover.

"Go for it. While you're back there, pass up the yellow pack in my gear bag," he instructed, checking out the rear entrance of the massage parlor through his binoculars.

Chief and Mack changed into their operations clothing, black cargo pants and a black T-shirt for Chief and black cargo shorts and a camo tank top for Mack. Chief attached his sidearm holster to his webbed belt, clipped his tactical flashlight and two folding pocket knives onto each pocket and replaced his athletic shoes with black tactical boots, complete with a long fixed-blade boot knife.

"Ah, this is so much better," Mack sighed, gearing up with his weapons and throwing on his tactical vest and gloves, topping it off with clear protective glasses and an American flag bandana.

"Delta Team, this is Echo Team. We can see the parlor's neon sign. We're seconds away," Johnny spoke into his mic as they walked.

"Roger that, Echo Team."

As they moved in, Johnny gave Switch a few pointers to make sure he was ready. "Try to make your eyes look like they're glazed over—pretend like the ladies bodies are the only thing on your mind. That's how the men looked whenever I did brothel busts on the vice team."

"Really?" Switch asked.

"Yeah, they look similar to a druggie."

"That does make sense though. Before we left, I did some research on sex trafficking and discovered that it's basically an extension of porn, and porn releases the same chemical reaction as drugs do in the brain. I'll try my best to channel in that look," he replied as they walked the street close to the brothel.

The brothel was housed in a two-story commercial building with a flat roof, two large plate glass windows, and a single entrance door, each tinted pitch-black and outlined in neon lighting. A green awning protruded out a few feet over the windows and several young Asian ladies were seated outside at a few round tables, hoping to attract male customers walking by.

"Hey, booooooy...come inside! Give you massage you never forget!" an older Asian woman in her early 60s addressed them in a suggestive tone. She sat at one of the tables puffing on a long, skinny cigarette. As she spoke, two other Thai girls, both in their late teens, got up from the tables and alluringly approached Johnny and Switch. They carried the same flat smiles they had seen on nearly every girl in Pattaya.

The girls were dressed in short, yellow dresses and their hair tied into double-sided ponytails, each with a puffy, cheerleader type-bow tying it off.

Switch held his eyes on one of the young lady's body without blinking and his lips formed a devious smile, giving his best acting performance, which wasn't entirely difficult since he was a man with eyes.

"We like military boy!" the older woman stated as the soft neon glows mixed with the bright street lights emphasized her vibrant blue eye shadow, hard wrinkles, and blatant love handles.

"Dat wasn't long," Bling stated, overhearing the conversation.

"Hi there...we'll be right back. Just gonna get some drinks first," Switch indicated in a nerdy tone as he pointed across the street, innocently stepping away toward an outdoor bar.

"No go far...many girl...you choose!"

"Delta, we're not seeing any American girls," Johnny spoke into his mic as he and Switch strolled up to the bar. "We've moved about 10 meters across the street to a local bar. We'll give it a little time. She might be inside, over."

"Roger that. We're in the rear parking lot. We've got eyes on the exit," Chief replied.

Several minutes transpired and Switch noticed some unusual activity at the front of the brothel. All the girls rushed back inside and the neon open sign suddenly went dark.

"Something's going down at the brothel. We're going in," Johnny spoke into the radio as they walked across the street.

"Roger that.," Chief replied.

Johnny and Switch stood in front of the massage parlor's darkly tinted glass door and slowly pulled it open, doing their best to appear like a couple spellbound Navy boys. The round bell that hung over the door loudly announced their entrance and a single red light bulb dangled from the ceiling, creating a red glow on everything they could see—the dingy walls, the commercial tile floor, and even the clear bowl of breath mints; it was like they were standing inside a photographer's darkroom.

"You know what I find odd?" Switch asked as he looked around. "Every place in this city is drenched in an odd reddish-colored light?"

"You noticed that, huh?" Johnny replied. "When I was on the force, we called them lust lamps or the red haze...nearly every brothel I've been to uses them. The red haze effect is from the neon signage and red bulbs the brothels use to set the mood for the men."

"And what about the disgusting smell? Do they all have that as well?" Switch cringed as he drew in a whiff of the peculiar odor permeating the foyer. It was as if a machine shop was attempting to mask its metallic and musky aroma with cherry air freshener trees—the kind you hang on your rearview mirror. The copper penny and cough syrupy smell was so thick it seeped into Switch's taste buds, initiating his gag reflex.

"Yep, hate that smell," Johnny kept his voice low as he scanned the small foyer that wasn't much larger than an average closet. "When I worked the task force back in the States, the burnt cherry smell was always one of our first indicators of prostitution."

"It's giving me the willies."

"Another common sign of illegal activity were ATMs like this one," Johnny stated, walking over and pulling a recent receipt from the dispenser. "The brothel pimps want quick cash. Plus, the johns don't necessarily want Gigi's Massage Parlor showing up on their credit card statement for their wives to get a hold of; cash provides a level of anonymity."

Switch nodded, contemplating Johnny's words.

"This brothel is typical of every brothel I've helped raid," Johnny stated. "Several security cameras, a second gated entrance, and look…" Johnny reached out and pulled back the curtain hanging behind the barred secondary door, revealing several girls moving around in skimpy clothing.

"So the gated door is to keep these girls trapped inside?" Switch's voice sounded more agitated by the second.

"In many brothels, yes, they use barred doors to keep the girls under their control, but those running them will excuse them away. They'll say they're only to deter thieves."

"Is that true?" Switch asked, pressing the doorbell.

"It's partly true, but burglars target brothels because they have lots of cash on hand and are already involved in illegal activity, which means they are much less likely to notify the police. So, in a way, they bring it on themselves."

"Hello!" Johnny spoke through the bars, realizing someone should have answered the door already. "We're here for a massage…happy ending…"

"The girls we saw out front—their job is to wait outside to attract the men, but the brothel goons are always watching. The older woman we saw is the madam, a type of manager who watches over the girls."

"Really?"

"Yep. But if we were to ask her, she would say that she's just the cleaning lady. That's what they always told us."

"I'm guessing that didn't work too well."

"Nope. It's about evidence, not words. People will say anything to not get caught."

Johnny pulled back the curtain again and caught a glimpse of some ladies running around as though they were anticipating a raid. He quickly called it in. "Chief, I've got something. Two male perps are escorting a girl out the rear…do you copy, over?"

"Roger. We see them. Hold your position."

"Copy that."

"Looks like we spooked 'em," Chief proposed as he spied through his binoculars, watching two men hurry a young lady out the back door of the brothel into a boxy, black 1980's Ford Crown Victoria. "I've got eyes on the girl…she definitely looks American. Correct height and build, but she's a brunette."

"Dark hair. Are you sure?" Mack leaned in, straining to look out the windshield, but he was only able to see dark shadows moving about in the dim alleyway.

"I'm positive, but it could still be her. We don't know what lengths they took to disguise her. The perps escorting her—one is definitely Asian and the other looks Eastern European."

"Well, you called it, Randall, looks like them commies are involved," Mack spoke up. "I wonder how deep this here traffikin' stuff goes."

"Deeper than most realize," Randall indicated.

Bling didn't say a word, but his lips were moving fast as though he was in prayer.

NINE
RIVER OF DEATH

Days Earlier

Mike had tried to enter the river feet first, but he fell awkwardly, violently slamming into the river's shallow, rocky bottom, twisting his ankle and lacerating his feet. Disregarding his ankle's sharp throbbing pain, he stayed submerged, swimming under the briskly-moving water, eventually resurfacing exactly where he had hoped, directly under the bridge and out of TJ and his goon's sight, but when he popped up, Sam was nowhere to be seen.

He frantically scanned the surface of the diarrhea-colored water—the kind that comes during the first few days of the flu and with about the same odor—but there was no sign of her. He closed his eyes tight and dove back under, trying to swim against the current to where they had plunged in. He fiercely thrashed his arms, searching for anything solid, but felt nothing but the occasional floating stick and foam cup. Moments later, he resurfaced, but this time he was completely exposed to TJ and his goons.

When he popped back up, Sam had already resurfaced several yards away, closer to the shore and under the bridge. She appeared a little dazed, but she was able to swim.

Mike finally spotted her. "Oh, thank God!" he uttered under his breath as he swam toward her. "Sam, I'm right here!" He yelled to get her attention. She turned around and saw him and was immediately relieved.

"Mike, look, a boat!" she shouted, pointing to a 10-foot long, wooden canoe beached on the shore not far from them. Somehow Mike hadn't seen it before and it was exactly what he needed for some motivation.

They swam through the brownish-green river, angling to the canoe and using the swift-moving current to propel them forward, reaching it moments later.

"Sam, get in, I'll catch up," he insisted, helping her into the boat. TJ's men had already slid down the embankment on the opposite side and were only seconds from reaching them. TJ looked on from the bridge with a sadistic smile, already thinking of the extreme torture he would inflict on them for attempting to escape.

"Row, Sam, Row hard!" he yelled, removing one of the oars and digging his feet into the mud, disregarding his pain, and giving the canoe a hard shove. As she floated off, he gave her a look as though this could be the last time he ever saw her.

She was a good 25 feet away when TJ's goons caught up to Mike. He clutched the oar in his hands and waited on the shoreline, his eyes fierce. He mentally gathered his remaining strength, channeling it into his hands, ready for a battle to the end. This was it; he was fighting for Sam, fighting for survival, fighting for everyone who these goons had taken advantage of— and he was prepared to die doing it.

TJ's goons tramped through the last portion of the river up the muddy shore, their axe handles in tow, but they strained to find solid footing. They kept their eyes on Mike as they stepped into the gooey mud, the river water rushing around their feet, causing an unsteady stance.

Mike gripped the oar tightly, his knuckles pale white as Sam watched in horror. The goons approached him, tapping the axe handles in their hands to intimidate him, but before Sam could see what would happen, she disappeared behind some thick reeds at the bend in the river.

"Mikkkkkkke!" Sam screamed at the top of her lungs as she rounded the bend, jolting the birds out of the canopy of the nearby trees and startling the goons. That's when Mike took his opportunity to strike.

Thunk! He jabbed the blade end of the oar into the goon's neck, pinching his juggler vein and pummeling him backward into the river.

The other goon had gained some ground and maneuvered behind Mike, but when he did he met the oar full force at his knees, his legs flying out from under him. Mike finished him off by slamming the oar down on his back, face-planting him into the fly-filled muck.

TJ stood watching on the bridge, his face red with rage and nearly shaking, shouting obscenities in his native tongue and reaching for his cell phone.

Once Mike saw that the threats were eliminated, he moved as quickly as he could down the edge of the shore to where Sam had disappeared, but when he got there she was gone, but he wasn't out of hope. A few yards away he saw another canoe abandoned on the shoreline. He darted toward it, maneuvering around wild bushes and vines, his bare toes digging into the mud.

He crawled inside the canoe and rowed hard down the river, trying to catch up with Sam. He rowed at a decent pace for several minutes, the landscape around him blurring into an endless sea of greens and browns. He hadn't noticed them before, but the shore was littered with various-sized crocodiles basking in the sun, nearly as long and wide as his canoe, their jaws open, exposing rows of conical teeth. As he pushed on, all he could think about was how Sam was probably freaking out at the sight of the ferocious-looking reptiles.

Mike rowed a little further, stabbing his oar deep into the water to get some good thrusts when his strength suddenly vaporized, zapped away as though his blood sugar had nose-dived into kryptonite. It was like every muscle in his body instantly became gelatin.

He sat on the canoe's bow seat, taking a break to collect himself, but it didn't help; it was only getting worse—and then the dizziness set in, the clouds and trees spinning wildly. He closed his eyes and nearly fell out of the boat, but he somehow managed to grab the edge and collapsed into the hull, his head throbbing in pain. He had the urge to vomit but did his best to hold it back to keep from losing precious fluid.

He rested on his back, floating along and thinking about Sam, when something bumped up against the canoe. Whatever it was pulled him off into another direction and gave him a slight bit of shade from the beating sun. He opened his eyes and sat up to get a look.

"Oh, Mike! Thank God you're alive!" Sam nearly shouted as she climbed in his boat, leaving hers behind. "I saw a canoe floating with a body in it. I…I knew it was you, but I didn't know if you were…" she spoke fast but couldn't finish her sentence. Relieved, she put her hand over her nose and mouth and bawled.

Still fighting against his dizziness, he moved next to her and held her tight while she continued sobbing.

"Sam, I…I lost my pack," he hung his head as though he had done something wrong. She did her best to get control of her emotions, wiping the tears from her cheeks, trying to stay strong.

"It's okay, we'll figure it out," she quietly reassured him, placing her arm around him, just glad he was alive.

"It had my tent and snack bars. Now, we don't even have food."

Sam remained quiet, not sure what she could say that would make any difference. Seconds later, Mike perked up a bit. "If we're going to make it out of here, at the very least, we'll need some decent water." He was clearly drained, but his statement indicated he still had fight left.

"I would give anything for a bottle of cold water and something…anything to eat," she mentioned, but he stayed quiet, not wanting to entertain the food conversation and add to his stomach rumbling.

They continued floating the ever-widening river that was now about 50 feet across. Mike returned to resting in the hull while Sam searched the river's shoreline, hoping to spot a tree with some hanging fruit, but there was nothing but unending mangrove and palm bushes that had assembled to form a dense jungle. Large willow trees were mixed in, their draping vines flowing over the edge of the river like a massive wig, providing sporadic shade.

As they drifted along, Sam had a strange feeling come over; it was as though every noise had been drowned away. She saw the gulls pecking at dead fish carcasses and the locusts gulping up the swarms of gnats hovering over the water, but she couldn't hear them. She couldn't even hear the leaves rustling in the light breeze or the slight roar of the mildly-moving river. In the midst of her silence she began to feel shame that she was somehow responsible for everything. She became hyperaware of herself, focusing on her partially dried and now coffee-colored tank top that dripped putrid river water onto her legs. Her sense of smell was heightened as well, consumed by the unbearable scent of her own body odor and the nauseating aroma in her hair, a smelly combination of sweat and fishy river water. She pulled her ponytail into a bun to keep her malodorous hair from flopping into her face, but it did little to help.

"Mike, are you asleep?" she asked quietly, wanting to break the silence of her thoughts.

"No, my mind won't shut off...what's up?"

"I, uh, I just want to say that I'm sorry. If it weren't for me, we wouldn't have gotten into this." She hung her head.

"Listen, Sammy, don't be so hard on yourself," he reasoned, sitting up and putting his hand on her knee. "I can make my own decisions...and I'm the one who decided to come. What's done is done."

"Can I ask you a question?" she asked timidly, unsure how he would respond.

"Go for it."

"Well, when we were at the market, you noticed something that kept us from walking straight into TJ's goons."

He nodded his head as he looked around the river's edge, his eyes adjusting to the bright sun and taking notice of a flat clearing with some rice paddy fields and a small irrigation stream.

"What did you see? More than likely it saved us."

"This is going to sound crazy, but—" he paused, not sure if he should share.

"What is it? Tell me. I want to know," she insisted, her gaze fixed on him as she leaned in closer.

"It's pretty depressing, honestly; it's part of the reason why I've been so negative with you from the beginning."

"It's okay, Mikey. I was hard on you, but you were right. I'm truly sorry. I want to know. Please share with me," she smiled from the corner of her mouth as though to convey sympathy and to persuade him to share.

He finally relented. "Okay, look, two nights before we left to come here, I uh…I had a dream. At first, I didn't think much of it, but the next night I had the exact same dre—" he abruptly stalled mid-sentence and his demeanor became uneasy.

"Sam, paddle to the left…"

"Why? What is it?"

"Look at the bridge up ahead."

Sam swiveled around in her sear to see a rickety bamboo footbridge connecting the dark jungle to the flat farmland about 50 yards downriver.

"What am I supposed to be looking at?" she asked nervously as they paddled to the edge of the river.

"Look at the left side…it looks like the front end of a motorbike."

Sam shielded her eyes from the sun with her hand and caught a glimpse of the bike, and almost immediately, her mind took her back to the conversation she had with Kylee in the brothel.

"Oh God, what should we do, Mike?"

"Let's try to paddle back to that rice field. I saw a small stream running along the edge of it. We can rest there and they won't be able to find us. They won't wait there forever."

They rowed hard, nearing the stream a few minutes later, but as they did something whizzed by Mike's head, coupled with a loud crack. Then two more whizzes and two more cracking noises.

"They're shooting! Row faster!" Mike yelled.

They pushed out the last of their energy as they reached the area where the river linked up with the stream and Mike checked the bridge. When he did, he observed TJ and several other men dressed in camouflage, their rifles resting on the bamboo railing, aiming in their direction.

"Quick, Sam, jump into the river!"

"What about the crocs?"

"It's a chance we have to take...those are soldiers!"

Lacking options, they jumped into the river and hid behind the canoe, dragging it along for cover. Mike drug it from the bow and Sam pulled it near the stern, kicking their feet to reach the stream, their eyes scanning between the shore and the water's surface, staying low, but also searching for anything in the water that might eat them.

Ratatatat! Ratatat! The soldiers fired their rifles for several more seconds, kicking up mud and debris around the kids and then, suddenly, everything went quiet.

Mike figured they were reloading, but when he scrutinized the bridge he saw the back of an army transport vehicle turning around.

"Sam, hold on, I think they're leaving."

Sam pulled herself up and peered over the top of the canoe, catching a glimpse of the military truck driving off. Her heart rate slowed a bit and her short, inconsistent breaths were becoming longer and smoother, but her anxiety wasn't altogether eliminated. She still feared what could be in the water, so she hurried to hoist herself up into the canoe, pulling herself in, nearly tipping it over in the process. Mike followed, plopping into the canoe that had been riddled with bullet holes near the top, but not far enough down to cause leaking. He inspected it for any holes and rowed into the stream, trying to ignore his dizziness and pain.

"I can't believe TJ has connections to the military," he stated in disbelief, maneuvering the canoe upstream through the four-foot-tall weeds.

"I'm glad they left when they did, Mike, look—" Sam pointed back to the area where the stream met the river. On the bank were a handful of sunbathing crocodiles waiting for an afternoon snack.

"What's your plan, Mike?"

"I think we should see where the stream takes us. It'll be safer than the main river. Hopefully, it will take us near some food and water."

Sam slumped forward without blinking, still considering the crocodiles and how the military was now tracking them.

"Sam, are you okay?"

"Hello, Sam? Are you still with me?"

"I'm still here…I guess," she replied flatly.

"Hey! Come on. I need you. Hang in there," he put his hand on her shoulder, her eyes refocusing on his.

"I…I just don't see how we can escape this. Are you seeing what I'm seeing? I mean, the freakin' military is after us!"

"I know, I know, but we can't lose hope. If our mind goes, we go. We can do this," he did his best to encourage her as she listened.

Mike paddled the canoe up the six-foot-wide stream, feeling the rocky bottom with his oar. Soon they would be forced to ditch the canoe and go at it on foot, which would bring a new set of issues. While he rowed, Sam stood in the middle of the canoe to get a peek over a row of weeds that separated the stream from the rice paddies. As soon as she did, she saw something that gave her hope.

"It looks like there's a village on that hill!" she exclaimed, talking so fast her words nearly overlapped.

Mike ignored his dizziness and stood in the canoe, his balance unsteady. She held onto him as he strained his eyes and eventually saw several one-room shanties on stilts, spattered on the side of a distant hill.

"I see it; it might be an option for us."

"But won't TJ will check for us there?"

"I don't think they saw us enter the stream. They probably think we went back upriver, but it's only a matter of time before they check it out. Still, if we don't get water, it won't matter if they find us anyway. We need to get to that village."

TEN
RESCUE OP

Days Later

C hief gripped the binoculars tightly, his arms becoming slightly heavy as he focused on the perps forcing the young lady into the rear seat of the Crown Vic. He considered moving in for the rescue but changed his mind after discovering they were sporting leather shoulder pistol rigs.

"We can't take out Comrade and his partner here," Chief surmised. "Their packing heat and we'd cause too much of a scene. Randall, I don't want to put you in that position. I'm sure your government wouldn't appreciate us conducting a covert operation in the heart of their most lucrative tourist area."

"I have quite a bit of pull, but you're right about that. It would be better to take them down outside the city if possible."

"Bling, when they pull out I want you to trail them, but don't make it obvious," Chief instructed.

"Yo, you got it—er, I mean copy dat," Bling replied, still getting used to the team's lingo.

"Echo Team come in, over," Chief hailed Johnny and Switch.

"Copy, boss," Johnny checked in for both of them.

"Listen, y'all find some transportation and hang tight. I'll let you know where we're at so y'all can meet up, over."

"Roger that, Delta."

The Crown Vic turned on its headlights and pulled away from the rear of the brothel onto the main road and Bling followed them about three car-lengths behind.

"Echo Team, we're on Pattaya 3rd Road heading west out of the city, over," Chief indicated.

"Roger that. We found a taxi. We'll head that direction, over," Johnny replied.

Bling trailed the car on a two-lane highway for about 15 minutes when it turned off on a pitch-black county road.

"Chief, that road is a dead-end," Randall reported, reviewing a map he had pulled up on his phone.

"Bling, pull over here," Chief instructed. Bling edged off the highway, stopping at a wide spot in the road where it intersected with the dirt side road. All they could see of the Crown Vic was a small portion of its red taillights, obscured by a cloud of dust.

"Echo Team, we stopped. I'm texting you the coordinates."

"Copy that," Switch replied.

"According to my map, the road dead-ends into an old farm," Randall indicated.

"Chief, what's the plan here?" Mack asked, "You know I'd like nothin' better than to bust in and rescue that girl, but if they're mafia they'll take her out before they hand her over."

"You're right...we need to think this through," Chief replied, removing his cowboy hat and scratching his head as though deep in thought. "Echo Team, what's your ETA? We need Switch to get the drone in the air to give us eyes on a farm where they've taken the girl. We could have a situation with several players."

"Copy that, we're five mikes out."

"Make it four," he replied with a sense of urgency in his voice. "Mack, I've gotta feeling we'll need the night-vision. Give it a check while we're waiting."

"You got it," Mack replied, rummaging through the gear bags, searching for everyone's night-vision and checking the function on each one.

Moments later, the taxi dropped Johnny and Switch off and they met up with everyone back inside the Rover.

"Alright, team, listen up," Chief stated firmly. "We don't know what type of resistance we'll meet at this farm, but I feel like it's connected to our girl. If we're gonna be successful, we need to make a hard move on it tonight."

"Assault op? We're all with you," Johnny wrung his hands, speaking up as though no one else had a say in the matter.

"Rescue op, Johnny. We're not shooting unless fired upon."

"Yeah, sure, boss, whatever you say."

"I don't care how it looks or how long it takes, I'm down, brother," Randall stated as everyone gave an affirming nod.

"Good," he replied, "Switch, get the drone in the air so we can get some recon on that farm."

"Already on it, Chief," he replied, configuring the drone for night-vision and launching it out the window, following the dirt road to the farm.

A few minutes later, Switch had the drone hovering over the farm, sending images back to the team as everyone watched on the Rover's screens.

"The only buildings I'm seeing are two single-story, cabin-like houses, both of them a little larger than a two-car garage. They're situated facing each other with a small courtyard in-between and surrounded by at least 50 acres of dense vegetation on all sides except the west. Westside has thin vegetation, mostly sporadic palm trees. I can also make out a gated entrance and a couple barking dogs."

"What do you see on infrared?" Chief asked.

"Switching over now," he replied, zooming the drone's camera out for a wider view.

"I can make out two male subjects…but I can't see inside the building. If you want to take the time, I can hack into their security cameras or laptops for a closer look."

Bling spoke up. "Yo, I thought them infrared cameras be seein' through walls."

"That's only in the movies. Infrared can't even see through glass; it acts as a mirror."

"How long would it take to hack in," Chief asked, drawing a schematic in his notebook of what he saw and heard.

"Assuming they take the bait email, maybe an hour, but more like three or four."

"We don't have that kind of time. Keep an eye on it and report back. 15 mikes max."

"Copy that."

Switch kept the drone hovering for several minutes, watching for any movement when a door opened on one of the houses.

"Chief, I've got something," Switch reported. "A perp left the door open. I can see multiple subjects in the north house...hang on...looks like several females on a bed. Wait, there's another male subject and he appears to be recording them."

"Figures...we talked about that earlier," Randall stated, feeling anger rise up. "They're selling the girls through prostitution and using them to make porn...big money enterprise here."

"Those sick sons of—" Mack shouted, hitting the seats in front of him.

"Alright, let's keep it together guys. So far we've got four MAMs...most likely all armed," Chief indicated.

"Mams?" Bling interrupted, tilting his head with a confused look.

"Military Age Males," Johnny interpreted, shaking his head at the lack of Bling's understanding.

"Guys, I want everyone in their vests—including you, Bling. The one advantage we'll have is our night-vision and the drone's overwatch. Bling, you'll be in the Rover with Randall. Switch, leave the drone hovering on autopilot and Randall can report what he's seeing to us."

"Copy that," Switch replied.

"You got it," Randall affirmed as Switch maneuvered the drone several feet higher for a fuller view of the farm.

Chief turned to the team and held up his notebook, continuing his instruction. "Bling will drive us in and drop us 200 meters

94

from the farm. We'll enter the wooded area here on the east side. That should provide us with plenty of cover. We'll improvise as we go, but I want to make it clear that the goal is to eliminate the threats quickly and quietly—and without unnecessary carnage."

"Quiet is my middle name," Mack replied with a loud belch as everyone slipped on their vests, adjusting the straps and securing the smoke grenades, flashbangs, and tactical flashlights.

Everyone except Chief and Mack had their favorite sidearm attached to the front of their vest directly under the extra 9mm ammo magazines for their MP5 submachine guns. Johnny carried an all-black SIG pistol, Switch his Beretta, and Randall his police-issued Glock. Chief had a drop-leg holster with his favorite .45 caliber 1911 semi-auto pistol, complete with custom deer stag grips and an extended ammo magazine, which he figured was enough firepower for nearly any situation. Mack, on the other hand, went overkill. He was decked out with three sidearms, a .357 revolver with an 8-inch barrel attached to his right hip, a silenced .22 caliber semi-auto on his left, and a snub-nosed .38 strapped to his ankle.

Bling's sidearm was quite different and of the less-lethal variety—a bright yellow stun gun—the kind that looks like a pistol and delivers 50,000 volts of incapacitating electricity into the perpetrator via propelled probes. He had never been trained with it, but Chief still wanted him to carry some type of protection other than his daily prayers.

"Delta team, y'all need your night-vision on and ready to go," Chief insisted, removing his cowboy hat and slipping on a black skull cap, fitting the night-vision rig on over it and tilting the goggles upward, ready for the assault.

"Boss, ready to rock and roll," Johnny responded, inserting a 40-round banana-like ammo magazine into his MP5. He slapped the cocking lever forward, engaging a round into the chamber.

"Ready," Switch responded, staring out the side window through his clear safety glasses, his eyes determined.

"Ditto," Mack replied in his usual cool demeanor.

"Good, Bling, take us in."

ELEVEN
DESPERATE PRAYER

Days Earlier

Mike and Sam pulled their oars into the canoe to conserve what little energy remained and floated along the stream that cut through the middle of two hundred-plus acre rice paddy fields—each one rectangular in shape, about half the size of a football field and enclosed by foot-high natural levees to keep them flooded with a few inches of the stream's water.

As they floated, they searched for suitable shelter to get out of the blazing sun, but the tallest objects around them were the four-foot-high weeds lining both sides of the stream and the slightly taller rows of rice stalks.

They continued floating the stream when the canoe's underside scraped against the rocks. Mike put the oar in the water and pushed off, but it was too shallow to progress further.

"We're gonna have to walk the rest of the way," he indicated as he stood in the nose of the canoe, wobbling a bit, hoping to shift their weight and float a little longer.

"Can you walk?" Sam asked, looking at his swollen ankle.

"The village is only a few hundred yards away. I think I can make it if we take it slow."

"Hey, do you think we could drink this water?" she asked, looking at her distorted reflection from the gently-moving stream that was slightly less murky than the river.

"You read my mind. I watched one of those survival shows one time where someone used their shirt to filter the river water—maybe we can do the same."

Sam recoiled at the thought, scowling as she examined his sweat-stained shirt, almost scolding herself for mentioning it, but she had no other option. Death was circling overhead and it was smart and cunning. If they were to live, they would need to stay at least one step ahead of it—and that would require doing uncomfortable things.

Mike knelt down and soaked his shirt in the stream, ringing it out repeatedly. He didn't have a modicum of spit in his parched mouth, but the thought of drinking the water aroused his glands and saliva rushed over his tongue, coating the insides of his cheeks.

"Sam, you can go first if you want."

She nodded with a hard gulp, not the least bit excited but also determined not to die.

"Let me try it," she replied, straightening up and mentally preparing her mind. He dipped his shirt into the water and wrung it out into her mouth.

The flavorless water hit her taste buds and they all fired off at once, her tongue tingling like it had been touched by a gob of rich frosting, both revolting and refreshing at once.

"Only drink a little and we'll rest here before we take off to the village. We need to make sure our bodies won't reject it like before."

"Good idea," she affirmed, talking through her drinking and bemoaning its flavor.

Mike went next, but as he tipped his head back to drink, he had a flashback of getting sick at the well and a wave of anxiety hit him. He pushed through it, taking in his fill, his body perking up as though it were a flower licking up the morning dew.

"What do you say we flip the canoe over and lay under it in the stream? We can use it for shade and the water will keep us cooler," Mike showed a bit of enthusiasm at the sound of his own idea.

"Um, rest here? But what about the crocs?"

"They're busy basking in the sun back by the river. You can rest first and I'll keep an eye out for any reptiles. We should be good with an hour of rest. What do you think?"

"Okay, I guess I can do that, but only if you're the lookout."

"You got it," he replied as he reached for a nearby stick. He turned the canoe over, propping it up so Sam could rest under it. She rolled under and he sat down on the mud next to the canoe, keeping as much of his exposed skin within the small amount of shade the canoe provided. It wasn't long after that they both drifted off into a light sleep.

Mike rested for a few minutes when he heard two male voices speaking Burmese. He opened his eyes wide, darting them back and forth.

Please don't let it be TJ or his goons he thought. The voices didn't sound excited or aggressive, but they were getting louder, along with the sound of feet splashing in the stream.

Mike sat up to see the silhouette of two village men, the sun beating down on their pointy, umbrella-like hats. Their loose-fitting shirts and pants, which were tied off by at the waist by a towel-like sash, blew in the light breeze.

"Sam, can you hear me?" he asked as he spoke under the gap of the canoe, his voice rushed and anxious.

"Yes, what's wrong?"

"A couple villagers are coming…They've already seen me. I'll try to get them to take me into the village for some food and I'll come back as soon as I can. Whatever happens, stay hidden."

"I…I don't know if this is a…is a good idea," she stammered in the darkness, unable to see outside.

Mike didn't respond. He was busy biting his lower lip and caressing his ankle, hoping the men would take notice of his injury and offer help.

The men remained silent, their hardened eyes studying every inch of Mike's sunburnt body, puzzled as to why a fair-skinned foreigner was resting in their irrigation stream. What Mike didn't know is they had heard the gunfire and knew he had been running from the soldiers.

The villagers helped him up, placing his arms around their shoulders and then pulled him through the wet rice paddies. They slogged along for several minutes, splashing through the water and stepping over the miniature levees, but Mike was so dehydrated that his legs weren't cooperating; they were heavy and his feet had become numb. He took a few more steps, desperately trying to get his body to line up with his mind, but he had nothing left. Seconds later, the darkness swallowed up his vision and he fainted.

Splash! Mike slumped down into the wet rice patty and his body shook violently. The villagers stopped and picked him up, carrying him the rest of the way.

A few minutes later, they entered a small, three-sided bamboo hut on the outskirts of the village. They laid him on a pile of discarded rice sheaves and Mike opened his eyes but everything was blurry. He could see the outlines of the men and the light brown thatched roof but nothing more. Although he was unsure where he was, he felt somewhat safe, and when he closed his eyes again he fell into his deepest sleep since arriving in Burma.

What's that smell, Mike wondered, the clean, starchy aroma stirring him from his rest. He had smelled it before but couldn't pinpoint it. He rolled to his right and opened his eyes. This time the blur was mostly gone. Sitting next to him on the dirt floor were two medium-sized wooden bowls, the steam still twirling above one of them. His mouth salivated at the thought of satisfying his intense hunger. He imagined slices of fresh pizza, a bowl of finely sliced Philly steak or maybe even some General Tso's Chicken.

No, he knew what was in the bowl, and as he inched closer he got a peek at the clumpy, slightly sweet-smelling white rice and the bowl of clean water next to it. Normally, rice would have been his last choice, but here, in his condition, it was more than food; it was life itself.

He stared at the bowls, wanting to dig in, but the fatigue was so heavy he wasn't sure he could reach his hand to his mouth and he continued slipping in and out of consciousness. If he was going to make it to Sam before nightfall, he had to force himself to stay awake long enough to take in some food and water.

Mike reached for the bowl of water, using all his strength to cup his hands around it to bring it to his lips. He would have stuck his face in and lapped it up if he thought he wouldn't lose some of the precious liquid in the process.

He drank a little, holding the bowl between his hands, staring longingly at the rice. The steam was already gone and flies were camped out on it, but he didn't care. He grabbed a handful, squeezing it together to make sure he didn't lose even one granule and bit down on it, chewing slowly to break it down, knowing his digestive system would need all the help it could get.

After he had eaten about half, he took the rest and pressed it together as tight as he could, placing a clump about the size of a tennis ball into his pocket. He finished his water and rolled over on his back, thinking about the terrifying dreams he had seen before they had left for Burma—nightmares he never told Sam, but wish he had.

***

Sam lay under the dark canoe, wondering if Mike had already made it to the village. If he had, she imagined him eating something scrumptious and was happy for him, and at the same time jealous, but her most overwhelming emotion was the loneliness she was experiencing. It was one thing to be in a survival situation with another person, but being alone was altogether different—and she didn't like it. She worried that if he didn't return soon, she might lose her sanity.

The darkness, solitude, and unpredictability ate at the fibers of her soul and she could no longer fight against them; anxiety overtook her mind and she shuddered at the thought of some creature creeping under her dark aboveground grave, wanting her for a snack—plus, she needed to relieve herself.

She closed her eyes and tried refocusing her thoughts, but the anxiety was too overwhelming. In a moment of panic, her body involuntarily jerked like it had been startled from a nightmare and she kicked the stick out of place, sending the canoe crashing down on her knee.

"Arghhhhhh!" She screamed as the intense pain shot through her knee, intensifying her already throbbing headache. In a fit of rage, she pushed the canoe off and tried to stand up, but when she did her knee popped and buckled, dropping her face-first into the stream.

Blood poured from her nose as she rolled over and sat up, taking a deep breath, angry at her stupidity, angry at the canoe, angry at TJ, the world, their situation…even angry at God. She snorted out some bloody mucous, wiping it away with her already tattered shirt, wondering if Mike would return before nightfall. In her mind, he had to return before nightfall.

***

Mike was still in and out of sleep when a cool breeze tickled across the peach fuzz hair on his cheeks. He thought someone might be standing over him, so he sat up and looked around, but the hut was empty. The sun had descended behind the small hills several miles away and, in its absence, made everything slightly cooler. He had slept for several hours and nightfall was fast approaching.

He checked his ankle and saw that the swelling had gone down considerably, so he tried standing to check his strength. He felt better, but he wasn't a hundred percent; still, he knew he had to get back to Sam before dark.

He stood at the edge of the hut and peeked around the corner, getting his first view of the village. Everyone had gone inside for the night, which meant it was a good time to slip away.

***

Come on, Mike, where are you? Sam wondered as dusk rapidly approached. The light breeze slowed to an odd stillness, and if it weren't for the setting sun, the heat would have been intolerable. She propped herself up, using the canoe as leverage to look out over the weeds to see if she could see him returning from the village, but all she saw was a sliver of the red sun peeking over the hills and endless rice patties becoming darker by the second.

She checked her knee to see if she could move, but when she put her weight on it, it buckled again.

I've got to keep moving somehow, she thought. *Maybe the canoe will float upstream with only me in it.*

She slipped her hand under the canoe's lip, attempting to flip it over, but her upper body strength wasn't enough, especially in her condition. She had to use her legs, which meant it was going to hurt. She got down in a squatting position, her back against the canoe's wooden frame and placed both hands under the edge, her knee already throbbing in pain.

"Arghhhhhh!" She screamed, not caring who might hear, managing to flip the canoe over. She fell to the ground and clutched her knee, the pain deep and intense, and she could only hope the struggle would be worth it.

She rested for a minute, crawling inside and laying across the middle of the canoe to distribute her weight evenly. Then she grabbed the oar, reaching her arm over the edge and pushed off, but it didn't move. She wanted to cry, but she wasn't done yet. She dug the oar deeper into the stream's stony bottom and used her entire body to push the canoe forward.

Scrape! Swoosh! The canoe started floating in the dawdling stream, and although it wasn't moving fast, it was taking her closer to the village, but only a few minutes of low light remained and Mike still hadn't returned.

Scrape! The canoe once again came to an abrupt halt on the stream's gravel bottom, sounding as though fingernails were dragging across a chalkboard. The canoe could go no further. She sat up to see how far away the village was, but all she could see were the weeds and an eternity of darkness. Feeling a wave of defeat, she slipped back down into the canoe's hull and closed her eyes, resorting to the only thing left she knew to do.

"God...I...ummm...haven't done this in a while," she quietly prayed, "and I'm sorry about that. I guess I'm also sorry that I'm only talking to you now because I'm in trouble...but, God, if you're out there...if you can hear me, please help me get out of this nightmare. Please be with me and Mike. I don't want anything else. I only want to get home to my family alive...amen."

She finished her desperate prayer and it wasn't but a few moments later when a renewed energy settled over her. She sat up and felt around for the oar to use it as a crutch.

Finding the oar, she placed the handle portion under her armpit and gently eased her weight onto it, pushing herself up, trying not to focus on the worsening pain.

She stood and paused to get her bearings, remembering that whenever she looked at the village in the daylight, it wasn't far from the right of the stream. She figured she could walk until the steam ended and it should lead her to the outskirts of the village.

She carefully put her good leg outside of the canoe and moved the oar along the ground. Her knee throbbed intensely, but she was making progress—and the more she moved, the better she felt.

With every step, Sam scanned her dark surroundings, unable to see beyond a few feet. She kept her eyes to the ground, watching the edges of the weeds for creatures while trying to stay on course, the darkness a new enemy to her already overwhelmed and anxious mind.

She moved further upstream until it dwindled down to only a trickle of water. The sound the water made as it swayed over the rocks along with the constant chirping of crickets and croaks of bullfrogs would have almost been mesmerizing if she hadn't been in her predicament.

She looked to her right where the village should have been and noticed a candle glowing off in the distance. As she stared at its flickering, she thought she heard something rustling in the weeds behind her. She chalked it up to the light wind, but then she heard it again.

Shissssshhhh! Splash! The rustling noise was accompanied by the sound of sloshing water and it was getting louder. She dropped behind the weeds on her good knee and held her breath, her heart beating fast. She closed her eyes tight, concentrating on the sound, listening to determine if it was man or beast. Then it went silent, followed by a new noise, this one much further away and sounding like engines revving.

Glancing over the weeds, she observed three sets of lights emerging over the hills a few miles away, the vehicles traveling at a high rate of speed. She heard the engine's roar getting louder and it wasn't long before the lights illuminated part of the rice patty.

The lights grew bigger and brighter, lighting up more of the rice patties around her. Now that she had a little light, she checked behind her to see what had been moving through the weeds. She caught only a blur of something moving, but before she could fully make it out, the vehicles turned into the village.

Oh, God, please don't let this be TJ or the soldiers, she prayed silently.

The brakes on one of the vehicles screeching loudly and she poked her head up again but couldn't see anything but the lights. Seconds later, a spotlight from one of the vehicles illuminated the bed of a military jeep in front of it and the two men who were standing in it. One of the men was older and taller, dressed in full military fatigues. He carried himself as though he was a high-ranking military official, maybe even a general, and the other man was TJ.

The general removed his pistol from its holster and pointed it up into the air, shooting three times, the shots eliminating anything remotely peaceful. The general scanned the area and shouted something in Burmese. Sam didn't understand the words, but she knew his tone, and could tell he was furious.

The villagers slowly emerged from their huts with their heads down and bodies slumped inward, clearly fearful of what would happen to them. As Sam cautiously looked on, another spotlight lit up, searching a section of rice patty near where she was hiding. She ducked down, but before she did, she saw the general turn in her direction.

Oh, no, did he just see me? she wondered. The spotlight lit up a full section of rice stalks surrounding her. She laid on her stomach, inching her way back down the stream, but as she pushed backward, something brushed against her boot. Startled, she yanked her leg back and held her hand over her mouth to hold back her painful scream. Then she turned around to see who or what was behind her, praying it wasn't a croc or a tiger, but all she saw was a shadow. She froze in place, unable to run or fight back, so she closed her eyes, content to meet her fate and bring the drama to an end.

TWELVE
GIRL BONES

Days Later

Bling drove the Rover along the dirt road and stopped a few hundred meters outside the farm, dropping Chief, Johnny, Mack and Switch near a thickly wooded area, the only light coming from a crescent moon. They trekked into the dark woods, passing through a grassy berm and a sprinkling of wild orchids which scented the night air with a delicate aroma.

"This here humidification so bad it got my dungarees sweatin'; reminds me why I like dry West Texas," Mack whispered as he hiked into the woods.

"Team," Chief backed against a tree, garnering everyone's attention, "Turn on your night-vision—and turn off the chatter." Everyone rotated their night-vision goggles down over their eyes and they instantly had several hundred meters of green-tinted visibility.

They marched through the flat, woodsy terrain, stepping over rocks and leafy underbrush, holding their suppressed MP5s, spying out anything that might pose an issue. Moments later, they came to a five-foot-high barbed wire fence not far from the farm.

Chief held out his arm, silently signaling the team to hold their position while he removed a pair of mini-bolt cutters from his vest, clipping through the rusty fence wire one braid at a time.

Back at the Rover, Randall caught something moving on the drone's camera and urgently radioed in. "Delta Team, hold your position, over."

Delta Team sensed a problem and everyone dropped down to one knee, surveilling the courtyard area a few meters past the barbed wire fence, waiting for more instructions from Randall.

"One MAM heading right for you guys, over."

Chief didn't respond; he already had eyes on the large-framed Eastern European man sporting a military-style haircut, his muscles bulging under his black T-shirt and brown leather shoulder holster.

"Don't come this way, Comrade; you don't want this," Chief thought, watching as he approached, figuring him to be the same man he had seen escorting the girl from the brothel. He got within a couple meters of the cut fence and stopped.

The hair on Chief's arm stood on end as he leaned against a tree, his all-black gear blending into the shadowy background. He fixed the red dot scope in the middle of the Russian's large head, gently resting his gloved index finger on the trigger, gliding it along the metal ridge, ready to squeeze it.

Zzzzzz Zzzzz! A mosquito dive-bombed Mack's ear and in the process of swatting it away, he inadvertently stepped on some dried leaves, the crunching noise in the calm night sounding like a mini-explosion.

Comrade jerked his head toward the sound, his hand simultaneously crossing his body and reaching for a pistol hanging under his armpit. He held his hand on the gun's grip for several seconds, straining to see into the gloomy woods. Delta stayed as still as a statue, their eyes pinned open and refusing to exhale, waiting for Comrade to make his move. If he pulled his pistol, it was lights out.

Chief studied him intently. There was no sweat on his forehead, no twitching of his forearm or triceps. He was clearly guarded but not overly anxious. Not jumpy.

"Come on, don't pull it," Chief thought as the weight of his seven-pound MP5 suddenly became apparent. He kept the

scope's dot on Comrade, anticipating his move. Seconds later, a common treeshrew about the size of a small squirrel scurried over the fallen leaves, darting past Mack into the grassy courtyard.

Comrade noticed the tiny varmint and removed his hand from his pistol, shaking his head, surprised at his own uneasiness. Then he pulled out a cigar and lit it up, the tobacco's red glow illuminating his square jaw as the white smoke churned into the woods. He puffed on it for a minute or so and all was quiet until he let loose a deep, hacking cough, the kind that produces snotty phlegm. He spat on the ground and turned away, strolling back through the courtyard.

"Switch, you and Mack check out the north house. Johnny, you're with me," Chief whispered, relieved that they hadn't needed to blow their cover to take out Comrade.

Everyone sounded off as Johnny followed Chief, stalking through the courtyard, their MP5s shouldered and ready to fire. Moments later, they reached the house, taking up a position near a small window at the side. Chief got close to the window, glancing inside, being careful not to be noticed.

"Two MAMs seated at a table in the center—one is our guy from earlier—AK rifles at their side," Chief quietly reported to everyone listening in. "Switch and Mack, y'all move to the other house. We'll cover you. Once you get in position we'll make our move, over."

"Roger that," Switch replied.

"Randall and Bling, y'all pull up to the farm. Be ready to provide us with a diversion, over."

"You got it, Chief," Randall responded as Bling put the Rover into gear and drove to the farm.

Switch and Mack reached the north house, aiming their weapons at the door and gave Chief a thumbs-up sign from across the courtyard, indicating they were ready.

"Delta, we're in position, over," Randall indicated.

"Copy that, pop some noise," Chief replied.

"Roger that."

Randall stepped out of the Rover with a flashbang stun grenade and approached the gravel driveway, but before he could throw it he was met by two growling guard dogs. He stood motionless, watching the whites of the dog's eyes and canine teeth floating toward him like ghosts. He backed away, pulling out the grenade's pin, but as he did he stumbled over a large rock at the edge of the driveway and dropped the grenade only a few feet from him.

Boom! The device emitted a bright flash and a loud bang similar to a crash of close thunder. The blast jolted Randall and sent the dogs whimpering away.

The Russians in the house jumped up, knocking the table over, and grabbed their rifles, checking their security monitors. Moments later, Comrade raced to the door, carelessly rushing out.

Whack! Chief rammed his weapon into the side of Comrade's head, his body slumping down into the doorway. The other Russian yanked his pistol from its holster, but before he could aim it, Johnny stepped in, firing his MP5.

Phttt! Phttt! Phttt! He shot the Russian twice in his chest and once in his head, the suppressed 9mm rounds sounding like a sock-covered ball-peen hammer hitting a cinder block. The perp instantly dropped to the cedar flooring, his eyes turning dark and hollow and his crimson blood amassing into a pool around him.

"Room clear," Johnny yelled as sweat dripped from his forehead, barely flinching at the sight of the carnage.

Chief placed his knee in the middle of Comrade's back, hogtying his feet to his hands with zip ties and placed tape over his mouth.

"Mack, status update?" Chief requested, his breath coming back slowly.

"We ain't got nothing…no movement."

"Pop smoke!"

"Copy that!"

Switch kicked open the door and Mack rolled in a smoke grenade.

Boom...phsssssh!

Switch and Mack waited on both sides of the open door with their weapons ready. They heard intense coughing coming from a back corner of the house and anxiously waited for the perps to be overcome by the smoke and rush out, but they never did.

As the smoke dissipated, Mack motioned for Switch to move in. He cautiously entered the building, Mack behind him, both of them sweeping their weapons back and forth to clear the room. Once fully inside, they saw the beds and recording equipment along with several cages half the size of a prison cell lining one of the walls.

Mack pressed on through the churning smoke, but Switch stood still, gawking at the cages, shocked that anyone could be so cruel. As he stood there, a dark silhouette advanced toward him. He placed his red dot scope center mass, ready to fire, but as he was about to press the trigger he got a good look at her—a short, Asian teenager wearing nothing but a white nighty that only reached to the top of her thighs. Her eyes were red and swollen, makeup smeared, and she had a look of complete desperation.

Switch lowered his gun, letting it hang down on its three-point sling and stepped forward to assist the girl, but as he did a perp charged out of the smoke, his face and nose covered by his shirt, holding a pistol in his hand. His slit-shaped, Asian eyes were filled with rage as he leveled the pistol at the girl and shot her twice in her upper torso. Johnny entered a second later, retaliating with a barrage of full-auto gunfire, cutting the perp down where he stood.

The girl slumped into Switch's arms, her mouth dropping open and eyes rolling back into her head. Switch stood motionless, overcome by the rush of mixed emotions as he held onto her limp body, the warm blood trickling out onto his gloved hands.

Switch rested the girl on the floor, but before he could get up another perp brandishing a large machete rushed out of the swirling smoke, bolting straight for him. He reached for his MP5, but before he could aim it, the perp swung the machete, hacking a good-sized gash in his upper thigh.

Switch fell against the wall and the perp raised the machete above his head as though to deal a final blow, but before he could bring it down, Chief entered the building and lodged two bullets in the perp's chest and one in his head.

Clank. The bloody machete hit the wooden floor and the perp plummeted next to it, his cloudy eyes still open and staring at Switch, giving him an eerie feeling.

"You alright, nerd?" Johnny asked, shouldering his gun as he entered the house. Chief removed his wound kit and poured in a blood-clotting agent to stop Switch's bleeding and covered it with a gauze patch and medical tape.

"I guess I'm supposed to live," he replied, attempting to stand to his feet, but when he did his knee buckled under him.

"Woah, easy there, brother," Chief stated, helping him to his feet.

"I'm good," he replied, wobbling as he stood up, putting most of his weight on his good leg. "I just need some fresh air."

"It's a pretty good gash, but it shouldn't take you out of commission," Chief indicated as Switch hobbled out the house, plopping down in the grassy courtyard.

"Guys, got something back here," Mack shouted. Chief and Johnny rushed to the back of the house where four girls were huddled together in the back corner, rubbing their eyes and coughing from the smoke. All of them were dressed in the same short nightgowns and displayed the same blank look on their faces.

Chief rotated his weapon behind his back and held out both his hands as a sign to the girls that they were now safe. Realizing they had been in a horribly traumatic situation, Mack knelt down on one knee to lessen any intimidation.

"Ladies, my name is Chief, and we're here to help," he conveyed to them as kindly as he could. He moved in closer to the girls but as he did they spun away from him, whimpering in

111

fear. The smoke had all but left the house and they had a full view of the dead girl lying in the doorway. They glanced at her and then at Chief, surveying his military garb, wondering if he was a rescuer or another abuser. One of the girls who appeared to be about ten years older put her arms around the younger girls and they began to sob.

"Bling, we need your help, over," Chief spoke into his mic.

"What's up?" he asked, forgetting to use the military lingo.

"I need you in here… leave your vest and get in my pack and bring some of the survival blankets…and an HRP," Chief instructed, figuring the girls would be less frightened by someone who didn't look like he had just stepped out of a war.

"HRP?" Bling radioed back, quite confused.

"Human Remains Pouch…a body bag…bring a body bag."

"Yo, are you for real right now?" he asked, unable to contain the shock of his request.

"Can you handle that?" Chief asked, becoming slightly irritated.

Bling stayed quiet for a moment, finally responding. "I gots it…on my way."

A few minutes later, Bling entered the house with several heat-sealed baggies containing the folded blankets and one body bag.

"Yo, Chief, I'm here," he announced as he entered, seeing the puddle of blood and carefully stepping around it like it was holy.

"Good," Chief replied. "I need you to do a couple things. First, get the deceased girl into the body bag and stay here with the other girls. We're gonna continue our search and pick y'all up before we leave."

Bling didn't answer. The girl's stiff body had his full attention, and he wasn't at all interested in placing her in the body bag.

"Bling, we don't have time for this. I need you fully engaged. Can you handle this or not?" he asked firmly, observing his hesitation.

"Yeah, okay, sure…er…roger—" he replied.

112

Chief pat him on the shoulder to reassure him and then walked out into the courtyard and stood next to Switch, checking his status and making sure Comrade was still where he had left him. He was still there, squirming around like a snake.

"Team," Chief announced to get everyone's attention.

"Yeah, boss," Johnny spoke up as he and Mack make a tighter circle.

"That girl's got to be here somewhere. We're not leaving until we find her."

"Understood," Johnny replied. "Maybe we should check the Crown Vic's trunk."

"Good idea. Check it out. Mack and I will continue searching around the houses."

"What about me?" Switch asked as he lay on the ground, waiting for his pain reliever to kick in.

"You sit there and rest. We've got it under control," Chief replied in an almost fatherly tone.

Johnny took off to the entrance where they had last seen the Crown Vic, but before he could get out of the courtyard, he heard Bling shouting.

"Yo, guys, get in here!"

Chief darted back to the house, his gear keeping him from running fast.

"What is it?" he asked as he rushed in, Johnny and Mack filing in behind him.

"Da girl here has sumptin' she wants to say."

Chief let out a long sigh. "Bling, next time use the radio. You nearly gave me a heart attack."

"Yeah, sorry 'bout dat, I got a little excited when she opened up to me."

"Go ahead, shorty," Bling nodded at her. "It's okay."

The oldest girl gradually stood up in the middle of the others and timidly stuttered "Ah...ah...mah...more...guh...gurl here."

Chief's eyes lit up at the sound of her unpolished English.

"Can you take us to her?"

113

"Ya…yes," she replied, her voice and hands still shaking.

"Good," he smiled. "Take your time. Do you need us to help you?"

"I…I no need help," she replied, taking a step forward, her balance unreliable as the other girls hung on to her tightly. She spoke something to them in her language and they sat down as she shuffled forward, her feet curled inward.

"What's your name, young lady?" Chief asked, standing next to her to make sure she didn't need assistance.

"My nuh…name?"

"Yes, what do they call you?"

"Call La…Lawanna."

"We appreciate you helping us, Lawanna," he stated, ripping open the silver survival blanket and wrapping it around her.

Lawanna led Chief, Johnny, and Mack several meters into the wooded area behind the south house and stopped in a small clearing in the trees, her body becoming rigid and mouth opening a bit.

"What's wrong, darlin'?" Mack asked, noticing her uneasiness.

She remained silent, putting her head down and clasping her hands together as though she were praying.

The team studied the girl's body language and they all had the same thought—that she was likely taking them to a girl who was already dead, but no one was willing to say it. Chief draped another blanket around her, not for warmth, but to reassure her safety as Johnny and Mack searched the area.

"Boss, we got something here," Johnny reported as his flashlight lit up a sheet of plywood lying on the ground. He swiftly brushed away the dirt and leaves that were camouflaging it.

"Oh my Lord!" Mack gasped as he lifted the plywood from over the large hole, the stench prompting him to tuck his nose into the crook of his elbow. He stepped away, not wanting to examine the contents further.

"Please don't tell me that's what I think it is," Johnny stated as he watched Mack's solemn facial reaction.

Chief shined his flashlight into the hole, the white beam of light exposing everything he was afraid it would be—a mass grave with at least eight decomposing bodies, one of them bloated with maggots and the rest in advanced decay, their long, black hair the only indicator that they were indeed girls.

"Many girl die here. They...they kill girl and dump when no more use," Lawanna's voice quaked as Chief removed his night-vision rig as a sign of respect.

"I'm so sorry," Chief replied. "No one should have to go through what you and these girls experienced here."

"Randall, are you still in the Rover," Chief called out on the radio.

"Still here monitoring on the drone," he replied.

"Listen, we've got a major situation here. Mass grave with several decayed bodies. We won't be able to stay quiet about this one, over."

"Copy that. When we leave, I'll call my sergeant. Not sure how I'm going to explain stumbling onto this, but I'll work it out."

"Good. I hate putting you in a bind, but this is too evil not to report."

"I'm with you, Chief."

"Thanks, Randall."

"Mack, cover the grave back up...we don't want animals getting to them before the crime unit does."

As Chief turned to walk back to the courtyard, Lawanna spoke up again.

"More girl here," she stated, pointing to the ground a few feet away. Johnny and Mack stared at her for a moment, amazed by her fortitude.

"Listen, Lawanna, I understand. I know there are probably many graves here. We're calling in investigators and they will find everyone—all the families will be notified. They will all get a proper burial and the whole world will know what these horrible men did to y'all."

"No!" Lawanna forcefully cried out, taking a step back as though she had no intention of leaving.

"Boss, I think the girl is flipping out."

"You no listen. Another girl here…ah…alive," she pointed down, making a circling motion with her hand.

Chief stepped back, taking a long, deep look into her eyes, hoping she was right. He clicked on his light to search the area, but the only thing he could see were endless pine needles and fallen leaves.

"Boss, I think it's the trauma speaking. I don't see anything," Johnny spoke up as he scoured the area with this light.

"Hold up, boys," Mack called out from few feet away. "I've got fresh prints here. Looks like someone placed these leaves here to cover something."

Chief focused his light near Mack and caught the reflection of light off a metal hinge sticking out of the ground. He rushed over and brushed the leaves away, exposing two solid metal doors about six feet in length, secured by a padlock in the middle.

"Guys, I've got something," Chief called out.

"Looks like a cellar or bunker," Mack surmised.

"Seems like the water table would be too high for that here," Johnny suggested.

"Unless it's one of them waterproof bunkers," Mack indicated.

Chief reached into his vest for his bolt cutters, cutting the padlock's u-shaped bolt and removing the lock.

"Y'all ready?" Chief asked as he held onto the latch to pull the door open.

"Ready, boss," Johnny replied as he and Mack hoisted their MP5s to their shoulder and aimed at the door, their faces more determined than ever.

THIRTEEN
SMALL SOLDIERS

Days Earlier

S am played dead, hoping whatever had brushed up against her boot wasn't a dangerous animal. Whatever was there hadn't left because she could still hear it. Then it kicked her foot and she was sure it was human. She turned and saw an elderly village man with a baffled expression standing over her, his triangular hat hung around his neck and a stringer of several recently-caught fish draped over his shoulder.

With terror laced deep within her eyes, she braced herself, waiting for the villager to yell out her location, but he never did. Instead, he pointed downstream as though to tell her to keep going.

Sam used the oar to stand up, hobbling back down the stream where she had left the canoe. Whenever she saw the spotlight scanning in her direction she knelt down to not be seen. It was a slow go, and even though she wanted to get away from TJ and the soldiers, she didn't want to leave Mike behind for fear of never seeing him again.

Sam trudged through the stream to hide any footprints, her feet squishing in her heavy, water-logged boots. She could hear the clacking bats as they swooped inches above the rice patties, scooping up their nightly fix of newly hatched mosquitos. As she considered the swiftly soaring creatures, she fanaticized having her own wings to lift her away, never to see Burma again.

A few minutes later she reached the canoe. She dug her good leg into the mud and pushed off with what little strength she had left until the canoe floated. She jumped in, looking back at the soldiers who were getting closer. They had already reached the village and it wouldn't be long before they spotted her.

She rowed hard, but even at her hardest, she crept along due to her lack of energy. Nearly completely drained, she paddled a few more strokes and let the canoe float.

As she rested to gather her strength, the spotlights lit up the last few huts. She put the oar down and slumped into the bottom of the canoe, closing her eyes and saying another quick prayer as she drifted off into a memory of her and her family.

"Sam!"

A familiar voice interrupted her musing and she remained still, wondering if her mind was playing tricks on her.

"Sam!" the voice repeated more forcefully this time, coupled together with a hard thud on the canoe. She opened her eyes and saw Mike standing over her.

"Mike?" she muttered.

"We've got to go!" he insisted, giving the canoe a good push and jumping inside.

"Mike, where…where have you been? Why did you leave me for so long?!" She was relieved, but also a little angry.

"No time. I'll explain later!" he stated, grabbing the oar and rowing as fast and hard as he could manage.

"Row, Sam, row!" he yelled as he watched the spotlights light up the bamboo hut where he had been resting.

Seconds later, a deep, raspy voice reverberated through the night air, penetrating the kids to their core. The general found evidence that Mike had been in the hut and barked orders to his soldiers to split up and search the area.

Two of the vehicles reversed and went back down the road, but the jeep TJ and the general were in drove toward the stream,

118

their spotlight skimming the rice patties, getting closer to their location.

"They're gonna find us, Sam!" his facial expression changed from emotionless to terrified as the spotlight lit up the rice patty a few feet from them. They stopped rowing and ducked down, hoping they wouldn't be seen.

The jeep rolled to the edge of the stream and the spotlight dispelled the darkness, illuminating the canoe like it was daytime.

"Maungg!" The general furiously shouted, indicating to his soldiers to drive the jeep down the stream and apprehend Mike and Sam.

Mike plunged his oar into the water, engaging every muscle, but he had pushed so hard that he tipped the canoe over, causing them and the oars to fall out into the shallow water.

The stream had risen up to Mike's knees as he hooked his arm with Sam's, trying to help her into the weeds.

"Arghhhh!" she cried in agonizing pain.

"What's wrong?" he asked with wide eyes.

"It's my knee," she explained, trying to hobble into the weeds. Her knee popped with every movement, sounding like someone was twisting packing bubbles. He didn't know what had happened, but she certainly couldn't keep up, and there was no way he was going to leave her behind again.

TJ and the general clung to the light bar in the back of the jeep as it straddled the stream, bouncing around vigorously. When they saw the kids fall out of the canoe, the general ordered the jeep to stop and he and TJ raised their rifles, aiming directly at Mike.

Ratatat! Ratatat! Ratatat! They fired several times, cutting the weeds and rice stalks around them in half.

"What do we do?" Sam cried, staying as low as possible.

"We have to get back in the canoe; it's our only chance!"

Ratatat! Ratatat! Ratatat! The bullets zoomed inches above Mike's head as they waited at the edge of the weeds.

"We'll make our move when they reload!" he yelled.

He no more finished his sentence when the shooting ceased. Seeing their opportunity, he stayed as low as he could, pulling Sam by her shoulders to assist her back to the canoe, reaching it seconds later. He helped her into the hull of the canoe, grabbed one of the oars, and sat down, moving them along at a decent clip.

"Why aren't they shooting?" Sam asked as she watched the spotlight erratically bounce around them.

"They're on the move and can't get a clean shot. My guess is they don't want to shoot you. If they wanted to they could have taken us out by now anyway."

"You think so?"

"Yeah, the bullets haven't landed anywhere near you. They're trying to take me out to force you to give up."

As he was speaking, Sam felt water on her legs. She looked down into the canoe and saw that her boots were nearly covered in water. "Mike, we've got a major problem, here," she stated in a panicked tone. "The canoe is filling with water!"

Mike hurried to remove his T-shirt and handed it to her. "There's gotta be a bullet hole somewhere. Find it and plug it with my shirt. We just need it to get across the river."

Sam slipped her hands into the water, rubbing them along the wooden hull until she felt a few splinters. She plugged the dime-sized hole with her finger and felt another next to it.

"I found them!" she replied, placing his shirt over the holes and pressing as hard as she could, but she was so fatigued it felt like she was trying to hold down an elephant from rising up.

"Mike, I'm super weak. I…I can't keep the water from coming in," She closed her eyes, trying to get her bearings.

"Hang in there. We only need it to float another 50 yards." He did his best to motivate her as he continued to row hard.

He looked over his shoulder again to see where the jeep was, ready to make a final stand, but it was no longer giving chase; it was bogged down in the thick mud.

"Finally, we get a break," he uttered under his breath, but he hadn't even finished his statement when he spotted the lights and heard the sound of a diesel-engine truck heading their direction.

The truck met up with TJ and the general and they jumped inside, passing in front of the stuck jeep. When it did, Mike got a good look at what they were dealing with—a boxy, six-wheeled, open bed, military troop transport truck full of soldiers—and it effortlessly maneuvered through the thick mud.

The truck barreled down the stream, the diesel engine sounding as though a semi-truck was bearing down on them from behind.

"What's that?" Sam asked, hearing the whining and clacking engine noise. Before he could answer a more distressing sound erupted.

Ratatat! Ratatat! The soldiers fired their weapons and one of the bullets hit Mike in the back of his hand. He instantly dropped the oar in the water, clutching his hand in agony as the canoe left the mouth of the stream and entered the river. Sam turned to see blood gushing out of his wound, mixing with several inches of water that had intruded into the canoe. She climbed up and sat on the bench seat, swinging her body around to help him, but he pulled back, refusing her aid.

"Not now. I'll deal with it later. Just row, Sam!"

"With what?"

"Your hand!"

"I'll try," she replied, dipping her hand into the water and cupping it to move as much water as possible.

Mike reached his good hand into the water and helped paddle, grimacing in pain. They got about halfway across the river when Sam observed something like a snake slithering toward them. It was several feet away when it disappeared under the black water, the spotlight catching the soft, white underbelly. At the last second, it twisted its body, revealing its rough, spiky tail.

"Mike! Crocs!" she cried out, yanking her hand out of the water. Mike nervously pulled back as well, and almost immediately the crocodile bumped up against the backside of the canoe, testing it to see what it was.

Mike and Sam scoured the water's surface, watching for their newest enemy, but they had forgotten about the water intruding into the canoe; it was now higher than their ankles and they had only moments before it sank.

"We're almost to the bank!" Mike called out, seeing some stubby ferns on the slightly elevated shoreline. Terrified, he reached his hand back into the water and continued rowing, but as he did the canoe began to list sideways.

Vroom! The military truck cut through the stream near the river and parked in one of the adjacent rice patties where a dozen soldiers with rifles filed out and lined up along the riverbank, the general barking out his orders to them.

Mike looked back and studied the troops who were about 30 feet away, noting their short height, bowl-style haircuts, and smooth, bronzish-colored skin. Their garb and weapons shouted military, but everything else, including their high-pitched voices and hairless faces, suggested they were no more than 12 or 13 years old.

"Give up! There no place go!" TJ stood at the riverbank and shouted across the river. The general, an Asian man in his mid-50s, sporting a bushy mustache and typical olive-drab green fatigues and matching patrol hat, stepped out and stood next to him, his eyes narrowed and jaw clenched.

Like prey backed into a corner, Mike reached into his waistband and grabbed the pistol, aiming for TJ. TJ stumbled backward but the general didn't budge. Mike aligned TJ's body in the pistol's front and rear iron sights as his dad had taught him to do so many times in their backyard and then pressed the trigger.

FOURTEEN
SECRET BUNKER

Days Later

Chief held his flashlight and pulled open one of the bunker's doors while Johnny and Mack pointed their MP5s toward the ground.

Creakkkkk…Bam! Chief let go of the door and it slammed against the ground, dust and leaves flying into the air.

"Ugh! What is that smell?" Johnny cringed as he pulled the handkerchief hanging around his neck up over his nose and mouth to help block out the combination of musty body odor, urine, and mold.

"Hopefully, ain't nothin' dead," Mack choked the words out, finishing with a cough.

Chief pulled his pistol out and shined his flashlight into the dark bunker, lighting up ten or so steps when Lawanna bolted toward the steps, intending to run inside, but before she could reach the steps, Chief blocked her from entering.

"Hold up, Lawanna," he stated. "Let us check it out first."

"Gin…Ginger in here!" she passionately replied.

"Let us take it from here. We'll find her."

"Mack you're with me," Chief instructed as he stepped down into the bunker. Mack pulled his .357 revolver and followed closely behind.

Chief reached the bunker floor, but the ceiling was so low he had to duck down to go any further.

"Mack, watch your head coming down," Chief warned. "Low ceiling."

Chief scanned his light around the small, concrete room, no larger than a typical bedroom. In one of the corners, he noticed a paper bowl with a small portion of untouched white rice. Human feces were in another corner—a sign that someone had recently been in the bunker. The only other items were a couple 55-gallon drums and some cardboard boxes.

Chief and Mack moved the heavy drums and dusty boxes around, checking for clues or hidden compartments. Mack saw that one of the drum's lids was ajar and lifted it off.

"Chief, I've got something here," Mack called out as he inhaled a whiff of a strong chemical odor and caught a glimpse of a bundle of long jet-black hair. He stepped back, gazing at it for a moment, not really wanting to investigate further.

Chief shined his light inside the plastic barrel, using the end of his pistol to move her hair back. When he did, it exposed her pale skin and a small Asian symbol tattooed on her neck. He pulled his phone out to take a picture, but when he did he saw movement.

Is this girl alive or did I bump into the barrel, Chief thought. He stepped back with a bewildered look and when he did she looked up, her beautiful, light green-colored eyes connecting with his. Then she stood up and both Chief and Mack's mouths dropped open.

"Woah, how'd you even fit in this here drum," Mack asked rather rhetorically, seeing she was rather tall.

"Take it easy, young lady," Chief spoke softly, helping her out of the drum and noting her rigidness. "We're not going to hurt you."

"Your name is Ginger, right? Are you American?" he asked. She didn't respond. She stared at the dirt floor, shifting her eyes rapidly, quite unsure about Chief and the team's intentions. He could see that she had been through a horrible ordeal and took it slow.

"Come on, young lady, let's get you cleaned up," Chief stated as he and Mack draped her arms around their shoulders and helped her up the bunker's steps where Johnny and Lawanna were waiting.

When she stepped out, Lawanna ran over to her, embracing her tightly and weeping loudly. Ginger broke down as well.

"Guys, this is the girl we saw at the brothel," Chief spoke quietly. "They must have dyed her hair while we were doing recon."

"That would explain the nasty chemical smell in the drum," Mack replied. "Do you think this could be the girl we're after?"

"Not sure, but it's possible. Lawanna said the girl's name is Ginger, so probably not. Still, I'm sure someone is looking for her."

"No doubt," Mack replied. "If this is as far as we get, we've done a solid mission."

"Indeed."

Lawanna turned to Ginger and spoke softly. "I think they help." Ginger turned around to look at Chief, Mack, and Johnny, studying them closely, eventually nodding in agreement.

"I…I need a shower," Ginger spoke for the first time, still nervously looking around.

"Anything you need," Chief replied, looking at Lawanna, "Young lady, can you take her back to the house and help her with a shower?"

Lawanna nodded, hooking her arm through Ginger's and they walked together to the courtyard, everyone else following behind them.

Chief, Johnny and Mack met up with Switch and Bling in the courtyard while Ginger cleaned up in the north house's shower.

"Yo, Chief, where we gonna take these girls?" Bling asked.

"Working on that now," he replied as he pulled up some hotel options on his cell phone, searching for a good place to take the girls.

As they were talking, Randall spotted some lights on the road and zoomed in with the drone to get a closer look.

"Chief," Randall radioed in, "we've got company. Looks like one cargo-style van heading this way. About three mikes out, over."

"Good copy, can you hide the Rover in the woods? There's a path on the backside," Chief instructed.

"Roger that."

"Switch, can you move?" he asked as Johnny took off to the north house to retrieve Ginger.

"Yeah...I think so...," he replied, using his MP5 to help stand up.

"Good. Wait inside the south house. I'll put Comrade in there with you."

"Roger that," he replied, hobbling to the house.

"Bling, Ginger is coming out now. Get her and those girls into the woods. Randall should be there with the Rover," Chief spoke fast. "Y'all wait there for further instructions."

"Got it, Chief."

Chief, Johnny, and Mack trampled through some tall weeds and hid a few feet behind some trees near the farm's driveway, waiting for the van to arrive.

"Here's the plan," Chief instructed. "We'll wait for them to pull up and try to get the drop on them. I'll step out and cause a diversion while y'all get behind them and take them out."

"Roger, boss," Johnny replied and Mack nodded.

Randall radioed in. "Chief, Lawanna informed me that there are two Burmese men in the van. She says they transport kids from Burma every two weeks."

Chief exhaled through his nose and his face reddened with anger. "Alright, copy that."

"Man, I wanna shoot these pieces of trash so bad," Mack whispered.

"Boss, I can see the lights," Johnny reported, looking in the direction of the road, his weapon shouldered and getting the itch to fire.

"Hold your position and follow the plan," he instructed as the van pulled up and parked behind the Crown Vic, not far from where they were hiding.

They flipped down their night-vision, watching as two middle-aged, Eastern European men exited the van and moved to the back and opened the rear door.

Great, more Ruskies, Chief thought.

"You sure you ain't wanna shoot these ol' boys," Mack whispered as he held his red dot on the back of the van, waiting for them to appear again.

"Hold tight," Chief whispered as his finger gravitated toward the trigger.

The transporters finally appeared with their shipment, three young Asian teen girls and one Asian boy, none of them more than twelve or thirteen years old. The Russians pulled them by their rope-tied hands, dragging them across the gravel driveway, lacerating their bare feet and leaving behind long ruts.

Chief motioned with his hand and Johnny and Mack slipped out from behind the weeds, moving stealthily to the back of the van. Johnny reached it first and covered Mack until he caught up with him.

Once they were in position, Chief stepped out of the weeds with his MP5 leveled directly at the closest Russian.

"Don't move!" Chief yelled.

One of the Russians reached for a pistol under his shirt, but before he could pull it Johnny and Mack stepped behind them, jabbing the barrel of their MP5s into the middle of their backs, dropping them down to their knees on the gravel driveway. They followed up with a blow to their heads, knocking them out cold.

The kids stopped and huddled together, refusing to look up out of sheer fear.

"It's okay everyone. We're here to help," Chief conveyed as Johnny and Mack put their knees in the Russian's backs, zip-tying their hands together.

"Man, that was too easy," Johnny stated.

"Yeah, didn't even get my heart rate up," Mack replied. "What are we gonna do with these guys anyway?"

"Maybe we could bury them in the graves," Johnny suggested.

"No, put them in the bunker," Chief instructed.

"That'll work, too."

"Alive."

"Yeah, boss, I got it," he stated, checking the Russians for the keys to the van.

"Alright, Rusky, let's go," Mack sternly commanded, lifting one of them to their feet by the zip ties and leading them to the back of the van.

***

"Lock it tight," Chief replied, watching as Johnny and Mack threw Comrade and the Russian transporters into the dark and fetid bunker. Johnny swung the doors closed and Mack inserted a crowbar through the eyelets to make sure it would stay closed until the authorities arrived.

"At least they'll get a little taste of what they put these girls through," Johnny stated.

"Not really," Chief replied solemnly. "These guys—even the dead ones—are getting off easy compared to what they did to these girls."

"You sure is tellin' the truth on that one, Chief," Mack replied.

Bling looked on from several feet away as he leaned against the Rover. "God will make it right in da end."

"What did you just say, Bling?" Johnny glared at him.

"I said God will make it right," he repeated even louder.

"You sure do have some nerve bringing God into this—why didn't he step in and—"

Chief interrupted him. "Johnny, we're not doing this right now." Johnny shook his head and stepped away, huffing out an exaggerated breath.

"Team, listen up," Chief addressed them. "Bling, we won't all fit in the Rover, so you'll drive the van and Switch will ride shotgun. Mack, I want you in the back to make sure the kids are good. Everybody understand?"

"Hold up, Chief," Bling had a disagreeable look on his face. "So, I gotta drive that Chester-molester van?"

"It's only temporary, Bling."

"I've gotta question," Mack asked somberly. "What is we gonna do with that girl in the body bag? We ain't leavin' her out here is we?"

"We'll put her in the house on the way out and notify the authorities."

Randall spoke up. "We'll make sure she gets a proper burial," he assured him as he handed the controls of the drone over to Switch.

"Maybe we could say a few words over her first," Mack suggested, considering the finality of her young life and all the torture she had to endure.

"Yeah, good idea. Bling, you're up," Chief instructed.

"Yo, why do it gotta be me?" Bling asked with a touch of uneasiness in his voice.

"Because you're the religious guy with all the answers," Johnny answered as they hovered over the black body bag. "Besides, if you can't do this why did we even hire you?"

"Nope, ain't religious—and I certainly ain't got all da answers," he replied, removing his sequined Chicago Bulls ball cap and looking down at the bag, contemplating what he should say.

"Yeah, whatever, Bling, you gonna say some words or what?" Johnny asked firmly.

"I'll say sumptin'. Just give me a second. Everyone gather 'round," Bling replied, swallowing hard.

Chief unzipped the bag so only the girl's pale and bluish-colored nose and cheeks were exposed. Ginger, Lawanna, and the rest of the kids immediately looked away.

"Dear Lort," Bling began as everyone bowed their heads, "These here is always tough and ain't no one got da right words, but I, uh, I thank you for protectin' da team and these other girls and da boy standin' here. Lort, death make us think 'bout our own lives. Help us to see dat life is short and real life is found only in You," Bling paused and continued. "And dis girl here who ain't make it, she...uh..."

"Her name Dara," Lawana interjected, her eyes shut tight.

"...Dara...Lort...make it right. She's a victim of horrible evil...and we axe for justice, Lort, In Jesus' name, a—"

"And help us send these other evil mothers straight to hell," Johnny interrupted.

"Amen!" Mack exclaimed.

Bling narrowed his eyes at Johnny, irritated that he had finished his prayer so disrespectfully.

Chief saw the tension and cut in. "Alright, team, let's wrap this up and get on the road," he stated as the team removed their tactical vests and placed their weapons in the Rover. "And y'all make sure Ginger rides shotgun in the Rover."

"Copy that, boss."

***

Chief drove the Rover away from the farm with Ginger in the passenger seat. She stared out at the nearly pitch-black darkness, not fully grasping that her nightmarish ordeal had come to an end. Johnny, Mack and Randall sat behind them, quietly contemplating what they had experienced in Pattaya and the farm.

They made it onto the highway and Chief attempted to strike up a conversation with Ginger. "We're going to get you a plane ticket back to the states in the morning. Is there someone you want to call?"

Ginger glanced at Chief and was overcome with emotion for the first time and couldn't answer.

"It's okay, take all the time you need."

She cried for a few moments and finally caught her breath long enough to answer.

"I...I...need to call my...my mom," she sputtered out the words.

"Absolutely," Chief replied, reaching into his pouch for his cell phone, sitting it in the console's cup holder. "Call when you're ready."

Ginger stared at the phone for a few seconds and once again erupted in uncontrolled sobbing.

"That's perfectly okay. No rush."

"I...I don't know if I'll ever be ready," she sniffled, holding back more tears. "But I've gotta make the call."

Chief nodded, affirming her emotions.

Ginger, still sniffling, grabbed the phone and dialed the number. She pressed all the numbers and held the phone in front of her face, gazing at the white numbers on the screen without initiating the call. She didn't know what to say or how to say it.

After several seconds, she finally initiated the call, but no one answered. Feeling overcome with emotion, she lowered the phone and bawled.

"Try it again, sweetheart...it's okay."

She looked at the phone and slowly redialed the number again. This time someone answered.

"Hello, ma—mom...it's...it's Ginge—I mean, it's Kylee..."

FIFTEEN
STALKED

Days Earlier

Click! Mike pressed the pistol's trigger but nothing happened. He shook the gun violently and pulled the slide backward, revealing the problem—it was caked with mud. TJ scowled and the general scurried back to the truck, grabbing an AK-47 assault rifle.

The general hustled back, making sure a round was loaded into the chamber and raised the rifle, aiming it across the river. TJ could tell by the intensity in his eyes that he was intent on killing both Mike and Sam, but he couldn't allow that; he had already told the Russians about Sam and if he didn't deliver her within a couple days his life would end at the bottom of the lake like everyone else who got in their way.

TJ stepped in and lifted the rifle's barrel as the general pressed the trigger. "Rattattattatt!" The bullets ripped through the tops of the jungle's palm leaves across the river, missing the kids by several yards.

Enraged, the general turned his rifle on TJ and fired several times, striking him in his stomach. TJ clutched his midsection, his eyes showing disbelief that the general had shot him. Seconds later, he collapsed to the ground and rolled down the riverbank, his head and torso coming to rest on the mud and his legs landing partly in the water, an irresistible temptation for the crocs.

The water in the canoe was now past Mike and Sam's shins when the bow ran aground into the mangrove shoots on the opposite side of the river. Sam rocked the canoe as she stood near the bow, searching for deadly creatures. She gazed under the mangroves into the shadowy water but it was too dark to see anything.

"Sam, jump now!"

Against her better judgement, she took a deep breath and dove for a cluster of mangroves, landing safely on them, but feeling the pain in her knee more than ever. Mike followed, grabbing his shirt from the hull and jumping off as the canoe slipped under the muddy river waters.

Ratatatatatatat! The general emptied his rifle, striking the mangroves around them, so close they could feel the vibrations in their feet, but he had completely missed them, and it wasn't for his lack of trying.

Mike helped Sam traverse through the mangroves until they reached solid ground a few yards away, taking cover behind several rows of green bamboo stalks and short palm bushes. With a fresh magazine and a renewed frustration, the general aimed into the jungle and mowed down the first row of bamboo stalks, but didn't come anywhere close to hitting the kids.

The general shouted to his boy-soldiers, ordering them to swim across the river to apprehend Mike and Sam, but their fear of the water and all its creatures kept them from moving in. He angrily repeated his command once more, but they remained obstinate.

With frustration and fury, the general pulled his service pistol from his holster and leveled it at one of the boys.

Pow! He shot the boy in the head and his body slumped to the edge of the river, his blood mixing into the murky waters. Seeing the grim result of their defiance, the other boys reluctantly waded into the river, their bodies shaking as they entered the watery hell filled with reptilian demons.

Mike put his river-soaked shirt on and they hiked into the lush jungle, but the combination of his bare feet and recovering ankle, along with Sam's injured knee, they were barely gaining any ground.

They navigated about 30 yards into what felt like a new world, a world untouched by human hands where it appeared that God had run out of every crayon but green. The trees boomed higher than several story buildings and tangles of vines dangled down from above, snaking through the jungle floor in every direction like a network of interconnecting cables.

The jungle's air was different as well; it was heavier and had an almost sweet, garden-fresh smell. A variety of insects and birds traded sounds back and forth, piping out peculiar speeches and songs of which only they and their Creator knew.

They journeyed a little further in and the jungle became so dense they could only see a few feet in front of them, losing their sense of direction. Overcome with uncertainty, Sam's body became numb except for her throbbing knee and she collapsed from sheer exhaustion.

"I…I can't go on," she stated, her breathing shallow and unreliable. "I've got nothing left in me."

Mike helped her rest against a nearby tree and sat down a few feet away. The scorpions and snakes had spared his bare feet, but he was flicking off leeches by the dozens, leaving behind slimy, mucous trails of blood on his legs.

"We'll rest here for a couple minutes so I can check my hand, but we have to keep going…hey, I've got something for you. Can you eat?"

"You've got food?!"

He reached into his pocket and pulled out a clumpy ball of river-saturated rice. Her eyes grew big as she cupped her hands together to make sure she collected every last grain.

"This tastes so good right now," she mumbled through her slow chewing, savoring every bite. "I never thought I would say that about bland rice."

Resting against one of the trees, Mike examined his wound; the bullet only nicked the flesh between his thumb and pointer finger and the bleeding had nearly stopped. He thought briefly about wrapping it with his waterlogged shirt, but he didn't want bacteria seeping into his open wound.

They continued resting, waiting for Sam to get a little strength, listening to the almost mesmerizing jungle noises. Moments later, they were interrupted by blood-curdling screams and muffled sounds of something like twigs snapping. They gazed at each other in silence, having never heard something as horrendous as an ensemble of crocodiles ripping through human limbs coupled with desperate screams and sporadic gunfire. Sam closed her eyes and plugged her ears wanting it all to end.

Off in the distance, lightning from a looming thunderstorm illuminated the dark sky, followed by a few low roars of thunder.

"One Mississippi, two Mississippi, three Mississippi…thirty-five Mississippi," Mike counted the seconds from the lightning strikes to the report of the thunder.

"Okay, I divide by five," he mumbled to himself. "The storm is about seven miles away. Maybe the rain will scare off these relentless skeeters." He turned to check on Sam but she was already sleeping.

He studied her intently, looking over her shiny, pale skin as it almost glowed amid the darkness. She barely had enough energy to sit upright, let alone continue trekking through the thick jungle, and although he more energy than her, he wouldn't be able to carry her for any distance. The only feasible option was to let her rest and get some strength back.

Mike closed his eyes to rest, but his mind was going wild, wondering if any of the soldiers had made it across the river. If they had, it would only be a matter of time before they encountered them, and they didn't have enough strength to fight back. Unable to rest, he got up and trekked back toward the river, making sure he wasn't too far from Sam. He had to be close enough to hear her if she woke up and called out for him.

He walked back for a couple minutes and found a good spot to hide behind a tree where he had a decent view of the river.

He waited, scouring the jungle and watching for the slightest movement. As he watched, he heard the distinct sound of the military truck's engine. He moved some leaves and saw the headlights as the truck backed away from the river. The general and his soldiers were leaving.

After they left, he returned to where Sam was resting and hid behind a leafy bush, keeping watch over her. Sporadic raindrops fell from the sky and the thunder got louder as he considered their nearly hopeless situation—especially with a deranged military chasing after them.

In between thunderclaps, he heard the crunch of some leaves. He opened his eyes, shifting them back and forth, staying as still as possible. Then he heard the rustle of palm leaves behind him. He spun around to see two shadowy figures sweeping through the trees, moving straight for them. As they got closer, he could see that it was the boy-soldiers.

He watched a few seconds longer, making sure there weren't more. As far as he could tell, there were only two, both armed with rifles and tracking on a path straight to Sam.

Mike crouched down on all fours and crawled toward them, using the claps of thunder and pounding rain as cover. He got to within a couple feet and stood up behind them.

Thump! Mike used the butt end of the pistol and hit one of the boys on the back of his neck, dropping him to the ground. He cocked the hammer of the gun, the foreign noise reverberating off the damp vegetation. The other boy turned to see the barrel inches from his head and dropped his assault rifle into the mud, trembling like it was winter.

"Get up, both of you, and stand against that tree," Mike stated, low and firm. The boys nervously backed away while he picked up one of their Kalashnikov rifles and then chucked the impotent pistol as far as he could into the jungle's foliage.

Sam heard the commotion and opened her eyes, startled to see Mike holding two soldiers at gunpoint. She sluggishly stood to her feet, sliding her hand up the tree to help steady her balance.

"What are you going to do, Mike?" she called out. He had a menacing look in his eyes that suggested he might pull the trigger at any moment.

"I'm not sure. Grab the other rifle," he asserted, adrenaline coursing through his body.

She picked up the rifle and aimed it at them. When she did, one of the boys flinched and closed his eyes tight.

"Mike, these aren't hardened soldiers. They're just boys."

"Right, boys who tried to kill us."

"We don't know that."

"Then who shot at us back at the river?" he asked sternly.

"Maybe they were forced to shoot at us—we don't know."

As she spoke, one of the boys dropped to his knees and put his hands together as though to ask for mercy. The other boy followed his lead, hanging his head, his tears adding to the jungle's already moist soil.

"What if they were forced into soldiering?" she asked, staring deep into the boys' dull eyes, sensing they had been through a terrible ordeal.

"Let's assume you're right. What should we do with them then?"

"I...I don't know, but we can't just kill them or leave them out here."

"And we can't let them go either," he protested. "But here's what I do know. Earlier, I heard a train. I want to find that train and see if it can take us out of this hellhole country."

"Trah—trah—ain?" One of the boys spoke up, copying Mike.

"Yeah, you know like Choo-Choo," Mike replied with a tinge of arrogance.

"Choo-choo?" the boy pressed his lips together, his eyes growing wider, realizing he understood.

"Yeah, choo-choo. Do you know where?" Mike asked firmly, holding up his hands as though he were asking a question.

Without warning, the boy enthusiastically jumped to his feet, pointing at the tree line, nodding his head. Surprised by the quick movement, Mike fumbled the gun and boldly aimed it at the boy's head, his finger partially squeezing the trigger, nearly blowing his head off.

The boy froze in place, throwing his hands up as high as he could and closed his eyes tight, realizing he had moved too quickly.

"Mike, stop! I think he knows where it is," she suggested, pleading with him. He thought for a moment and slowly lowered the rifle's barrel.

"Well, he did point in the same direction that I heard the train earlier, I'll give him that much."

"How far?" Mike asked the boys, still glaring at them, but they didn't understand his words.

"How far, dammit!" Mike yelled.

"Mike, are you…are you okay?" she asked, placing her hand on his shoulder. She had never heard him curse before and figured it was the stress speaking. He didn't respond, but instead placed his forehead on the tree and broke down, the salty tears running over his lips, his emotions overtaking his will to remain composed. Sam put her arm around him to embrace him, but he swiftly pulled away, wiping away his tears with his arm.

"Get up!" Mike pointed the gun and yelled, using the rifle to make an upward motion. The boys stood up and looked at each other, terror filling their eyes as they waited for Mike to completely snap and shoot them.

"Sam, are you able to stand up? We're gonna try moving you. We need to get some distance from the river."

"Yeah, I think so."

Mike knelt down and she put her arm around him. Then he motioned for one of the boys to come around the other side to help. Sam put her arm around the boy's shoulders and Mike pointed at the other boy to take his place.

"Are you okay with this, Sam?"

"I'm okay, but I can't do much—they're going to have to drag me along."

"It's okay, we'll go until they can't."

Mike kept his eyes on the boys as they carried Sam through the jungle, dragging her in the mud, over fallen logs, leafy vegetation, and through sharp, bamboo vine thorns. Her cargo pants had been ripped to shreds at the ankles by the jungle's prickly barbs, causing small pin drops of blood to form on her skin.

It wasn't long before they came to a wide clearing in the jungle and stopped at the tree line, peering out into the wide-open space no more than a football field wide.

"Is that a building?" Mike asked out loud, squinting through the rain and newly formed fog. Sam traced her eyes along the outline of the mysterious-looking, six-story high edifice, recalling something she had seen online before they had left.

"Looks like a Buddhist monastery," she suggested.

"Okay, we'll rest here for now. It should be safe enough, and I need to find us some water."

Mike motioned for the boys to lower Sam to the ground and they rested her against one of the trees while he sat opposite her, the rifle clutched firmly in his hand.

"Where are you gonna get the water?" she asked. "We can't get enough from the rain and you're not leaving me again."

"Don't worry, I'm not leaving. I've got an idea."

With determined eyes, he motioned for the boys to remove their solid-green military shirts. When they took them off Sam gasped.

"Mike, look!" She winced, pointing to the multiple foot-long scars on their backs. "Those are from a whip or a cane—they've been tortured."

Mike didn't look or even respond as he tied their shirt's sleeves around two trees that were close together, spreading the shirts out so they angled down over a couple sticks he had stuck into the mud.

"What are you doing?" she asked as her eyelids became heavier.

"It's going to sound gross, but once the rain fully saturates the shirts the water will drip off the end for us to drink."

"That is beyond...gross," she replied sluggishly, struggling to keep her eyes open and pausing between her words. "Where...did you come...up with that?"

"I don't know. I'm just trying to survive," he replied, checking one of the shirts. "Here, lay down; it's already starting to drip."

Sam slid down the tree under one of the shirts, opening her mouth under the small drip. As she took in the water, Mike removed the shoulder strap from one of the rifles and tied the boys together around a tree.

After the boys were secured, Mike rested a few feet from Sam and opened the carriage bolt on one of the rifles, ejecting the banana-style magazine and removing the bullets one-by-one.

How are there only six rounds between two guns? he thought, knowing the magazines should have had 25 or 30 rounds each. He grabbed one of the bullets to put back into the magazine, but he had difficulty pressing them back in with his sore hand. He finally got one round in the magazine when he heard a rustling noise in the nearby brush, about 15 yards away. Sam and the boys heard it too. Something was coming up behind them.

Sam and the boys both looked at Mike, wondering what he would do. He placed his pointer finger over his mouth, signaling them to stay quiet while he carefully loaded a bullet directly into the rifle's chamber, but not racking the chamber closed for fear that the noise would give away their location.

Sam moved around the tree so the trunk was between her and whatever was stalking them. She spied through the vegetation and caught a glimpse of what looked like a face mask, but seconds later she saw its entire profile and struggled to catch her breath. She frantically waved to get Mike's attention, pointing at the nearby brush. When he finally turned, it was so close its yellow eyes had locked on to his.

Can we not get a break, God?! Mike uttered a hasty and arrogant prayer through gritted teeth, concentrating on the massive cat; its orange and white-stripes breaking up the jungle's green monotony as it prowled only a few yards from them, its velvety black-striped tail pressed against its back thigh, twitching vigorously.

The boys panicked as they struggled to free themselves from the rifle strap, yanking, pulling and whimpering like caught prey. The tiger smelled their fear and angled its body at them, ready to pounce. Sam saw its intentions and prayed her own silent prayer

Spak! Mike racked the gun's bolt and the tiger faced off with him. Sam opened her eyes, watching as the tiger crouched down on all fours, glaring intently at Mike, its eyes locked in onto his. He carefully brought the gun up to his shoulder, aiming at the tiger's head, wondering if one bullet would be enough to take it down, and hoping it wouldn't misfire like the pistol.

SIXTEEN
INTEL

Days Later

Yeah, mom, I know. It feels like a dream, but I'm...I'm alive. I'm flying out soon," Kylee sniffed, her eyelids clamped tight to hold back the cascade of tears, a few drops sneaking out. "No, I don't want to talk about it right now...mom, don't cry...I know...just...just, I'll share more later...No, there's nothing you need to do," Kylee reiterated as she looked at Chief to be sure that was accurate. Chief nodded, silently agreeing that they would take care of getting her back home. "Okay, I've gotta go now. I love you..." she finished, trying hard to keep from breaking down.

Kylee hung up the phone and leaned back in her seat, exhaling loudly, relieved that her mom knew she was safe—a moment she had longed for but doubted would ever be a reality.

"So, it's Kylee, right? Chief asked.

"Yeah," she replied quietly.

"If you don't mind me asking...how did you end up—"

"How did I end up being prostituted?" she interrupted him candidly.

"Umm...well...only if you want to share."

"I'm really just stupid for letting myself get into it..."

"Stupid?" Chief slowed down, edging over to the side of the road. He turned and locked eyes with her. "Listen to me. You're

142

anything but stupid, you're a brave survivor. Not many people could have endured what you did…the fact that you stayed alive helped us in our rescue operation. We saw you in Pattaya and we followed you to this farm. We couldn't have rescued anyone tonight if you hadn't been brave." A single tear rolled down her cheek as she thought about the night's events and how she would still be in that horrific bunker if it wasn't for Chief and his team.

"I, uh, well, it's been more than a year ago when I saw this ad for the beautiful Burmese islands on one of my social media accounts; I can't even remember which one now. I was living in boring Ohio and I wanted an adventure. Anyway, it wasn't long after that I met this guy online. He called himself a tour guide and told me I would have a blast at all the clubs and the beaches and what not…oh, and that the little bit of money I had saved up from babysitting would stretch a long way in Burma. It was a good hook, and I bit hard."

"So, your parents were fine with you leaving…and you left by yourself? That's bold," Chief inquired as he turned on his phone's voice recorder and pulled back onto the road, the van shadowing their moves.

"No, no, not at all. At first, I left with my boyfriend. I told my parents I was going to New York, but instead, we left to, you know, travel the world…I told a few friends back home so someone knew where we were going."

"Sounds familiar," Johnny spoke up from the behind them.

"So, you and your boyfriend left for Burma, what happened to him?" Chief asked, glancing at her.

She remained silent for several seconds and finally spoke. "We…we left together and arrived in Burma. We didn't meet up with the tour guide right away. We were supposed to, but I just wanted to do my own thing for a while…you know, that rebellious teenager stuff. So my boyfriend and I got a cheap motel and toured the city for a couple days. I loved the Burmese people and culture—everyone was so nice—but my boyfriend, he didn't care for it. One night, he was acting like an idiot, so I called up the tour guide and—"

143

"Can you tell me this guide's name?" Chief interrupted, "And I didn't mean to cut you off…keep going."

"His name, yeah, I can tell you; I'll never forget it. His name is Tuan…sometimes they call him TJ…he's got a few names really."

"Okay, go on."

"So, um, I called up Tuan and I told him where I was staying. I just wanted to hang out with someone else who wanted to have fun…But If I knew then what I know now…that…that call would have taken my boyfriend's la…li…life—" Kylee stuttered, unable to finish the sentence through her sobbing.

"These thugs gotta go," Johnny mumbled as he watched her break down.

"Kylee, you're not the one to blame here. I wish you would have stayed stateside, but you're not to blame for what happened to you or your boyfriend…that was Tuan and his men," Chief reiterated as nicely as he knew how.

Kylee remained quiet for a few moments, dropping the visor mirror to look at herself. It was the first time she had seen herself in a mirror since the Burmese brothel and she still had her elaborate makeup.

"I know this is hard, but keep sharing if you can…I think it will do you good. Any info we get could help put an end to their operation—and you're the key to getting it done."

"Okay, I'll try," she replied through her sniffles. "I…I met up with Tuan outside my motel in Mandalay and he took me to this bar in the city…it was awful, and I should have known better, but he just seemed so nice, ya know? We danced for a while and then he asked if I wanted to go to a nicer bar. He said we could drink as much as we wanted…that's pretty much when it all unraveled for me."

"Do you remember the name of the bar?" Chief asked.

"No, I don't even know if it had a name."

"Remember any identifying details about it?"

"It was dark out, and I already had some drinks in me. All I remember is the creepy feeling I had when I first walked inside

144

and saw some other girls dancing seductively for a bunch of men. I looked in their eyes and it was like someone had turned the lights off; that's when I knew I had made a terrible mistake. I know that probably doesn't make much sense."

"Makes perfect sense. I've seen it. Kylee, about how many men were there?"

"That first night…I honestly can't remember, but on any given night there were probably 40-60 guys coming through there."

"How many were running the place?"

"At least three at all times—sometimes more."

"Okay, that helps."

"So, yeah, I…uh…I waited for a while, building up the courage to leave," she paused, looking straight ahead, wiping the tears from her cheeks.

"You're doing great…giving us a lot to go on," Chief encouraged her.

"I finally built up the courage to walk out, but when I did they trapped me…circled around me and for several hours they…they had their way with…with…" She placed her hand over her mouth, trying to hold back her emotions.

"Hey, listen, take a break. You don't have to continue."

"No, I…I need to get this out…to help put them away," she paused and then continued. "I guess it was the next day when they put me into a room and padlocked the door. They took my clothes, money and all my identification and left me with a see-through nighty and some laced hard liquor."

"Drugs…figures," Randall spoke up.

"Yeah, they gave us drugs to keep us sedated so we wouldn't cause a problem. I faked taking it most of the time, but sometimes I took it to numb my mind to forget what was happening to me."

"Monsters," Johnny muttered under his breath.

"Chief, with your permission, I'll pass that info on to my narc commander," Randall confirmed. "He knows someone high up at Interpol. Maybe we can put some heat on these guys and help shut it down."

"Good. That's why I'm getting as much info as I can. We definitely need to get this operation shut down...Kylee, do you remember how many entrances or exits?"

"Two. One in the front and one in the rear. There were windows too, but they were all boarded shut."

"Sounds like a hellhole," Johnny suggested.

"More than you know. They kept me locked in the room during the day, except to use the restroom, which is also where I got my drinking water...out of a stagnant bucket."

Chief shook his head, disgusted at what he was hearing, but also feeling helpless to do anything about it.

"At night, I was forced to dance for the men...and to, you know, give them fa...favors," she cringed, placing her hand over her mouth again.

"We know, Kylee...we're so sorry for what they did to you, and I promise they'll pay," Chief reached out his hand to put it on her shoulder, but stopped himself at the last second, giving her time to process.

"You told us a little about your boyfriend. What happened to him?" Chief inquired.

Kylee exhaled for several seconds and nodded. "Yeah, Jake. I guess he started asking around about me when I didn't show back up at the hotel. I had already been at the brothel for at least a few days. I didn't really know how long because there were no clocks and I had no view of the outside. I only knew it was a new day when the men showed up by the droves at nighttime. Pretty soon it all ran together into one endless night without sunrises or sunsets, only a creepy red color everywhere all the time."

Chief looked at her sympathetically, watching as she struggled emotionally, but not having the words to console her. Moments later, she shared again.

"So, yeah, somehow Jake, he ended up at the brothel. He came in one day, maybe four days later and I...umm...I was dancing on the stage and he...he saw me," she paused, bursting into tears.

She took a moment to concentrate on her breathing and eventually continued. "Jake, he uh, he went crazy, grabbing chairs

146

and throwing them at the men…they umm…they…" She paused again, the emotion too powerful to speak.

"They hurt him bad, didn't they?" Chief asked and she nodded through her whimpering.

"Every guy took turns beating him, and they dum…dumped him…la…la…lake," the words tumbled from her lips.

Chief pulled the Rover over again and she curled into a ball. He looked her over like a loving father would a daughter, wanting to hold her.

Chief looked to the rearview mirror and locked eyes with Randall. "I think it would do Kylee good if someone could come and speak to her—maybe provide some guidance before she heads back to the States?"

"Sure, Chief. Absolutely. I'll call up my friend who runs the non-profit in Pattaya. I'm sure she'd be glad to assist."

"Good," Chief replied as he reached for his phone. "Tell her that we'll be at the Kameo Hotel in the Chon Buri District, maybe she can meet us there."

"I'll call her now."

"Great. Thanks."

"Ch…Chief?" Kylee whispered, "Can I ask you a question?"

"Yeah, darlin', anything."

"Did my…my parents hire you?"

"To be honest…" Chief hesitated for a second to find the right words, "…we didn't know about you. We were hired by another American family whose daughter left for Burma a few days ago, but no one has heard from them. I'm worried she ended up in a situation similar to yours…But I want you to know that we're glad we found you. You made our mission."

Kylee sat up straight, her eyes staring ahead about as wide as she could make them.

"Them?" she asked.

"What was that, darlin'?"

"You said them. Was it an American girl traveling with her boyfriend?"

"Yes," Chief paused, his eyebrows creased, retracing his words but not recalling mentioning a boyfriend. "Wait, do you know something about that?"

"It's the reason I was in the bunker...I ran into an American girl at the brothel in Burma. I helped her and her boyfriend escape."

"You helped them escape?" Chief asked, putting the Rover's gear into park and taking out his notepad and pen.

"Yeah, Tuan was furious, because she's a blonde, ya know? He would have killed me for it, but I brought in too much money for them. Anyway, when they found out what I did they brought me here and locked me in the bunker. They only let me out to work in that brothel. It was supposed to be punishment, but at least I got to see some daylight."

Chief stared at her, slightly confused. "You said she is a blonde. Did that mean something to them?"

"Yeah, the first natural blonde they ever got. The men here go crazy for blondes because they're so rare. They would dye the Asian girls' hair blonde sometimes, even tried dying my red hair blonde because they said red hair is scary to Asian men, but all they did was turn it pink."

"Do you remember the girl's name?"

"Yeah, she told me her name was Sam."

Chief's mouth fell slightly agape as he turned to look at Johnny who was nearly as shocked.

"Listen, Kylee, anything you can think of to share about her and what you saw when she arrived would greatly help us right now."

"All I know is they managed to escape and I remember Tuan bringing the military in to help. I'm not sure if they made it out alive because the next day Tuan got a call like someone had located them or something and they rushed out of the brothel...then a couple hours later they blindfolded me and transported me here. That was a few days ago. That's all I can tell you."

148

"You mentioned a lake," Johnny poked his head up from the back. "Do you remember the name?"

"I was trying to remember…it's a weird name…"

"Keep trying Kylee," Chief encouraged her. "It could make all the difference."

"Wait! It was something about a man. Something the man lake. I remember that much."

"That helps more than you know," Chief smiled, "I'm going to let you rest, but if you remember anything else…"

"I'll let you know for sure," she rested her head against the window, thinking back on the events of the night as Chief pulled back onto the road, thrilled for the big break, but also concerned with what awaited them if they continued the mission.

"Chief, can I ask one more question?"

"Ask as many as you need, darlin'?"

"Just one more. Are you…are you gonna get those creeps?"

Chief remained silent for a moment, looking at her and thinking about her incredible bravery. "One way or another, I'll make sure they pay."

"Good."

"I…I don't know how to thank you for rescuing me," she formed a half-smile.

Chief smiled back. "You already have."

SEVENTEEN
THE MONASTERY

Days Earlier

Mike eased his finger toward the rifle's trigger, waiting for the right moment to shoot the tiger. He kept his eyes locked on the large, intimidating cat, watching as its back legs rose up slightly, its body poised to pounce, but before it could attack one of the boys managed to get free and its attention shifted to him.

As the boy cautiously backed away, the tiger caught a whiff of the fear emanating from him and licked its chops. The boy panted heavily, extending his arms with his palms facing it as though he could somehow temper the wild within it. He persisted backward, stepping through the dense foliage and multitude of insects swarming around him until he completely disappeared behind a cluster of thick palms, the rustling leaves and his heavy footsteps the only indicator that he was still nearby.

With the boy out of its sight, the tiger turned its attention back to Mike, studying him intently, its eyes tracing the outline of his body, curious as to what he was holding.

Grrraaawwwwrrrrrrr! The tiger let out a deafening roar and turned back toward the boy who hurried through the unforgiving jungle, the leaves making a swooshing sound as he ran through them, attempting to escape his fate. The tiger abruptly shifted its body weight and the muscles under its striped fur moved like an

150

ocean wave as they collected together, empowering a huge leap and gallop through the jungle.

"Shoot it, Mike!" Sam yelled, but he refused, not wanting to make any noise that would give away their position.

The tiger ripped through the jungle's thick vegetation like tissue paper and within seconds they heard a chilling scream. The tiger followed with a short growl and then the jungle went eerily silent.

Sam gasped aloud, lost in the thought of the boy's brutal death, but Mike acted as though nothing happened. He grabbed the shirts and knelt down to help her to her feet when she finally spoke up. "What about the other boy?"

Mike glanced at him, still shirtless and hugging the tree. "We're leaving him here as a distraction."

"Are you listening to yourself?" she asked, surprised that he would leave the boy to die.

He snapped back. "We don't have time for this! What if it's him or us?"

"Mike, we don't want that on our conscience," she retorted, hoping he would be sensible.

"Oh, whatever," he replied, tramping over to the tree and unstrapping him, not wanting to deal with Sam's nagging. Once he got free he put his hands together and bowed down to Mike to thank him for saving his life. Mike remained apathetic, motioning with the gun's barrel for him to pick up where he had left off with helping Sam walk. The boy picked her up under her shoulder and they moved into the grassy area surrounding the monastery, getting a full view of the massive complex for the first time.

The temple's reddish-gold, triangular spire was nearly 75-feet tall, an almost ominous presence set against the backdrop of the moon's soft, glowing light and the hazy fog produced by the recent thunderstorm. Several other buildings were connected to the main temple, accessible by a wooden decking that wrapped around the exterior. As they got closer they could see the temple

151

was propped up on stilts and every edge was gilded in gold with small Buddhist idols carved into them.

"Where is the entrance to this thing?" Mike mumbled as they moved under the structure, weaving in and out of the stilts until they finally reached a limestone entryway with several moldy steps leading to the temple structure. The top rails had been cut to appear as though it was either a slithering snake or a dragon and a few sets of thong sandals had been kicked off nearby.

"We can rest here until morning. I think it will be safer than staying in the jungle," Mike suggested as he tried on the sandals, eventually finding a pair that nearly fit, a welcome relief for his shredded feet.

"Rest...that sounds good to me."

They gently laid her on the steps and she closed her eyes, quickly dozing off to the sleep, the day's stress and fatigue fully catching up with her.

Mike directed the boy to sit on the bottom step and he slumped down next to Sam, his rifle resting across his lap. Not trusting the boy, he fought against his drowsiness for several minutes, but his weariness was like anchors pulling on his eyelids, and before long he was snoring.

***

The sun's powerful rays cut through the light fog, climbing above the treetops and whisking across Mike's face and then Sam's. Mike gradually opened his eyes, his hand still firmly clutching the rifle's pistol grip. He glanced across the stone steps to where the boy had been resting opposite him, but he wasn't there.

"Sam, wake up!" He shook her shoulders. "The boy's gone!"

"Huh, what?" she asked, startled from her sleep.

"We have to find the boy! He knows we're heading to the train station. Ugh! If only I would have kept my eyes on him," he scolded himself as he stood to his feet.

Mike was still speaking, mumbling incoherent words when the still shirtless boy suddenly appeared, his hands clutching a wooden bowl of water and freshly picked vegetables from the monastery's nearby garden. Mike stared at him for a moment, wondering where he had gotten the bowl and realized he had been wrong about him. To show his thankfulness and as a way of apology, he gave him back his nearly dry shirt.

"My name is Mi-ke...Mi-ke," he slowly annunciated, pointing to himself repeatedly as he lifted the bowl of water, drinking some of it and being careful not to spill any.

"May-k...may-k," the boy repeated.

"Close enough."

"Sam...Sam," she patted herself on the chest several times.

"Sum."

"Very good. Very close," she smiled.

"Nyan...Nyan," the boy pointed to himself.

"Nyan. Good," Mike extended his hand and Nyan gawked at his fair skin for a moment, finally bowing to him.

As Mike and Nyan exchanged pleasantries, Sam drunk the rest of the water and pulled back the green husks on one of the corn cobs, chewing on the yellow kernels it until she had ingested every last one. Mike grabbed one and did likewise.

"Onions!" Sam muttered. "I've always hated onions." She reached into the pile and bit down on the end of the long, skinny green onion stalk, relishing the strong taste and nearly equally powerful odor.

They ate until they were full and then rested against the limestone wall. Mike was much more relaxed and within a few seconds he had dozed off to sleep again.

While he rested, Sam considered her surroundings, studying the east side of the jungle where the tiger had stalked them the night before. She recalled the previous day's events, her mind still reeling from the trauma they had been through. She stared at some chirping birds in a nearby palm tree, becoming lost in a daydream of home, but she quickly snapped out of it when she heard what sounded like a door opening.

Creaaaaaakkk! The monastery's large 20-foot high wooden doors swung inward and the sun lit up the dust that had kicked up in its wake. Sam lifted herself to see over the last step, cautiously peering into a dark corridor, waiting for someone to appear.

"Mike, wake up!" She whispered, rousing him from his light sleep. He opened his eyes and saw her scrutinizing the temple.

"Look!" She pointed to the open doors.

He looked into the dark corridor waiting for someone to appear but they never did.

"Sam, someone is here. Monks maybe. We should see if they can help," he suggested, standing up. "Maybe the open doors are a sign."

He didn't wait for her reply. He ascended the steps and stood at the door's golden threshold, but before he could step through Nyan hurried in front of him, waving him off. Mike paused for a moment, curious as to why he blocked his way, but ultimately moved around him into the shadowy corridor.

Mike cautiously stepped inside the temple, the vintage flooring groaning and the dusty, mildew smell tickled his nose, tempting him to sneeze.

As he continued on, his eyes adjusted to the darkness and he noticed the stilts he had seen the night before, protruding up through the floor and lining the corridor on both sides, acting as the temple's pillars, each painted in a reflective gold to hide its irreverent mediocrity.

He stepped deeper inside, his hands held out in front to feel for anything he might stumble into but it wasn't long before the sun had raised high enough to completely illuminate the corridor. He felt the sun's warm rays across his back and stepped to the side, the light hitting a life-sized, golden Buddha at the rear of the temple, making it appear as though it was the lost treasure of the temple of doom. He gazed at the religious effigy for a moment, unable to shake the unholy thought of how it reminded him of crispy egg rolls at his favorite Chinese restaurant.

On the floor, directly in front of the Buddha, was a crimson-colored symbol he couldn't quite make out. At first, he thought it was a splotch of blood, but it was more uniform than that. He stared at it for a moment and moved in closer, and that's when he recognized it—the same Asian symbol he had seen since arriving in Burma.

He stumbled backward, his eyes wavering, expecting something evil to pop out of the shadows and attack him. Sam stood at the threshold, watching curiously as he nervously backed away and turned to run out.

"Sam, we gotta go!" he insisted, struggling to find a decent breath. He grabbed the rifle from her hands and placed her arm around his shoulder, helping her move down the steps.

Her curiosity turned to confusion as she wondered what he had seen. "Mike, what's wrong?"

"No time to explain," he huffed out.

Nyan grabbed Sam's other arm and they moved through the clearing to the west side of the monastery, entering the opposite side of the jungle. They walked past a couple rows of trees when Sam purposely slipped off their shoulders, dropping to the ground.

"I'm not going another step with you until you tell me what you saw," she stated firmly. "You have the same look you had at the market. What's going on?"

He didn't respond. He faced a nearby tree, resting his arm against it and closed his eyes.

"Mike, I…I just want to know what you know," she spoke gently.

He let out a long sigh and was about to tell her when he felt a sharp stinging pain on his ankle. He looked down and his bare legs were littered with several large, red fire ants.

"What else is going to go wrong out here," he grumbled through his gritted teeth, lifting up his foot and brushing away the biting ants. When he did he saw that he had been standing on a small ant mound and quickly stepped away.

"Mike…" She wasn't letting him escape this time.

"Okay, alright…I keep seeing the same Asian symbol everywhere," he replied with limited information, still checking his legs and feeling the itch set in.

"A symbol? Can you describe it?"

Perceiving that she wasn't going to be satisfied with a general response, he told her everything. "It's something like an Asian letter with a circle around it. TJ had the symbol tattooed on his arm; it was on the outside of the brothel, at the goon's cafe, and now on the floor in the monastery. Whenever I see the symbol, something bad happens."

"So, it's like a premonition or something?" she asked, her eyes conveying a look of bewilderment, still prodding him for more details.

"No, more than that. It's like someone is speaking to me. I don't know how else to explain it," he replied, checking to be sure they weren't being followed and scratching his ankle from the ant bites.

"Before you said something about a dream. Is it connected?" she asked, leaning against one of the trees. Nyan watched their body language, trying to figure out what they were discussing.

"I think so. A few days before we left, I had a dream; that's when I first saw the symbol. I brushed it off, but when we were sleeping on the plane, I had another dream and saw it again. Then, when we got off the plane, I saw TJ's tattoo—the exact same symbol. I should have told you…I should have never let us go with him."

"Don't blame yourself. I think God's giving you a message. Hey, look at it this way, if God keeps giving you this message it means He's still with us, right?" she proposed, putting her arm around him.

Mike stayed quiet, listening to her suggestion.

"I'm wondering if the symbol is connected to something larger—like an organization that's behind all of this," she stated, her forehead wrinkled as though in deep thought. "Maybe the monastery is part of it. I remember reading an article before we left about radicalized Buddhist monks who were working with the Burmese Military. They were persecuting Christians in the Rakhine Province. It's one of the most dangerous areas in Burma. I memorized that area so we wouldn't travel there."

"Ra...Ra-keen" Nyan stuttered out the name, his eyes becoming large and shaking his head no. He put his hand near his head and made a circling motion with his pointer finger as though to say the place is crazy.

"You're probably right, Sam, but as far as I can tell, we've been in Rakhine since we got here. We just need to get to the train and hitch a ride out to Thailand."

"I was thinking about that. How will we get a ticket without money?"

"We'll have to improvise."

He could tell by the look on her face that she wasn't sure they could even get on the train.

"Look, it's not a perfect plan, but I know we won't last long out here. We need to make some distance while it's daylight. I'm not sure how far away the train is and we don't want to be in the jungle another night."

"I'm with you on that," she replied. "Let's just take it a step at a time. My knee is feeling better. I think I could walk on my own if I had a stick as a support."

"Good idea," he replied, searching for a decent stick for her to use, finding one close by.

With her new stick as a support, Sam took her first steps on her own through the jungle's wild tangles and overgrowth, but they were moving too slow to get out before nightfall.

They trudged along for a few hours when Mike heard the faint sound of a train whistle again, relieved that they were still heading in the right direction.

"Mike, I hate to say it but I need to rest again," she hesitated to speak up, but her injured knee was on fire and her other leg wobbled as it bore the brunt of her weight.

"It's okay. I could use some rest as well."

Mike cleared a spot, checking for fire ants and snakes and helped her down to the damp ground.

"What time do you think it is?" she asked as her eyes became heavy, her words becoming softer and quieter.

He looked up through the trees and saw a tinge of light shining through.

"Judging by the sun, I'm gonna say around noon...or maybe a little later."

She was already asleep when he replied—and so was Nyan.

Mike sat against the tree and removed the gun magazine and bullets from his pocket. He pressed the first round into the magazine, cringing through the pain in his hand until he had all five bullets loaded. He inserted it into the gun and laid it next to him. Moments later he closed his eyes to rest and drifted off into a light sleep.

They rested for several minutes when Mike was awakened by an odd noise. He turned his ear to the sound, unsure if he was in a dream, but then he heard it again.

Snap, swoosh. He sat still, grasping the gun's wooden grip tightly as he skimmed the area.

He examined the nearby trees and vines, catching a glimpse of reddish blur near a cluster of palm bushes several feet away. He looked intently, unable to see past the thick vegetation, but noticed the sound had faded. Still, he figured he should wake Sam.

He gently tapped her leg and she opened her eyes. When she did, she saw him squatting in front of her with his finger over his mouth and pointing in the direction of the noise, letting her know something was nearby.

She was nervous—and with everything they had been through, she had every right to be.

Mike woke Nyan up, and together they carefully pushed further into the jungle, moving around the wild vines, trying to be as stealthy as possible.

They walked for a short time when Mike heard the noise again—and this time it sounded closer.

Creak, crack, swoosh. Sam and Nyan heard it as well. They knelt down on the jungle floor, hiding under the vegetation. Mike readied his rifle as sweat poured from his forehead, waiting for whatever was there to come into view.

EIGHTEEN
DEBRIEFING

Days Later

Y ou'll be safe here," Chief spoke softly to the girls and the boy as they stood outside their hotel rooms, Lawanna translating for him. "We'll be in rooms on both sides of you and Bling will be back soon with some clothes for y'all. Until then, you can cover up with the sheets and blankets."

The kids didn't say anything as Chief put Kylee and Lawanna in two separate rooms, splitting the kids up between them.

"Team, once Bling gets back, we'll have a quick debriefing in my room and then y'all can get some sleep. We've had a long day."

"Roger that," Johnny stated as everyone anticipated a good shower and a clean bed.

***

Not long after, Bling arrived, carrying a trash bag full of clothing, his face displaying a rare frown.

"What's this Bling?" Johnny laughed as he dumped the clothing out onto one of the beds, "Smells like mothballs. You rob some old lady's wardrobe?"

"Sumpin' like dat. Chief done sent me out on a wild chick chase."

"You mean a wild goose chase," Randall replied.

"Nah, man, a wild chick chase…I had to find some chick and pay her for da clothes in her closet…probably thought I'm some freaky creep, rollin' round in da Chester van askin' for girl's garments in the middle of da night."

"Did she give you any toddler clothes you can change into?" Johnny snickered as Mack and Switch had a good laugh.

"Good enough, Bling, good enough," Chief stated. "Drop the clothes with the kids and meet us back here."

Bling didn't respond as he piled the clothes back into the bag and walked out.

***

Chief began the debriefing. "First, I want to commend everyone on a job well done. If you want to know how well the mission went today, go take a look at the beautiful prizes sitting in the rooms next to us."

Everyone nodded and smiled while Bling lifted his hands as though to give thanks to God.

"We had a pretty stressful day…lots of shooting. We also lost a girl. Let's go around the room and everyone can share what's on their mind."

Everyone was quiet until Switch finally spoke up. "I'll go first, I guess," he mumbled, sitting on the edge of one of the hotel's double beds.

"Go for it," Chief stated.

"Well, I thought we had a good mission, but I didn't expect to be sliced by a machete. Laugh if you want, but that friggin' hurt. And, yet, it was worth it to rescue all these girls…and that boy."

Mack chimed in next. "Yeah, rescuing them sweethearts—that's a good ol' fashioned feelin'—and I didn't mind cracking some shots off at them perps either."

"Yo, I know I ain't have much of a role tonight, but it felt really good what y'all did," Bling stated.

"What you did as well, Bling. You did your part," Chief replied.

"Yeah, good job with the girl's clothing," Johnny teased.

"Not now, Johnny," Chief countered.

"To be honest, Chief, I had a little flashback," Bling looked down, uncertain if it was the right time to speak up about it.

"You? You had a flashback?" Johnny gave him a sly look, indicating his disapproval. "What triggered your flashback? Saw a gun and got scared?" he finished with a lighthearted chuckle. Mack followed with a hearty laugh, but Bling didn't respond.

"Look, I'm not trying to bust your brass here, Bling, but when you see someone blown apart…" Johnny looked down, "…and you were the one who did it—it's slightly irritating to hear someone talk about PTSD who has never been to war."

Bling turned and locked his eyes with Johnny, addressing him candidly. "You eva see a guy get a shank to his eyeball? You eva live in a cage the size of a closet for years or see horrible stuffs in da group showers? I gots all the respect for ya Johnny, but other peeps been through different wars but got da same stress."

Chief cut in. "Hey, come on Johnny, let's hear him out."

"Thanks, Chief," Bling replied. "It's just dat when I saw them girls…" Bling paused, his voice a little shaky, "How they trapped like dat, them cages and ever'thin', it sorta took me back to my time in the pen."

"That's a bit of PTSD creeping up on you, but you kept it together," Chief stated, affirming his emotions as Johnny rolled his eyes.

"Not really. For a few moments, I lost it. It could have been a problem for the mission. I heard y'all talkin' 'bout dat girl in da bunker and I 'membered how they put me in da hole for something I ain't even do."

"Bling, I know a bit about post-traumatic stress," Randall spoke up, propping himself up on the wall across from one of the beds. "I've also spent some time behind enemy lines in a prisoner camp for a short time. What matters is you overcame and stayed on mission…You're a good man. Your faith will help you sort it all out."

"Yeah, you right. My faith gots me. I'm also thankful to be on da team and workin' wit' y'all. Helps keep da focus off me."

"We're glad to have you, Bling, really we are, right guys?" Chief asked, glancing around the room.

"A bit preachy, but yeah, you're a teammate," Switch smiled.

Mack hesitated but eventually nodded.

"You talk about faith, Bling, but—" Johnny started in and Chief quickly cut him off.

"Hey, come on, Johnny. We're all tired. Let's just get through this and get some rest."

"No…no, you set this up to get stuff off our chest and I gotta get this question settled; it's causin' me PTSD," Johnny smirked. Mack shook his head as Chief looked down and held out his hand, palm up, suggesting to him that he could go ahead with his question.

"Here's my issue with you, Bling. Your faith in this supposedly good God. Why would your God allow innocent girls and that boy to go through such pain and torture? If He's real, why does he allow this type of evil to exist in the world?" Johnny crossed his arms, figuring he asked a question Bling couldn't answer.

"I thought 'bout them questions before, Johnny, but theys worded different. I ain't ask why God allow others to do all da evil; I asked Him why He ain't take me out when I did all my evil. I ain't got no right to ask Him why He allows evil when I know I've been part of it. Lyin', stealin', fornicatin' and worse…I've heard some of your war stories; maybe that could apply to you as well."

Johnny contemplated for a moment, staring at Bling, the room silent as everyone could feel the tension thickening. Chief shook his head and stood up, placing his gear bag on the small table for an inventory check as he listened in.

"Yeah, well, I haven't done anything like what we encountered tonight. You're right, I have been to war, but I was raining down justice on the enemy."

"So, since God is a God of justice and all, I guess you was actin' for Him in da war," Bling countered. "Either way, we still back to God and now you workin' for Him."

Johnny glared at Bling, stunned by his thoughtful response and unable to reasonably counter.

"I guess I'll give you that, but what about Adolph Hitler…why didn't God stop him from killing all those people? Why would he allow that? Where was your God of justice then?"

"What 'bout Walt Disney?" Bling refuted.

"I'm not following."

"You wanna give an extreme evil, so I gave da opposite. If you gonna blame God for evil, you gotta give Him credit for the pleasure as well, but you probably ain't wanna go there since dat ain't fittin' your narrative."

"Man, Bling, you're throwing it down tonight," Switch suggested, lifting his glasses. "I didn't know you had all this in you."

Johnny narrowed his eyes at Switch, silently conveying to him to stay out of the conversation. "Okay, whatever, Bling." Johnny frustratingly replied. "I can tell you don't want to answer my questions."

"Actually, Bling, I want to run something by you that's similar to what Johnny asked," Switch reentered the conversation, garnering everyone's attention. "This has been on my mind for a while, but it came back to me today when I saw what the perps were doing to those girls at the farm."

"Sure, axe away," Bling replied, slightly curious as to what was on his mind.

"Well, years ago, when I came back from Afghanistan, a neighbor-mom from the apartment complex I lived in asked if I would help find her 13-year-old daughter who went missing. She met someone online who she thought was 17, but it turned out he was a nasty old man. Anyway, we searched for over a year and came up empty. But then I…uh…well, one day I stumbled across a video of her on a porno website," Switch paused for a moment, looking down. "Guys, this girl was in dozens of videos that had been uploaded to this site and she had been coerced into doing stuff I don't even want to describe—and I was the one who had to break it to the mom."

"Wait, I think I heard this on the news," Johnny replied. "If I remember right, the perp got her pregnant as well—made her get an abortion."

"Yeah, you're right," Switch replied.

"So, how come no one at the abortion clinic asked questions?" Mack furrowed his brow. "They could've rescued her then."

"That's common here," Randall indicated.

"It's common in the States as well," Johnny confirmed.

"Seriously?" Mack asked, surprised that something like that would happen in America.

"Absolutely. The pimps take the girls to the abortion clinics to keep them walking the streets, but no one asks any questions. In fact, the clinics will encourage the girls to work the streets 'from the waist up' while their healing. It's sickening…and it's all about money."

"Then the way I see it, them clinics is part of the problem," Mack replied.

"That would be an accurate assessment," Randall agreed. "Switch, you did a good job locating her. I can't imagine what that mom was going through…and discovering her on a website like that…horrible!"

"See, that's the thing. The mom wanted to know how I had found her, but I lied and told her I had a hunch. The truth was that I was surfing for porn when I came across her."

"Woaaaaaah," Mack blurted out, unable to constrain himself.

"Exactly, but that motivated me to get help. I didn't want to play any part in supporting sex trafficking, so I prayed that God would take away my porn addiction. I uh…I figured if God was real and all, it would've been an easy thing for him to do, but he never came through, and that was a real blow to my faith. Now, I'm not even sure he exists."

"That's because he doesn't," Johnny mumbled.

"I get it, Switch," Bling responded, disregarding Johnny's off-hand comment. "But can I be blunt wit' you?"

"Sure, please do."

"First, what dat girl went through is tragic, and I'm glad y'all found her. Secondly, you already know God is real, but you was treatin' Him like He a genie. You wanted da easy road, but dat ain't how it work. You rode in full donkey wit' dat porn, but you went half-donkey wit' God, and half-donkeys ain't gonna carry dat heavy load, brother."

"Half-donkey? That's not true. I pleaded with God to take it away."

"And is dat what you did to get into da habit…you pleaded into it?"

"I'm not following."

"Right. Let me help. When you got into porn, you thought about it and then you went online and sought it out. After dat, you put in yo credit card info. Then, for hours after hours and days after days you searched for da right female pictures and videos to feed yo appetite. You had to find da right girl wit' da right skin tone, perfect size waist, right kinda legs, big—"

"Hey, okay, I get it," Switch interrupted. "I definitely gave porn a lot of time and money. Damn, man!"

"But somehow you expected to just pray to get out of it? Dat ain't even commonsense, brother. But I'm curious now, how you did get out of it?"

"I, uh, I read some books and learned how to build up my willpower," he replied, sticking his chest out a bit.

"Yo, willpower ain't gonna get you full freedom. Wit'out God's Spirit, there ain't no true freedom. I'm guessin' you still seduced by it—probably still dabblin' in it."

"That's where you're wrong, man; I'm a hundred percent good," he responded, checking to see if Mack was listening.

"You sure about that?" Mack giggled, tearing into a stick of beef jerky, listening harder than Switch had assumed.

"Mack!" Switch angrily addressed him and stood to his feet as though to intimidate him from saying anything else.

"What you got on him, Mack?" Johnny asked with an inquisitive smile as everyone listened closely, waiting for the grand finale.

"Shoot, not even a week ago, I walked in on this chump surfin' online department store ads—he was lookin' at ladies' britches and bikinis." Mack and Johnny erupted into laughter, and Randall and Chief were struggling to hold it in.

"Maybe he was buying a gift for his mom," Johnny teased.

"Man, shut up," Switch heatedly retorted, but shame began dominating his anger and he soon hung his head.

"Guys, let's take it easy," Chief spoke up, still going through his gear but clearly eavesdropping.

"Yo, Switch, I ain't tryin' to poke fun, man, but I knew you was still dealin' wit' it. Many people come to God for help, but few do what's necessary for freedom. Even if God would've taken it when you axed, you still woulda lacked character. Yo, you gotta put something good in place of da bad—and da only One good is God. You gotsta replace them demons spirits wit' God's Son and da power of da Holy Spirit, yo."

"Oh, brother—" Johnny smacked his lips and rolled his eyes.

"Can you teach me how to get that freedom you're talking about?" Switch asked, talking over Johnny.

"Most of it you already know. You gotsta surrender to God and make Him yo life in da same way you gave yo life to dat porn. Desire Him and give Him your time and resources. Pretty simple, yo. He gives da Spirit to those who ask."

"I guess that makes sense."

"Sure it do. Da same keys dat locked me up in da prison cell are da same ones dat set me free. Seek God with dat same drive and you'll find Him. When you do, He'll draw near to you. Oh...and fill up dat idle time surfin' da net with da things of da Lort."

Switch lifted his head a bit.

"I've never heard anything like this before," Switch replied, still deep in thought. "All I've ever heard from a religious person is that I needed more church or religious activities."

"Freedom comes only through God's Holy Spirit. Everything else is a weak substitute. You gotta have Him in yo life, cuz He not only gives freedom, but He also builds character in you to stay free."

"Can you explain that a little more?"

"Sure. Your porn use cut trails in da forest of yo brain and every time you tempted, you naturally gravitate to dat same trail 'cuz it's already been cut down. It's an easier walk. Yo, you gotta cut new spiritual trails to override dat flesh, man, to where it's more natural to take da high road."

"Makes a lot of sense, Bling. Thanks."

"Spirits and ghosts…sounds like hocus pocus to me," Johnny snorted out a laugh.

"Nah, not hocus pocus, abracadabra," Bling smiled widely.

"Man, Bling, you're crazier than I thought," Johnny shook his head.

"Abracadabra is a combo of the Hebrew words for da Father, Son, and Holy Spirit—and dat's what Switch needs right now, him, you, and everyone in dis room."

"If you say so, buddy," Johnny sneered.

"It's only for those who have ears to hear."

"Alright, I'm gonna redirect y'all because this is only going to get worse and we have a more pressing issue to discuss," Chief sternly interrupted.

"Hey, you started it, boss," Johnny replied.

"And I let y'all hash it out, but now I'm finishing it," Chief's eyes were intense.

Everyone stayed quiet, knowing better than to respond.

"Listen up, I need to ask y'all a serious question. The American girl we rescued today, her real name is Kylee. I interviewed her and it came out that she was locked up with Sam in a brothel in Burma."

"You're kidding?" Switch responded.

"No, I'm not. We also have an approximate location. This is a huge break, and we have another opportunity to make a real difference. I'd really like to shut these scumbags down for good, but I need everyone's take on it."

"What we waitin' fer? Let's get the damsel and flip the switch on them perps," Mack asserted, still chomping down on his jerky.

"I wish it were that simple. There are some issues I need to run by y'all." Chief rubbed his hair and blew out a long breath. "Apparently, along with the Russians, the Burmese Military is also directly involved. If we continue, it will be extremely risky."

Chief looked around the room, but everyone was silent.

"Look, if we call it now we've already had a successful mission, but I'm fairly certain we can finish what we came to do. What are you guys thinking? The floor's open."

"So, we'll be leaving for Burma?" Johnny inquired.

"Correct. We'll leave in the morning, but only if everyone is on board."

"As long as we're not going to Ramree Island, I'm down," Johnny crossed his arms, looking at the floor, a subtle hint that he didn't want to explain further.

"Ramree Island?" Switch mumbled. "What are you talking about?"

"Something you want to let us in on, Johnny," Chief asked, noting Johnny's apprehension.

"You know what. Never mind. It's nothing, really. I…I'm good to go…just me rambling, boss." Johnny talked faster than normal and Chief sensed he was holding something back, but he left it alone.

Seconds later, everyone agreed to the mission.

"Alright. Good," Chief replied, "Randall has a bush pilot who can get us to Burma by 18:30 tomorrow. That will leave us with a few hours of daylight when we arrive."

Randall gave a confirming nod.

"Switch, after you get your rest, I need you to do a search on all the lakes near Mandalay that have the words *the man* in them. According to Kylee, there's a karaoke bar at the edge of the lake where she met Sam and it's operating as a brothel. Also, I recorded Kylee's statement and I'll be playin' it when we get on the plane so everyone is up-to-date," Chief scanned around to make sure everyone understood and moved to the front of the room, extending his hand to Randall.

"Randall, you were instrumental in our operation today and we want to thank you for all you did to help us," Chief stated as Randall firmly grabbed his hand.

"My pleasure. It's not every day I get to rescue trafficked kids and help shut down a criminal ring," he replied as Chief removed a stack of hundred dollar bills, slipping them into his hand.

"I trust you'll take good care of the kids and get Kylee to the airport?"

"Absolutely. Sandra from the non-profit will be here in the morning. She wants to run trauma protocol with Kylee and then I'll personally take her to the airport."

"With everything she's endured, she'll need some good counsel, I'm sure."

"What about them other damsels and that boy?" Mack asked, his eyes showing concern.

"We're gonna take good care of them," Randall confirmed. "I've already spoken to a few of the girls. Some told me they got into this when they aged out of the foster system and others were sold into it because of family debts. These are difficult situations, but Sandra has a safe house where they can stay and learn life skills and make a new family. I'll make sure they're well taken care of."

"That's great," Chief replied. "If Sandra needs any support, tell her to call and I'll arrange to provide some assistance. Guys, what do y'all think?"

"Yo, anything they need," Bling replied.

"You can have half my take," Mack agreed. "I'd just buy more guns anyway, and you can only shoot one at a time."

"I'd be willing to donate," Switch stated.

Johnny nodded in agreement.

"Good. That's settled. Let's get some rest and eat a good breakfast. We'll be wheels up at 1100 hours."

"Roger that," Johnny replied.

NINETEEN
UNLIKELY COMBATANTS

Days Earlier

Mike eased back on the rifle's charging handle, bracing for the loud clack, wondering why he hadn't learned his lesson to keep a round in the chamber.

Spak! The rifle's bolt closed and the foreign, metal-on-metal sound ricocheted throughout the jungle, temporarily silencing the numerous melodic birds and buzzing insects.

Mike gazed into the vegetation where he had last heard the sound, noticing that the large palm leaves were swaying—and it wasn't from the wind. There was absolutely no breeze in the stifling hot jungle. Something was definitely there—and they could only pray it wasn't the tiger.

Mike looked down the rifle's peephole sight, aiming it at the shivering foliage, waiting for whatever was there to make its appearance. Seconds later, the leaves parted and three bald monks in crimson-colored robes and thong sandals stepped through the greenery, their hands held out to signal that they meant no harm.

Nyan's eyes expanded and he lost his breath. He turned to Mike and Sam, waving his hands in a manner that suggested the monks weren't to be trusted. Mike stood up, studying their nearly solemn body language, intrigued as to why they had followed them into the jungle.

Sam and Nyan stood as well, their eyes studying every inch of the monks as they bowed at their waists in unison, one of them motioning with his hand in an attempt to get the kids to follow them. Mike stepped back, sensing something was off. He remembered the symbol in the monastery, but he also wondered if maybe he could have been wrong. They hadn't shown the slightest aggression and there was an undeniable peace about them. He decided to disregard his uneasiness and embrace his intrigue, leaning the rifle against a nearby tree as a token of peace, hoping that maybe they could help them get home.

The middle monk stepped up and bowed again, reaching out his left hand and holding his palm up, his fingers curled upward, not moving or saying anything. Mike and Sam glanced at each other, silently conveying the oddity of meeting the monks in the heart of the jungle, but Nyan wasn't impressed in the slightest. He was already nervously sweating.

Mike curiously stepped forward to inspect the monk's hand and caught a glimpse of the same Asian symbol, but this one was branded into his palm. Before he could react, the monk reached out and grabbed him, turning him around and wrapping his arm around this throat, choking him.

"Mikkkkkkkeeeee!" Sam screamed as the other monks reached beneath their long robes, each pulling out a large, curved machete, raising them into the air, poised to attack.

Nyan stood motionless, remembering how they had raided his village with the Burmese Military and used their martial arts to subdue anyone who resisted.

Mike gasped, struggling to get a breath, but as he did the monk's grip became tighter, cutting off his airway completely. It would be only a matter of seconds before he passed out—or worse.

"Wait, wait! You don't have to do this," Sam yelled, limping closer with her hands raised as a sign of surrender, hoping they would be reasonable, but they didn't flinch.

Nyan saw how the monks were focused on Sam and dove toward the rifle, reaching it as they wielded their machete at him,

172

swinging it through the vegetation, missing him by inches. He pointed the gun at the closest monk and fired a shot, missing him completely, but sending hundreds of birds resting in the treetops into flight, a sound similar to the crackling of a ravaging fire. With his hands shaking profusely, he aimed again and fired, this time striking the monk in his shoulder, the machete dropping from his hand and stabbing into the jungle's lush peat soil.

The other monk battled toward Nyan with his machete raised high, but before he could strike, Nyan shot him in the chest. The monk collapsed to his knees, his eyes rolling back into his head as he slumped over, blood gushing from his wound.

Only one monk remained—the one holding Mike hostage, his arm still tightly clamped around his throat, choking him out.

Mike's peripheral vision was fading as he neared passing out. In a desperate act, he grabbed the monk's forearm with both hands and pulled down, rotating his chin into the monk's elbow area to get a little air. The monk squeezed tighter, but it didn't stop Mike from stepping out and shifting his body weight to pull the monk off balance. With his left hand, Mike reached up and spread out his fingers wide, jabbing them into the monk's face, hoping to hit his eyes. He followed up with multiple downward hammer fist strikes to the monk's groin area, eventually striking gold.

"Arghhhhh!" the monk groaned—the first sound any of them had made—and he promptly released Mike. Mike turned and kicked the monk in his mid-section, knocking him to the ground, making sure he was down for good.

Nyan threw the rifle to Mike and he aimed it at the monks, his face full of fury while Nyan grabbed the machetes.

"Mike, no," Sam hobbled to him, placing her hand on top of the gun and pushing it down gently. He raised it back up and she stepped in front of him, off to the side of the rifle, gazing into his eyes. She stood there for a second, not saying a word, her eyes silently speaking to his soul. He didn't really want to shoot them, but he was tired of the relentless attacks. He finally lowered the gun and the two monks who were still alive put their hands together, bowing repeatedly as they backed away, grabbing the dead monk by his feet and dragging him back to the monastery.

Sam gazed at the trail of blood from where they had dragged the body and couldn't hold back her emotions any longer. She openly wept. Mike knelt down to console her, but he was barely holding it together himself.

As they sat together, an ominous cloud settled over the jungle and everything got darker, including their thoughts. Just as they were about to lose all hope, they heard the faint sound of a train whistle. Mike tilted his head, making sure he heard correctly. Then he heard it again—and it was getting louder.

"The whistle sounds close—probably no more than a mile away!" Mike jumped to his feet. He was worn out, but also determined to get to the train. He looked into Sam's beautiful eyes and saw that it was still there—the sparkle of hope he had seen before. She wasn't ready to give up and that gave him a fresh drive.

"Think you can go a little further?" he asked as he helped her to her feet, putting her arm around his shoulder to assist her.

"I think so," she indicated as Nyan followed, eventually taking the lead with the machete and cutting a path through the bushy undergrowth and a myriad of poisonous plants.

As they navigated the jungle, mud and pricker thorns stuck to Sam's boots and torn pants. Some of the green coloring from the vegetation had rubbed off on her shirt, which made her feel small and helpless—almost as though she was assimilating into the massive, unforgiving jungle. With foreboding thoughts invading her mind, she struck up a conversation to keep from wandering further into despair.

"Mike, I don't understand? Why did those monks attack us? I thought they were peaceful and religious? Is everyone here out to kill us?"

"It sure seems like it."

"It feels like someone is trying to break us," she suggested. "I mean, it's probably easier to name something that hasn't tried to kill us…Maybe there's some type of—" she paused, carefully considering her words.

"Some type of what?"

"I don't know, this sounds crazy, but maybe there's something supernatural at work here."

"Like God?"

"May…maybe…I guess…I don't know," she looked down, doubting her response.

"I'm not even sure I believe in God anymore," he stated.

"What do you mean? We were raised in the church. Surely, you believe in God."

"Look, now that I'm older, I'm thinking for myself. All those stories in the Bible. Have you seen anyone live that stuff out in real life?"

Sam stayed silent.

"I'll help you. We don't know any giant killers or people who lived through a fiery furnace or shut the mouths of lions. Everyone from our old church is a boring pew sitter. Politicians and scientists do more to help the world."

"Well, I guess you sort of have a point there," she spoke softly as they trudged along.

"Yeah, and do you remember Old Man Jenkins—the guy who taught the kid's Sunday school class?"

"Don't remind me."

"Dude's a big perv—the sheriff caught him with child porn on his computer."

"I remember."

"Exactly. The church is full of a bunch of fakers."

"Yeah, but what if…"

"Look, Sam, you can believe those fairy tales if you want, but I can't see how there's a God. I mean, if there is one, he must be evil to allow us to go through all this hell. Think about that girl back at the brothel and tell me a loving God would allow that."

"I see your point, Mike, and I've had those thoughts too, but what if God's allowing it for some greater purpose."

"A greater purpose, Sam? What great purpose is behind a girl trapped in a brothel forced to do things I don't even want to mention?"

"I…I know…I guess it's all about perspective, Mike. Maybe we're just seeing the ugly strokes of the painting and when we see the big picture it will all come together."

"Yeah, nice thought, but I'm not buying into it."

"Well, what gave you all those warnings then? We might be going through hell, but those warnings have kept us alive—that much you can't deny."

"Believe what you want, but I'm not buying into the whole God thing," he replied with a tinge of irritation in his voice.

"I…I'm not trying to get under your skin, Mike. I just wanted to talk it out—for my own sake. I'm not even sure about—" she paused without finishing, not really sure it was the best time to declare that she wasn't sure God existed—especially since they were lost in a jungle with a deranged army chasing after them.

They plodded through the jungle's volatile terrain as the bright slivers of sunlight slowly disappeared from the jungle's canopy. Nightfall was upon them and there was no end to the shadowy forest enveloping them—one that was getting gloomier by the second.

Mike and Sam were drained and Nyan wasn't fairing much better, their feet feeling like they were dragging anchors, but they continued on, remembering how they were nearly a late-night snack for a tiger the night before. They were almost to the point of collapse when they heard the sound of moving water.

"Sam, listen…"

"Sounds like the river!" she exclaimed, hoping they were truly at the end of the jungle.

Nyan sliced through the last of the jungle's vines and they stepped into a wide-open grassy berm at the edge of the river. He swung his machete low, shredding a path through the slender, knee-high grass, checking for snakes. Mike and Sam followed after, but they were soon cut off by the river's swiftly flowing water.

"Sam, look, do you see that?" Mike pointed to a metal sombrero-looking lampshade with a single bulb illuminating a small building a couple hundred yards to their right.

"I see it. Looks like it could be a small train depot!" she exclaimed with a touch of excitement in her voice. "But how are we going to get across the river?"

"I'm thinking this is the same river we crossed before. At least it's not as wide here," he replied, kneeling down, trying to determine the depth of the water and checking to see if there were crocodiles nearby.

"Mike, you're not thinking about swimming that, are you? I'm definitely not." she insisted, crossing her arms. Nyan looked at them and shook his head no. He remembered what had happened to the other boys who were attacked by the crocs the last time he had crossed the river.

"But Sam, we're so close."

"Absolutely not! My mind is made up!"

"Ugh...alright. We'll have to look for something to use to get across then, a log maybe, but it's too dark out to find anything."

As they stood at the edge of the riverbank trying to determine how to get across, they heard a train approaching.

"Man, we could be on that train!" Mike grumbled, pointing across the river, growing more frustrated by the moment. He knelt down and punched the ground and pulled the back of his hair, thinking of a way to get across. He had a fleeting thought of going back into the jungle and searching for something to use, but he wasn't too keen on that idea.

"Sam, think! There's gotta be a way across!"

"I am thinking, but maybe we should rest awhile and collect ourselves. That might be the best thing we can do right now."

"Ugh! I'm just ready to get out of here!"

"I know. Me too, but maybe we could use a break." She leaned in and put her hand on his shoulder.

"Yeah, maybe you're right. Once we get some rest, we'll think clearer."

Mike and Nyan used the machetes to clear an area of grass between the jungle and the river and checked for any creatures that might want to snack on them. Then they found a spot to lie down for the evening.

"Mike," Sam whispered as she rested on her back, staring up at the glistening stars and swatting away the relentless bugs. "Do you think our parents are looking for us?"

"Maybe yours, but my folks don't have much money. I don't know if they could afford the plane ticket and the time off from work to come over here."

"I keep thinking about my dad," she replied. "I know he would search for me. He might already be here. I...I don't know though."

"Let's get some rest, Sam. We've got a big day ahead," Mike's voice got quieter as he attempted to change the subject.

"Right. I can't think about it too much anyway," she replied, her eyes becoming heavier by the second.

Mike listened to the strange jungle noises behind him, thinking about how close they were to the train depot. He turned and saw that Sam and Nyan were already sleeping, but his mind wouldn't shut off; he couldn't stop thinking about how to cross the river. His mind rambled, thinking about logs and swimming and bridges, but it wasn't long before the stress caught up to him and he drifted into a forgotten dream.

TWENTY
OVERWATCH

Days Later

I ain't sign up for no hikin' adventure, Chief," Mack griped, placing both hands on his hips and gazing up at the rocky hill with some sporadic pine trees mixed in.

"You know there's no way we could have landed in Mandalay with our weapons," Chief explained. "The pilot said we couldn't get closer than this without causing a commotion. Besides, you could use a little exercise."

Johnny snickered and Mack rolled his eyes.

"Yo, at least it ain't quite as humid," Bling inserted, staying positive.

"Chief, the pilot was right," Switch reported as he unfolded a paper map, checking their location. "There should be a small village on the backside of this hill...about a klick and a half away."

"Good. How's your leg?"

"Still hurts, but I'll manage."

"Keep me updated. If we need to help carry your gear, it's not a problem."

"Appreciate that."

"Team, let's get going. We've got a lot of ground to cover," Chief stated as everyone grudgingly hoisted their gear bags over their shoulder for the ascent.

179

Chief and the team hiked nearly halfway up the hill when Mack got winded and lost his footing on some loose rocks. He stumbled around a bit and everyone got worried that he might fall.

"Mack, you alright over there," Chief called down from several feet ahead.

"I just need a…a sec to catch my…my uh…"

"One too many biscuit breakfasts, Mack," Johnny laughed. "See, this is why I'm always on you to get back in shape."

"Well, I ain't know we'd be humpin' it up no mountain…I thought Burma was full of soggy jungles," he replied, dawdling up the steep incline.

"This reminds me of that mission when we babysat those bureaucrats in Brazil," Chief suggested. "One day we were floating in the Amazon jungle and the next we were camped out in the mountains. Y'all remember that?"

"I remember," Mack huffed out the words. "I signed up for that op 'cuz of the beautiful scenery…but this ain't like that."

"You could have fooled me," Chief chuckled. "I thought you went for all Brazilian ladies."

"Them damsels was foxy…you can't deny that," Mack recalled, continuing a gradual ascent.

"That makes perfect sense, Boss," Johnny paused for a moment, his expression oddly serious. "I just now figured out why everyone calls him Mack…it's short for Mack Daddy." Johnny laughed almost hysterically, the sound echoing around them, but everyone else just smiled and shook their heads.

"Back in my hipster days, maybe…" Mack played along in good fun. He climbed a couple more steps and stopped to take another rest, bending over with his hands on his knees, still struggling to get a breath. "But hey…John-boy…I don't recall how…how you got your name," he finally huffed out the words.

"Maybe another time," Johnny called back.

Switch called up from a few feet behind them. "C'mon, Johnny, tell us a story while we finish our stair climber work out."

Bling chimed in as well. "Yo, I could go for a good story."

"It's not that interesting, guys, but I supposed I can share."

"That's the spirit," Switch replied.

"Well, after I graduated Ranger training, they shipped me off to Afghanistan. It was right after the terrorists took out the twin towers and I was furious for what those ragheads did to us," Johnny paused for second and continued. "When I got in-country, I begged the commander to let me operate the 50 caliber minigun on the Humvee."

Mack smiled widely. "Them are some amazin' weapons…I don't blame ya."

"It didn't do it for the gun. I wanted to operate it so I could mow those Taliban cowards down until they were unrecognizable—until the coroner had to put a John Doe tag on their big toe…that's how I got my call sign."

Everyone but Bling looked at him and nodded, giving him a silent affirmation that his actions were acceptable.

"I don't think I ever knew that, Johnny," Chief broke the silence as they continued climbing, reaching the 1,800-foot summit a short time later.

Standing at the top, they removed their binoculars and scanned the valley below, getting a partial view of a few dozen thatched huts at the base of the hill and a two-lane dirt road extending from the northeast, running along the backside of the huts and proceeding southwest.

"We need to get a vehicle…and hopefully a translator," Chief stated as they heard the sound of a motorcycle moving along the dirt road, approaching the village.

The team hiked down the hill, sliding their gear bags behind them on the blanket of pine needles that covered the ground, a light breeze blowing through the towering pines, keeping them from being completely miserable. Moments later, they arrived at the tree line and a several meter clearing that separated them from the village.

"Johnny and Bling," Chief called out, "Y'all go into the village and see if anyone will rent us a vehicle. We'll wait here."

"Copy," he replied as Bling followed, swatting away the swarm of gnats he had walked into.

Chief, Switch, and Mack stayed behind a row of trees, waiting for Johnny and Bling to return when a motorbike taxi driven by an elderly village man rolled up and stopped behind the huts.

"You've gotta be kiddin'," Mack muttered, laughing at Johnny and Bling who were scrunched up in the rear of the taxi.

Chief and Switch stepped out from behind the tree's shadows to meet them and Mack stayed concealed, carefully surveilling the area, looking for threats.

"Look, boss, this is the best we could do. There are no large vehicles here."

"There's no way this will hold everyone," Chief replied, rubbing his forehead.

"Okay, look, here's what we're gonna do. According to the map, there's a larger town about nine klicks away. I'll take Bling and we'll get a vehicle, and hopefully a translator," Chief addressed them, hopping into the back of the taxi.

"Johnny, you're in charge. Watch over our gear. We'll be back soon."

"Roger that, boss."

Johnny gave some instructions as the taxi zoomed off. "Alright guys, let's move Chief and Bling's gear bags behind the trees and keep our eyes open."

As they moved back to the trees, Switch caught a reflection of light coming near the backside of one of the huts.

"Johnny," Switch whispered to get his attention.

"What's up?"

Being careful to hide his hands, Switch motioned toward the hut and Johnny turned around, walking backward, pretending to talk with the rest of the team while he examined the area where Switch had pointed.

"Boss, come in, over."

"Go ahead, over."

"We've got one MAM on a cell phone. He's watching us pretty hard. I also saw him when we entered the village…acting strange then, too. What do you want us to do, over?"

"Do not engage. Stay hidden and move 200 meters to the southwest," Chief replied. "We'll turn around and head back."

"Roger that."

Johnny and Switch moved down the tree line while Mack climbed up the hill a few meters, finding a good spot behind some rocks to provide overwatch on the village and the dirt road.

"It's real quiet out here, boys. I ain't likin' this one bit," Mack spoke into his mic as he panned back and forth between the village and the road with his binoculars.

"Everyone needs to gear up," Johnny instructed. "And keep your eyes open."

For the next few minutes, Johnny, Switch, and Mack unpacked their vests from their bags, strapping on their gear and making sure their weapons were ready.

Moments later, Mack noticed movement and radioed in the report. "Guys, I've got what looks like a three-vehicle convoy approaching the village from the north. They're traveling at a good clip. Can't make out any details yet."

"Roger that, Mack, keep us updated, over," Johnny responded.

Chief listened intently on his radio, finally getting the driver to understand his hand motions to stop and turn the taxi around.

Mack radioed back in. "I've got a visual. They're definitely military…two drab green jeeps and a small, camoed-out Mazda pickup. The jeeps have vehicle-mounted machine guns and all of them have some type of Asian symbol on the doors…Unable to confirm number of personnel, over."

"Boss, you getting this, over?"

"Copy that. Maintain your posi...we're turn…around…head back…the vill…"

"Boss, you're breaking up, over?" Johnny stated, trying to hear through the static, but Chief didn't respond.

"Not reading you, boss. Do you copy, over?"

Silence.

"Boss?"

"I copy," Chief confirmed as the driver finally turned the taxi around and they returned to radio range.

"Them jeeps just drove up," Mack radioed. "I'm counting six soldiers total. One of them is definitely the commander, but the others look like…like kids."

"Tatmadaw…aka Burmese Military," Chief replied as the taxi driver dodged large potholes in the road. "They're known for forcing children into soldiering…world's largest child force."

"More human trafficking!" Mack mumbled into his mic. "This stuff is getting on my last nerve."

"What's the plan, boss?" Johnny asked, keeping his voice low.

"Rules of engagement. Don't shoot unless you have to. We're only a few mikes out."

"Roger that," Johnny let out a long sigh, not liking what he was seeing.

The soldiers filed out of their vehicles and searched the wooded area immediately across from the hut where the villager had called in the coordinates, but after not seeing any sign of the team, they turned back.

As they returned, the commander, a man in his early 40s and wearing green fatigues, stood in the back of the jeep behind a machine gun, talking on a satellite phone. When he saw his troops returning with their guns slung around their shoulders and walking casually, he shouted something in Burmese and pointed them back into the woods.

The boys removed the rifles from their shoulders and held them at the ready position, grudgingly marching back into the woods.

"Boss, they're returning. They'll be on to us at any moment."

"Guys, I got an idea, over," Mack radioed in.

"Let's hear it," Chief replied.

"Them boys ain't seasoned military. They gonna fill they drawers if we neutralize their commander, over."

"Do it, but keep it quiet."

"Roger!" he replied, moving out from behind the rocks and studying the best location to get a drop on the commander.

"I'm at the clearing...got the commander in my sight. He's still on the phone, facing away. I'm crossing the road now. I'll come up from behind them huts for the drop, over."

"Copy that," Chief replied. "Johnny, we're one klick out. We'll stop at the outskirts of the village. Let us know when it's clear to move in, over."

"Roger that, boss."

The boy-soldiers canvassed closer to Johnny and Switch as Mack crossed the road and came up behind the commander. With as much speed and stealth he could employ, Mack snuck up at the rear of jeep, stepping up on the tire and wrapping his arm around the commander's throat, dragging him backward off the jeep and choking him until he felt his body go limp.

"Target's dreamin', over," Mack indicated.

Mack reached down to remove the commander's sidearm when he caught a shadow in his peripheral vision. He jerked his head around, but didn't see anyone.

Click. Mack recognized the peculiar sound of a gun's hammer being pulled back. Someone had gotten the drop on him. He closed his eyes, mumbled some incoherent words, and slowly raised his hands.

"Don move!" the middle-aged village man angrily insisted as he stood behind Mack. Mack looked at him from his peripheral vision and saw his hand shaking profusely.

"Boss, big problem here, over," Johnny radioed in, keeping his voice low.

"What's going on?"

"That villager we saw earlier got the drop on Mack and he has a pistol trained on him."

185

TWENTY-ONE
WAR TRAIN

One Day Earlier

The sun peeked over the horizon, chasing away the dark black and blue shadows, signaling an ensemble of melodic birds and insects. The crake birds initiated their tune first, followed by the lapwings and crickets until the entire jungle awakened from its nightly coma.

As the sun continued to rise, the sky blushed with shades of magenta and tangerine until its golden rays caressed the tall grass. Sam peeked through her partially opened eyelids, hearing the wild jungle behind her and what sounded like male voices coming from the river. She swiftly crawled through the grass, staying behind some long reeds at the edge of the riverbank, checking the river. When she looked down, she saw two male villagers in a long canoe attending to their fishing nets, preparing for a new day.

She looked back to get Mike's attention, but he was gone—only Nyan was there, still sleeping. She nervously scanned the area, but there was no sign of him. She backed away from the riverbank to the matted grassy area where she had been sleeping and seconds later a dark silhouette, backlit by the morning sun, approached from several yards away. She contemplated waking Nyan, but there wasn't enough time.

"Morning, Sam!" Mike called out with a renewed vigor, erasing her nervous suspicion.

"Mike! Why did you leave me again?" she snapped angrily.

"Hey, calm down. You were never out of my sight. I took a quick stroll to see if I could find a way across the river."

"Yeah, well, why you were out strolling, some villagers floated by on the river. They could have helped us."

"Nope. I already tried. They just stared at me when I motioned them over to me."

"Well, maybe that's why I should have done it. Of course, they're not going to come over to some foreign guy holding a rifle. Probably thought you were a serial killer or something. You should have got me up; I could have helped," she chided, still slightly annoyed.

"C'mon, Sam. Give me a break. You were still sleeping and I didn't want to disturb you."

"I'm not really mad. I was just…just scared is all."

"Hey, I get it. I do. I didn't mean to scare you. I wanted to get a jump on the day while you finished resting."

"So, what's the plan?" she asked as Nyan woke up. "I could really go for a bowl of cereal or some syrupy pancakes right about now. Any chance you found a free cafe on your little stroll…or maybe some clean water? I'm just so thirsty."

"Nope, but we'll have all of that soon," he replied, sounding optimistic. Sam brightened up as he continued filling her in. "I found a part of the river that's narrower and looks fairly shallow. I think we can cross it easily and be at the depot in no time."

"Wait, so you expect me to swim across?" she recoiled at the thought.

"We're gonna wade across, Sam…and I checked for crocs; there's nothing down there."

Her body language silently disapproved, but it was their best option.

Mike helped her up and Nyan followed them as they walked through the tall grass to the river, reaching it moments later.

"Are you ready?" Mike asked her. She stood silent, her face a little pale as she skimmed the lily pads that looked like green dessert plates floating at the river's edge, praying no creatures were hiding under them.

Anxious to get across, Mike grabbed her hand and they stepped into the muddy water. They waded in and at first the water only reached their knees, but it quickly rose to their waists and continued until only their head was above water.

"You said the water wasn't deep," Sam snapped, trying to keep the filthy water from rushing into her mouth.

"It didn't look this deep!" He took another step and suddenly lost his footing, plunging under the water. Sam spun around in the water, searching frantically for him. Seconds later, he popped back up, gasping for air.

"Careful, Sam...big drop-off!" he shouted, treading water to keep from sinking. He felt around with his feet for the river bottom but he wasn't able to find it.

"Sam, come on. You'll have to swim. We're only a few feet away from the other side," he yelled back, eventually reaching the sandy shore.

Sam cautiously slid her foot along the bottom of the riverbed, bracing herself for the drop-off. She did well until she thought about crocodiles and hurried a little too fast, becoming inundated by the river.

"Come on, Sam, swim!" Mike yelled, crawling up on the sand. She eventually resurfaced, but when she did she was flapping her arms like she was drowning. She could swim well, but the combination of fatigue and panic was dragging her under.

Nyan watched as she struggled, wanting to help, but he wasn't a good swimmer. He remembered what had happened at the river with the general and gulped hard, not wanting to revisit the thoughts.

"Throw me the gun!" Mike shouted across the river to Nyan, pointing to the rifle and motioning with his hands. Nyan chucked the rifle across and it landed in the sand.

"Grab the gun, Sam," he shouted, holding the rifle barrel and extending the buttstock out into the river. She kicked with all her might but she was still sinking, the water covering over her eyes. Completely depleted, she gave up and slipped under the water, the blue sky suddenly becoming a murky blur as she continued to sink. Her body jerked violently as she descended into a watery grave.

Mike saw her slip under and rushed back into the river. She knew she would be dead within seconds, so she used her remaining time to pray. Suddenly, a shadow partially blocked out the light above. It was the rifle's buttstock. With a quick burst, she reached her hand up and clutched it. Mike felt the weight on the end and pulled her in.

He helped her up the sandy shore and she struggled for a breath, gasping and coughing up the brown, gritty water, the taste earthy and organic. Mike stood over her, patting her on her back, making sure she was okay.

Moments later, he motioned to Nyan to enter the river, but he just stared at the swirling water, his body arrested by fear.

"Come on, Nyan!" Mike motioned, holding the rifle out into the water. Nyan reluctantly waded in, inching forward until he reached the drop-off. He ran his foot along the river floor, going as far as he could walk. Then, mustering up all his courage, he bent his legs at his knees and leaped into the turbid water, landing about a foot from the outstretched rifle. He grabbed ahold and Mike pulled him in. Then they climbed to the top of the embankment, all of them collapsing at the top in exhaustion.

"Are you alright?" Mike asked Sam.

"Give me a minute," she replied, still breathing deeply.

They rested until Sam was breathing normal again and then they helped her to her feet, taking off in the direction of the depot.

"Do you have a plan for getting on the train?" Sam asked as she walked on her own, her knee feeling quite better than the day before.

"I'm thinking we can wait in the trees and when it rolls up we can sneak into a boxcar or something."

"I really hope you're right about that, but don't you think we need to ditch the gun?"

He silently looked it over, not really wanting to leave it behind, but Sam was right. They needed to blend in. Seconds later, he chucked the gun into the river, watching it sink under the water.

"I didn't think you'd give it up that easy."

"It was caked full of mud. I doubt it would have worked anyway."

Moments later, they made it to the depot, which was nothing more than a thatched roof covering a few benches bolted down to a concrete slab; it looked more like a beach tiki hut than it did a public transportation building. The only indicator that it was a depot was a small chalkboard with train times written on it, hanging on one of the four corner posts.

Mike stepped across the tracks and entered the depot, checking the chalkboard, but was unable to understand the Burmese writing; it didn't really matter; they were intent on catching the first train that came along.

Sam made her way around the back and saw a blue plastic barrel and a pipe hanging over it with a brass spigot and knob. Her eyes expanded as she considered the possibility of fresh water. With a burst of optimism, she turned the knob and heard some gurgling noises, but no water came out. She opened up the valve as far as she could and within seconds water gushed out into the barrel.

She stared at the free-flowing water as the sun glistened off it, almost mesmerized by it. Her severely chapped lips and parched mouth quivered as her brain sent expectant signals that her personal drought was about to be cured.

"Look!" Sam shouted, calling his attention to the yellowish-brown water that poured into the barrel below. She let it run for several seconds and eventually the rotten egg smell dissipated and the water ran clear. Mike stood next to her as they gazed at the barrel, recalling how they had gotten sick on the water at the well, but they didn't care anymore. They cupped their hands under the water and drunk deeply. Nyan saw their excitement and walked over, dunking his head into the barrel to cool off and drinking some of the water as it poured from the spigot. They drank as much as they could handle and moved to the nearby benches to rest.

Mike sat on one of the benches, staring up at the pipe that coursed along the roofline, thankful that someone had installed a water line. Sam sat opposite him, removing her waterlogged hair tie. With her nappy hair spread over her shoulders she got up and went back to the barrel, hanging her head over it. She nearly dipped her head in, but before she did she caught her distorted reflection and it gave her pause.

Drip! A drop fell from the pipe, sending a shockwave through the tranquil water, erasing her reflection.

"Mike, do you...do you think this is the end?" she asked, turning to him.

He opened one of his eyes and closed it again to show that he had heard her but wasn't ready to have that conversation. Sam sat down and smiled, thanking God for the blessing of life and hoping it truly was the end of their drama.

They rested for several minutes, the calm early morning breeze and shade a welcome relief from the muggy jungle they had left the day before. They nearly dozed off again when Mike heard the faint sound of a train whistle.

"Sam, do you hear—"

"I hear it!"

Mike motioned for Nyan and they walked to the edge of the trees a few yards away, waiting patiently for the train to arrive. As the whistle grew louder, three villagers appeared out of nowhere, balancing atop one of the track's metal rails and stopping under the depot's roof, waiting for the train.

"Once the train stops, we need to look for a place to get on," Mike stated with a touch of eagerness in his voice. "The rear of the train should be the closest to us."

They took off through the trees and progressed to the tracks, hiding behind some overgrowth for cover. Mike stepped out of the trees briefly and saw the front end of a yellow-colored locomotive as it roared down the tracks toward them.

"Okay, this is it!" Mike shouted over the loud rumble. Moments later, the train's braking system initiated and it screeched stridently, bringing it to a gradual stop and producing a strong, burnt metallic smell.

They were about to make their move when Nyan grabbed Mike's arm, pulling him back into the trees. Stunned, Mike spun around and stared at him, wondering what was wrong this time. Nyan pointed at the railcars and Mike's eyes grew wide in disbelief.

The locomotive looked like any other he had seen before, but the dozen or so railcars it was pulling were painted a military-green and its windows were covered in flat armored slats. Near the middle of the train was a flatbed car with an anti-aircraft cannon and two cars at the end carried armored personnel vehicles. If all that wasn't enough to give them pause, each of the railcars also bore the same Asian symbol that Mike had come to despise.

"That train is military," Sam stated as they stepped back behind the cover of some palm shrubs to not be seen, but it was too late. Several soldiers had caught a glimpse of them as the train rolled by and before the train could stop, an entire squad had disembarked from one of the railcars, their pistols drawn and sprinting directly at them.

"Raut! Raut!" The troops shouted as they spread out to surround them.

"Sam, go, I'll stay behind and do what I can to fight them off," he spoke fast, but before she could move one of the soldiers fired his pistol into the air and she froze in place.

TWENTY-TWO
HOSTAGE

One Day Later

Mack's in a tight spot. We gotta be smart about this," Chief asserted, speaking into his mic as the taxi dropped them off at the edge of the village. "Johnny, you and Switch move across and take cover behind the huts when you can. We'll converge on them from both sides, over."

"That's a good copy, boss...we're moving across now."

"Yo, we ain't bustin' caps in them kids is we?" Bling asked Chief as they reached one of the huts, crouching behind it.

"If they wanna hold a gun like a man, they should be prepared to face another man with a gun," Chief replied, peering around the corner of the hut to get a look at the villager holding the gun on Mack.

"What you gonna do with that old pistol?" Mack growled at the villager, advancing toward him. The villager nervously gripped the gun, which caused him to accidentally disengage the gun's magazine. As it dropped to the ground, Mack reached out and grabbed the gun by the slide, ripping it from the villager's hand while stepping behind him, causing him to stumble to the ground.

"Hmmm...not bad for an old man, eh," Mack sneered as he hovered over the surprised villager, holding the gun on him.

"Guys, Mack got the drop on the villager, but we gotta provide a distraction or the troops will have him surrounded," Chief instructed, motioning for Bling to step out from the huts into the clearing.

"Roger that, boss. Lead the way."

"Heyyyy! Heyyyyyyy! Over Here!" Chief and Bling both yelled, waving their hands to get the boys' attention while Switch and Johnny aimed their rifles at them from the cover of the trees. The troops turned to see the commotion and fanned out in an attack formation.

"What now?" Bling asked as he and Chief stood in the grassy clearing with no cover.

"Not sure."

"Well, ain't dat great."

The boys moved in swiftly, their rifles held ready. Chief raised his hands in surrender and Bling followed his lead. Within seconds, they were surrounded.

"Play it easy, Bling."

"Ain't nothing else to do," he replied, noting the extreme aggression on the boys' faces and the Asian symbol painted on all of their green, Vietnam-era helmets.

Mack brushed off the gun and inspected it. "World War 2 Nambu pistol. Last time I seen one of these here was in a museum," he smiled, pulling back the slide to eject the bullet on his newly acquired toy, but he had forgotten about the commander who had regained his energy.

"Whack!" The commander sucker-punched Mack from behind and he fell face down into the dirt. He groaned in intense pain as the commander zip-tied his hands together. With the help of the villager, they placed Mack into the front seat of the jeep. Then the commander punched him again, knocking him out cold.

"Boss! The commander has Mack in his jeep. Permission to engage."

"We need to deal with these boys first," Chief replied into his mic as he and Bling dropped to their knees.

"Bling, lay down flat," Chief whispered as he carefully pressed the radio button again. "Do it now, Johnny!"

Phttt, phttt, phttt! Johnny and Switch fired their MP5s from their crouched positions behind the trees, shooting the boy-soldiers in their legs, cutting them down to the ground.

Blood poured from their wounds as they screamed in agony and Johnny and Switch hurried out of the woods, helping Chief and Bling disarm them.

After watching his troops go down, the commander jumped into the jeep's driver seat and backed away as fast as the jeep would drive.

"Chief, he's leaving!" Johnny shouted, raising his gun to shoot.

"Aim low!" Chief ordered.

Johnny selected his MP5 to fully automatic and pressed the trigger, sending a stream of bullets at the jeep, emptying his magazine within a couple seconds. He popped several holes in the jeep's radiator and blew the front tires, causing it to swerve erratically.

"Bling, keep an eye on these boys," Chief ordered, "Johnny and Switch...y'all are with me!" he finished as they spread out to engage the commander.

With the jeep riding on its rims, it slowed considerably, but before they could reach it, the commander backed into the middle of the last few huts, disappearing out of sight.

"What's he doing, boss?" Johnny asked as they moved in.

"Not sure," Chief panted, "But there's an M-60 in the back of that jeep. Stay alert."

"Roger that."

The team reached the hut where they had last seen the commander and Chief motioned to Johnny and Switch to move around the back to get the drop on him. They started around the hut when they heard the distinct sound of loud diesel engines coming from near the hillside road. Johnny checked it out, but couldn't see anything.

"Take cover until we can see what's heading our way," Chief instructed them. They backed in between the huts, watching the road as three black and gray-camouflaged armored personnel carriers appeared, traveling at a fast clip, producing a trail of dust behind them.

"This isn't good…those are APCs," Johnny called out as the vehicles continued in their direction. Each armor-plated carrier had a beveled front end, six wheels, and a 360-degree gun turret with a 25mm canon—basically a tank on wheels.

"What's the plan, boss?"

"Y'all cover me!" Chief yelled as he ran to the other jeep a few meters away. He climbed in the back and swiveled the machine gun around, aiming it in the direction of the APCs. Johnny and Switch hurried near the jeep, kneeling down next to it and making sure their weapons were set to fully automatic—ready to provide Chief with cover fire.

Standing in the rear of the jeep, Chief pulled back on the machine gun's charging handle, but it wouldn't engage. He looked it over and saw that the clip had been inserted incorrectly. He removed it, but before he could reinsert it, the APCs stopped and opened their rear doors. Johnny and Switch watched attentively as several troops rushed out, fanning out as though to attack.

"RPGGGGGGG!" Johnny shouted.

Chief spied a group of six older soldiers standing at the rear of the APC, one of them aiming a Russian-made RPG rocket launcher at them.

Swoosh! A burst of fire and a plume of smoke erupted from the rear of the launcher. The rocket blazed inches from the jeep, careening into the hut near where Bling had been watching over the boys, blowing the hut to smithereens. When it blew, a three-inch piece of grenade shrapnel struck Bling's forearm and blood poured out, running down to his hand.

Phtt, phtt, phtt. Johnny and Switch fired their MP5s, striking three of the soldiers, prompting the others to retreat behind the APCs.

Johnny and Chief turned to each other, but neither said a word; they didn't want to do it, but they were in a tough spot and their only option was to pull back. With one last effort, Chief racked the machine gun again—and this time the bullets loaded into the chamber.

Bratatatatatatatatatat! Chief squeezed the trigger and the bullets flew out at the APC.

Sing…ping…pang! Chief squeezed the trigger for several seconds, emptying the 100-round ammo can, but all it did was dimple the vehicle's armor.

Seconds later, the APC's autocannons rotated toward the jeep.

"Take cover!" Chief shouted as he jumped to the ground and knelt down behind an adjacent hut.

Boom! Boom! Boom! The cannon's armored-piercing rounds zipped through the air, slicing through the jeep and the wooden huts, tearing everything in its way to shreds.

Once the firing ceased, Chief dashed through a haze of smoke and jumped into the nearby pickup truck, the keys still in the ignition. He pressed the clutch pedal and turned it on, putting it into gear and slamming the gas as the autocannon rotated in his direction.

Boom! Boom! Boom! Boom! The autocannon fired several times and a few rounds penetrated the back of the pickup's bed as Chief drove between the boys who were still lying on the ground. Bling waited for him, sitting against a pile of debris, cringing in pain.

"Johnny and Switch, fall back to our position, over!" Chief radioed as he called out for Bling to get into the truck's cab. Johnny and Switch rounded the corner, aiming their weapons behind them as they climbed into the pickup's bed.

Once they were inside, Chief burned off down the road and got about 200 meters away when the engine sputtered like it was running out of gas. Eventually, it stalled, leaving them exposed on the open road.

"Piece of——" Chief cursed, visibly irritated. He waited a moment and turned the key again.

Johnny watched for threats and caught a glimpse of the nose of one of the transport carriers coming around the edge of the hut.

"Boss, we gotta go…now!" Johnny yelled.

"I'm trying!" Chief yelled back, engaging the gears for the fourth time.

Vra…vra…vroom! A plum of white smoke filled the air and the pickup jerked forward, causing Johnny and Switch to slide into the back of the bed.

Chief gradually stepped on the gas and the engine smoothed out, moving them down the road as the transport carrier's autocannon engaged them again.

Boom! Boom! Boom! The bullets whizzed over Johnny and Switch's heads as Chief drove in a zigzag pattern, hoping to stay out of its line of fire.

Phtt, phtt, phtt! Johnny and Switch fired back, but the 9mm rounds did nothing to the armored vehicle.

"Save your ammo!" Chief yelled back. They ceased firing and got down as low as they could as the autocannon continued firing at them. One of the bullets hit the upper corner of the pickup's back glass, shattering it, missing Bling's head by about an inch. It finally stopped firing when Chief drove around a bend in the road, moving out of its sight.

"Everyone all right?" Chief yelled back.

"We're good!" Johnny yelled as he and Switch laid flat in the pickup's bed.

"I'm ai'ght," Bling responded, staring at the shrapnel in his arm and thankful to be alive.

Chief drove about a kilometer from the village and pulled to the side of the road, checking to be sure the APCs weren't pursuing them. Then he backed into a wide spot in the trees to get some cover while Johnny and Switch jumped out and knelt down near some trees, their MP5s aimed at the road.

"Yo, Chief," Bling cringed through the pain. "What we gonna do about Mack? We aren't leavin—"

Chief cut him off. "Of course we're not leaving him! Mack's mission priority now," he stated as he shifted the truck into park, leaving the engine idling in case they needed a rapid escape. He jumped out and moved around the truck, opening Bling's door and called for Johnny and Switch to fall back to the truck.

"Look, y'all know Mack is priority, and the good news is that there's little chance those APCs will pursue us. Their top speed fully loaded is about half of what we can do. The bad news is that it looks like they're Chinese 551s and they hold about 12 troops each—so we could be dealin' with 30 plus soldiers when we go back."

They looked at each other without saying a word, but they couldn't hide their facial expressions. They were in one of the toughest spots they had even been in as a team and all they could think about was rescuing Mack.

"Johnny, I need you to bandage Bling up. Switch, I need a visual on that convoy. I don't want to roll in there not knowing what we're up against."

"Chief, the drone is in my gear bag back in those woods."

"I was hoping you still have your tech buddy who could get us a satellite image."

"I can try," he replied, pulling out the sat phone from his vest.

As Switch dialed, Bling removed his tactical medical kit from his pocket, handing it to Johnny.

"Congrats, Bling," Johnny smiled, "I see you met Mr. Henry."

"I ain't know no Henrys," Bling replied somewhat sharply, making sure Johnny understood he was in no mood for humor. Johnny looked at him and snapped the pliers in his face. Bling flinched and when he did, Johnny yanked the metal shrapnel from his forearm.

"Ahhh! Yo, you knows what you doin?"

"Calm down! Would you rather I get you a pediatrician?" Johnny laughed.

Bling narrowed his eyes at him.

"Look, in all seriousness, I've been in your same spot before. I met Mr. Henry—aka Henry Shrapnel—in Afghanistan when a grenade exploded under our Humvee and a chunk of metal wedged into my leg."

"Is Henry Shrapnel da guy who first got hit by a grenade or sumptin?"

"No, he invented the concept of frag grenades. A couple hundred years ago, Henry took a cannonball and hollowed it out, filling it with lead pellets—super nasty invention. The RPG shrapnel is a variant of his design."

"Well, then, I'm not really fond of Mr. Henry right now," Bling responded.

"Yeah, I've heard a lot of soldiers curse the day he was born. It didn't help that he was also from our neighbors across the salty pond," Johnny indicated as he placed a blood clotting wrap over Bling's wound. "Tea and crumpets and explosive ordinances. I've got mixed feelings about his invention, but I've also taken out a bunch of bad guys with it."

Switch paced back and forth in the woods, holding up the phone. "Chief, there's no signal up here. I need to get away from these woods with a direct line of sight."

"Go for it. We got ya covered."

Switch stepped out into the clearing near the road, holding the sat phone and staring at the screen, waiting for a signal.

"No signal yet…wait, hang on. I've got something. Okay, I'm connected!" he exclaimed with a hint of optimism. Moments later the call was answered and he was able to relay his request to his contact. Switch listened as he got the update.

"Chief, my guy has an image, but it's four hours old," Switch reported as he moved back into the wooded area. "The satellite won't be in position with an updated image for another hour."

"We ain't got no hour! Alright team, everyone back in the pickup."

Chief placed both of his hands behind his head, interlocking his fingers and contemplating their next move. He wasn't keen on rushing back into a firefight, but the grim reality that they may never see Mack again was unacceptable—and there was only a small window of opportunity to get him back.

"We don't have any options, here. We have to go back now. Lock and load, boys."

"We're ready, boss," Johnny replied. Bling closed his eyes and uttered a silent prayer and Switch racked his MP5, indicating his agreement.

Chief pulled back onto the road and drove to the edge of the village, stopping to let Johnny and Switch out. Their goal was to move to the tree line and flank the soldiers. Once they were in position, Chief drove behind the first hut and turned off the engine. With the engine off, he noticed an eerie silence. There was no movement in the village and no sounds of diesel engines or troop chatter.

"It's quiet down here," Chief spoke into his mic. "Y'all give an update as soon as you see something, over."

"Copy, boss," Johnny replied, watching the village from behind the first row of trees.

"Roger that," Switch replied, his gun pressed against his shoulder, scanning the area as he hiked up a path, reaching a clearing several meters up the hill and hiding behind some rocks for a good view of the village.

"Boss, I'm not seeing any movement...and the boys we shot are gone."

Switch reported in next. "I can see the backside of all the huts. Nothing here either. No sign of APCs or the commander."

"Keep your eyes open until we clear the area."

"Copy, boss."

"Roger that."

Chief pulled out onto the road and drove to the front of the village, watching for potential traps. He got to the edge of the village on the north side, but there were no soldiers, no convoy, and not even any villagers. Worst of all, there was no sign of Mack.

"Alright guys, the place is empty—and it's creeping me out. I don't know where everyone went so quickly but let's get to the woods and get our gear. We need to find out where they've taken Mack. "

Chief pulled the pickup around to the back of the village and met up with Johnny and Switch, helping them load up the gear.

"Chief, my contact is calling," Switch relayed, answering the sat phone.

"What do you have for me?" Switch asked, listening intently. "Are you sure about that?" He rubbed his forehead, running his hand down his face and letting out a long sigh, pacing back and forth as Chief studied his gloomy facial expressions, bracing for the bad news.

"Chief, it's not good. My guy says the convoy is about 20 klicks north and they've met up with a helo. He can't be certain, but there's a good chance they put Mack on the chopper. The last image he has is the helo taking off and flying in a southeasterly direction. I've got the coordinates and he'll keep us updated."

Chief backed against the side of the pickup and took a deep breath.

"What are you thinking, boss?" Johnny asked somberly.

No one could be sure of Mack's fate, but Chief didn't hesitate. "We're gonna drive southeast until we hear back on the helo's coordinates."

"Roger that."

Anyone could see that Chief was deeply troubled by the day's events, but he also wanted to remain strong for everyone else. He had heard stories of the brutality of the Burmese Military and he could only hope that somehow Mack would still be alive by the time they reached him.

As the darkness fully descended upon the village, Chief drove the pickup down the dirt road and Switch navigated for him, making sure they were traveling in a southeasterly direction. He drove for a few hours, stopping to fuel up, and then switched places with Johnny, taking a break to get some rest and waiting for an update from Switch's contact.

TWENTY-THREE
YOUR RESCUER

Hours Earlier

Mike looked at Nyan and had an idea. He raised his hands raised in surrender and nudged the rifle at him with his foot, motioning with his head and eyes for him to pick it up. There was no reason for Nyan to be doomed along with them, he thought—and maybe he could find a way to free them later.

"Sam, turn around and act like we're Nyan's prisoners."

"Do what?"

"Just raise your hands. There's no way we can outrun them."

Nyan hesitated for a moment, hanging his head as though he was ashamed of what he had to do, but eventually picked up the rifle and pointed it at them. As soon as he did, the troops rounded the trees and Nyan quickly rammed the rifles' buttstock into the back of Mike's knees, dropping him to the ground.

"Ahhhh!" Mike groaned and Sam fell to her knees beside him as Nyan angrily yelled at them in Burmese, saliva dripping from his mouth, playing the part a little too perfectly. He grabbed Mike by his ear, standing him up and poked him in his back with the rifle's barrel, prodding him to move to the train.

Escorted by Nyan and several other boy-soldiers, they grudgingly moved along the drab gravel to the rear of the train. With every step, Sam scrutinized the menacing military locomotive. Then she heard a raspy and hideous voice—one she had heard before; it was the general.

The general sauntered toward them with a crooked smile, his shoulders back and gait smooth. Every few seconds he pulled his stogie from his mouth and puffed out a plume of white cigar smoke into the steamy, late morning air.

"I am General Htun. Do not forget name," he snarled in broken English. "You run long time, but you mine now." He stepped up, his body nearly touching Sam's as he attempted to gently caress her cheeks with the back of his hand. She jerked her face away, her eyes watering up, thinking of his intentions.

General Htun grasped Sam's chin, squeezing tight as he turned her head to look her in her eyes. His hands were rough like sandpaper and the combination of his rank body odor and halitosis was nauseating. As his grip tightened, the pain jolted through her jaw to the back of her neck like a surge of electricity. She pulled back with all her might, her tears helping her slip from his grip.

"You fight girl…I like," he growled, his face contorting as though an evil spirit was controlling him. "But you break soon."

In a fit of rage, Mike balled his fists and gritted his teeth, prepared to fight back, but before he could one of the soldiers discerned his intentions and rammed the rifle into the middle of his back, dropping him to the ground, his body curling up in a fetal position.

Mike moaned in agonizing pain as General Htun drew long on his cigar, sucking in as much smoke as he could and knelt down, blowing it into his face. "Ah, yes, you cause much trouble for me, boy. I should kill now," he suggested. He stood up and turned as though to walk away, but before he did, he slammed his boot down on Mike's wounded hand, twisting his foot back and forth on his open gash. "I have special plan for you. I feed you to dragon."

Mike remained on his hands and knees, saliva dripping from his mouth as the penetrating anxiety surged through him, supposing the general intended to feed him to the crocodiles. As he contemplated his brutal words, he collapsed to the ground, thinking of a way to take himself out before he would allow that to happen.

General Htun called for Nyan and he promptly stood straight at attention, his chin up, chest out, and shoulders back. Then he motioned for him to approach and Nyan clicked the back of his military boots together, marching forward and being careful not to look him in the eyes. General Htun looked him over, patting him on his head as though to say he was a good little boy and then Nyan clicked his boots together once more, bowed and performed an about-face, walking away from the general, refusing to acknowledge Mike and Sam.

The soldiers bound Mike and Sam's hands and led them to one of the metal boxcars. They slid open the door and a malodorous mixture of body odor, urine, and feces rushed into their faces, causing them to turn away and gag. Two of the soldiers lifted Mike into the car, sliding him forward, sharp splinters from the wooden plank flooring jabbing into his cheek and arms.

Sam was next, but before they loaded her into the car one of the soldiers, a lieutenant in his late 20s, stepped in front of them, stopping them. He strolled over to Sam, smiling seductively and tracing her body with his eyes. Her entire body shook when he reached out to touch her blonde hair, lifting it up and fanning it out.

"Don't touch her!" Mike shouted furiously, his voice echoing through the boxcar. He wiggled around, struggling to get to the edge of the car, but it was useless.

The lieutenant grinned at Mike as he continued stroking Sam's hair, brushing his hands along her shoulders and down her arms. Sam's eyes were welded shut, trying to think about home, but when he whispered into her ear she couldn't take it any longer. She lifted her boot and raked it down his shin. Stunned, he stepped back and narrowed his eyes, backhanding her across her face.

"Arghreech!" She let out a high-pitched shriek as blood dripped from her nose onto her shirt.

"Sam? Sam, are you okay?" Mike's voice sounded muffled from the rear of the car. "You better keep your hands off of her you sick son of a—"

Chooooooo! The train's whistle blew, interrupting Mike's angry outburst and the lieutenant's perverted intentions. With the train about to depart, he commanded the soldiers to load Sam into the car, tying her and Mike up at opposite ends, about 50 feet apart.

Slam! The door closed, purging the light and ending the slight breeze that had been swirling through the car.

"Sam?" Mike called out, his voice cutting through the thick darkness and ricocheting off the metal walls.

"Yeah, I'm here, Mike. I'm okay."

"Oh, thank God."

"What's going to happen to us, Mike? What did he mean by feeding you to a dragon?"

"I...I don't...I don't know," he stuttered, finally getting the words out, not wanting to think about it.

"Sam?"

"Yeah, Mike."

"I...I don't want to say this, but I need to be honest. I...um...I can feel my mind...giving....giving up."

"I know. I can feel it, too," she spoke softly. "I don't know what to do. We need to keep talking though."

"It's like when you're about to pass out, you get tunnel vision...that's what it feels like in my mind...like a curtain is closing and the light is fading."

"I don't know what to say, Mike," she replied, barely holding it together.

They did their best to console each other but it wasn't long before the train's steel wheels rotated on the metal tracks and all they could hear was a constant, thunderous rumble.

Unable to see or even speak to each other, Mike slid down onto the floor, his hands tied to a metal rail above him. Sam did the same. Seeing nothing but darkness, she cried and screamed as loud as she could, but he couldn't hear her over the noisy rumble. She cried for a while, her tears eventually running dry. With nothing but darkness and despair, her body shut down and she faded into a light sleep. Mike followed soon after.

The train bowled down the tracks for several hours, crossing a variety of terrain and then gradually slowed down. The train's brakes were applied and Sam was awakened by the ear-splitting screeching sound.

"Mike?" she called out.

Mike opened his eyes, but it was so dark it didn't matter. "I'm still here," he replied.

"What do you think is going on?"

"I don't know. I'm trying not to think about it."

As they talked, they heard several faint gunshots and women screaming. For a few seconds the sounds became louder, but then they faded off until all that was left was an unnerving stillness.

"Mike, that general is crazy. We've gotta find a way to escap—

Sliiiiiiiiiiiiide...Slam! The doors on both sides of the railcars slid open and an array of flashlights lit up the interior of the car. It was the first time Mike had laid eyes on Sam in more than half a day. Her nose was black and blue and dried blood covered her cheeks and neck, except where her tears had paved trails through it. Fury seized his emotions as he fantasized killing the soldiers and escaping with her, but they were only thoughts; he had no viable plan.

They sat in the dark car, straining their eyes to see out of the doors, but the moon only provided a sliver of light. All they could see were a couple soldiers standing guard, their rifles slung over their soldiers, waiting on something. Moments later, they heard high-pitched screams and crying; it became louder until more soldiers appeared, escorting over a dozen girls and several boys into the railcar—all of them juveniles—and all of them crying and whimpering.

Off to the side, Mike saw the orange-red glow of General Htun's cigar. He was watching, making sure the soldiers did his bidding. As he directed his soldiers to load the children, one of the boys fought back and broke free, but before he could get more than a few yards away, the general pulled his sidearm from his holster and aimed into the darkness.

Boom! General Htun shot the boy in his back. The boy stumbled a few feet more, but soon collapsed to the ground. The cold-hearted general casually spun around, taking an extra-long drag on his cigar, the glowing embers highlighting the hard lines on his wrinkled and scarred up face. Then the boxcar's doors slammed closed and the children's cries intensified.

"Mike?" Sam called out over the cries and whimpering. "These men are sick in the head. I think they took these kids from their village."

"That's why we have to stay strong. We have to escape and tell someone what's happening here."

As they spoke, the train's whistle blew and the boxcar jerked forward, moving them down the tracks until the rumbling became so loud it drowned out the crying and made talking impossible once again.

The train barreled down the tracks for a few more hours, crossing through thick forests and over rice patties until it eventually stopped again.

Mike, Sam, and the children sat in the darkness, unable to see anything, but they heard the soldier's hard footsteps as they approached, the gravel crunching under their boots. Their bodies tensed up, unsure of what was coming next.

Sliiiiide! The railcar's door slid open again and two bright spotlights lit up the interior, prompting everyone inside to shield their eyes. A military transport truck backed to the door and Mike could see the general's silhouette as he stood at the edge of the tailgate, barking out orders to his troops.

Two soldiers in the back of the truck dragged an older man and slid him into the car, his body heaped over as though he were already dead. One of the soldiers prodded him with a gun in his rib cage and the old man let out a yelp. Then the soldiers hogtied his hands and feet together and stepped back onto the truck, placing a spotlight on him. His eyes were swollen shut, face and arms badly bruised, and his white beard was matted together by dried blood.

"This you rescuer!" General Htun addressed Mike and Sam, his voice booming through the boxcar. "We feed him to dragon first, then you." He let out a cruel laugh and the door slid closed, the darkness once again enveloping them.

"Hello? Sir? Is it true? Did you come to rescue us?" Sam spoke quickly, hoping she could get some information before the train pulled away, but he remained silent, the only noises coming from the soldiers' muffled movement and the whimpering children huddled in the middle of the car.

"Sir? Thank you." Sam spoke again, trying her hardest to initiate a conversation with him.

"Fer...wat?" the old man struggled to reply, his voice hoarse and nearly unintelligible.

"For trying to rescue us."

The old man groaned and let out a deep sigh.

"My name is Sam. My boyfriend's here also. His name is—"

"Mike," The old man barely got it out as he finished her sentence. Sam's eyes expanded, a rush of emotion flooding her mind.

"Mike, he really did come to rescue us," she shouted across the railcar.

"It doesn't really matter, now does it?" Mike replied cynically, his hope all but lost.

"But maybe they'll send others!" She exclaimed. "Sir, what's your name?"

Sam's voice bounced throughout the metal car and seconds later the train's whistle sounded.

"They call me...Mack...and they're already—"

Before Mack could finish, the train's wheels turned on the tracks and the loud rumble thundered into the car, shutting down their conversation.

Sam turned her ears in Mack's direction and shouted as loud as possible.

"What? They're already what?"

"Hello? Can you hear me?" Sam continued shouting, but the train's rumble was too deafening to communicate.

Frustrated, Sam slumped down against the wall. She wanted needed to know more information, but just him being there with them gave her a flicker of hope. They were no longer alone in the fight to survive, and that made a difference to her. She also assumed more than one old man was searching for them.

The military train chugged on, passing over trestle bridges and traversing through mountain tunnels until it eventually stopped for the last time. The door slid open once more and the dawn's powerful early morning rays and fresh, woodsy air sliced through the malodorous car, a welcome relief to their senses. Then, a large, six-wheeled, military-green troop transport truck backed up to the door.

Mike and Sam's mind whirled, wondering who would be loaded in next. They stared out the door as four teenage soldiers dropped the truck's tailgate and climbed into the railcar, but they weren't loading anyone, they were unloading it. They untied Mike and Sam and ushered them along with the frightened children into the truck, corralling them in the front, near the truck's cab.

The soldiers loaded Mack on last, grabbing the rope and sliding him on his belly into the bed of the truck while the others held their rifles, ready to fire if anyone attempted to escape.

After Mack was loaded, the soldiers plopped down on the benches at the rear of the truck, slamming the tailgate, acting as though everything was business as usual.

Soon after, the truck revved its diesel engine and a plume of black smoke billowed from the vertical exhaust pipe, floating into the air and settling over the back of the truck, causing everyone to cough, including the soldiers.

As the truck drove the desolate dirt road, every few moments it hit a large pothole and everyone bounced up and down. Sam gripped one of the wooden slats, doing her best to stay upright, but her legs had become increasingly weaker. She hadn't had sufficient food or water in days and her body had redirected its energy to support her vital organs.

I need to get to Mack to find out about the rescue plan. I know there's a plan, she thought, glancing at Mack lying on the floor of the truck's metal bed and checking on Mike who had slouched down on the opposite side, about eight feet away. He sat lifelessly, his skin pale and eyes glazed over as he stared at the truck's wooden slats. Sam called out to him to get his attention, but it was no use, the trauma had shut him down.

The soldiers sat on a bench seat at the rear of the truck with their brown and black AK rifles resting on their laps, watching the road behind them. Sam slid along the wooden railing, past the children, keeping her eyes on the soldiers. Once she got past the children, she saw Mack lying on his stomach. She thought she heard him moaning, but it was hard to tell over the noisy diesel engine. She dropped down to her knees and called out to him, hoping the soldiers wouldn't hear.

"Mack?"

He turned his head, unable to see her through his swollen eyes.

"Mack, is there…is there a rescue plan? Is someone else coming?"

"Poss…possible. Argh!" Mack clutched his side, the pain intensifying.

"Can't be…argh…certain."

As she attempted to get information from him, one of the soldiers caught them speaking and stood up, jabbing the rifle's barrel into his side. He rolled to get away, but any movement he made was horrendously painful. Then the soldier pointed the gun at Sam, motioning for her to get back to the front of the truck.

Sam stood with her hands raised, gradually moving backward to the front of the truck and the soldier sat back down. She slid down behind some of the children and peeked out in-between the wooden slats on the side of the truck, noticing that they were crossing an old bridge and a decent-sized body of water.

Once across the bridge, they turned down a muddy lane that ran through the middle of the swamp, the rotten-egg like smell permeating the moist air. Lining both sides of the lane were an assortment of lush tropical palms, bulrushes, and weeping willows, so thick they blocked out most of the sunlight and made it appear as though it was dusk.

The truck's diesel engine whined loudly as it bounced over ruts and kicked up mud, startling dozens of turtles and crocodiles resting on the banks, encouraging them to slip under the algae-covered marsh. It continued on for a short time further and then slowed down for a military checkpoint where they were met by two middle-aged soldiers standing guard on both sides of a red stop arm gate. The truck never stopped as the soldiers motioned for them to continue on.

The truck advanced another few hundred yards and a spotlight turned on, shining down on them. Sam stepped back for a better view, but she couldn't see through the blinding white light. Then she heard what sounded like an iron gate swing open and the truck gradually pulled up behind a concrete wall; it was at least 20 feet high and topped off with sharp, glistening razor-wire and several stone-faced armed guards. Sam figured they were entering a prison or a heavily-fortified military installation and her spirits fell, along with her hope of ever getting home.

TWENTY-FOUR
CROCS

Present Day

Together the team drove the dark Burma roads for several hours, doing their best to make up time. The sun rose a few hours later, the black expanse giving way to a navy blue hue and then a bright white, like the sun's reflection off a snowy field in the winter.

As the dawning sun saturated the Burma landscape without invitation, Bling drove the uneven dirt road, throwing on a pair of sunglasses while the rest of the team slept—everyone except Chief; he couldn't stop thinking about Mack.

The dirt road soon gave way to sporadic concrete and solid blacktop as they approached a larger town. Moments later, Switch was awakened by his sat phone. He sat up and wiped his blurry eyes, looking at the call screen.

"Chief, my contact is calling," he yelled from the back.

"Bling, pull over up here," Chief insisted as they approached a gas station at the edge of a small town.

"Talk to me, brother," Switch answered as Chief stepped out of the cab to listen in.

Switch listened closely as his contact filled him in on Mack's last known location. "Alright, we're gonna write this down," Switch spoke aloud as Chief clicked his pen to write in his notebook.

"A military train stopped near the town of Magway," Switch repeated. "Can you spell that for me? Okay, M-a-g-w-a-y. ...large truck heading toward an island...okay, give me the coordinates...perfect. Listen, thanks for your help. If you get anything else, let me know."

Switch hung up the phone and filled them in with the glum news. "It appears they put Mack on a train that's heading to a covert military installation on Ramree Island in the Rahkine Province...The good news is that he's still alive."

Johnny's eyebrows drew together. "Absolutely not! I am not going there!"

Chief studied Johnny's body language and tone, curious about his unusual demeanor. "What's up, Johnny? I know Rahkine's been in the news, but—"

"I don't care about Rahkine," Johnny cut him off. "It's Ramree Island that's the problem."

"Why would that be a problem? I've never seen you react to a mission this way."

"Yeah, well, we've never been to Ramree." Johnny turned his back on them and they all stared as though he were off his medicine.

"So you mean to tell me no one here has heard of Ramree?" Johnny put his hands in his pockets and kicked a rock. "Arghhhh!" he yelled, hitting the tailgate with his fist and mumbling under his breath. "Somehow I knew this was gonna happen. The one place—the only place—that I didn't want to go."

"Johnny, fill us in here, what's got you so bothered, brother?" Chief asked in a calm tone.

"Boss, this is gonna sound odd, but I have nightmares of that place."

Everyone stared at him like he was an alien from another world, not saying a word.

"Look, when I was a kid, my folks would send me to my grandad's place over in Louisiana for the summer. At night, he'd take me out to the swamps to catch gators. Anyway, one of his friends would always tag along—a British guy named Bruce," Johnny paused, looking at the ground.

"I don't see what this has to do with us," Chief stated, becoming slightly irritated at the limited information.

"I'm getting there," Johnny spouted. "Bruce fought in the Second World War, and every time we'd go out gatoring grandad would ask him to share his crazy Ramree Island battle story. I bet I heard it at least 20 times..."

Switch interrupted him. "So, let me get this right. You're worried about a battle that occured on Ramree Island more than half-a-century ago?...What am I missing?"

"If you stop interrupting me, I'll tell you...Listen, Bruce told us that when he and the Brits arrived at Ramree they encountered nearly a thousand Japanese troops. They eventually overpowered them and ordered them to surrender, but they refused. Instead, they waited for nightfall and retreated through Ramree's swamps to link up with reinforcements further inland. Anyway, he said during the night of the retreat, he and the rest of the Brits heard random gunshots and bloodcurdling screams coming from deep in the swamp. They didn't know what was happening, but when the sun rose the next day, they only found 20 of the thousand Japanese still alive."

"20?" Bling gaped at him.

"Yeah, his horror story sent shrills up my spine every time he told it. Grandad always got a laugh at my expense, but I'd have nightmares for days. Still hate gators because of it."

"Yo, so what killed them troops? Gators?" Bling asked moon-eyed.

"Worse. Bruce said it was Salties."

"Salties?" Switch inquired, "As in saltwater crocodiles?" he asked, his forehead wrinkled.

"Yeah, unfortunately. Salties are much larger than alligators, and they're the most powerful apex predator in the world. Some grow as big as an SUV is long, and they weigh twice as much as a grizzly bear. Oh, and Bling, you'll appreciate this fact: they all have 66 teeth—one digit short of the mark of the beast. If that isn't a sign that they're the spawn of the devil, I don't know what is…and Ramree is infested with those monsters."

"Sho' do sound like sumptin' from da underworld, dat's for sure," Bling surmised.

"Sounds like you're an expert on these things," Chief replied, still trying to gauge Johnny's apprehension.

Switch looked at Johnny and it still wasn't adding up for him. "So, wait, let me get this straight. You're telling us that you're known for blowing bad guys apart, but somehow you suffer from reptile PTSD from some story your grandpappy told you as a kid?" He finished with a snarky laugh.

"It's not funny," Johnny retorted heatedly.

"How do you know it isn't just a myth?" Chief asked.

"It's all over the internet. Have Switch check it out on one of his geek devices. It's even in history books. The place is literally hell on earth."

"Okay, look, Johnny, regardless of whether it's true or not, this ain't the 1940s," Chief insisted. "And we're not trudging through any swamps. We're gonna do some recon on the installation and see if we can come up with a plan to safely extract Mack. From the coordinates that Switch received the installation is on the edge of Ramree. If it were so dangerous, I doubt they would have a military compound there."

"Unless it's part of they security," Bling chimed in.

"Crocs don't discriminate, Bling. The military would get eaten as well." Chief replied.

Strangely curious, Switch reached into his gear bag and pulled his electronic tablet out, checking for an internet connection.

"I've got a weak signal, but I think I can pull it up." Switch mumbled as he typed the name Ramree into his search engine.

"While you got a signal, check out the meaning of that Asian symbol we saw on the military vehicles," Chief instructed.

"You got it."

Switch scrolled through the first few internet entries on Ramree and a sudden coldness gripped him.

"You weren't kidding, Johnny," Switch gulped hard. "This is crazy…Guinness called it the deadliest animal attack on humans ever!"

Chief smacked his lips. "C'mon, guys, enough of the campfire stories. According to my map, we've got another three hours to Magway. We gotta get back on the road."

"Hang on a sec, Chief." Switch replied with his mouth slightly agape, scrolling through the entry. "Let me read this short insert to you guys. I found Bruce's account; it's scary stuff, but there's another report from a captain in the British Navy that we may be able to use."

"Read it, but then maybe we can get on with rescuing Mack."

"It's really short. This is from a captain who was in the conflict on Ramree. He says, and I quote, '[The island is] dark during the day as well as during the night, acres of thick impenetrable forest; miles of deep black mud, mosquitoes, scorpions, flies and weird insects by the billion and—worst of all—crocodiles. No food, no drinking water to be obtained anywhere—'"

Chief broke the fear-laced silence. "I'm more worried about the mosquitoes, to be honest…and speaking of stories, did y'all know the most notorious military commander was killed by a mosquito?"

"Alexander the Great?" Switch proposed.

"You got it. Some historians speculate he contracted malaria; that's our biggest concern with Ramree—not crocs."

"Right, let's be sure to dope up on mosquito spray," Switch replied.

"Yo! All dis talk 'bout gators and water—I've gotta run into the little boy's room." Bling pointed to the gas station.

"Go ahead…hurry back!" Chief shouted to Bling who was already halfway to the station.

"Johnny, while we're waiting, do a weapons and gear check. Let me know what Mack brought along. I'm gonna run inside and see if we can get some spray paint to cover this camo so we don't stand out so much."

"Roger that. Good idea," Johnny stated, carefully unzipping Mack's black gear bag.

A few minutes later, Chief and Bling returned with six bright red spray paint cans. Chief popped the lid off one of them, shaking it vigorously, and then sprayed a wide swath across the door.

"Candy Apple Red?" Switch laughed.

"Hey, it's all they had. Grab a can and help spray this down. Johnny, what's the deal with Mack's gear?"

Johnny remained silent with his head down, his hand resting on Mack's unzipped bag. "Feels weird going through his stuff, boss."

"I know it does, but he may have something we can use. Besides, he'd go through your gear if you were in the same spot."

"Especially if you had weapons in there," Switch interjected with a snicker, listening in as he and Bling continued spraying the truck.

"When you put it that way," Johnny opened the black flap and peered inside. "Looks like he's got pretty much everything in here…meal bars, his breakdown sniper rifle, a couple glow sticks, matches and bug spray…oh, and a tube of hemorrhoid cream."

Johnny shook his head and everyone giggled. "Hey, hold on a sec. There's something else in here…a smaller case."

Chief smiled broadly. "That's what I was hoping for… Attaboy, Mack," he mumbled as he opened the case, leaving behind red fingerprints on it. Inside were six fragmentation grenades, two smoke grenades, and two flashbangs.

Johnny reached into the bag and pulled out Mack's 7.62mm sniper rifle—a blacked-out Remington that had been broken down into three pieces.

"Boss, Mack's got a night-vision scope mounted on his sniper rifle with a few dozen rounds of ammo. He's got another five mags for the MP," Johnny continued.

"Hey, what's in this pack?" Switch asked as he reached into Mack's bag, removing a fanny pack. He unzipped it, exposing a curved plastic box with two spikes sticking out of it.

"Woah! Nice! He brought a Claymore."

"Ain't look like any type of clay I've ever seen," Bling surmised as he threw his empty spray can into the pickup's bed.

"Claymore...as in Claymore mine," Johnny indicated, rolling his eyes at Bling's ignorance. "It's named after a huge medieval-era Scottish sword—and for good reason. They're super nasty; it's loaded with C-4 explosives and when it's detonated, hundreds of ball bearings shoot out at the enemy."

"Yo, so it's like a big ol' shotgun then," Bling suggested.

"I guess you could say that."

"This is gold," Chief stated. "A Claymore can take out half a football field wide of enemy personnel in seconds."

"There's another one in here," Johnny reported.

"Good job, Mack!" Chief exclaimed.

As they finished rummaging through Mack's gear, Switch used his tablet to search the internet for the meaning of the Asian symbol they had seen. "Chief, I think I've got something on that symbol," Switch called out, still reading the online content.

"What's it mean?"

"This is odd; it's not Burmese; it's an old Chinese symbol that means dragon."

"Dragon?" Chief tilted his head, seeking more information.

Switch shrugged his shoulders. "That's all I've got; there's not much information about it."

"Not sure if that's significant, but we'll keep it in mind. It definitely has something to do with their trafficking operation. Kylee had the same symbol tattooed on her neck—and it wasn't professionally done," Chief concluded.

"Yo, it could be like a pimp's brand," Bling surmised. "Back in the day, we tattooed the girls we was runnin'. Shows ownership."

"Good info," Chief stated. "Alright, let's get back on the road. Y'all make sure you get some water and a meal bar...and some rest if you can. We've got a long day ahead of us."

TWENTY-FIVE
THE INSTALLATION

The five-ton military transport truck drove into the massive compound, stopping in front of another gate inside the square sally port. The gate behind them banged closed and they were surrounded by concrete and steel on all sides, the truck barely fitting inside.

Two soldiers circled the truck, examining it closely, looking for anything that was out of place. Sam ducked down behind the wooden slats and looked up at catwalk where a handful of soldiers with rifles slung over their shoulders paced back and forth behind circular razor wire. She locked eyes with a boy who was probably a year or two younger than her and he reached for his rifle, but Sam darted her eyes away, slipping down to the truck's bed and then moved over to check on Mike.

"Mike," she called out, keeping her voice low, but he didn't respond. He was slumped over like he was dead.

"Mike!" She nearly yelled, but he didn't budge. She tried again, and this time she got a response, but it wasn't from him—one of the soldiers heard her and moved swiftly in her direction. She attempted to move back to the opposite side of the truck, but it was too late; the soldier rammed the butt of his rifle into her back, dropping her to her stomach.

"Argh!" She let out an agonizing scream, keeping her eyes on Mike, but he still hadn't moved. She had to know if he was alive, so she reached out and placed her hand on his back, feeling the

220

warmth radiating from his body. Seconds later, the soldier slammed the butt of his rifle into her head and everything went dark.

Sam felt the jagged gravel stones digging into her skin as the soldiers dragged her through the compound. She opened her eyes briefly, but she soon lost consciousness again. She was in and out for few minutes when she felt a mosquito biting her and finally woke up, realizing she was no longer being dragged but lying on her back on the slightly cooler dirt ground.

She looked around to see where she was, but everything was blurry. Her ears rang horribly and her head felt like it had been squeezed in a clamp. She rubbed her eyes to clear the blurriness, but it didn't help. All she could make out were dozens of fuzzy bamboo poles and pervasive darkness.

Sam got up on her knees, feeling around like she was blind, her sense of smell reawakening. Almost instantly she was met by a wave of body odor combined with a dank, fishy smell, prompting her to pull her grimy tank top over her nose, but she soon realized that her own body was part of the fetid odor.

She closed her eyes and opened them repeatedly, her eyesight beginning to return to normal, but as it did everything around her spun wildly and her head throbbed in pain. She reached up and felt a several-inch long gash and a swollen knot where the soldier had struck her. It wasn't long before the spinning slowed and her vision returned, but it was so dark it didn't matter.

Sam grabbed the bamboo bars at the front of what she figured was a crude holding cell, sliding her hand along them to help her stand up. Once she got to her feet, she scanned the rectangular building. Three of the four sides were lined with hundreds of skinny bamboo sticks, including the roof, which was covered with dried palm thatches. The back wall was made of concrete, which she figured was the compound's exterior wall and the front had a section cut out for a door, secured closed by a stainless steel chain and a heavy-duty padlock.

As she continued surveying the crude cell, she heard faint whimpers coming from behind her. She turned and looked into the gloominess, expecting to see the children from the truck, but, instead, she saw several other young girls huddled in the back of the cell. They were her age and younger—possibly as young as 11 or 12 years old—all of them dressed in dirty, skimpy T-shirts that barely covered their bottoms.

"Hel...lo...does anyone speak English?" she asked softly, unsure if anyone understood. She waited for a moment, but all she could see were the girls' backsides and their long black hair.

Not hearing anything from the girls, she turned back to the front, pressing her head to the bamboo sticks. She studied the compound, searching for Mike and Mack, but she couldn't see much, only another bamboo and thatched-roof holding cell, about 20 feet long, identical of the one she was in, and several metal boxes to the right of it, each one slightly larger than a casket.

"Tha...that buh...boy holding place," a soft, high-pitched voice stammered from the rear of the cell. With her eyebrows raised, Sam turned to see who was speaking, but she couldn't see due to the darkness of the cell.

"Who...who ish shpeaking?" Sam asked, her speech still slightly slurred from her concussion.

"Must be careful," the girl whispered. "If see you look, they hurt." Sam didn't wait for the girl to show herself. She moved into the shadows, eventually catching a glimpse of an Asian girl who had broken away from the huddle.

Sam studied the girl's skinny frame, noting the only piece of clothing she was wearing, the same skimpy oversized T-shirt. She looked to be about Sam's same age, but it was difficult to tell because her hair was disheveled and her face dirty, except for the ruby red lipstick that had smeared from the corner of her lips across her right cheek.

"My name is Sam, what's yours?" she asked delicately.

"My...my name...no...no matter...I no exist," she replied, hanging her head.

Sam stepped closer and saw that her arms and wrists were badly bruised and swollen.

"Hey, no, that's not true. You do matter."

Sam softly touched the girl's shoulder, but as soon as she felt it, she pulled away.

"I suh...sorry...but you no unstan," the girl replied, choking back tears. "You just got here. You no see yet. Make feel like nothing. They use place to break us...very evil place."

As they were speaking, Sam heard men talking in what sounded like a Russian dialect. She moved to the bamboo bars, peeking through the slats, catching a glimpse of two heavyset white men with high, broad cheekbones and short blondish-colored, crewcut-style hair. They were walking with General Htun and approaching the holding cell and Sam quickly backed away into the darkness, not wanting to be seen.

"White man take girl from here every week," the girl indicated. "No let them see you look."

"How long have you been here?" Sam inquired, wondering how she knew so much information.

"Four month...I...I think."

"Four months? That's a long time."

"Most girl leave here, but I no pretty enough for palace."

"Palace?" Sam speculated.

"That what they call where take girl. They make seem great place. No great, but better than here."

"How...how did you get here?"

"Most girl take from village, but I...well...how do you say...I escape from home."

"Do you mean you ran away from home?" Sam inquired, her head tilted slightly.

"Yes. Yes. Ran away."

"Why did you run away from home?"

"Papa no good. He—um—he abuse mom. He abuse me in different way. Mom take, but I no take. But look at me now," she replied, burying her face in her hands and quietly sobbing.

Sam looked into her brown, watery eyes with empathy, but didn't really know what to say. "I'm…I'm so sorry," she paused, wanting to hug her, but she wasn't sure if it was the right time. "Hey, but I really would like to know your name."

"My name, Shein, but I no matter. The men here say I no good. They use me for bad thing."

Sam closed her eyes, desperately trying to hide her emotions. "They treat you like that because they only see your body and how it can please them. They don't know how important you are to God. But you do matter, Shein."

Shein looked down, unconvinced by Sam's words.

"Shein is a very beautiful name. What does it mean?"

"Mean? I no unstan."

"Umm…well, does your name maybe symbolize something?"

"Ah, symbol…yes…symbol of reflection. Mirror."

"Oh, reflection…that's beautiful. My mom—" Sam abruptly paused mid-sentence, thinking about her parents and whether she would ever see them again. A tear slipped down her cheek and she continued. "My mom, she always told me that people are special because they are made in God's reflection. That means you're special, Shein, because you reflect God."

"I reflek God? But I no have big belly like Buddha." Shein's forehead wrinkled, unsure if she understood correctly.

"No, Shein, not like Buddha," Sam giggled for the first time in days. "Buddha was just a man. God is a spirit and He gave us part of Himself so we could know Him personally. That's who you were made to reflect. His image is hidden in us…invisible"

"Person…invisible?" Shein looked confused.

"My mind isn't the sharpest right now, so hopefully this makes sense, but it's like He gave us a built-in radio that we can tune in to His station—to hear Him and speak with Him. I wish I wasn't so rebellious and listened to him better before coming he—" She stared ahead, trailing off.

"God speak me?" Shein wondered, her eyes glistening.

"Yes, and more than that," Sam glowed. "His reflection on us is why we're able to write beautiful poetry and love songs and have faith and hope. It's where we get our sense of right and wrong and why we seek justice for victims and hold evil men accountable. Does that make sense to you?"

"I think I get. You say lot," Shein half-smiled.

"Yeah, I guess I did," Sam smiled out of the corner of her mouth and looked down. "Shein, I'm sorry. Here I am being all positive, but I haven't been through what you have. I guess I'm trying to keep hope alive in my own mind."

"No say sorry. I like you words. So what symbol you name?"

"My name?"

"Yes."

"Mom always told me my name means God listens...and you know what, I don't think I ever truly considered the meaning until now."

"Sam, if we special to God, why he allow get trap here with evil men?"

Sam stayed silent for a moment, retracing her thoughts back to when her and Mike had the same conversation.

"I...I...don't...don't kno—"

"Sam...shhhhh," Shein abruptly interrupted and faced the wall. "They come. No talk." Sam didn't say a word as she backed into the darkness, listening to the sound of soldiers marching closer to the cell, their heavy boots thumping the ground with each step. Seconds later, they heard a key being inserted into the padlock and the chain clanking against the bamboo bars. Sam peeked at the door to see what was occurring, but when she did Shein tugged at her shirt.

"No look," she whispered. Sam swiftly turned around, her heart pounding fast. Two soldiers, one a portly lieutenant in all-green fatigues and the other his boy-assistant, strolled into the cell and stood behind Sam, the lieutenant's warm breath so close it disturbed her hair.

"Girl!" the lieutenant's deep, powerful voice arrested her attention. "Take off cloth. Put on shirt."

Sam recoiled, her body rigid as she pondered his request and considered what evil he had in mind for her. Then he threw a crumpled up yellowish-white shirt on the ground—one that matched Shein's and the other girls—and pointed to it with his rifle.

"Take off cloth now!" he demanded, nearly shouting. Sam flinched and shut her eyes tight, bracing for the worst. Seeing no way out of it, she begrudgingly lifted her soiled tank top over her head, pulling it off and dropping it to the ground.

The man stood behind her, his breath wheezing like nails on a chalkboard in her ears. He poked the barrel of his rifle into the small of her back and traced it down her spine until it rested on the top of her shorts.

"Take off all cloth!" He whispered seductively into her ear.

Trembling and teary-eyed, Sam held one arm over her bare chest and used her other arm to unclasp the button on her shorts. It took a few seconds, but when she got it, they slipped down her legs and fell around her ankles. He stood behind her, lustfully gawking at her for what seemed like forever. Then the heavy breathing stopped and she heard the chains being wrapped around the cell door and the padlock locking closed. They had left, but the trauma had already taken root.

Sam snatched up the oversized shirt, throwing it over her head and pulling it down, tears streaming down her cheeks. The shirt left part of her bottom exposed and smelled like several girls had worn it before her.

Shein could tell Sam was struggling with her new reality and tried her best to encourage her. "Sam, you must be strong. They do to every girl...even worse things. No give up."

"I uh, I...I need to relieve myself...where...where do you do that at?" Sam asked, her eyes unfocused.

"Bucket," Shein indicated, pointing to a corner at the rear of the cell, about 15 feet away. Sam couldn't see anything, but as she got closer her eyes adjusted to a white bucket nearly full of urine and excrement. A few rats squeaked away as they saw her approaching and a flood of rancid odor crossed her nostrils. Almost instantly the muscles in the back of her throat contracted, causing her to gag.

Sam stopped moving and gazed down at the bucket, her mind overwhelmed. She tried to take a step, but her knees buckled under her and she dropped to the ground, convulsing. The stress and anxiety from the horrendous conditions dominated her body. Shein raced over and placed her hand on her back, trying to console her.

"I...I can't do...I can't do this..." Sam stumbled over her words. With glazed eyes, Sam stretched her body out on the cell floor, laying her head on the dirt, her tears mixing with a string of saliva from her lips, dripping into a small, muddy puddle.

"No cry, Sam. No let them take hope. You give me hope."

Sam didn't say another word. She was too exhausted.

As she stared out the bars, she fanaticized about Navy Seals repelling down from hovering helicopters and gliding in on airboats, blasting the enemy and rescuing her and Mike. It was an entirely irrational thought, but it helped eased the pain, so she let her mind take her there.

As she could fantasize no further, she closed her eyes and rested her head on the ground, the anxiety and trauma nuzzling up next to her, slowly squeezing the life from her like a famished python attacking a paralyzed victim.

TWENTY-SIX
ROAD SNIPER

Chief and the team traveled Burma's backcountry roads to lay low, knowing the military would be watching for them. They continued for several hours, taking turns driving and resting until they came to Datkon, the last sizeable town before entering the Rakhine Province.

Chief instructed Bling to pull off the road so he could give everyone a quick briefing.

"Alright, guys, we're gonna gas up in the town up ahead; it'll be our last stop before we enter Rakhine on the way to the military installation in Ramree."

"Oh good, I guess that means we're calling in a rescue team to pick up Mack and we can wait here at a nice hotel," Johnny spoke up quite seriously.

"Are you still worried about Ramree?" Switch asked, his head propped up on his gear bag, but Johnny didn't reply.

"Listen, guys. The road we're on is the only way into that installation. In about ten klicks we'll hit the Arakan Mountain Range and the road will become narrow, steep and slippery, but my main concern is coming across a military convoy. We'll have no place to go if we're spotted. Keep your eyes open...and Johnny and Switch, y'all make sure to lay low back there."

"Copy that, Chief."

"Roger that, boss," Johnny replied unenthusiastically.

After fueling up and grabbing a few extra gas cans, Chief switched places with Bling, driving the pickup back onto the two-lane road. They drove through the winding mountainous roads for about an hour when they came to a particularly high peak covered in fog. As they climbed higher, the old Mazda sputtered horribly, having trouble ascending the steep road with everyone in it.

Chief held his foot to the gas pedal, but they were barely moving. "C'mon, you piece of—!" He swore. "We could have gotten an elephant and moved faster than this!"

"Sounds like it could be a fuel pump issue," Johnny shouted from the back as they continued up the wet and foggy road.

"Switch," Chief yelled back. "Give me some navigation here. I need to know how much longer till we're out of these high peaks."

"Roger. Give me a sec."

Switch unfolded his paper map to chart their location.

"Looks like maybe five or six more klicks."

"Good, because I don't think it will make it much further."

As Chief was speaking, dark storm clouds settled over them, blocking out most of the light, making it appear more like midnight than the early afternoon. Seconds later, a set of headlights appeared as a large vehicle crested over the mountain's peak a few meters away. Johnny grabbed his binoculars and looked over the cab, spotting what appeared to be the bumper of a large military truck pushing through the dense fog.

"Boss, we've got a problem—at least one military truck approaching, possibly more." Chief slowed considerably, nearly coming to a stop as a light mist settled over them.

"Guys, get low and stay ready!"

Johnny and Switch grabbed their MPs and rested them on their stomachs, hoping they wouldn't be seen.

"Looks like only one troop transport truck, unless there are more behind it," Chief reported as the truck barreled through the fog in their direction. "Everyone stay calm. It's about to pass us."

The transport truck got to within only a few meters and Chief and Bling were able to see the soldiers inside the cab. They quickly looked away, hoping they wouldn't be made.

"Phew...that was a little tense," Chief announced, turning around to see Johnny and Switch on their backs, still laying low.

"Yeah, wasn't sure how that was going to go, boss. There were several troops in the back."

The pickup continued sputtering up the mountain, reaching the summit a short time later. As it did, it became enveloped in the dark clouds, but only a few seconds later, the road leveled out and they began descending out of it.

"Ah, here we go. Getting some speed now," Chief yelled back.

"Yeah, well, we're gonna need it!" Switch shouted. "That truck is following us!"

Johnny grabbed the binoculars and sat up to get a better view.

"Boss, they'll be on us any moment!"

"Can you see into the cab...look for anyone on phones or radios?" Chief stressed.

Switch yelled up, "There's no reception up here. Unless they have a sat phone they can't call anyone."

"Johnny, get on that sniper, just in case!"

"Copy that, boss!"

Johnny dug through Mack's gear bag, pulling out all the pieces of the breakdown sniper rifle. He attached the barrel to the receiver, installed the bolt and handguard, and inserted the magazine to chamber a round.

"Ready, boss!" Johnny shouted, sitting against the back of the pickup's cab and making some adjustments on the scope.

"Yo, we gots another problem!" Bling shouted as he looked through Chief's binoculars at the transport truck. "Them soldiers got heat on us."

Johnny looked through the scope and spotted five boy-soldiers, no more than young teenagers, their rifles resting over the top of the cab, aiming in their direction.

Ratatat! Ratatat! The soldiers fired their weapons in unison, a few of the bullets striking the tailgate and the top part of the cab.

"Fire!" Chief shouted, checking the rearview mirror and seeing the truck only a few meters behind them.

Dhak! Johnny fired the suppressed sniper rifle and checked his target.

"Man, I missed! All this swerving!" Johnny fumed. He looked through the scope again and one of the soldiers was holding a grenade launcher.

"RPG!" Johnny shouted. Chief slammed on the brakes and the transport truck rammed them from behind, but they were so close that the soldiers weren't able to fire down on them.

"Johnny, you got this?" Chief asked.

"I'm ready. Go for it!" Johnny asserted as his heart bear faster and breathing became shallower. When Chief pulled away, he would have only a split second to align the scope's crosshairs on the soldier to take him out before he fired the rocket.

Chief stomped on the gas pedal and pulled away from the truck and when he did several rain drops hit the windshield.

Dhak! Johnny fired again and hit the soldier in the head, the RPG falling from his hand into the back of the truck.

Phttt! Phttt! Phttt! Switch fired his MP5, taking out two more soldiers while Johnny pulled the sniper rifle's bolt back, extracting the spent brass and reloading for another shot. He looked through the scope into the truck's cab and spotted two more soldiers. One of them, the driver, was in military fatigues, and the other was an older officer.

Johnny concentrated the crosshairs on the officer's head and pressed the trigger, but he was slightly off target and the bullet hit him in his neck, his blood splattering across the windshield. It wasn't a perfect shot, but it took him out and stunned the driver, provoking him to pull over. Chief slammed the brakes, nearly locking them up, and then angled the pickup to block the road.

"Bling, stay inside," Chief ordered as he Johnny and Switch jumped out with their MP5s, sweeping toward the truck in a staggered column formation.

Johnny climbed a nearby rock structure to get a view of the transport truck's bed, anticipating a fire fight, but when he reached the top and peered over, it was empty, save the three dead bodies and a couple wooden crates. He looked down the road and three soldiers—all of them teenagers—were sprinting away, their bodies nearly disappearing into the thick fog.

"Boss, I got three boys in green fatigues retreating...they appear unarmed...about 10 meters out!" Johnny shouted.

"Stop them!"

Phttt! Phttt! Phttt! Johnny fired his MP5 and the bullets danced in front of the boys, kicking up a fine mist on the slightly saturated and pitted asphalt. With no place to go, they stopped and raised their hands in surrender.

Chief and Switch caught up with the soldiers moments later, and when they did, two of them broke down in tears.

"Chief, these boys aren't hardened soldiers; they're like the ones we ran into at the village," Switch observed.

"Yeah, I can see that," Chief indicated. "Let's make sure they're fully disarmed and load them into the back of the truck."

"What's the plan here, boss?" Johnny asked, shouting down to Chief as he descended from the pile of rocks. "Have the boys remove the bodies from the truck and clean the blood off the windshield. We're gonna use the truck as cover to get closer to the installation. We'll let one of the boys drive and we'll stay low."

"Great idea," Switch suggested.

Johnny nodded. "That might just work."

As he was speaking, a small civilian car rolled up. The passengers saw the dead bodies and stared straight ahead, stepping on the gas to speed by as quickly as possible.

Johnny climbed into the back of the truck, using his boot knife to pry open and inspect the wooden crates that were pushed against the truck's cab.

"Bling, you can come out now," Chief shouted.

"Boss, we got a weapons cache here...several AKs, a couple RPGs with a half-dozen grenades—hang on, I've got something else. Holy mother of—"

"What is it?" Chief asked.

"There's a heavy machine gun with several ammo belts…looks like a Dushka."

Chief climbed into the truck and peered into the crate at the no-frills weapon—a six-foot-long metal barrel connected to a receiver box and two wooden handles with a butterfly trigger in the middle. "Man, I haven't seen one of these since Afghanistan—this beast shoots 12.7mm light-armor piercing rounds at 600 per second."

"600 rounds? Nice!" Johnny smiled widely as Bling climbed into the truck to see what they were gawking at.

"Yep, this meat chopper is basically a .50 cal. machine gun. Me and my squad got pinned down by one during an operation in Iraq. Not fun. Let's hope it works."

"Yo, what's so special about it? Looks like one big hunk of metal to me," Bling proposed.

"Super basic design, like most Soviet weaponry, but it's effective. Johnny, help me lift this thing up."

They lifted the bulky gun from the crate, exposing a tripod for anti-aircraft use.

"Looks like we struck gold here," Johnny surmised as he set up the tripod. "Good, load it up. We need to test it out."

"Roger that, boss," he smiled.

"Bling, there's a lake about 40 klicks from here. You're gonna drive the pickup and ditch it in the water," Chief instructed. "And go ahead and transfer our gear bags into the transport truck."

"I'm on it," Bling replied, "And good call puttin' me in the pickup. I'd rather let y'all ride in the big truck wit' them dead bodies."

"Actually, Bling—" Chief paused.

"Don't even say it, yo!" Bling responded, crossing his arms.

"Well, we gotta put the bodies somewhere. Don't worry, we'll ditch the pickup before they start stinkin'."

"Man, c'mon. This is whack," Bling replied, sulking like a child.

"Bling, the lake is only 25 mikes from here. You got this," Switch indicated.

"Then why ain't you do it?" Bling asserted.

"Ah, no. That won't work. I've gotta navigate for Chief."

"Man, dis ain't right," he stormed off, hopping down from the truck. He transferred the gear bags from the pickup into the transport truck and reluctantly sat in the pickup's driver seat, gazing into the rearview mirror as the boy-soldiers discarded the dead officer into the pickup's bed, his limp body making a hollow thud as it hit the thin sheet metal. Then they did the same with the other bodies, piling them on top each other, the blood's peculiarly sweet-metallic aroma giving Bling a woozy feeling. He did his best to stay focused, but he was consumed with how their lives were snuffed out so quickly and how he would be the one to dump them in their watery grave.

"Boss, gun is ready," Johnny confirmed, rotating the gun on its turret and peeping through the dual-ring sight, aiming at a small tree about 30 meters behind them.

Chief rounded the corner of the truck and saw Johnny standing in back, situated behind the weapon, the clip of large bullets dangling into an ammo can sitting next to it. He stepped back a few feet and shouted up. "Give it a try."

"Roger," he replied as everyone plugged their ears with their fingers.

Bratatbratatbratat! Johnny squeezed the trigger for several seconds, severing and the tree in half, the top falling halfway across the road.

Chief nodded his approval. "Alight, good, now let's get on the road."

"Roger that, boss…I can't imagine what Mack must be going through right now."

"We're not going to talk about that. Let's stay focused," Chief commanded.

"Copy that"

Chief and Switch climbed into the truck's cab while Johnny stayed in the bed, keeping an eye on the three boy-soldiers in the back.

"Alright, Bling, you're good to go, over," Chief instructed, speaking into his mic on his recently charged radio.

"Ain't nuttin' good about this; I keep hearing noises from the back; givin' me the heebies...but, okay, copy dat."

Chief looked at Switch and they both cracked a slight smile as Bling put the pickup into gear and pulled away. Chief followed about 30 meters behind and they drove for about a half-hour when they came upon Auk Lake, outside the town of Ann in the Rakhine Province. The lake was situated about 30 meters from the road, behind several trees and some brush.

"Bling, Auk Lake is on your left," Chief indicated. "Pull over and we'll help you push the pickup into the water, over."

Bling pulled off the road and put the pickup into neutral as Chief and Switch ran up. They did a quick check of the area and together pushed the pickup down the hill, sending it splashing into the still waters, watching until it was completely submerged.

They climbed back up the small hill and Switch's sat phone rang again. He answered and listened as his contact provided an update, his face turning solemn.

"What is it?" Chief asked, noting his serious expression.

"Mack's at the Ramree installation."

"I figured as much, but don't say anything to Johnny. He's already on edge about that place."

"Good call."

"I need a new ETA on those coordinates."

"You got it."

Switch got the map, charting the distance from lake to the coordinates he had received from his contact and Bling climbed into the back of the truck with Johnny.

"About two hours from here," Switch replied, staring down at the map. "There's a tiny village called Ma-ei about four miles from Ramree on the mainland. Looks like the installation is just past Ma-ei River."

"Okay, great intel. Can you check with your contact and see if they have an image of the military installation?"

"I was just getting ready to inform you of that. I already asked. They can confirm that there's a compound, but they can't get a sat image because there's too much tree cover."

"Not what I wanted to hear. We can't form a plan without knowing what we're up against."

"I know it's risky, but I've got a five-mile range on my drone and it's fully charged. We could stop outside the compound and fly it in for an image."

"It's super risky, but at this point, it's our only option. We've gotta see what we're dealing with."

"Copy that," he replied as they got back into the truck.

Once everyone was loaded in, Chief slammed the gas pedal to the floor, pushing the transport truck to its mechanical limits. While he drove, he desperately tried to come up with a practical plan that wouldn't result in sacrificing the entire team for the sake of one man.

TWENTY-SEVEN
TANNIYN

C hief drove for about an hour when the environment drastically changed. The mountain's comfortable temperatures had given way to flat marshland and a disagreeable mugginess. Seeing they weren't far from the island, he pulled over to brief everyone.

"Man, this humidity is the worst yet," Switch complained as he opened the truck's tailgate and pulled himself up, dangling his feet over the edge.

"Yeah, the sweaty armpit of Satan—as Mack would say," Johnny joined Switch on the tailgate, smiling from the corner of his mouth but still keeping an eye on the young soldiers. Bling stood behind them, leaning against the wooden slats.

"Alright guys," Chief began. "We've got maybe 20 mikes before the sun will disappear behind the trees. The map shows we'll cross over a large river separating the mainland from the island and then the installation should be a few kilometers beyond that."

"Ramree...just great," Johnny mumbled under his breath.

"Mack's life is worth more than your anxiety, Johnny. I need you ready to go."

"You're right, boss, I'm good. I'll...I'll get it together before we get there.

"Good. The plan, for now, is to have two of the boys in the cab with me. Hopefully, we can pass through their security checkpoints without any issues...Johnny, Switch and Bling... throw a tarp over the Dushka and make sure no one can get a look at y'all from behind. The one advantage is that it'll be dark soon and we'll have some cover."

"Copy that, boss," Johnny confirmed as Switch and Bling bobbed their heads, signaling that they understood.

"Alright guys, let's stay alert. From here on out, we're entering the lion's den."

Chief ushered two of the teen boys into the cab and positioned himself opposite of them, near the door. One of the boys moved into the driver's position and nervously stared at the steering wheel and gearshift.

"Great, I hope one of y'all can drive this thing," Chief mumbled under his breath. He looked at the boy and nodded at him to begin driving.

The boy wiped his sweaty hands on his pants and placed them on the steering wheel, slowly shifting the truck into gear. The truck jerked forward, jarring everyone, and nearly dumping the Dushka out the back. Chief was about to take over when the boy eventually got the hang of it. He drove for a short time when they came to their first test—a security checkpoint.

Chief reported in, speaking into his mic. "Alright team, we're coming up to a long bridge and a checkpoint manned by two soldiers. I'm gonna take cover on the floorboard. Be ready for anything."

"Roger. We're ready back here, boss."

Chief drew his pistol as the boy slowly drove up to the outpost. The outpost soldiers recognized the boys and raised the gate arm and waved them through. Relieved, Chief gave the boys a thumb's up and got back up on the seat as they traveled across the bridge to the island. Once across, he pointed to the boys to stop the truck at a dirt road nestled between a dark jungle and swamp on both sides. They stopped and Chief reached across and turned off the diesel engine.

"You hear all those birds?" Johnny asked with his eyes open wide, staring into the thick darkness.

"You alright, Johnny," Switch asked, seeing his nervousness.

"I'll be alright."

"Switch, I need you up here," Chief spoke into his mic.

"On my way."

Switch jumped out and met up with Chief.

"Are we close enough to the installation to use the drone?" Chief asked.

"Let me see…yeah, according to the map, the installation is only four klicks away; it shouldn't be a problem."

"Good. Make it happen."

Switch moved to the back, dropped the tailgate, and slid his gear bag to the edge, setting up the drone with night-vision. He took a few test shots and launched it into the darkness.

**

"Sam, wake up!" Shein exclaimed. Sam opened her eyes and closed them again, hoping she had been in a horrible nightmare.

"Sam, water."

Sam heard the word water and opened her eyes wide. Someone could have offered her a million dollars, but she was so parched she would have traded it for a gallon of fresh, clean drinking water. She gazed through the bamboo bars at a small jeep parked in front of the boys' cell, watching as a soldier fed a hose from a large plastic tank through the bamboo bars.

"When soldier come, each girl drink fast," Shein stated. "Must stand line." She pointed to the girls who were already lined up single-file, ready for their few seconds under the hose.

Sam sat up, trying to get her bearings, but when she tried to stand, her legs buckled beneath her. Shein saw her struggling and helped her into the line.

The soldier in the jeep drove to the girl's cell, rapping the bars with his black baton to get their attention. He stopped near the door, slipping a black garden hose between the bamboo bars. The first girl put her mouth up near the hose and murky water gushed out in her face. She drank for several seconds and moved away so the next girl could drink.

Shein pulled Sam behind the last girl in line and got her ready to drink. After the last girl went, she sat her under the hose. Sam looked up as the water poured out on her head—the coolness a welcome relief to the stifling humidity. She stuck her tongue out, but as soon as she did, the soldier removed the hose and hopped back into the jeep, but it didn't stop Sam from getting some water. She was so thirsty that she got down on all fours and stuck her face in a small mud puddle beneath her, lapping up the water like a dog.

"No, Sam, no drink that. No good for you," Shein insisted.

"Not to be rude, but nothing has been good for me since I got here," she muttered, flipping over on her back.

As she rested, a soldier approached the cell, carrying a bucket. He stopped at the bars and scooped out a cup of dried field corn kernels, throwing them into the cell. The girls scampered around, seizing as many of the kernels as they could. Sam watched, disgusted that they were being treated like animals, but she was so hungry that she soon joined in. She scooped up a half-dozen kernels, placing them in her mouth one at a time, closing her eyes and savoring the bland flavor. After crunching on them, she rested against the bamboo bars and closed her eyes again, thinking about home. Then she heard an unusual noise.

Bong, bom! Bong, bom! The sound resembled tribal bongo drums. At first, the drums were faint, but then they got progressively louder.

Sam gazed out the bars waiting to see what was happening. "What is that?" she asked Shein, noticing her head had dropped and appeared quite somber.

"Tanniyn is coming," she replied quietly.

"Tan-een?" Sam faced her, her forehead wrinkled, wondering deeply.

"Tanniyn island keeper. The soldiers feed."

Sam's mind quickly traced back to General Htun's words about feeding Mike to a dragon and her eyes grew wide.

"Is…is Tanniyn a crocodile?" Sam asked, horror filling her eyes.

"No, no crocodile. No sure how tell. They make watch when feed. It sa—sad time." Shein looked at the ground and continued. "Some men come with you. They next feed."

Penetrating anxiety rushed over Sam like she was about to face death herself.

"Wha—what did you say?"

"See boxes?" Shein pointed to the metal casket-looking containers next to the boys' cell. "Two men came with you. They there…and they feed to Tanniyn."

Sam stumbled up to the bamboo bars, gripping them tightly, staring at the metal boxes.

"Are…are…they de—dead?" Sam stuttered.

"No dead, but horrible spot…they probably wish dead," she explained. "They put in dark, hot box for hour…Every few minute guard walk by and hit with stick. Sound make deaf and shake whole body. Never know when hit come…make go crazy."

"Did…did they put you in the box?" Sam barely got the words out through the intense stress.

"I try escape and they put me in box for whole day. Tell me they feed me to Tanniyn if I try again."

As they spoke, two soldiers marched by the cells with large bongo-style drums. They smacked their hands on the canvas creating a loud tribal beat as though they were part of a grand ceremony. Several more soldiers marched behind them in a military formation, their rifles slung over their shoulders, marching in unison to the beat of the drums.

***

Switch navigated the drone, following the road to the installation's coordinates, dropping below the tops of the trees to get a good image.

"Chief, take a look at this, there's another small checkpoint leading to the installation, two soldiers, but the compound itself looks like a fortress surrounded by mangrove swamp on all sides," Switch indicated, zooming in on the large concrete structure.

"Reminds me of Louisiana and gators," Johnny muttered, curling his lip.

"Man, sho do look like a prison to me," Bling suggested, standing on the tailgate and watching the tablet's screen. "Big walls, razor wires, guard towers, security gates. They either keepin' sumpin' locked up or sumpin' locked out."

"Or both," Chief surmised.

"Check out the huge symbol on the exterior," Switch zoomed in closer. "It's the same one we saw on the soldier's helmets and vehicles."

"See if you can get an infrared image inside the compound," Chief instructed.

"Converting over now."

Switch flew the drone higher, angling the camera to get a shot of the interior.

"Perfect! Stay right there," Chief watched, sketching out a diagram of the compound on his notepad.

"Let's see the backside now."

Switch flew the drone over the soldiers who gathered between the holding cells beating their drums, stopping at the rear of the installation.

"What is that?" Johnny asked, his eyes focused on a three-story-tall, square limestone structure about 15 meters from the rear of the compound. It had steps leading to the top from the compound's rear exit and a ramp on the opposite side.

"Looks like a massive platform," Switch submitted.

"Lookin' like an altar or a shine to me," Bling chimed in.

"Sure does," Chief agreed. "Okay, Switch, we've got what we need, bring it back," Chief instructed, making a few final notes while Switch flew the drone back to the truck.

"Alright team, listen closely. There's no way to be certain how many soldiers we'll be dealing with or their firepower. Y'all saw the compound—it's a rectangular structure with a sally port main entrance and an exit at the rear. I'm speculating here, but it looks to be about a football field long and half as wide. There are four guard towers at each corner and multiple guards walking the elevated catwalks. There are also four sets of elevated, ballfield-style halogen lights surrounding the complex."

"Boss, I counted at least a couple dozen soldiers," Johnny spoke up.

"Right. At least—and all of them are carrying small arms."

"Yo, so what was them soldier's doin'? Looked like they was gettin' ready for a ceremony," Bling interjected.

Switch nodded his head. "Yeah, that was odd—some of them were beating on drums like they were gearing up for a parade."

"Whatever it was, I'm hoping it's a distraction that can work to our advantage," Chief replied, holding up his notepad to show everyone his sketch of the installation. "This is a rough look at what we saw from the drone. These two buildings in the front look like make-shift stockades and there's a good possibility it's where they're holding Mack."

"What are those square buildings in the back?" Switch asked.

"My guess is that they're soldier's barracks. Behind them are two APCs. We'll need to keep an eye on them."

"How are we breaching?" Johnny asked.

"That's the thing. This will sound crazy, but I'm hoping they will see the boys and open the gates."

"That's super risky," Switch replied.

"It is, but it's our best shot."

"Boss, that tiny building in the front—is that the generator room?" Johnny asked, studying the sketch.

"I think so. Once we infiltrate, we'll need to take it out. That will give us tactical advantage—especially with our night-vision."

"Good call," Switch responded.

"Johnny, you'll be on sniper overwatch outside the compound. Be prepared to drop out of the truck. On my command, you'll take out the towers and soldiers from the catwalks. Switch, I need you in back on the Dushka. Johnny will give you a quick primer on how to use it. Make sure it's loaded and ready to rock. Your job will be to take out the bulk of their soldiers. Hopefully, they'll still be bunched up in the middle of the compound like what we just saw."

"Roger that."

"Does anyone have any questions before we roll out?"

"Yo, what's my job here, Chief? I ain't staying behind. I can do sumptin'," Bling stated.

"I thought you'd never ask. I need you to do what you do best…be flashy. You're gonna roll out with Johnny. Now, I ain't gonna ask you to shoot no one, but I do need you to take a gun and a couple grenades. You can fire the AK into the water for all I care. I need you to make a lot of noise when I tell you to and then move quickly from your position. And it's probably gonna require you to get wet. You down for that?"

"I'm not!" Johnny defiantly raised his chin.

"I can do flashy, Chief," Bling replied, interrupting Johnny's stubbornness.

"Good. We're rolling in five."

Before Chief finished speaking, Johnny moved to the edge of the dirt road and stared down the embankment at the swampy water. Three cranes stood at the edge of the brackish water stalking out worms in the rich, black soil.

"C'mon John boy, we haven't even started the op and you're already checkin' for reptiles," Switch smirked.

"Well, I need to get down there for some homemade camo, but, yeah, I'm no dummy. There's gonna be all kinds of stuff here that can kill us besides those kid-soldiers."

Against his better judgment, Johnny slid halfway down the embankment and dipped his hand into the stinky, black soil, keeping his eyes on the swamp as he spread the mud over his pants, shirt and face. After he was sufficiently covered, he raced back up to the truck and uncovered the Dushka to give Switch a basic rundown of its operation.

"Okay Switch, it's a little tricky at first," Johnny mentioned, opening the gun's receiver. Switch tried to focus, but he was distracted by the fact that he could only see the whites of Johnny's eyes and his pink lips, plus the disgusting smell.

"Yo, Johnny you rank bro!" Bling exclaimed, waving his hand back and forth in front of his nose.

"Try having it on your face. Hey, come on, Switch, pay attention here. In fact, you do it. Lift the metal receiver plate and load the belt. Close it down and pull back this charging arm and slam it forward."

"Easy enough," Switch replied, doing as Johnny instructed, successfully arming the gun.

Moments later, under the cover of darkness, the truck started up and backed out from the dirt path and pulled onto the road leading to the compound. They were only moments from their rescue attempt, and everyone silently questioned if it would be anything more than a suicide mission.

TWENTY-EIGHT
BREACHING

The boy-soldier drove the truck toward the installation, reaching the muddy lane that intersected with the main road a few minutes later. Chief motioned for him to turn down the road and as soon as he did he pushed off the truck's headlights.

The boy drove the truck down the lane, traversing over the deep ruts until the checkpoint came into view, but when they got closer they saw that it was unmanned. They continued on, slowing their speed considerably, keeping their eyes open for anything.

"Johnny-Bling, this is your exit. Watch for landmines, over," Chief communicated into his mic.

"Roger—and crocs," Johnny replied as he and Bling jumped out of the truck, heading in opposite directions and scanning the ground for tripwires and pressure switches. Bling carried an AK rifle with a grenade and flashbang clipped to his belt and Johnny carried the RPG and sniper rifle with the Claymore strapped around his waist in the fanny pack.

Bling reached the edge of the road and slid down the embankment, splashing into the shallow swamp water. A family of swamp rats scurried away, swimming stealthily through the water. Sweat was already dripping off Bling, but being around the stagnated water made it stifling; the air was so humid he could taste the mold as the smell crept into the back of his throat. He trudged through the mud, recalling Johnny's Ramree horror story and thoroughly checked his surroundings. He slogged through the water until it was up over his knees and eventually saw a sandy knoll protruding out of the water near a few trees, located about 20 meters from the left side of the compound.

"Chief, yo, I'm in my spot, over," Bling checked in.

"Copy that, Bling, wait for my order."

"Copy."

Johnny stealthily maneuvered down the side of the road for about 50 meters when he saw a massive tree close to the road that had a well-developed canopy, perfect for resting in its branches to overlook the compound. The only issue is that he would have to slog through about 15 feet of knee-high swamp water to get to it.

We won't be trudging through any swamps, Johnny muttered in a snide tone, recalling what Chief had told them and how it was now a lie. He stood at the edge of the stagnant swamp water, gazing at the green algae floating on top, scouring it for the slightest ripple or bubble. Seeing no movement, he cautiously stepped into the water and reached the tree several seconds later.

After he reached the tree, he removed several screw-in steps from his pack, placing the first one about three feet from the bottom. He rotated the step clockwise, drilling the screw into the tree's flesh until it grabbed hold. He repeated the process until he had climbed to the top of his overwatch spot.

"Team, we're at the front of the compound, but something's not right," Chief reported into his mic as he looked through his night-vision binoculars. "The lights are off and there's no movement of any kind. No guards in the towers, no one on the catwalks—even the sally port is empty, over."

"Roger that, I'll have eyes in a second," Johnny indicated from his perched position as he made a few adjustments on the sniper rifle's scope.

Now, this is odd. Where did everyone go? Chief mumbled to himself, gazing at the dark compound.

"Hold on, team. I've got something," Chief anxiously spoke into the mic, peering through the double-gated entrance.

Chief adjusted the zoom, trying to see through the slats of the gate and saw two torches at the rear of the compound, but it was too dark to see much else.

"Boss, I've got eyes on the compound," Johnny indicated as he positioned himself high up between two of the tree's branches, getting a look at the installation through the night-vision scope. "There's uh…there's some strange stuff goin' on behind the compound, over."

"Yeah, I can make out some of it as well, what are you seeing, over?" Chief asked as Switch and Bling listened intently.

"The troops we saw earlier are amassed in a large column near the rear gate, about three dozen boy-soldiers. They're staring out into the swamp at that altar-thing we saw. I can also make out a couple older, higher-ranking officers at the front of the column. One looks like the commander who took Mack, over."

"Good chance Mack is here then," Chief replied.

"Boss, something else. They're shouting something, but I can't make it out…Hang on, I'm seeing some movement near the stockades, over."

As Johnny was speaking, Chief reached for the truck's keys dangling from the ignition and turned it off, hoping to hear what they might be yelling.

"I hear the shouting as well. Sounds like they're repeating the word canteen, over," Chief cocked his head slightly, assuming he misheard their chant.

The soldiers marched in place in column formation, stomping their feet and shouting while a few soldiers carried torches in some type of ritualistic ceremony.

Sam watched the soldiers as they moved like zombies, their faces expressionless and eye's glazed over. Directly behind the column, separated into their own row, two soldiers fell out of formation. They weren't in rhythm and they didn't appear to be shouting. She squinted through the compound's dimly lit courtyard until her eyes relaxed on a familiar figure. It was Nyan and another boy-soldier.

"Sam, no stare. Soldier let us out soon," Shein insisted. "Can you walk?"

Desperately wanting to get out of the cell, Sam gathered all her strength and reached for Shein's outstretched hand, holding on to it tightly. Then she gripped one of the bamboo bars and a large tree roach crawled onto her hand. Unfazed, she shook it off and continued gazing into the courtyard, curious as to what was occurring.

"When get out, must shout Tanniyn, okay?" Shein advised.

"What? Why? I don't understand."

"Must say Tanniyn name and bow when soldier bow...or—"

"Or what?" Sam clenched her jaw, repelled at the thought of bowing down to an animal.

"Or feed you to Tanniyn."

Chief ushered the two boys out of the truck's cab and made them climb in the back with Switch, zip-tying their hands to the wooden planks next to the others. Then he hurried back to the gate with his bolt cutters, being careful not to be seen.

Pop! The lock snapped in half and he removed it, swinging the gate open. He hopped back into the truck, started it up, and drove into the sally port, stopping in front of the second gate.

"Tanniyn! Tanniyn! Tanniyn!" The soldiers shouted as they bowed in unison. The chants got louder and four soldiers broke off from the main group, two of them marching to the boy's stockade and two toward the girl's. When they reached the stockade they turned and stood with their backs to the barred doors. Then two more soldiers broke away and marched to the metal sweatboxes, opening one up and forcibly removing a young teen boy. The boy kicked and screamed furiously as they tried dragging him to the rear of the compound.

"What are they doing?" Sam asked Shein as she watched the soldiers tie the boy's feet together.

"He try escape, too. They feed him to Tanniyn."

Sam gulped hard, choking back tears as she considered Mike's fate.

Switch spoke into his mic. "What's going on up there, Chief, over?" he asked as his hands cramped from holding the Dushka's handle.

"They don't know we're here. They're lost in the ceremony. Right now, some soldiers have unlocked what looks like a sweatbox and pulled out a teen boy. Just be ready."

"Copy that," Switch replied as Johnny and Bling listened to the report.

Chief continued watching through his night-vision binoculars as the soldiers hogtied the boy, dragging him to the back gate. Once they reached it the gate swung open and another soldier carrying a two-foot-long wooden torch marched into the swamp ahead of them.

The soldier waded through waist-deep water until he reached the altar. Once there, he climbed onto the first step and ascended to the platform, lighting up two torches connected to it, each one about ten feet apart. The soldier lit the torches as the other two dragged the boy to the top, securing him to the platform with ropes.

"Looks like they're strapping the boy down for some type of backwoods' sacrifice," Johnny suggested.

Switch and Bling listened closely, stunned by what they were hearing.

"Tanniyn! Tanniyn! Tanniyn!" the column of soldiers shouted at the top of their lungs and stomped their feet in unison almost as though they were building up to a climax. Then, out of nowhere, a lurid, blood-curdling sound boomed from the swamp near the altar, interrupting their chants. The ghastly sound echoed off the compound's walls and everyone who heard it shuddered.

Sam stepped away from the bars, her eyes bulging from her head. "Wha…what was that?" she stuttered out, but Shein didn't answer.

"Guys, you hear that?" Johnny asked as he checked the swamp, waiting to see what had made the horrifying noise.

"Yo, it sounded like sumtin' from dem Jurrasic movies?" Bling was the only one to respond, his head on a swivel as he scrutinized the swamp that surrounded him. "Y'all gots me in dis here bayou knowin' creatures be killin' black folk first."

"Keep it together, guys. We'll gonna make our move and be out soon," Chief replied, looking out the back gate and silently questioning what could have made the strange sound. As everyone considered the possibilities, the noise erupted again—this time even louder. Its shrieking was so horribly loud that Johnny's chest cavity vibrated like deep bass from a concert loudspeaker.

"Hey, um, boss, I've got eyes on the swamp area just past the altar. Something big is out there and it's moving fast…it's causing the mangrove vines to sway in the water."

"Copy that. Hold your position, over."

"Copy."

Chief surveilled the altar closely, somewhat mesmerized by the events that were unfolding. He wanted to believe that whatever they were hearing was a typical jungle animal, but after hearing the strange sound and recalling Johnny's crocodile story, he couldn't help but speculate if they were about to see a creature unknown to the modern world.

Chief reached for his cell phone and opened the video recorder, zooming in as far as he could. He propped the phone up on the truck's dashboard and attempted to focus in on the altar, but the low light was making it difficult. As he waited and watched, two more soldiers broke away from the column and marched toward the girl's cell.

"Boss, I've got movement at the other stockade, over."

"Copy that," Chief replied, keeping one eye on the phone and the other on the soldier's movements.

"Sam, head down," Shein whispered as one of the soldiers unlocked the stockade door, swinging it open for the girls to exit. The girls arranged themselves in a single-file line at the stockade door as Sam clung to the bamboo bars.

"Sam, must get line!" Shein whispered a little louder, but she didn't move. She didn't have the strength, plus she didn't have any intentions of worshipping some animal.

The first girl exited the cell, moving alongside the outside of the column of soldiers as though she had done this several times before. She stepped to the front of the column into the courtyard between the stockades and stopped while the other girls moved in behind her, staying in line. With one last attempt, Shein tugged on Sam's T-shirt as she walked out, but she wasn't budging.

Furious at Sam's refusal to comply, the soldier entered the cell and grabbed her shirt, throwing her down to the ground and ripping it in the process. She rolled to the back of the cell and he followed after, kicking her in the ribs. Then he removed the rifle from his shoulder, aiming at her head.

"Htwatswarr!" the soldier shouted angrily. Sam cringed from the pain and gasped for breath as the soldier yanked her hair, forcibly pulling her out of the cell into the courtyard.

Johnny spotted her first. "Boss, you gettin' this, over?"

"Roger, blonde hair—"

"Do you think she's our girl?"

"Possible, but Mack is still our priority. Everyone hold your position."

"Copy that," Switch replied as Bling considered the chatter.

The soldier escorted Sam from the cell, leaving her in the middle of the courtyard while two other soldiers unlocked the opposite cell, releasing a dozen boys and lining them up behind the girls. Then the soldiers moved to one of the sweatboxes and unlocked it. Chief looked on, wondering if Mack was inside. They lifted the metal lid and reached down and grabbed Mike by his hair, pulling him out. He was lying on the ground, barely moving. They bound his hands together and kicked him in his stomach and then moved to the other sweatbox.

One soldier held his hand on the lid and the other removed his rifle from his shoulder, aiming at the box.

This isn't a typical prisoner; it's someone dangerous—someone, like Mack, Chief thought. They opened it up and confirmed his suspicions.

"Boss!"

"I see him!" Chief exclaimed.

Switch jumped up and peered over the cab of the truck, getting his eyes on Mack for the first time. It was clear by his bruised, swollen, and bloodied body that he had been beat up pretty severely.

"Guys, Mack...he...he's in bad shape...I doubt he can walk," Chief struggled to get the words out, watching as they hogtied him like the other boy. "I think they intend to take him to the altar."

"Not gonna happen, boss!"

"Johnny, when they start dragging him, that's your sign to take out as many as you can from that catwalk."

"Roger that! My pleasure, boss!"

TWENTY-NINE
BONE CHILLING

C hief kept his eyes on Mack and Sam, but he couldn't stop thinking about the mysterious sound that had come from beyond the altar, wondering what kind of creature could have made it. As he considered different large animals, the beast crawled up from the swamp onto the altar's ramp, its every step sounding like a sledgehammer slamming down on concrete.

The beast climbed to the top of the altar and stared down at the soldiers and prisoners who were still shouting and bowing down before it.

"Boss, you getting this?"

"I am."

"What is y'all talkin' 'bout?" Bling asked, already creeped out by the creature's eerie shriek and the swamp in general.

"Yeah, what's making that pounding noise?" Switch asked, still waiting behind the Dushka.

"Y'all just hold your position…and your fire," Chief replied, trying to calm their uncertainties. "We'll make our move soon."

"Yeah, copy that," Johnny replied, his eyes glued to the altar.

Chief checked his phone to be sure it was still focused on the altar, zooming out and back in again to get the best shot. As the video came into focus, he caught a glimpse of two glowing red circles a foot apart, each about the size of tennis balls. Chief knew he was looking at the beast's eyes, and he had never seen anything like them before. Each circle had dark black slits down the center, similar to a snake's eyes, and they were oddly mesmerizing. As he zoomed in closer, he caught a blurry image of the large-framed beast. Chief's pupil's dilated and his skin turned clammy as he attempted to focus further, but before he could the creature backed away.

Chief kept his eyes fixed on the altar and it wasn't long before the beast's glowing eyes appeared again, the torch's flickering flames briefly reflecting off of them as it once again observed the soldiers and children who had bowed down before it. Chief could make out the outline of its massive body, but nothing more.

The creature stood over the boy, lowering its head to inspect him and Chief and Johnny watched in suspense, almost refusing to blink. Then it bowed down at the top of the ramp, flaring its nostrils wide as it inhaled the musty scent of the frightened boy who was squirming with every last ounce of energy to get free. It shook its head and snorted out so powerfully that it appeared as though a slight mist of light shot out from its snout. Seconds later, it twisted wildly and swung its massive tail, slicing through the darkness and slamming it into both torches, cutting them in half, the lit sections falling into the swamp, instantly snuffing them out.

With nothing but thick darkness surrounding it, the beast let out a jolting roar and snatched the boy into its jaws, clamping down with an inconceivable amount of force, ripping apart the thick rope and snapping the boy's bones in the process. The boy cried out the most horrifying scream anyone had ever heard from a human, and then everything went silent—eerily silent.

The soldiers who had been holding onto Mike and Mack checked the knots in their ropes one last time, preparing to take them to the altar. Nyan watched helplessly, but there was nothing he could do to stop it. He looked at Sam but her vacant stare indicated that she had already checked out—her mind protecting her from what she was about to endure.

The soldiers parted the column again and they began dragging Mike and Mack to the altar. That was the sign. Johnny aligned his scope's crosshairs on one of the unsuspecting soldiers who stood nearly hypnotized on the catwalk. He calmed his breathing and gradually squeezed the rifle's trigger.

Phttttt. The bullet spun out of the sniper rifle's suppressed barrel and pierced the soldier's head, a fine pinkish mist exiting the back of the wound like paint expelling from a spray can.

Phttttt. He aimed at the next soldier, firing again with the same result. Within seconds he had silently neutralized several soldiers, their bodies flopping down on the suspended catwalk.

Nyan couldn't hear the gunshots, but he saw the soldiers dropping into heaps of flesh. His heart raced as he turned to see who was firing, but saw no one. He darted to the girl's stockade for cover, scanning the compound and noticing the truck in the sally port; it hadn't been there before the ceremony started and he wondered if the American military was there to rescue Mike and Sam.

General Htun noticed the dead soldiers on the catwalk and scurried behind one of the nearby barracks, screaming out commands to the dazed soldiers. It took them a few seconds to break out of their worshipful gaze, but they eventually took cover, their rifles aimed in every direction and blind-firing sporadically. They couldn't see Johnny and had no idea where the attack was coming from. Seconds later, the large halogen lights flickered on, emitting a soft, yellowish glow.

"Bling, throw your grenade now!" Chief commanded, knowing the compound would be lit up like daytime within a few moments.

"Roger!" Bling pulled a pin from flashbang and flung it into the water.

Kerplunk! The flashbang submerged into the water but it didn't detonate. He waited a few seconds, but nothing happened so he pulled the pin of the frag grenade and hurled it at a tree that was about 10 meters away and then followed up with several bursts from the AK. He fired it into the air while plodding through the swamp, back to the road.

Boom!

Sam heard the grenade's explosion and dropped to the compound's dirt floor, laying on her stomach and frantically moving her body around on all fours, attempting to see what was happening. As the lights grew brighter, the soldiers fired in the direction of the explosion while Johnny continued sniping, his body count rising into near double digits.

He put the glowing crosshairs on another soldier's head when the creature shrieked again, this time more aggressively. The soldiers momentarily stopped firing and checked to be sure the beast wasn't anywhere close and then returned to scanning for the armed ghosts hunting them.

With the soldiers temporarily preoccupied, Nyan saw an opportunity to help Sam find cover. He weaved through some soldiers and placed his arm around her, helping her move back into the stockade. She knelt down behind the bamboo bars and traced her eyes through the courtyard hoping this was the rescue of which she fantasized.

Mack barely heard the gunshots through his excruciating pain, but he knew Chief and the team were assaulting the compound. He rolled to his side to get a better view, looking through his puffy eyes at the transport truck in the sally port. He covered his eyes with his hand to shield the light and could see Chief sitting behind the wheel.

Moments later, Chief drove the truck forward past Mack, angling it to provide him with a temporary shield.

"Switch, get ready to give me a hand with Mack," Chief indicated.

"Roger," Switch replied.

"Johnny, give us some suppressive fire, over."

"Copy," Johnny affirmed as he pulled the bolt back on the rifle and chambered another round into the gun, peering through the scope and scanning the courtyard for immediate threats. Not even a second later he had his first target, a soldier who crept up to the truck and waited at the rear corner to get the drop on Chief.

Phttt. Johnny squeezed the trigger, sending a bullet downrange and striking him in the temple, his young body crumpling under the tailgate.

"Now, Switch!"

Switch jumped out and he and Chief grabbed Mack, pulling him to the rear of the truck.

"Hey, old man, it's us!" Chief shouted over the noise of the gunfire.

"About time," Mack grumbled, trying to disguise his intense pain.

Tink, tink, ping. Three soldiers fired on the truck from the rear of the compound as General Htun hid behind them barking out orders. Johnny saw them but was busy taking out two other soldiers armed with RPGs.

The soldiers marched into the courtyard, forming a v-shaped pattern, firing their weapons in every direction, and one of the Russians ran out behind them, armed with a heavy machine gun. He pulled the gun's bipod down and set it up on the ground under the legs of one of the soldiers. As he readied the weapon, the soldiers each threw a grenade into the middle of the courtyard.

Boom!

Boom!

Boom! The grenades sent shrapnel ripping through the courtyard, cutting down most of the boys and girls and even a few of the soldiers.

Sam peered into the courtyard as the smoke settled, hoping Mike and Shein made it through the blasts. Amazingly, because Mike was huddled near a concrete barrier, he had been spared, but Shein had taken a direct hit to her leg and blood was spurting everywhere. Without thinking, Sam hobbled out of the cell to help her, but when she did the Russian fired the heavy machine gun.

Bratttatttattttatt! A barrage of lead spilled from the automatic weapon, tearing through some of the children in the courtyard and filling the transport truck with gaping holes. Chief ducked down in time, but a bullet sliced through the slat and hit Switch in the leg.

"Argh!" he yelled through the intense burning sensation. The bullet had hit the front of his sat phone that had been strapped in his cargo pocket and missed his leg, but it damaged the battery, causing the acid to spill out.

Switch quickly pulled out the phone to stop the burning. "Oh, thank you, phone. Phew!" Switch wiped his brow and climbed the steps on the passenger side of the truck to get an elevated view to the compound to fire back, but when he did, he saw that the boy-soldiers in the truck had been killed, their blood filling the wooden bed.

"Chief, the boys are gone, over."

"Copy. Stay on mission."

"Rog…roger that," Switch replied solemnly, pulling the boys out to the ground and retraining his gun on another target.

Johnny listened in and focused the scope's crosshairs on the Russian, but before he could fire, three soldiers closed up around him and they all moved back to one of the barracks, hiding behind it.

"Boss, the Russian is using guerrilla tactics. If you get back in the truck, he's gonna take all of you out, and I don't have a shot, over."

"Copy, that. What's his position, over?"

"Behind the right barracks."

"Copy. Keep shooting at them!"

"Copy that."

Chief grabbed a grenade from the pouch on his vest and edged to the rear of the truck. He was going to use the grenade for the generator, but the Russian was a more pressing problem.

"Switch, give me some cover."

"Got it."

Switch pushed his eyeglasses further up his nose and rested his MP5 on the truck's cab, checking the area and motioning to Chief to move out.

Chief stepped out, but as he was about to throw the grenade two soldiers confronted him, raising their guns, but before they could fire, Nyan took both of them out, firing on them from behind the bars of the girl's stockade. Stunned, Chief turned to see who had fired from inside the dark cell. Seconds later, Nyan stepped out into the light, Sam's arm draped over his shoulder. Chief nodded as he pulled the grenade's pin and threw it as far as he could toward the barracks and then ran to help Nyan get Sam to the truck.

Boom! The grenade blew near the target, but it was slightly off target, exploding at the front side of the barracks, blowing open the door.

"Boss, the grenade missed, but I think I can hit it with the RPG, over."

"Do it!"

Johnny climbed down the tree and reached for the launcher resting on the limbs and climbed back into his overwatch. He raised the launcher, resting the hollow metal tube on his shoulder and aimed at the target through the iron sights.

"Boss, I'm in position with the launcher."

"Fire!"

Johnny pressed the trigger and a ball of fire erupted from the rear of the tube, sending the rocket zooming over the wall, past the truck and finally detonating about 20 feet from the barracks. A plume of black smoke billowed from the explosion as Chief assisted Sam into the truck.

"Switch, give me a hand with Mack," Chief yelled.

"Roger!"

Switch climbed down and moved to the tailgate, helping Chief hoist Mack into the truck.

"Boss, it's a miss, over."

"Copy that. We've got Mack and the girl. You and Bling get ready for extract, over."

"Copy," Bling replied from his crouched position at the side of the road, watching the front of the compound and the swamp behind him.

"Copy that. I've only got a few rounds left. I'll provide cover as long as I can."

"Switch, get on the Dushka…get ready!"

"Roger."

Chief climbed into the truck, engaging it into gear as sporadic gunfire ricocheted off the truck from the soldiers who were hiding at the edges of the buildings.

Nyan stood behind the truck, firing back, but he soon ran out of bullets. He thought about climbing into the truck, but he knew they needed help. Putting himself aside, he scrambled for another gun lying on the ground.

Ratat! Ratat! Ratat! An array of bullets erupted from the rear of the compound as the Russian and the other soldiers moved from one building to the next, encroaching several meters closer to the truck. Nyan grabbed another rifle and tried to fire back, but the gun had jammed. He pulled the charging bolt back to clear it, but before he could, one of the soldiers popped out from behind the left barracks and shot him in the shoulder, severing a major artery. He collapsed to the ground, screaming in agony.

"Chief, the girl is going ballistic back here. She's trying to jump out. Something about her boyfriend only being a few feet away," Switch pressed the mic button as he tried to hold her back.

"I see him. Hold on!"

Chief turned the truck to create a barrier between Mike and the soldiers and jumped out.

"Give me a hand here, Switch!" Chief yelled as he ran along the back of the truck.

"Roger!"

He jumped out and met up with Chief, waiting at the edge of the truck, watching for anyone who would try and attack them. As they waited, a fine mist settled over the compound and within seconds the sky opened, releasing a moderate rain on them.

"Boss, the Russian's back!" Chief listened through his earpiece as Johnny's agitated voice pierced through the sporadic popping of gunfire and the light rainfall. He and Switch dropped to the ground as Johnny placed the sniper rifle into his shoulder pocket again, aiming at the group of soldiers who had amassed around the Russian and his machine gun.

Phttt! Johnny fired into the group, taking out two soldiers who were standing staggered behind one another. Switch also fired, hitting one of the soldiers. He checked his shot and fired again, eliminating another soldier until only the Russian remained. With his cover gone, the Russian bolted from behind the machine gun back to the barracks.

Phttt! Johnny fired his last sniper round, missing the Russian by only millimeters.

Disregarding the danger, Sam collected her energy and climbed down from the truck, moving through the courtyard past Chief and Switch who were on their stomachs, their guns aimed at the corners of the barracks, waiting for the Russian to pop back out. Sam stumbled over to Mike, and when she reached him, she slid down next to him, placing her hand on his cold, wet arm.

"Mike! Come on! They're rescuing us!" She yelled, but he didn't move.

A couple soldiers popped out from the barracks and Chief and Switch provided cover fire for her as she tried to get Mike to move, but he was incoherent and nearly lifeless. Chief looked over at him, examining his eyes, seeing it before Sam did. They were dull, almost as though his soul had left him. There was no way she could get him back to the truck on her own.

Chief checked for soldiers, and seeing it was clear, darted over to Sam, reaching the concrete barrier. He ducked behind it, resting his MP5's barrel on the barrier and scanned the courtyard for combatants.

Every few seconds, sporadic gunfire erupted, zooming over their heads as the soldiers hid behind the barracks, continuing to blind-fire their rifles.

With no time to waste, Chief grabbed Mike under his arms and dragged him toward the truck. Sam followed close behind but had difficulty keeping up. Seconds later, Switch met up with Chief and they slid Mike's wet, limp body into the bed of the truck.

Sam stepped up onto the truck's bumper and looked back to see if she could find Shein. Her eyes looked past the now heavy rain, skimming over piles of bodies, bouncing her eyes off the blood and severed body parts until she finally located her. She was knelt down, her black hair covered in blood. Sam stared at her for a moment, holding her breath for any sign of life. Finally, she saw a slight movement. Without thinking, she stepped off the bumper and made a move toward Shein, but Chief saw what she intended to do and grabbed her from behind.

"No, it's too dangerous!"

"I'm not leaving her!" Sam angrily countered, trying to yank her arms out of his tight grip.

"Look back there!" Chief spun her around so she could see a handful of soldiers who were treading through the muddy compound to the armored personnel carriers.

"Once they get on those autocannons, we won't stand a chance…none of us will make it out of here! I want to rescue everyone, but we can't right now!" he exclaimed, his eyes conveying the severity of the situation.

Not fully understanding the danger they were in, Sam pursed her lips in defiance and attempted to take off to help Shein. Without saying another word, Chief blocked her and lifted her into the truck. She kicked and screamed like a little child, but deep down she knew Chief was right. It was too risky. Shein was on the other side of the courtyard and she likely wouldn't live even if she were rescued.

"Lay down! If you jump out, I'm not coming back!" Chief shouted intolerantly, slamming the tailgate closed and moving back to the cab.

"Switch, get in!" Chief exclaimed.

"Copy," he replied, climbing into the back.

Chief climbed into the cab, putting the truck into gear while Sam knelt down near the tailgate, fixated on Shein. She stared at her through the moderate rain and did the only thing within her power. She prayed.

"God, Shein has endured horrible things here. Please help her through this. I don't know what else to say. Amen." Sam finished her short prayer and a strange peace enveloped her. She called out to Shein and she slowly twisted in her direction, her face bloodied and dirty. With all the strength she had, Shein formed the heart sign with her hands. Sam pressed her hands together to tell her to pray with the remaining time she had left. Shein pressed her hands together and then her chin suddenly dropped to her chest as though her soul had left her body.

THIRTY
CONVOY

Chief eased the truck into the sally port, checking the catwalk above them for soldiers, but Johnny had done a perfect job at eliminating them. As he drove through, Sam rested against the tailgate, still thinking about Shein. She looked back into the compound one final time and when she did she saw the other Russian standing at the back corner of the boy's stockade, aiming his rifle at the truck. She ducked down, bracing for gunfire.

Ratatat! Ratatat! The Russian fired at the truck repeatedly, striking it multiple times and barely missing everyone inside.

"Switch!" Chief shouted into his mic. "Take him out!"

"Copy!" Switch rotated the Dushka, aligning the corner of the barracks in the round sight and then pulled back the butterfly trigger.

Bratatatatatatatat! The large, anti-material bullets rained from the heavy machine gun, obliterating the stockade and cutting down the Russian standing behind it, taking him out of commission.

The weapon's thunderous cracking sound resonated through the dark, swampy jungle, producing a sustained echo, but it wasn't close to being the fiercest sound out there. Seconds later, the creature bellowed out a sharp, deafening, shriek. It was so loud it seemed only a few meters away.

"Russian eliminated, over," Switch indicated, ignoring the creature's horrifying screech.

"Boss?"

"Yeah, I heard it. Johnny, get down from there."

Johnny didn't respond. He had caught a partial image of the beastly creature as it swiftly maneuvered through the swamp water, heading straight for the compound.

Switch radioed in. "Chief, I've got movement on the APCs. We'll be taking fire any second, over!"

"Copy that!" Chief yelled, stomping on the gas pedal and sending a plume of dark smoke billowing out of the truck's exhaust as he drove the rutty lane.

Both of the APC's gun turrets rotated and locked onto the truck.

Boom! Boom! The autocannons fired simultaneously, hitting the compound's walls and the front gate seconds after Chief drove through.

Brataaatbraaaataaaaatbraaaaat! Switch unleashed the Dushka, bombarding the APCs with bullets, but they did nothing but dent the thick armor.

Johnny descended from the tree, contemplating the horror he had seen. He got a foot from the bottom step and looked down at the shallow swamp water and a deep panic came over him. He paused momentarily, attempting to disregard the feeling, but it happened again, this time much stronger, almost as though his body was having one big muscle spasm. Seconds later, Chief drove up and Bling climbed into the truck, but Johnny was nowhere in sight.

"Johnny, come in, over?" Chief spoke fast. "We've gotta go now!" he finished as he removed his tactical flashlight and scanned the swamp where he had dropped him off earlier. Eventually he located him clinging to a tree a few meters from the road.

"Johnny? What's goin' on? We gotta go!" Chief called out, but he didn't respond.

"Switch," Chief radioed. "Something's wrong with Johnny. Grab an RPG and take out the first APC that comes through the gate, over."

"Copy that," Switch replied as he rummaged through the crates, finding the launcher, but before he could set it up one of the APCs pulled into the sally port.

"Hey, Sam, right?" Switch asked, raising his voice over the noisy engine, and moving behind the Dushka. "Can you help me here?"

She nodded, pulling herself up and situating herself behind the machine gun.

"Just keep this round sight on that vehicle and pull the trigger," he instructed.

"Umm...okay..." she replied, looking over the massive weapon.

"Do it now," he replied as he gripped the rocket grenade and loaded into the launcher.

Brataaaatbrataaaatbrataaaat! She held the trigger back and ten rounds of lead per second bludgeoned the APC, the bullets cracking its plated windows, but seconds later it stopped firing as smoke billowed from the end of the barrel.

"I think it's out of bullets!" Sam shouted, her ears ringing horribly from the loud gunfire.

"Everyone, get down!" Switch yelled as he stood near the truck's tailgate, hoisting the RPG to his shoulder. He took a wide stance and aimed for the APC.

Swooooooooooosh! Boom!

The grenade hit the APC's front tire and the side of the sally port, twisting the metal gate and crumbling the cinder blocks around it, eliminating the threat.

Johnny was still clinging to the large teak tree when Chief entered the edge of the swamp. He called out again, but after not getting a response, he slogged through the knee-high swamp water until he was only a few feet from him.

"Johnny!" Chief shouted as loud as he could to get his attention, but there was still no response. Chief walked around the tree to get a look at his face and noticed that his fingernails had dug into the bark.

"I don't know what's goin' on, but I'm gonna reach up and pull you down slowly. You gotta problem with that?" he asked, not waiting for a response. He reached up and gently tugged at his foot, hoping it would shake him out of his daze, but all he got was a reflexive foot stomp on his hand.

"Argh!" Chief yowled, shaking his hand.

"Chief, we got a problem here!" Switch shouted into his mic. "I can see the other APC's headlights—it's coming around the rear of the compound!"

Without saying another word, Chief jerked both of Johnny's feet from the steps, sending him splashing face-first into the swamp. Johnny lay on all fours face down in the murky water, almost as though he were dead. Suddenly, his head popped up and he drew in a deep breath, shaking his head while his eyes refocused. The caked-on mud he applied earlier slid off his face as he scanned the area, still in a daze. Then a moment of awakening hit him. Like a cat that had been thrown into a bathtub, every muscle contracted and he jumped up from the swamp and raced to the truck, climbing into the bed.

Chief grabbed the sniper rifle and followed closely behind, reaching the cab as the APC rumbled into the swamp, using its amphibious capabilities to maneuver through the water to the front of the compound.

Chief climbed back inside, listening to the APC's unique turbodiesel sound, knowing it was getting closer.

"Hang on, y'all," he yelled back as he pressed hard on the truck's gas pedal.

"Switch, you got eyes on that other APC?" Chief shouted into his mic.

"Negative, Chief. I hear it…but I also used the last RPG and I'm out of ammo on the Dushka. What do you want me to do?"

"Not sure yet. If you got an idea, now's the time to share," Chief indicated, trying to hold the truck on the rutty road.

"Johnny, what happened back there?" Switch turned to him as he gripped the truck's side wood slats to avoid being tossed around. Johnny was on one knee and his pale face showed a bit of color as it returned to normal.

"I—I guess I just...I froze up."

"I got that, but why? I've never seen you like that."

"That creat—that mon—monster—" his voice quaked.

"I heard it, Johnny. Sounded awful, but probably just some jungle animal—"

"Yo, dat thing sounds super creepy," Bling replied, sitting next to Mike, his head on a swivel.

"No," Johnny closed his eyes, shaking his head.

"What do you mean, no?" Switch asked.

"I—I saw the outline of it," Johnny paused momentarily, taking a slow, profound gulp. "It's terrifying—it moves like a monster croc but it's even larger—bigger than an elephant." Johnny stopped blinking and his eyes glazed over, recounting what he had seen.

"Johnny, come on—are you sure you saw that? I mean, it's really dark out here. Maybe your storytelling has you spooked."

"No, Switch!" Johnny angrily faced off with him, his eyes intense.

"Okay, okay, easy there," Switch deflected. "At least you're starting to come back to normal," he mumbled.

As they talked, the APC rolled up out of the swamp onto the muddy lane, pulling away from the compound, its headlights lighting up the road behind them.

"Chief, the APC is closing in on us, fast, over?" Switch relayed as he looked back at its headlights.

"Our only hope is to outrun them."

"Roger that." Switch replied as Chief drove the truck in a zigzag pattern so the APC couldn't lock its autocannon onto their position. Moments later, the truck bounced over a rut and an ammo can that Mike had been leaning against slid out from under him and hit Sam's foot. She recognized that it was for the machine gun and kicked it over to Switch and then helped Mike lay down on the truck's bed

"Good job!" Switch exclaimed, trying to keep his balance as he opened the can and stretched out two 50-round ammo belts.

"I've got this!" Johnny indicated, moving behind Switch and grabbing the Dushka's wooden handles.

"You sure?"

"I'm good."

"Well, alright then," Switch replied, moving out of his way. Johnny inserted a bullet belt and aimed low at the APC's front tires, squeezing the trigger and blasting through the first belt. Hot shell casings fell into the bed as the bullets shredded the APC's rubber tires. The APC quickly dropped back, unable to keep up with the truck.

Chief continued driving the truck as fast as he could, creating a nice gap between them and the APC, his wipers rapidly swinging back and forth. It wasn't long before they arrived at the intersection of the main road out of Ramree, but as he got closer, he could see that the road was lit up by vehicle lights. He slowed the truck to a crawl, cautiously nosing it out past the dense jungle trees to where he could see down the road. He peered through his night vision binoculars and counted two jeeps and a troop transport truck full of soldiers.

Ping! Sing! A few bullets hit the front end of the truck and a spotlight lit up the intersection as Chief put the truck in reverse, backing up behind the trees.

"We gotta problem guys," Chief announced over the radio. "Our exit out of here is clogged up by an oncoming convoy. We're gonna head the opposite direction and see if we can find somewhere to lay low until daylight."

Switch glanced at Johnny and he could almost see the anxiety flowing through his body, but they were out of options. Chief pulled out into the intersection and drove away from the convoy, pushing the truck as fast as it could go.

Whiz...whiz...sing...tink! Gunfire erupted from the convoy, zooming around them and hitting the truck's two rear tires on the right side, deflating them almost instantly. Chief continued driving as the rubber disintegrated and the rims rolled on the concrete. Sparks lit up as it swerved erratically, pulling them near a deep ravine leading to the swamp. Chief gripped the steering wheel and jerked it back, correcting their path as the last second. As they leveled out, Johnny aimed the Dushka at the convoy.

Bratatbratatbratat! Johnny squeezed the trigger emptying the last ammo belt, hitting one of the jeeps and sending it careening down the embankment into the swamp.

Swooooosh! A soldier standing in the back of the other jeep fired an RPG at the truck and the rocket exploded in the swamp water next to it, launching a geyser of mud into the night air.

"Boss, we won't stand a chance with this convoy behind us," Johnny radioed.

"Copy! There's another road up ahead. We'll turn down it and make our stand there. Get ready to jump out."

Switch looked at Mack and the kids who were huddled together and drenched from the downpours. He removed his pistol, racked a round into the chamber and crawled over to Mack.

"Hey old man, how you holding up?"

"Not...not so...goo—ahhh," he replied, his body almost as white as a sheet of paper. "Lots of pay—pain."

"Bling, toss me a medical kit!" Switch yelled, sitting across from him on the opposite side of the truck. Bling reached into Mack's gear bag and tossed him the kit. Switch pulled out a morphine syringe and poked it into his arm.

"You should feel better soon."

Mack nodded, still cringing in anguish.

"When we get to a good place to rest, we'll hook you up on a portable IV bag and get some liquid in you. Just hang in there!"

THIRTY-ONE
BAD OMEN

Chief turned down what he assumed was a road, but it was nothing more than an abandoned trail, strangled closed by thick vegetation, but there was no time to turn back. He slowly drove through the jungle's overgrowth, snapping vines and pulling down willows. He checked his mirrors, expecting to see the convoy's light, but they never appeared. He pushed on, but it wasn't long before the vegetation became too thick for the truck to continue.

Chief jumped out of the cab and moved to the back, his words rushed. "Listen up; we need to get out of here before that convoy gets here."

"Seems like they should already be here by now," Switch spoke up.

"They probably linked up with the other soldiers at the compound. In any case, they will be here shortly. Bling, you and me will move down the trail with Mack and the kids. Grab your gear and the machetes."

"Yo, copy that," Bling replied as he reached into his gear bag and pulled out a baggy pair of sweatpants, holding them out to Sam.

"Young lady, these is probably way too big and kinda hot for—" Sam snatched them out of his hand before he could finish, slipping them on over her tiny waist.

"Thank you," she spoke softly.

"Switch, take one of the Claymores and set it up a few meters from the truck. Johnny, cover him. Make sure y'all detonate it so it causes max damage. After it blows, the soldiers will be in shock and should give y'all enough time to fall back to us."

"Understood," Switch replied, digging into Mack's gear bag for the Claymore. Johnny didn't say anything; he was busy staring into the swamp that was only a few feet away.

Chief knocked on the truck's bed to get his attention. "You gonna be able to do this, brother?"

"Yeah…yeah, boss, no problem here," he snapped out of his gaze, reaching for his MP5 to provide overwatch from the back of the truck while Switch set up the Claymore at the side of the trail.

Chief threw his gear bag over his shoulder and crouched down to help Mack up. "Bling, I'm gonna need your help here. Think you can help me with Mack and still swing the machete?"

"I'll try my best, yo."

"Samantha, can you help your boyfriend?" Chief asked as the rain nearly stopped, sporadic drops pitter-pattering on the large palms above them.

"I think so…and you can call me Sam," she stated.

"Okay, Sam it is," he replied, holding up Mack with one hand and gripping the machete with the other. Bling draped Mack's other arm over his shoulder as he and Chief slashed at the thick vegetation, cutting a path.

Switch finished covering the Claymore with leaves and unraveled the detonation wire as he moved back to the truck. "Boss, Switch has the Claymore set."

"Roger that."

Chief and Bling hacked away at the undergrowth with their machetes, its air-slicing swoosh and metal-to-vine pinging filling the damp air along with the aroma of freshly cut foliage and the ground's rotting leaves.

"Boss, I can see spotlights—looks like the convoy," Johnny radioed to Chief who was about 10 meters into the dense jungle.

"Copy that. Make good use of that Claymore and meet up with us ASAP, over."

"Copy," Johnny replied, hopping down from the truck and moving behind a nearby tree, his gun concentrated on the convoy.

Switch squatted near the front of the truck, holding the detonator as the convoy lit the trail up with its spotlights.

"Chief, the convoy has stopped where the trail intersects with the road and I can hear voices; sounds like the troops are coming in on foot, over," Switch whispered into his mic.

"Copy, see if they group up and hit them with all you got!"

"Roger that."

Chief and Bling continued with Mack and the kids down the trail; it was a slow go, but they were making progress. Chief used the red light on his flashlight to guide their way, preserving his natural night-vision and helping hide their movements. Moments later, they came to a dead end. The trail was blocked by a tree and two smaller paths forked around it in opposite directions. Chief squatted down and everyone rested, waiting for Johnny and Switch.

"Sam, I'm going to give your boyfriend some smelling salts; it might shake him out of his daze," Chief stated.

"O—okay" She replied as Bling propped him up against an adjacent mangrove shoot. Chief ripped open the salt and waved it under Mike's nose but there was little response.

"Well, it was worth a shot, but he's not—" Chief paused. "Hang on…"

"I saw it, too!" Sam exclaimed, watching as Mike's eyes slowly dilated. Without any warning, he scrambled to his feet and took off through the tall weeds, stopping in front of the large tree at the fork in the trail, his eyes expanded wide.

"Son, are you okay?" Chief inquired as he stood behind him, watching intently.

"Mike?" Sam called out.

Mack opened one of his puffy and blood coated eyes to see what the commotion was about. He tried to pull himself up to get a better look at Mike but when he did coughed profusely.

"Mack, you okay?" Chief asked, kneeling down next to him with a rag to suppress the noise from his cough.

"I...I don't think I'll make it much long—"

"You gotta hang in there, ol' buddy...do you hear me?" Chief encouraged him, pulling out his cell phone to check for a signal, but they were too far into the jungle for any cell communications. Chief had to act fast. If they didn't get Mack to a doctor soon, they would be taking him home in a body bag.

"Bling, toss me an IV bag!"

Bling unzipped his bag and removed an IV kit, throwing it to Chief and Sam raced over on the opposite side of Mack to help in whatever way she could.

Chief handed the bag to Sam. "Hang this pouch on the tree limb," he instructed. She hung the bag and he tied a tourniquet around Mack's bicep to expose a vein, jabbing the cannula's needle into it to start the fluid drip.

As they attended to Mack, Chief looked over his shoulder to check on Mike. He was still standing in front of the large tree, his mouth partially agape.

Bling noticed him as well. "Yo, this boy still in da funk."

Sam stood and looked over Mike's shoulder to see what he was gawking at. She pulled back some of the vines and saw a partial circle with an Asian symbol in it—the same one she had seen on the side of the train and the one Mike had seen so many times before.

"Mike, are you okay?" she asked, placing her hand on his shoulder. Startled, he stepped back and fell over a fallen log, stumbling to the ground.

"Hey, hey, take it easy," Chief stated, helping him up.

"We...we have to get out of here!" Mike stuttered, the blood vacating his face as though a ghost were standing in front of him. Hearing him speak for the first time in over a day, Sam rushed over to him and gave him a hearty embrace, but he barely responded. His body was slowly exiting survival mode and he wasn't all there yet.

"Oh, thank God. You're back—"

"I—I'm super thirsty," he replied, taking a seat on the large log, still focused on the partial symbol.

Chief unzipped one of the three gear bags he and Bling were dragging, feeling around for a small, plastic water bottle.

"Here ya go, son, but don't drink too fast."

Mike ripped off the cap and chugged the water, defying Chief's suggestion in an attempt to satisfy his parched glands. Seconds later, his stomach rejected the ambush of water and he threw most of it up.

Back at the truck, the Burmese soldiers filed out of the vehicles, amassing on the trail into three fully-armed squads of ten troops each, all lined up in successive rows, pushing down the trail and coming closer to Johnny and Switch's position.

"Boss," Johnny whispered into his mic. "At least a couple dozen troops heading our way, over."

"Copy. Continue with the plan. Keep me updated, over."

Switch held the detonator as the soldiers pushed to within a couple meters of the Claymore. He waited a few seconds more and then closed his eyes, plugged his ears, and clamped down hard on the detonator.

Ka-boom! The Claymore exploded, lighting up the trail like it was high noon, but a half-second later the darkness swallowed it up again.

"Switch, get going," Johnny shouted as the smoke dissipated. "I'm right behind you." He motioned him down the trail while looking through the scope to see how many soldiers were left. As he scanned the trail, he saw body parts strewn everywhere, some blown into the tops of the trees. The few soldiers that remained scurried back to the convoy, many of them badly mangled from the blast.

"Boss, the Claymore did its job. Only about a dozen left standing," Johnny reported into the mic.

"Good. Fall back to our position, over."

"Wait, something is happening—" Johnny indicated, but before he could finish reporting, the APCs and several soldiers fired their weapons at the truck.

Swoosh...Boom! An RPG careened down the trail and blasted only feet in front of the truck.

Rattattatat! Rattattatat! Rattattatat! The soldiers stood near the convoy and fired everything they had, pinning Johnny down.

"What's going on, Johnny?" Chief asked as he heard the gunfire, but there was no reply, only static. Soon after, Switch met up with Chief, but Johnny wasn't with him.

"Where's Johnny?" Chief asked with a concerned gaze, peering over his shoulder.

"What? He was supposed to be right behind me!" Switch exclaimed, holding his hands up and spinning around. "I'll go back!"

"No, it's too risky," Chief replied, hearing the constant gunfire. "He's been trained for this. We have to stay on task."

Switch narrowed his eyes and with a rare defiance, responded harshly. "Yeah, and what's that task, Chief? I thought the job was to rescue people. I guess we're being selective about that."

"I want to help him, believe me, but this isn't the Marine Corp. You don't have an entire platoon at your disposal. It's just us. If we go back, we won't last a minute with the RPGs and autocannons. We have to keep going. Got it?"

"Yeah, Chief, I got it!" He responded curtly, kicking a bamboo shoot with his boot and swatting away some mosquitoes.

"Hopefully this isn't about protecting that girl for the money," he mumbled.

Chief spun around and grabbed him by the top of his vest, his cobalt eyes as serious as he had ever seen them. "What did you just say?" he asked through his clenched jaw.

"Nevermind."

"It ain't even like that," Chief replied, putting him down. "We're not even on that mission anymore; we're in a fight for our lives."

"Chief, listen, I spoke out of turn," Switch's eyes were downcast. "You're making the right call."

"Look, I get it. No need to apologize. I want to go back as well, but we have to be smart about this."

Switch nodded and Chief turned to address everyone. "Alright, we're gonna move down the trail. The right fork appears to be the least overgrown, so we'll head that way. Johnny is a good tracker; he'll find us."

Bling grabbed two gear bags and Chief knelt down to assist Mack, but as he grabbed him he noticed his body was limp.

"Mack?" Chief nudged his shoulder but he didn't get a response. He held his flashlight in one hand and lifted one of Mack's eyelids, noting his clammy skin, bluish lips, and fast breathing. Then he checked for a pulse. He held two fingers on Mack's jugular vein and illuminated his watch to start the count.

"Weak pulse, extremely fast heart rate, blue lips..." Chief muttered as he rubbed his head, his eyes revealing his concern. "Hypovolemic Shock...Mack c'mon ol' friend, don't give up now." Chief tried to encourage one last fight for life, but he was all but gone. Suddenly, Chief stood up, his facial expression switching from sullen to stoic. He didn't have the privilege of grieving; he had to hold it together for the sake of everyone else.

"Son, can you give me a hand here?" Chief asked Mike, panning over to him. He was still sitting on the log, staring at the symbol. Without saying a word, Mike stood and hiked back down the trail in the direction of the truck.

Chief raised his voice. "Son? What are you doing? You can't go back—"

"Mike?" Sam fretfully yelled. "Where are you going?"

"Switch, stop him!"

Switch turned around and saw Mike coming straight for him and he held out his hands to stop him. "Woah, boy, where are you go—"

"Swap!" Mike grabbed Switch's vest with his right arm and gripped his elbow with his left, pulling him downward. He stepped behind him, sweeping him to the ground with one of his

278

martial art techniques. Chief rushed over, somewhat shocked that the scrawny young man had taken Switch out so quickly. But the fight wasn't over. Laying on his back, Switch seized Mike's ankle and jerked it back as though he were performing a shoe-string tackle. Mike tried to step out of it, but he was too weak and fell into some leafy vegetation.

Chief ran to Mike and pulled his arms back, lifting him up by his belt.

"Son—"

"Let me go!" Mike angrily interrupted, his mind reeling in fear. He tried to stop trembling, but couldn't. "…I'm not going down that trail."

"Okay, Mike, calm down. Talk to me here," Chief softened his voice and released his grip. "I know you've been through a horrible ordeal, but this is our only option if we want to survive."

"You…you don't get it," Mike's voice quivered. "I've seen this symbol several times since I've been in Burma, and every time I see it something horrible happens soon after."

"Okay, Mike. I'm hearing you, but this symbol was painted all over the soldier's helmets, vehicles and even the compound itself…it's their logo. Switch, what did you say it meant again?"

Switch tilted his head trying to recall the meaning.

"Drag—" Switch paused without completing the word, his eyes expanding and mouth falling open as he and Chief simultaneously faced each other, realizing it was more than a logo; it was somehow connected to the beast they had heard. Sam saw their dumbfounded expressions and wanted answers.

"Drag?" She questioned. "What's drag?" Chief and Switch looked at each other, thinking of a way to deflect without causing her to panic, but before they could submit a decent explanation, they heard the sound of twigs snapping behind them. Chief pulled his 1911 pistol and made everyone kneel down. Switch reached for his MP5, rolling onto his belly and aiming in the direction of the sound.

"Boss, I'm coming up the trail—couple meters out," Johnny radioed in, pressing through the last bit of foliage to their position. Chief lowered his pistol and breathed a sigh of relief

Switch stood to his feet. "Where'd you go, Johnny? You were right behind me."

"You made it out before they released the fury. I was in a bad spot. They had the trail clogged up, so I rolled down the embankment and followed the edge of the swamp down the trail—and I'll have you know that I saw at least two crocs."

"We're just glad you made it." Chief patted Johnny's shoulder and nodded at him, a subtle indication that he had done well.

"You weren't gonna leave me out in this swamp, I know that."

"Chief!" Sam nearly yelled, jumping in between them, her voice firm and determined. "I want to know what you were talking about. What do you know about this symbol?"

"We don't have time right now," Chief deflected, glancing at Switch.

"Well, Mike and I aren't going anywhere until you tell us," she replied, reaching for his hand and holding her chin up in defiance.

"Look, Sam, I'll meet you halfway on this. When we start moving down the trail, I'll fill you in on what we know. Deal?"

Sam looked at Mike to get his take. His back was still to the group, determined not to move past the symbol.

"Son—er—I mean, Mike. Look, here's what I know. There's a deranged military waiting for us at the truck. They're probably already regrouping and rearming. If they get their hands on us, they'll torture us to no end. What I don't know is what's down this trail beyond this symbol, but at this point, I'd rather face the unknown than what I do know."

Mike remembered telling Sam something similar when they left the brothel and so far they were still alive. Chief saw Mike's averseness relaxing and took the opportunity to seal the deal. He reached inside Mack's boot and took out his .38 snub-nosed revolver, holding it out to him.

"Uh, Chief, you sure about that?"

"Know how to operate a gun, young man?" Chief addressed him in a military tone. Mike turned to see the gun in Chief's hand and stared at it for a second, eventually wrapping his hand around it.

"Good," Chief nodded. "Now, if you and Sam will help us with Mack, we can move much quicker. Switch you get on one side and Mike can take the other. Sam, if you could hold up the IV bag, it would be a great help."

"Sure...it's the least I can do for him."

THIRTY-TWO
MOZAMBIQUE DRILL

Chief led them down the skinny path that was no more than a foot wide, slicing away at the bushy flora. Johnny brought up the rear, watching for soldiers and also keeping any eye on the swamp only a few meters away.

They trekked for a short time when they came upon a large clearing, a circle about 20 feet in diameter. Chief stayed behind the trees, scrutinizing the area and taking an opportunity to douse himself in some bug spray that he had in his pocket.

"Look like sumptin' huge been here, Chief…bulldozer or sumptin'," Bling proposed as he inspected the splintered trees and matted down plants. Chief didn't reply; his head was already on a swivel, shining his flashlight in every direction. He cautiously stepped into the clearing and touched the sharp splinters of one of the broken trees, examining it closely. Then he saw some unusual prints in the mud—each one twice the size of a bear's print. He squatted for a closer assessment, tracing his fingers across what appeared to be claw markings that were longer than his hand. Something big had caused the damage, and it wasn't a machine.

Sam saw the prints and her eyes widened in horror.

"Listen, Chief. I'm not stupid," she stated, handing the IV bag to Mike. "I've been on hunting trips with my dad. Those prints were created by a very large animal. Tell me what you know…please."

"Team, we'll take a break here," Chief stated, using his boot to rake some leaves over the prints, disregarding Sam.

Switch and Mike put Mack down and propped him against a tree and Johnny knelt down to check on him, concerned by his shallow breathing. "Chief, Mack's not doing so well."

"His body is in shock...shutting down," Chief somberly replied. "He doesn't have much time...Switch, you think you got any battery life left on the drone?" Chief asked, trying to keep his mind off of Mack's grave condition. He briefly locked eyes with Sam to show that he had heard her but wasn't ready to disclose any information.

"I'll check," Switch unzipped his bag and searched for his tablet.

"Chief?!" Sam raised her voice, becoming more irritated that he was ignoring her and not delivering on his promise.

"Son of a—" Switch cussed.

"What is it?"

"I left the drone on...the battery is almost gone."

"Is there enough time to get some intel on the convoy?

"Possibly."

"Launch it out."

"Roger that." Switch launched the drone through the clearing, following the trail back to the truck, hovering above the convoy and watching the tablet's screen.

"Chief, take a look at this!" he exclaimed, flying the drone higher for a wide-angle view of the intersection. They both watched the screen, counting at least ten vehicles and dozens of plain-clothes men amassing with about two dozen soldiers.

"Who are those men? Those aren't military vehicles or soldiers," Switch asked, zooming in closer. Chief and Johnny looked at the screen over his shoulder.

"They're probably local military sympathizers," Johnny submitted, still surveilling the nearby swamp and trying to suppress his uneasiness.

"You're probably right," Chief agreed, watching as Switch zoomed in on General Htun and the Russian, both of whom appeared to be giving orders.

"Man, I wish I had the ability to call in an airstrike right about now!" Chief spouted and then addressed everyone. "Guys, listen up. Since the soldiers are regrouping back at the truck, our best shot is to continue down the trail and hide out until it's safe, but we need to keep our eyes op—"

"The tanniyn did this!" Sam furiously interrupted him, her eyes closed tight and fists balled up at her side. Chief tilted his head, marveling at her outburst.

"Tanniyn?" Chief repeated, remembering the soldier's chant at the compound and how it sounded similar.

"Okay, Sam, I'll make a deal here. You share what you know and I'll share what we know," Chief smiled at the corner of his mouth, giving her a slight nod.

"No way!" Sam's veins pulsed in her neck as she grabbed Mike's hand as a show of defiance. Chief wouldn't be able to evade any longer.

"Aright. You win. Here's what we know. The symbol Mike saw back there—" Chief paused and Sam stepped forward, anxiously waiting for him to finish. "The symbol is a word that means dragon."

"And?" Sam threw her hands up, expecting more information.

"And what? That's what we know. I didn't say anything because I didn't want y'all to panic."

Sam stood quiet, not blinking, realizing she had the information all along and knew more than anyone else.

"Can you tell us what tanniyn is?"

Sam didn't respond, contemplating stonewalling like Chief had done to her, but she gave in, hoping the information might be helpful.

"That's what the soldiers were chanting back at the prison," she replied, her mind recalling Shein's words and the last time she saw her.

"I kinda put that together myself. Is there anything else you can tell us?"

"I know they worship it. They...they feed it."

"Do you know what *it* is?" Chief emphasized.

"The commander—when he, uh, when he captured us—he said he was going to feed Mike to the—," she trailed off, gripping Mike's hand tighter, locking eyes with him. He smiled slightly and she finished. "He said he would feed Mike to the dragon."

When she said the word dragon, Johnny gulped and did a check of the gloomy swamp again.

"Look, surely we're not dealing with some mythological creature here. Asians can be superstitious. It's probably a very large, angry rhino or something like—"

"No, I saw it," Johnny interjected, still scanning the swamp. "It's not a rhino."

"Or something big like that—I don't know—but we gotta stay focused," Chief exclaimed, knowing full well it wasn't an animal he had seen before.

"Maybe it's a pack of animals," Bling suggested. "I mean, they fed it a whole human and they was gonna feed it two more. I ain't know 'bout no animal eatin' three humans in one sittin'."

"Good point," Switch suggested, landing the drone before it ran out of battery life.

"Hey, guys, listen," Sam cocked her head slightly, looking up into the dark sky. "Do you hear that?"

"Sounds like a helicopter," Mike suggested.

"Definitely a helo. Let's get moving," Chief commanded. "We're easy targets in this clearing."

Chief rushed over to help move Mack, but when he did he noticed the color in his skin was gone. He reached out and grabbed his hand and it was cold.

"Mack?" Chief shook him but didn't get a response.

"Mack!" He yelled louder and checked for a pulse. Johnny, Switch, and Bling huddled around him, perceiving the inevitable.

"Come on, Mack!" Chief yelled again and slapped his cheek. He rested him flat on the ground and began chest compressions, blowing air into his lungs with the CPR mask from his personal medical kit.

Everyone stood silent.

Chief continued CPR for a few moments when Switch gently placed his hand on his shoulder. Chief stood up without saying a word and stared at the ground. He broke his gaze when he heard the helicopter coming closer.

"Chief!" Johnny shouted. "Spotlight at three o'clock."

"Everyone take cover behind the trees!" Chief shouted as he and Switch pulled Mack under some green palm bushes.

Seconds later, the helicopter flew over the clearing, shining its spotlight through the thick vegetation in a search pattern; it hovered over the area for a few minutes and eventually moved on.

"Great. Now we have to contend with a heli—"

Shrieeeeeeeeeek! Switch was interrupted by the same spine-chilling sound they heard at the compound, but this time it sounded further away. Everyone stood still, their eyes darting back and forth, hoping the creature was nowhere near them.

"Might have more to worry about than a chopper," Johnny attested.

"We need to keep going," Chief instructed, his voice flat and emotionless as he unfolded a vinyl body bag and unzipped it. Switch, Johnny, and Bling lifted Mack a few inches off the ground while Chief slid the bag under him.

"We, uh, we don't have time to grieve as we should," Chief stated somberly, looking at Mack's stiff body. "But I do want to say some words." Bling took a knee and everyone else followed. A few tears leaked from Sam's eyes as she reached for Mike's hand.

"Mack, you were a good soldier...and an even better friend. I'm sorry you had to go out like this...I promise your death won't be in vain," Chief kept his voice low, choking back his tears. He looked at Johnny and nodded as though it was his turn.

"I'm not too good at this stuff, but, well, Mack was a hoot. Always had me laughing at the oddest stuff...We always joked with each other and he made a mean country breakfast. I'll miss you ol' man."

"I'll probably miss his bizarre antics the most," Switch spoke next, lifting his glasses to wipe a tear. "He sure was crazy. I remember the time he somehow convinced the city morgue to give him a cadaver for what he told them was research purposes…Man, he brought that old, naked and frozen corpse to the ranch and set it up on the range to see what different bullets did to it…crazy ol' man, but I'll definitely miss him…rest easy, buddy," Everyone shared in a slight laugh and nodded at Switch's sentiments.

It was Bling's turn, but he stood silent for several seconds, his lips moving fast as he mouthed an unspoken prayer and finally spoke up.

"I ain't have the pleasure of knowin' Mack all that long, but we always had some good conversatin'. He always be askin' me deep questions on da side. Questions about da afterlife and such. I couldn't answer all of 'em, but I know he's gettin' a good view now," Bling smiled and finished with a prayer. "Dear God, we wanna give tanks for da time wit' our friend. Please protek and guide us on dis here mission 'til da very end. In Jesus' name, amen."

Chief reached down to pick up his MP5 when Sam unexpectedly spoke up.

"The first time I saw your friend, Mack…" Sam paused, wiping the tears from the tops of her cheeks, "…was when they put him on the train with…with me and Mike. He had been roughed up pretty bad. When I saw he was American and had military gear on, I knew it was because of me that he had been captured and hurt so badly. I know Mack had a heart of gold because the highest form of love is sacrificing yourself for another—especially for someone you don't even know. Mack, I will never forget…never ever forget…your sacrifice for me."

"I couldn't have said it any better," Mike followed, nodding his head. "Thank you, Mack."

Chief stood silent for a moment and then broke the somber mood.

"We have to keep fighting...for Mack," Chief's face shifted from somber to brazen as he bent down to grab one of the straps on the body bag. Switch, Johnny, and Bling quietly followed while Sam and Mike corralled the gear bags together, slinging them over their shoulders.

Chief and Johnny took point, carrying the body bag's front straps in one hand and swinging the machete in the other. For the next several minutes, they hiked through the jungle until they came to another clearing. Chief held up his hand, silently signaling everyone to stop. He motioned to Johnny and they gently rested Mack's body to the ground.

"Y'all listen up," Chief whispered, connecting with everyone's eyes. "All of us are a team now. We have to depend on each other if we're gonna have any chance out of this. All of us—all of our lives—are the mission now."

Everyone quickly bobbed their head in agreement while Chief lifted the night-vision goggles that were hanging around his neck over his eyes and inspected the clearing.

"There's a hut in the clearing about 30 meters away. I can't confirm any movement from here. I'll go in and check it out. Everyone keep your eyes open. Johnny, watch our six."

"On it," Johnny replied confidently, moving a few paces back down the dark trail, aiming his gun into the darkness, ready for anything.

"Switch, give Sam a pistol and make sure she knows how to use it, and cover me as I go in," Chief instructed.

"Understood," Switch whispered as he pulled out his Beretta 9mm pistol and handed it to her. He knelt down and laid on the jungle's floor.

"Have you fired a gun before?" Switch asked in a gentle but instructive manner.

She knelt down next to him. "Yeah, I have; I was raised on a farm," she confidently replied. She assertively grasped the gun and racked the slide, ejecting a bullet from the chamber and causing it to land nose down in the dirt.

"Uh—oops," Sam mumbled beneath her breath, blushing from her overconfidence. "But I do know how to use it."

"Well enough, I suppose," Switch responded. "Just make sure you confirm your target before firing. And no leg shots. The torso is the largest target on a person. Oh, and if you need to be sure they're stopped, do a triple tap."

"A triple tap?" Sam questioned, blinking rapidly.

"Sorry...that's military jargon. Two shots to the body and one to the head; it's called the Mozambique Drill."

"Why is it called that?" Sam curiously whispered, swatting at mosquitoes as they watched Chief move closer to the hut.

"It's named after the Mozambican War of Independence in the 1960s. As the story goes, a mercenary shot an armed guerrilla twice in the sternum with his pistol but he kept advancing, so he aimed for his head and shot again, hitting him in the throat, severing his spinal cord. Stopped him dead in his tracks—pun intended—and now most militaries and police teach the drill to safely eliminate threats."

"Wait, so he shot a gorilla with a gun—like Planet of the Apes stuff?" Sam's eyebrows raised in innocent curiosity.

Switch let out a little chuckle. "No, not a monkey-gorilla; it's spelled differently. A guerrilla is a person employing military tactics to fight in a conflict, but they aren't professional soldiers. Usually they're villagers or rebels."

Sam closed her eyes and bit her lower lip, realizing the hilarity of her response. She knew the term, but it hadn't come to her in the moment. Switch didn't care, though, because she was helping him keep his mind off of Mack's passing and the stress of their situation.

Chief stalked near the hut, his MP5 pressed to his shoulder, silently sweeping around the rear. He traced his way along the wall and moved to the front, observing a dilapidated wooden deck that served as a type of porch, stretching the length of the front of the hut. The deck stepped down a 10-foot embankment to a long, skinny pier, no wider than a sidewalk; it jutted out several feet into the algae-covered, pea soup-looking swamp, ending at two large trees that provided the majority of its support.

Chief stepped onto the porch and the decayed boards creaked beneath him. As he got closer to the door, his heart pounded. The two-inch-thick wooden door had been forcibly ripped from its rusty metal hinges and was lying near the porch on the embankment. He examined it closely, taking note of four large gashes made by some type of massive claw or talon.

Staving off the anxiety, Chief peeked around the corner of the hut, cautiously observing the nearby teak trees. He scanned up and down, left and right, watching and listening for any type of movement. Moments later, he saw a slowly moving red object and he froze in place, recalling the creature's terrifying red eyes at the compound.

"Chief, you okay out there?" Switch asked, speaking into the radio's mic, straining to see where he had gone. All he could make out was Chief's dark, motionless silhouette. Chief didn't answer. His eyes were trained on the red dot near the tree line, waiting for whatever was there to make a move. He thought about his options. There was no way the MP5 could take out the beast without him being injured in the process. Even an RPG probably wouldn't stop it.

As he ran the scenarios in his mind, the dot suddenly spread its wings and flapped away into the jungle. Relieved, Chief wiped the sweat from his brow and radioed in.

"I'm good. I'm gonna clear the hut," he indicated, sounding quite out of breath.

"Roger that."

Chief entered the hut, sweeping his rifle around the entryway, his eyes concentrated down the gun's sights, waiting for someone or something to align itself in front of the barrel, but no one was home; it was abandoned. As his flashlight flooded the room, he noticed the wood-paneled walls and floor were covered in dried blood. Chief gulped, contemplating what had happened in the room. *Was someone murdered and dragged away? Was it the military? Could it have been the beast?* He tried to think about something else, but his imagination took over.

"All clear," he eventually announced. "Leave Mack and fall into my location with the gear. Keep your eyes open, over."

THIRTY-THREE
JUNGLE HUT

Y o, what's this place?" Bling asked as he squatted near the hut's broken door, running his hand over the claw markings, his mouth partially open.

"Are they bears up in here? Maybe that's what we heard."

"It's not a bear," Johnny sternly insisted, keeping his MP5 ready, but not offering any other suggestions as to what he had seen.

"That looks like a dock for a canoe or small boat. Maybe this was a fishing outpost for the villagers," Switch suggested.

Mike stepped up on the porch and entered the hut and Sam followed closely behind. Once inside, they saw the dried blood that had been splattered like it was a murder scene.

"Sam, look…" Mike pointed to the floor at the tiny dragon symbol that had been smeared in the blood—something Chief didn't even notice. A sudden coldness gripped Sam and she became overcome by the permeating smell of brackish swamp water, humidity, and rotting wood. She began coughing profusely and Mike helped her out of the hut for some fresh air.

"Hey, check that out!" Johnny exclaimed, pointing to the fully-matured swamp trees at the end of the pier. One of the trees had wood slat steps several feet up from the pier that ascended to a makeshift wood-plank platform, suspended about 20 feet from the water.

"Interesting," Chief mumbled, looking up into the trees. "That's a big platform—probably 15 feet across. If I didn't know better, I'd say it was some kind of unfinished treehouse. I wonder what they used that for?"

"I'm wondering why there are no steps at the bottom?"

"I saw that, too," Chief indicated. "The bottoms of the trees are missing bark. Maybe it's from deer rubbing their antlers against them during rutting season."

"...or maybe a dragon breathed fire on it and destroyed the bark," Switch suggested with an exaggerated smile, but no one was amused.

"Okay, everyone pay attention," Chief announced. "I hate to say this, but we don't know what's out here so we need to get Mack underground. If we don't, he'll draw out the animals."

"Hold up. I don't like this at all, boss," Johnny snapped. "He needs to be buried back home where he belongs."

"I agree. This is only temporary. We'll bury him at the edge of the swamp where the soil is easy to move and pick him up when we leave this place."

Johnny knew Chief was right and quickly surrendered his argument, catching up with Switch, Bling, and Mike who had already arrived at the body bag. Chief watched over everyone as they carried Mack near the hut, gently lowering him down the embankment. Switch stood one foot in the water and one on the shore, while Johnny used his collapsible entrenching shovel to clear away a shallow grave. They dug until it was deep enough and set the bag in the hole, laying Mack to a temporary rest.

"Chief," Sam whispered, standing near the porch. "Did you hear that?"

Chief nodded and placed his pointer finger vertically over his lips. Seconds later, they heard another twig snapping and he held down the radio's Morse code button to get everyone's attention. Johnny and Switch hurried to spread the black mud over Mack and crawled up to the top of the bank, reaching for their weapons.

Chief motioned for everyone to take cover behind the embankment while he slowly dropped back to the corner of the hut, scanning the trail through his night-vision goggles.

"Team, we've got company," he whispered. "Several soldiers on the trail. I'm gonna set up the last Claymore."

"Copy that," Switch replied.

"Boss, I'm gonna try to get to that platform and set up overwatch, over."

"Good idea."

Johnny traversed the pier and reached the tree, using it as cover while he quickly screwed in some metal steps.

"Everyone stay in place. Wait for them to come in close, over," Chief instructed, placing the Claymore's metal prongs in the dirt at the side of the porch and angling it at the trail.

"Copy, that," Switch whispered.

"Almost in place, boss. One more step to go."

As they waited for the soldiers to enter the clearing, Johnny heard the sound of splashing near the swamp. He clicked on the night-vision scope and peeked around the tree at the waters below.

"Big problem, boss!" Johnny whispered into his mic. "Soldiers flanking us from the edge of the swamp at 11 o'clock, over."

"Copy. Get to the platform and wait for my command."

"Roger that."

Switch looked into the dark swamp and saw the silhouetted outline of a squad of troops who were less than 20 meters away, wading through the water, their weapons shouldered and stalking closer.

As the soldiers approached from both sides, Chief stood with his back to the wall of the hut. He briefly closed his eyes, unable to think of a viable plan of resistance. He didn't have enough men or firepower to wage war on an entire military force that would only grow larger as the night went on. He embraced their fate, ready to go out in a blaze of glory, but as he was about to blow the Claymore, he glanced at the swamp and noticed the water was no longer stagnant; it was rippling—and it wasn't caused by the soldiers.

Chief focused on the shadowy swamp made extra-green by his night-vision and noticed the reflection of the moon on the water had been dashed into unrecognizable streaks. He followed the ripples and his eyes settled on something like a rudder flapping back and forth, causing a shining wake to rush toward the soldiers like a miniature Tsunami.

The soldiers pushed forward in unison until one of them spotted the movement and came to a halt, listening and observing the ripples with a horrified facial expression. He looked closer, waving to get his comrades' attention, but before they could react, the creature blasted out of the swamp like exploding dynamite, perfectly concealed behind a massive wall of water.

"Arghh—" The soldier bellowed out a hair-raising scream as the creature thrashed its tail, whipping his legs out from under him, sending him plunging under the water and muffling his cries. The other soldiers hurried out of the water and up the embankment, slipping on the black mud, not going anywhere fast. As they raced to find safety, one of the soldiers stopped climbing and wheeled around, defiantly pointing his rifle into the water, waiting for the beast to appear again.

Ratatttatat! He squeezed the trigger, emptying his magazine. With the gun's smoke swirling from the end of his barrel, the beast lunged from the water and bit the soldier's leg, pulling him underwater and out into the middle of the swamp.

Ratatttatat! More erratic gunfire and terrifying screams erupted, but this time they came from down the trail. The flashes from the gunfire lit up the jungle behind the tree line, but Chief couldn't see what was attacking.

Chief shouted at Switch. "Take Bling and the kids and y'all get up on the platform!"

While the soldiers were distracted by the creature, Switch led the group down to the pier. Sam reached the steps first, climbing

295

up as Mike and Bling followed. Switch was last to ascend the steps while Johnny provided cover from above.

"Johnny, how is that platform holding up?" Chief asked, still waiting at the edge of the hut.

"So far, so good, boss."

"Good. I'm on my way up. Cover me." Chief grabbed a gear bag and slung it over his shoulder, carefully making his way down the pier. He got halfway down and stopped, detecting something was wrong. Not only had the gunfire stopped, everything around him went quiet.

Chief scanned the swamp and the tree line, but there was no sign of soldiers. Not even the leaves on the trees moved—and it spooked him. He cautiously walked sideways on the pier, pointing his gun at the water, being careful not to step off the edge. He got about 10 feet from the tree when he observed the same flapping movement in the dark waters.

Phttt! Phttt! Phttt! Chief fired at the creature's scaly tail while Johnny targeted it from above, both of them emptying their magazines, but the bullets did nothing to deter it; in fact, it provoked it to move quicker.

Chief rushed to the tree, but before he could reach it the creature burst out of the water, its bulky body splitting the pier in half. Chief leaped for the bottom step, seizing hold of it as the pier dropped out below him, his legs dangling into the dark swamp water.

Pow! Pow! Pow! Johnny switched to his pistol, firing at the beast. Switch joined in the battle, firing his MP5 as Chief hung from the step, his gear bag and MP5 hoisted over his shoulder, swaying back and forth. With his last ounce of energy, Chief dug his boots into a small portion of bark still left on the tree, boosting himself up to the next step.

The beast thrashed around in the water, twisting back to the tree as Chief continued climbing up. He reached the last step and gazed down at the beast as it circled the tree like a predator intimidating its prey. Then, out of nowhere, it whipped its tail above the water and pommeled the tree, sending a shockwave coursing up the trunk, through Chief's hands and through everyone's body.

"Yo, what was dat?" Bling blurted out as he and Switch helped Chief to the platform. Once to the top, he nearly collapsed on the wooden planks, completely exhausted.

Slam! Slam! Slam! The beast violently smashed its massive tail into the base over and over, causing its acorn-size buds to splatter onto the platform and the swamp below like hail during a thunderstorm. Mike and Sam held onto each other, their bodies trembling, hoping the tree and platform would withstand the assault.

Chief peered over the platform's edge into the murky waters, somewhat mesmerized by the creatures' wild twisting; that's when he noticed the swirling pattern had changed; it no longer only circled clockwise; it was rotating in both directions.

"Guys, there's more than one of these things…whatever they are."

"Well, that's just great. This is getting worse by the second," Johnny grumbled.

"The good thing is that the soldiers are gone," Chief replied, staying optimistic for the sake of everyone else.

"Yeah that's odd," Switch spoke up," Where did they go?"

"Yo, them boys up and vanished like ghosts," Bling stated. "Probably ran back to the convoy."

"Boss, these creatures—whatever they are—they killed all those Japanese soldiers. We gotta think of a way to take them out or we won't make it," Johnny changed the subject back to their new enemy.

"Let's not get too far into the unknown, Johnny."

"I'm just trying to be ready is all."

"There's nothing wrong with that, but I want to make sure you're focus isn't being skewed by your fear."

"My focus isn't skewed!"

"Calm down there, brother."

"Look, I just want to get on with a plan to get out of here, okay? That's my focus."

"I'm with you on that. So, you have a plan?"

"Yeah, I do. I'm thinking we could use the Claymore on them. If we can get them both to line up near—"

Chief cut him off. "We could try that…if I hadn't dropped the detonator in the water."

"Seriously? Why did you do that! Damn, man!"

"Johnny, chill out a sec. There's no reason to get hyper yet. If we stay up here for a while, there's a good chance they'll move on to easier prey."

"20, boss! 20 Japanese soldiers survived out of nearly one thousand. They're not just going to let us walk out of here."

"I remember that part, Johnny. Do you know what those 20 did to survive?"

"All I remember is they spent one night on this same island and when they woke up the next day only 20 were—"

Chief cut him off. "Ok, then we'll concentrate on tonight. We only have a few hours 'til sunrise. We'll take this a step at a time."

Sam spoke up. "I think we can make it as well. God didn't bring us this far to take us out now."

"Good point," Bling chimed in. "Faith is what we need right now; it will see us through."

"Mike? How about you? You good?" Chief asked.

He slowly nodded, not saying anything.

"Good, everyone listen closely. We all need to get some rest so we can put our heads together and figure out how to get out of here alive. Johnny, you'll take the first watch. I'm not sure if the soldiers will return, but we need to be ready."

"Copy that," Johnny stated, sitting down on the platform, positioning himself so he could keep an eye on both the swamp and the trail. He looked into the swamp and the creatures had stopped circling, but they were still close by, resting with only their bony-ridged backside exposed above the algae-covered swamp, waiting like zoo animals for the kiddies to drop a snack.

Bling stretched out on the platform and removed his outer shirt, folding it over to use it as a pillow. He closed his eyes and was soon fast asleep.

"I don't get it, Chief," Switch whispered as he listened to Bling's light snoring. "How can he sleep so easily? My mind is going wild."

"I certainly can't sleep," Chief replied as he rummaged through his gear bag. "Probably has something to do with him not shooting any bad guys."

"That could be," Switch replied as Mike and Sam found a spot to rest near Bling. They rested on their backs, staring up at the rustling leaves that twirled elegantly in the light breeze.

Chief sat on the platform next to Switch and Johnny, unzipping his partially waterlogged gear bag, checking to see what they could use. He pulled out a few energy bars, one reusable water filter and bottle, a baggy of pain reliever tablets, some rope, extra socks, a small tarp, and one roll of toilet paper.

"Water is the most essential right now," Johnny submitted, glancing at the clear bottle, his mouth drooling at the thought quenching his thirst. He had a fleeting thought of racing down the tree to fill it up with water, but he also wanted to survive to drink it.

"I'd say TP is probably a close second…remember how everyone hoarded it during that global virus that broke out?" Switch's off-hand humor was a welcome stress relief.

"Yeah, the bathroom situation up here is gonna be interesting," Chief smiled slightly as he checked on Mike and Sam; they had both fallen asleep, their heads resting on one another.

"Guys, I'm going to go clear my mind on the other side of the platform. Johnny, I'll be back to relieve you in an hour so you can try and get some rest. Keep your eyes open for anything."

"Roger that, boss."

THIRTY-FOUR
EVIL EXPOSED

A shard of warmth crept up the tree behind Chief, settling on his hand. He cracked his eyelids to see the sun's bright light breaking through the swampland, radiating the hope of a new day and a new opportunity to live. Seconds later, he sprang to his feet. He had missed relieving Johnny.

"I...I overslept...I'm sorry I didn't relieve—"

"Don't mention it, Chief." Johnny interrupted his atypical apology. "You needed the rest more than any of us."

"You should have got me up. Have you been on watch this entire time?"

"Switch and I did the watch together."

"Yeah, I couldn't sleep," Switch indicated as Chief stepped to the edge of the platform and looked down at the soupy water.

"They went underwater about an hour ago," Johnny reported. "One second they were there and the next I only saw a bunch of bubbles. We haven't seen any indication of them for a while."

"That's a relief," Chief stated.

"Chief, what are we gonna do now?" Switch asked. "We can't stay up here forever."

"I don't intend to, but we can't get ahead of ourselves. We need to take a little time and study the creature's habits to outmaneuver them, but, more importantly, we need to get some water."

"I was hoping you would say that," Switch replied as Chief opened his gear bag and felt around for his water filtration bottle.

"Okay, I'll go first; we'll each take turns filling the bottle until everyone gets hydrated," Chief instructed. "Y'all watch my back."

"Hey, be careful, those things could still be close," Johnny advised.

"I will," Chief replied, hanging the water bottle's strap around his neck and slowly descending until he was only a few feet from the water. As he stood on the last step, he looked over his shoulder, sweeping his eyes across the swamp for any sign of the beasts, but there was nothing. No massive tails, no swirling, no bubbles…he couldn't even hear a sound. Everything was calm—maybe too calm.

Chief unscrewed the bottle from the lid and plunged it past the thick algae blooms into the murky water. It took only seconds to fill the 32-ounce bottle, but as he was topping it off, he saw two red eyes glowing under the water, ascending toward him. Panic set in and he rushed up the steps, stopping halfway up the tree to make sure he was seeing correctly. He turned to look back into the water but nothing was there. He shook it off and continued climbing to the platform where Johnny, Switch, and Bling were waiting.

"Yo, you ai'ght there, Chief?" Bling asked. "You look a little shook."

"I—I'm fine. Don't worry about me. Everyone drink a little and pass it around."

Switch didn't waste any time. He grabbed the bottle and sucked through the straw that doubled as a filter and handed it off to Johnny. Bling was next to drink and Chief finished off the last few swigs.

"Man, this tastes so good right now," Johnny stated as he closed his eyes for a moment to savor the blandness of the filtered swamp water. I'm glad you packed one of these in your bag, boss."

"Awesome invention," Chief explained, sitting down on the platform.

"Yo, what about the kids?" Bling asked.

"Let them sleep," Chief answered. "We'll get them water on the next go around."

"I guess it's my turn to take the plunge," Switch replied, grabbing the water bottle strap and throwing it over his shoulder. He stepped over the edge and descended the steps, but as he did Chief called down to him, his voice a little shaky.

"Hey, Switch—um—make it quick, alright?"

Switch looked up at Chief, noting his uneasiness, and then cautiously continued down as Chief and Johnny trained their MP5s on the water below.

Once on the bottom step, he lifted the bottle's strap from around his neck and reached down to fill it up. That's when Chief saw it again. The two glowing red objects. He rubbed his eyes, figuring he was hallucinating. He looked down again and one of the creatures thundered out of the swamp, sending a rush of water into the air like a geyser.

Switch clung to the step, trying to climb back up, but before he could get away the beast lashed its tail at him, the bony tip nicking his arm and snapping it in half, causing him excruciating pain.

"Argh!" Switch screamed, dropping the water bottle into the water. He gripped the step with his good hand while the other dangled like a worm, his skin the only thing connecting it to his arm. Hearing the commotion, Mike and Sam awakened and rushed to the edge of the platform.

"Oh, God…help him!" Sam uttered.

"Yo, hang on!" Bling shouted down.

"Johnny, you got a shot?" Chief yelled as he tried to locate the beast's head, watching as the bottle flooded with murky water and sank under the swamp.

"Can't get a bead on it! Thrashing around too much!"

As they attempted to target the beast, Switch managed to pull himself up to the next step. He was moving slowly but was out of the range of the beast's weaponized tail. Chief dropped his gun and got down on the platform, hanging over the edge to help him up as the beast maintained its wild thrashing. A few minutes transpired and the beast finally ran out of energy and calmed down. When it did, everyone got a clear look at its backside for the first time.

"This definitely isn't a croc," Johnny surmised, his eyes bulging out. "It's huge!"

Chief didn't respond. He was focused on the beast's reddish, bony spikes that extended from his back to the end of its tail, speculating what it could be.

"It's gotta be at least 25-30 feet long," Mike suggested as he and Chief watched it slowly submerge under the swamp.

"What else is going to go wrong out here?" Chief fumed, considering Switch's injury and the fact that they no longer had access to clean water.

"Why didn't you shoot it?" Switch gazed at Johnny, nearly fainting from the intense pain.

"We didn't have a headshot and its hide is too thick. Shooting it would've made it more aggressive," he replied, backing away from the edge and kneeling down to check his arm.

Switch slithered in pain, trying to hold it together when Chief handed him some pain reliever tablets. "Here, take these…we'll reset the bone and hold it in place with some of these small tree limbs."

As Chief was talking, Mike thought he heard a helicopter off in the distance.

"Hey, I think I hear the helo—"

Chief reached for his MP5 and backed up against the tree. "Everyone get close under the canopy!"

About a minute later, the helicopter hovered over the hut and eight soldiers repelled down from ropes. They hit the ground and fanned out, being careful not to get too close to the embankment. A few soldiers cleared the hut while the rest set a perimeter.

"Chief, I've got a soldier at the back of the hut," Switch whispered, but Chief already had his sights trained on him.

"Rann suu! Rann suu!" the soldier shouted to notify his comrades that he had spotted something in the trees. He dropped his binoculars and reached for the rifle slung around his shoulder.

Phttt. Chief squeezed the trigger and took him out, the muffled sound bouncing off the water and reverberating through the jungle, giving away their position. The other soldiers took cover at the side and the rear of the hut while Johnny, Chief, and Switch spread out on the platform, lying on their stomachs, ready for a firefight.

One of the soldiers moved along the edge of the hut and caught sight of the Claymore. He bent down to inspect it and saw the detonator wire leading into the swamp. He grabbed it, reeling it in and scurried behind the hut as Johnny shot at him, creating several holes in the porch and kicking up mud around him.

"Boss! They have the Claymore!" Johnny yelled.

"Concentrate your fir—" Chief yelled back, but he stopped mid-sentence, his attention abruptly interrupted by the most ferocious form he had ever seen.

"Boss?"

A sudden coldness enveloped him and he didn't respond.

Johnny had been viewing the soldiers through his scope when he pulled back to look at Chief. He was staring out into the swamp, his mouth wide open. Johnny panned out into the water to see what he was captivated by and that's when he noticed the beast gliding in the water up to the shore.

"What the—" Mike paused, gulping hard as they observed the beast slowly rise from the swamp at the edge of the embankment, about 40 feet away. Seconds later another emerged behind it.

"That's...the...tah...tah-neen," Sam stuttered, her eyes locked onto the frame of the immense beasts, everyone getting a full view of their terrifying splendor for the first time.

The tanniyn sauntered up the bank, moving its mighty limbs and broad, ellipsoidal body like a massively oversized crocodile. From its snout to its tail it was as long as a city bus, nearly as tall, and weighed even more. Its partially-webbed feet were as large as frying pans and were accented by eight-inch long, black claws that milled down into the mire for an unrelenting grip. Heavily armored scales covered its large triangular head all the way back to its spiny and muscular tail that swayed behind it. As it moved, its sharp-ridged underside left a path of deep scars in the embankment's mud.

"If I didn't know better, I'd say that's a dinosa—" Switch quickly trailed off, not sure how his absurd statement would be received.

"Yo! Dis mos' definitely Jurassic Park stuff!" Bling surmised. "Looks like a gator, but its gotta be ten times da size."

Mike's eyes showed both intense wonder and dread as the massive beasts roamed up the embankment, their long tails gliding behind them. He nudged Sam in her side to get her attention. "Those things look like something we studied in science class?"

"I remember!" Sam exclaimed, unable to get the lump out of her throat. "Wasn't it called an Ankylosaurus or something like that?"

"Ankle-saurus?" Bling shook his head. "Dat ain't sound right, but it do got big ankles…"

"Bling, how can you be so flippant at a time like this?" Switch asked, pulling his phone out to take a video, but discovering his battery was dead.

The tanniyn reached the top of the embankment and faced off with the quivering boy-soldiers, snarling aggressively as saliva dripped from their gigantic jaws. Their reptilian pupils locked in on their prey and their bluish-colored, forked tongues flicked out and back in, detecting the musty body odor emanating from their next victims.

In an obvious show of intimidation, the beasts slashed their tails wildly and opened their jaws about three feet wide, emitting an ear-stabbing shriek and revealing rows of ivory-colored, dagger-like teeth, clearly designed for tearing through flesh and crushing the thickest of bones.

Ratattatttatttatt! Rattattttattt! Two of the soldiers broke their gaze, firing directly at the beasts' tough, leather-like scales, emptying their entire magazines, but the bullets did nothing but agitate them. With the beasts' attack imminent, one of the soldiers squeezed the Claymore's detonator rapidly, but the water had flooded it, disrupting the connection, and it wouldn't fire.

Everyone on the platform looked on in terror as the tanniyn made a low growling sound and stalked the soldier who anxiously held the detonator up to his mouth, blowing hot air into it to dry it out. The tanniyn displaced their weight to their squatty hind legs that were directly set under their immense bodies, preparing to lunge forward, but before they could, the Claymore mine detonated.

Ka-boom! The device exploded and a veil of smoke concealed the barrage of steel ball bearings that pummeled the beasts. Everyone held their breath, waiting for the smoke to dissipate, hoping and praying the mine had worked.

THIRTY-FIVE
LEVIATHAN

The smoke pillared out of the clearing into the morning sky and everyone waited for confirmation of the kill. Soon, the smoke emptied out, but there was no sign of the beasts.

"Maybe…maybe there's nothing left of them," Switch replied optimistically, but he didn't even believe his own words.

"They're too big not to leave some type of carcass behind," Chief advised as he looked at the soldiers, their arms shaking so much they could hardly hold their guns up.

As they reasoned it out, the beasts roared louder than they ever had, sending a horrifying shock through everyone's body. They were still there, lurking behind a row of trees beyond the clearing, completely unscathed and more aggressive than ever.

The beasts lunged out of the trees, galloping at the soldiers like horses. Horrified, the soldiers scrambled for fresh bullet magazines, but before they could insert them into their guns, the beasts were face-to-face with them, their tails raised into the air, thrashing violently. Before the soldiers could react, the beasts' tails whipped at them, severing limbs and cutting some of them in half. Two of the soldiers attempted to flee but they beasts gave chase, catching them in their massive jaws and effortlessly chewed them up like wood shredders consuming twigs.

Sam clamped her hands against her ears to muffle the grisly sound of the tanniyn growling and ripping chucks of flesh from the boys' bodies. Mike placed his arm around her and held her tight, refusing to watch them feast.

"Chief, I've got a headshot. Permission to shoot," Johnny asked.

"Negative. Hold your fire."

As he spoke, they heard a familiar sound coming from the trail. A diesel-powered armored personnel carrier had pushed through the dense vegetation and nosed into the clearing. The tanniyn whipped their heads around, flicked their tongues rapidly and beat their mighty tail in the air.

The APC pushed through the last of the thick undergrowth and the tanniyns left the nearly unrecognizable human remains and moved in to inspect it. They ambled to the vehicle with their tails standing nearly erect, sniffing out its all-metal skin, their curiosity consuming them.

The vehicle's black diesel fumes spilled around them and their nostrils flared wide. Then they opened their massive jaws, shrieking so powerfully loud that the APC's thick-plated windshield glass cracked in several places.

The soldiers inside the APC rotated the autocannon at one of the beasts and fired.

Boom! Boom! Boom! The autocannon's thunderous blasts resounded through the jungle and everyone on the platform held their breath, but they didn't have to wait long to see that the bullets had no effect; in fact, they literally bounced off the tanniyns' armor-plated scales, obliterating the small hut behind them.

The beasts snarled aggressively, thrashing their tails in the air, the back-and-forth motion sounding like the loud crack of a whip.

Slam! Slam! Slam! They battered the APC with their tree trunk-sized tails. With their bodies shuddering from the intense pounding, the soldiers inside popped the hatch and exited the vehicle, attempting to jump off into the jungle, but the tanniyn intercepted them, grabbing them in their jaws and ripping them apart.

Once the cold-blooded beasts had their fill they returned to assaulting the armored vehicle, pummeling it until it resembled a massive, partially crushed soda pop can. Then they took off down the trail toward the convoy and sporadic gunfire and horrifying screams filled the late morning air…and then everything went quiet again.

Chief spoke up and broke the silence. "Guys, while the creatures are preoccupied, I'm going to swim across and get our gear bags. We can use the IV kits for hydration. Y'all cover me."

"I don't know if that's a good idea, boss," Johnny whispered, pointing at the trail. "Listen."

Chief turned his ear toward the trail and listened to the sound of snapping tree branches and the beast's heavy feet pounding the ground. The beasts were coming back. He grabbed his binoculars and got a close up look at them as they roamed back into the clearing, their jaws covered in blood.

"Is it me or do they look worn-out?" Switch asked, peering over Chief's shoulder.

"I think you're right," Chief responded as everyone watched them meander further into the clearing. They stopped halfway into the clearing and rested under the slivers of sunlight.

"Looks like they may be cold-blooded," Chief surmised.

"Yo, they mos' def cold-blooded…"

"I'm talking about their body temperature, Bling, not their temperament."

"I ain't seein' no difference, yo."

"Cold-blooded like crocs," Johnny suggested. "Which means they probably hunt mostly at night."

Switch spoke up. "Well, they just took out God only knows how many soldiers and tore through that APC in the middle of the day. I'd hate to see what they can do at night."

As the sun reflected off their body, their bony armor appeared as though it was metallic and gave off a dazzling rainbow color. Bling's bottom lip partially dropped open as he focused on their brilliance.

"I...I know what these is," Bling stammered, his eyes focused intently on the beasts.

"What do you mean?" Chief asked.

"Bling, what are you talking about?" Johnny asked sternly. "Nobody knows what these are...for all we know they really are prehistoric."

As they talked, Sam observed a large saltwater crocodile glide up out of the swamp and rest on the bank to soak in some of the sun's rays. One of the tanniyn sensed it and rose up, peering over the embankment, locking its large, red eyes with the crocodile's. The croc backpedaled a few inches and the tanniyn let out a low growl and opened its hideous jaw, its teeth still bloodied from when it had feasted on the soldiers. Not wanting any part of the immense monster, the inquisitive croc quickly scampered away, submerging itself into the swamp.

"These tanniyn creatures make salties look like puppies," Johnny suggested as he sat down on the platform.

"Let's assume these things are somehow related to crocs," Chief speculated. "Johnny, you're the expert on them; tell us what you know."

"I'm no expert. My knowledge comes from my fear as a kid, but I'll tell you what I know...Crocs are great hunters, but they have poor eyesight; they make up for it with other sensory features, like the small nerve-filled pits all over their bodies that can detect even a single drip of disturbance in the water."

"Poor eyesight; that makes sense," Chief suggested. "I guess that's why these things missed knocking Switch into the water. They have trouble targeting."

"I'd say they did pretty good, if you ask me," Switch replied, glancing at his throbbing arm.

"Crocs also prefer live prey and have almost a natural night-vision," Johnny continued. "They're at home in the water, but can run faster than a horse on land for a very short period of time..."

"I think we just saw some of that. Do you remember anything else?" Chief asked.

"Yeah, their metabolism is super slow, which means they can go without food for long periods of time; it allows them to stalk their prey for weeks at a time if necessary. But probably their most fearsome feature is their bite force. If I remember correctly, a crocodile has nearly 4,000-foot pounds of bite force—about twelve times stronger than a Rottweiler dog."

"Man, you really do know a lot about crocodiles," Switch remarked.

"Yo! Here it is. Listen to this," Bling excitedly interjected, flipping through the thin pages on his small pocket Bible.

"Hold up," Johnny interrupted. "Are you gonna tell us that these monsters are in your religious book?"

"Yeah, they ain't no crocodile. If you allows me to finish, I'll show you."

"Look, this is the last thing we need right—"

"You know what, Johnny," Bling deepened his voice and uncharacteristically cut him off, garnering everyone's attention. "I've been takin' lots of heat from you since I gots on da team. You always be cuttin' me down for my faith, but you ain't nevah got no good explations for nuthin'—just always talkin' 'bout how they ain't no God. I make a deal wit' you. If you got answers for dis here beast, I'll give you a listen."

Feeling the pressure to respond, Johnny forced out his best rebuttal.

"Nobody knows what these things are, Bling, let alone some dusty religious book."

"Well, I figures you ain't have no answers, but you called it a creature out yo own mouth. Have you thought dat maybe da Creat-or knows sumptin' 'bout da creat-ure?"

"I don't wanna hear jack of what your ancient book of fables has to say!" Johnny angrily countered.

"Johnny, stay cool, brother," Chief interjected, trying to keep a calm tone. "What can it hurt if he reads from the good book?"

"Boss, you can't be serious right now."

"I'd like to hear what Bling has to say as well," Sam softly answered. Mike nodded in agreement.

Johnny turned to Switch. "What about you? Surely, you're not on board with this religious stuff."

"I don't know one way or another," he responded. "But we did listen to your Ramree story; maybe Bling has some intel that's useful."

"You know what? Y'all have at it," Johnny responded curtly and then stormed off to the opposite side of the platform, slouching down against the tree.

"Wow, is it that serious, Johnny?" Chief asked, but he didn't respond.

"Go ahead, Bling," Chief stated, disregarding Johnny's sulking.

"Okay, well, there was dis righteous guy in the Bible named Job and he went through some extremely hard knocks. He ended up questionin' God about his horrible sufferin' and dis is one of God's responses to him: Job, can you draw out Leviathan with a hook or play wit' him like a pet? Can you shoot him wit' weapons?...Just one glimpse of this monster make all courage melt. No one is so fierce dat he would dare stir him up. Leviathan belongs to Me, so who den is able to stand against Me?"

Chief tilted his head, slightly confused. "So are you're saying these creatures are called leviathan?" he asked, looking out of the corner of his eyes at the clearing and observing the tanniyn still basking in the sunlight.

"Yeah, but there's more," Bling indicated as he looked back down at the Bible. He traced his finger to where he stopped and then continued, "What powerful legs, what a stout body Leviathan possesses. Who would try to open his jaw with his terrible teeth? His back is covered with shield after shield...His sneezings flash light and his eyes glow like da dawn...everyone trembles before him...When he raises himself up da warriors are afraid; because of his crashings, they are beside themselves. Weapons cannot prevail against him. His undersides are like sharp edges dat spread pointed marks in da mud, and he leaves a shining wake behind him. On earth, there is nothing like him, a creature dat has no fear...He is king over all da children of pride."

Sam listened as Bling finished and spoke up. "I don't know about anyone else, but that describes exactly what I'm seeing and feeling."

"Hey, Johnny, what do you think?" Switch asked, calling out from several feet away.

"I think he described a croc."

"A croc as in crocodile or as in he's full of crock?" Switch snickered, not expecting a response.

Chief shared his own thoughts. "When he first started reading, I thought he was describing a crocodile too, but he went on to say that the creature has no fear of anything. I've seen videos where a lion's roar intimidated crocodiles into retreating; it can't be talking about crocs."

"Regardless, boss, I don't see how the Bible is helping us here," Johnny murmured.

"I can see your point, Johnny, but I also know that book gives a lot of people hope—and I thought we could use some of that right now—especially if it somehow describes our situation."

"Chief, I can keep readin'. I ain't gots to da hope parts yet."

"That's good for now, Bling," Chief indicated, giving him a subtle look as though to back off a bit for Johnny's sake.

"I gots you," Bling responded, quietly flipping through the thin Bible pages.

"Hey, but I am curious about one thing, Bling," Chief replied. "Maybe you can clear this up for me. What was it that caused you to remember that this creature was mentioned in the Bible? The beasts walk out into the sun and it was like a light came on for you."

"When da sun hit its scales, it revealed da rainbow."

"I saw that, but what you read didn't reference anything about a rainbow."

"True. I'd have to collate it and break it all down for y—"

"Collate?" Switch's eyebrows rose. "Bling, that's a pretty big word there, buddy."

"It means to gather da text in order…Just cuz' I ain't speak all proper ain't mean I ain't smart."

"Bling, I know you're smart, man. I never meant to imply anything otherwise."

Johnny smacked his lips. "Look, you all can continue this Bible lesson if you want, but I need water…and I also need to relieve myself."

"We second that motion," Mike spoke up as though he were speaking for both he and Sam. She quickly jabbed him in the rib with her elbow to let him know she didn't approve.

"Hey, come on, it's true, right?" Mike sheepishly stated.

"Okay, look, here's what we're gonna do," Chief asserted, trying to unify everyone. "Bling, we'll break it down later. Right now, I need to know if anyone has any ideas on getting water— without us becoming a snack for the tanniyn…or leviathan or whatever it is."

"Well, it's gonna sound gross," Switch began. "But what if we dangle the rope in the water and let it soak. We could suck the water out of it."

"Yeah, that's certainly an idea," Chief frowned. "But we'll save that as a last resort."

As they were speaking, the tanniyns rose up and sluggishly entered the water several yards from the platform. Johnny watched through his scope as their tails maneuvered them out into the swamp and finally disappeared from sight.

Sitting by himself, he gazed at the spot where they had buried Mack. He lowered his head, looking quite despondent.

"Johnny, you okay over there?" Chief asked.

"Thinking about our friend is all."

"We all miss him."

Johnny didn't say anything more. He stood up, removed his boots, and walked to the edge of the platform.

"Johnny?" Chief called out, but he didn't answer. He sprung off the platform like an Olympic diver, plunging into the swamp and creating a huge splash.

Chief jumped to his feet, staring into the dark waters, but there was no sign of Johnny, only thousands of tiny bubbles. Several seconds later he finally resurfaced near the embankment.

"What the hell are you doing?" Chief spoke through gritted teeth to limit how far his voice would carry into the jungle, but he disregarded him.

Johnny raced up the embankment and maneuvered carefully around the soldier's mangled bodies. Then he saw what he was after—the gear bags. One had been crushed by the tanniyn, but the other two appeared untouched. He opened one up, pouring the contents into the other and slipped something shiny into his pocket. He removed a shovel and a few other heavier items to make the bag lighter and zipped it closed. As he did, Chief caught a glimpse of the tanniyn moving in the swamp water, rapidly approaching his position.

"Johnny!" Chief shouted. Johnny sensed the urgency in his voice and threw the bag over his shoulder, slipping down the embankment. When he did, he tripped over one of the pier's wooden stilts and scraped up his shin. Ignoring the slight pain, he jumped into the water, swimming as fast as he could.

Switch stood near the platform's steps, trying to ignore his throbbing arm, waiting to help Johnny any way he could. As he waited, he held the scope in his good hand and surveyed the clearing. It wasn't long before he saw something moving at the opposite side of the trail. He zoomed in and saw a cluster of reddish-green scales, but when he zoomed back out, he nearly lost his breath.

"Ch—chief…maj…major problem here," Switch stuttered. "I'm counting four more of those tann—"

Chief yelled over him, "Swim faster, Johnny!"

Moments later, Johnny reached the steps and pulled himself up, but the sopping wet gear bag weighed him down and he slipped off the bottom step.

"Lose the bag!" Chief yelled down, but he refused to let it go. Johnny got back up on the first step when the bag slipped off his shoulder. He reached back and caught it as one of the tanniyn shot out of the water, its four-inch long teeth scraping across the top of his arm, gashing it open and snagging the gear bag, ripping it out of his hand.

315

"Ahhhhh!" Johnny screamed in pain, but there was no time to lament; he moved as quickly as he could up the steps where Chief waited, helping him to the platform.

"What were you thinking?" Chief seethed in anger. He wanted to punch him and hug him at the same time. Johnny remained silent, thankful to be alive.

"The next time you want to pull a stunt like that, you had better let me know," Chief stated, still simmering.

"Yo, goin' afta dat bag was a bold move," Bling surmised.

"Sure was," Switch agreed, opening up his first aid kit and inspecting his wound.

"Too bad I didn't get it," Johnny replied.

"At least you're alive…and it missed your major arteries," he responded, cleaning the wound and wrapping it with gauze. "But it'll make one nasty-looking scar," Switch smiled. "Now you've got a new story to tell. How many people can say they basically lived through a dinosaur attack?"

"Yeah, right, and who would believe it? Besides, living is looking more elusive right about now," he stated, listening to the sloshing swamp water as two of the tanninyn once again violently circled the tree.

THIRTY-SIX
INSANITY

Mike stepped to the edge of the platform and sat down, his feet dangling over the edge, swinging them like he was a little kid again. He stared at the tanniyns as they swirled around the tree, mumbling some incoherent words, the stress causing his brain to misfire. Sam and Chief both watched him closely to ensure he wasn't relapsing back to his incoherent stupor.

"Yo, how many of these things are there?" Bling asked as he glanced over the edge at the sloshing whirlpool below.

"Six," Switch responded as Chief's eyes briefly connected with his.

Johnny sat in the middle of the platform, several feet away from everyone else when he spoke up. "Chief and Switch, can you guys come here for a second. I need help with something," he mentioned, keeping an eye on Mike.

They looked at each other, wondering what he was up to and walked over to him.

"What's up, Johnny?" Chief asked as they squatted down in front of him.

"Listen, guys," he whispered. "We...uh...we won't survive this if we just sit up here, but I've got an idea. I need you to hear me out because it's gonna require something we probably don't want to do—a necessary sacrifice if you will." Chief and Switch pulled back to look him in the eyes.

"What are you talking about, Johnny?" Chief asked as he focused intently on him.

"I'll just get right to it; we need to somehow convince Mike that the only way his girl can live is if he draws the beasts away from us," he whispered. "If he gets a good start into the woods, those beasts will chase him and we can take off down the trail back to the—"

Chief interrupted. "That's your idea?"

"Hey, you're the one who said he wasn't even part of the op."

"Are you listening to yourself?" Switch chided him, trying to whisper.

"Do you have a better idea? We did this in the military all the time. One takes the fall so the others can live. Look at him; he's not right in the head anyway."

"Hey, what are you guys talking about?" Sam questioned from several feet away. "Is there a plan?"

"Listen, Johnny, your idea isn't an option, are we clear?" Chief lowered his voice even more and then addressed Sam. "Yeah, we're trying to work it out. We'll fill y'all in when we figure it out," Chief raised his voice a bit as Johnny brooded again. He moved to the furthest edge of the platform, plopping down on the wooden decking, and then pulled a shiny flask from his pocket.

"Please tell me you didn't risk your life for some whiskey," Chief asked.

"Sure did," Johnny responded sharply, wiping sweat from his forehead and taking a swig.

"So you let us think you were doing a good deed trying to get the gear bags, but you went down there for some liquor?" Switch asked with disappointment in his voice.

"Ahh!" Johnny took an exaggerated swig. "And it was so worth it."

"That was really stupid!" Chief railed. "You know my policy for drinking on the mission anyway—not to mention you'll get even more dehydrated."

"Look, Chief, you can stop pretending we'll survive this. The mission is jacked. You don't have a plan, and you didn't approve of mine. Just let me have a little peace here, alright?"

"Ain't no peace in dat der stuff," Bling uninvitingly interjected. "It's gonna make things worse."

"Ah, yes, our gunless, hood preacher is now about to tell me the Bible has the answer for my peace as well," Johnny criticized.

"Yo, you can call me names all you want, but I know alcohol's effect betta than most. Them drinks is evil. They bite like a serpent. In my old days, I'd get hammered and go out and do all kinds of evil stuff. I ain't see da truth till they locked me in da penitentiary...Dat's where I found sumptin' much betta. And, yeah, I do know 'bout peace. I'm just tryin' to share Him wit' you."

"Good for you, but I ain't interested in your version of peace," Johnny snapped, checking to make sure the blood from his wound hadn't penetrated through his gauze.

"Johnny," Sam spoke up. "I'm curious to know about your plan."

"It doesn't matter; Chief shot it down."

"Guys, the tanniyn stopped circling...they're leaving," Switch reported as he examined the water below.

"Good. I'm just thankful these dragons ain't got wings," Chief responded as he broke off a low-lying limb from the tree to make a splint for Switch's arm.

"Roger that," Switch replied.

"Bling, I think I know what you're saying about peace," Sam responded, provoking the conversation to keep her mind off their grim reality. "I've watched you since we've been out here and you have so much peace and joy about you. Do you get that from God?"

"Sure do. I used to get my peace from da bottle like da rest of da world, but I learned dat's only temporary. Once I got a grip on real peace, I saw dat alcohol was a poor counterfeit."

"Real peace. I'd like to know more about that," she smiled at him.

"I don't," Johnny retorted, taking another swig. "I got all the peace I need right here."

"I'd be glad to share mo' wit' you, Sam," Bling replied, ignoring Johnny. "When I got sentenced to prison, I got hold of a Bible. Ain't have nuthin' else to do, so I read…and read. I got to dis part where da Bible say not to be drunk on alcoholic spirits but to be filled up on God's Holy Spirit. Since gettin' drunk was always one of mines hang-ups, I was curious about da Bible comparing God's Spirit to alcohol's spirits."

"Hmmm…that is interesting," Sam suggested, tilting her head in curiosity as everyone else listened. "I'm sorry, I didn't mean to interrupt."

"Yeah, so I started prayin' 'bout givin' up da drink. But not just givin' it up—replacin' it with God's Spirit. I figured if there was sumtin' dat could give me joy and peace without all da drama, hangovers and blackouts, I wanted it. I read where it say dat it's God's good pleasure to give us da Holy Spirit, so I asked Him every day. It wasn't long afta dat when I felt da presence of God so powerful on me dat I couldn't stand up."

"You couldn't stand up?" Mike asked, seeking more information. "How's that?"

"Yeah, I was in my cell and my bunkie said my speech was all strange. My lips was stammerin' and I had dis supa joy come all over me. I fell asleep dat night wit' so much peace and bliss and I woke up wantin' nothin' mo' than to live fo' God. Since then, I've been talkin' wit' God on the daily and got no desire for da Devil's counterfeit spirits."

"That is so cool, Bling!" Sam replied.

Mike didn't say anything, but his face showed his confusion.

"Oh brother," Johnny replied, taking another swig from his flask.

"Look, I know it sound crazy, but when God gave me His Spirit it was like I was drunk wit'out da bad stuff—I guess dat's why da Bible makes dat comparison. In fact, there's a Bible story 'bout dis happenin' with a bunch of peeps in da book of Acts. When God's Holy Spirit filled 'em up wit' His presence, they bodies couldn't handle God's power and they started actin' strange. Everyone who saw it thought they was drunk on alcoholic spirits, but they wasn't; it was God's Holy Spirit fillin' 'em up!"

"This is a little far-fetched, Bling," Chief interjected, finishing wrapping Switch's splint with gauze. "When I was a kid, I attended mass every time the doors were opened, but I've never had anything like that happen to me—never even heard about nothing like that."

"Well, I'll be honest wit' you. A lot of churches ain't even believe in dis here stuff, even though it's in da Bible…and while I ain't know everythin' 'bout it, I do know it ain't gonna nevah come if you satisfied wit' da Devil's spirits and don't got da faith for it."

"Bling, you're full of it," Johnny snarled. "Entire cultures drink alcohol as a staple in their diet. Are you telling me they're all wrong and that they're sipping on the Devil's spirits?"

"Entire cultures ain't allowed to eat cheeseburgers 'cuz they worship cows. Some tribes cannibalize strangers, but dat don't make 'em right."

Johnny didn't respond, but everyone could feel his scowl.

"Yo, look, every instance of peeps drinking to get drunk in the Bible is linked wit' evil. Every one of 'em," Bling stated. "In fact, God gave us a wise proverb dat condemns alcohol pretty boldly when it say dat wine is a mocker and strong drink makes a person rage. But even in dat, da Bible again associates alcohol wit' being filled with God's Spirit because da word for mocker means to speak in a stammering tongue—and dat's exactly what happened to me when God's Spirit fell on me in dat cell."

Chief stayed quiet, contemplating Bling's comments.

"That's fascinating," Sam replied, "I guess that's why they're called alcoholic spirits…and I had no clue that God's Spirit could cause a similar effect without the negative stuff. Thanks for sharing that."

"I'm glad to," Bling responded. "I can talk to you mo' 'bout it, if ya want. Jesus is real peace—believe me when I sat dat everythin' else is a fraud."

"So, you mean to tell me, you got drunk on God?" Johnny laughed almost hysterically. "Man, your religion has you messed up in the head."

"It's true, whether you wanna believe it or not. Not only dat, they've been millions of peeps all ovah da world wit' dis same experience. Ain't nutin' like conversatin' wit' God and knowin' your creator wit' da benefits of da Holy Spirit. It's wild, bro. You get peace and joy and ain't no drama or wakin' up throwin' up."

"Whatever, Bling. Keep gettin' drunk on Jesus. I'll be over here *conversatin'* with Mr. Jack Daniels." Johnny sneered. "And by the way, even your Jesus turned water into wine."

"You know what, Johnny, you right, He did. And do you know why He did dat?"

"I don't have a clue…I think He was celebrating at a wedding reception or something. Does it really matter?"

"Sure it do. Jesus always had a reason for doin' stuff. You focused on da drink 'cuz dat's what you like, but you missed da background."

"I ain't interested in the background."

"I…I am," Sam softly interrupted. As she spoke, a huge spider about the size of a man's hand crawled off the tree onto Switch's shoulder. Switch felt its hairy legs tickling his ear and he tensed up.

"Argh!" his girly scream echoed through the swamp, bouncing off the mirror-like water, the algae unsettled and pushed away by the tanniyn. "Get this thing off of me!"

"Hold still," Chief insisted as he smacked the spider off into the water.

"Ah, man, thank you. We've gotta get out here. The place is giving me the creeps!"

"Switch, your scream reminds me of my niece," Johnny laughed.

"Whatever, man. There's deadly stuff out here."

"Yeah, me."

"Then why don't you take out those beasts down there so we can get out of here."

Johnny didn't respond. He was crazy, but not that crazy.

"Bling, can you tell us more about what you were saying? About Jesus turning the water into wine and what that was all about?" Sam asked, redirecting the conversation to where they had left off.

"Absolutely. Turning da water to wine was Jesus' first miracle and was meant to be a symbol. To understand fully, you gotsta go back to anotha occasion when water was turned into blood."

"Wait…are you talking about what happened with Moses and Pharoah?"

"You on it, yo. I see you know a bit of yo Bible, too."

"Great! Another Bible study. I should have kept my mouth shut," Johnny responded sharply, but no one paid him any attention.

"Hmm…yeah, I know about Moses from Sunday School when I was a kid, but what does that have to do with Jesus?" she asked.

"Yo, you gotta look deeper. Da first public miracle dat God did through Moses to convince Pharaoh to let His peeps leave was turning all da water in da land into blood."

"So, let me see if I have this right. When Jesus turned the water into wine, He was giving something like an illustrated message?"

"Yo, you got it, shorty. Jesus was using a story peeps was familiar wit' to show dat His mission was like Moses'. Da first plague was when God worked through Moses to turn da water to blood, and eventually he was able to fully deliver da Children of Israel from Egyptian slavery through the blood of an innocent lamb."

"An innocent lamb?" she asked, trying to understand. "I vaguely remember that part."

"God told da Children of Israel to kill da lamb and put its blood on they houses, and when da death angel came dat evening, it passed over 'em, but it took out all da Egyptian's firstborn sons, 'cuz they wasn't covered in da blood."

"I remember now," she replied. "That's where the term Passover comes from."

"Right. When Pharoah saw dat his son died, he finally allowed the Children of Israel to leave—even though he later chased after 'em. In da same way, Jesus' miracles began with turnin' da water into da blood of da grape at dat wedding, and when He—da innocent Lamb of God—finally shed His blood on da cross, it opened da door to freedom over da slavery of sin fo' everyone who believes, for all who cover themselves in Jesus' innocent blood…by faith."

"See, told you we were getting another Bible study," Johnny snidely interjected. "Who can even understand this stuff?"

"It's only fo' those who gots ears to hear, Johnny."

"Bling, thanks for sharing your insights. I'm blown away right now," Sam replied, disregarding Johnny's antagonistic attitude.

"Sure. Oh, and one mo' thang. Jesus ain't turn dat water into no alcoholic wine."

"How do you know that?" Mike asked, suddenly perking up.

"Now this I gotta hear," Johnny chuckled.

"Laugh all you want, but like I done said, da wine was a symbol of Jesus' perfect, sinless blood. Alcoholic wine is fermented, which involves yeast and decay, both of which are biblical symbols of sin. Jesus wouldn't have used symbols of sin to represent His sinless blood. Dat's contrary to da message. He turned da water into da fresh blood of the grape—what da ancients held in high regard because it was so difficult to keep from turning sour. You gotsta remember dat they ain't have no refrigerators back then."

"Grape juice, Bling? You sound like a typical Christian— always trying to take away everyone's happiness," Johnny responded. "Bling, the old fuddy-duddy—won't kill nobody, but he sure will kill everyone's happiness."

"You gots me all wrong. I'm ain't even trying to stop you from drinking; I'm just trying to show you sumptin' real—sumptin' mo' betta. But since you brought up happiness, you should know dat it ain't da same as joy. Happiness is short-lived; it's based on what happens—da ups and downs of life. But joy, dat's entirely different. Joy is based on God's Holy Spirit—and because He is constant and everlasting, joy can be a constant for you without all da downers. Dat's why, even though we in a tough spot right here, I gots so much joy, and you have...well, you have dat drink in yo hand."

Johnny kept quiet, rolling his heavy eyes, becoming more and more intoxicated.

"I can see the symbolism, Bling!" Sam was getting excited. "That's gotta be why Jesus turned the water into wine at a wedding. It was another symbol that He came to restore our joy through a relationship with Him."

"Bingo! And there's much mo' to it than dat, but you on da right track. Da main point is to be completely filled up with da Holy Spirit, 'cuz when dat happens, you ain't gonna have room for no other spirits to cause havoc in yo life, and dat's a good thang."

"Man, you're both off your rocker." Johnny barked, taking another long, exaggerated drink of his whiskey. "I'm done with this convo. It's useless. Y'all leave me alone so I can get some rest."

Soon after, Johnny was snoring and everyone was careful not to disturb him.

THIRTY-SEVEN
RAINBOWS

O kay, guys, who can eat?" Chief smiled flatly. The dusk sky had all but erased the slivers of light and night was intruding fast.

"Are you seriously asking that question?" Switch replied.

"I certainly can," Mike blurted out. "I'm almost ready to drop the rope into the swamp to get some water."

"We could always drink our own pee," Switch grinned wide, unconvinced of his own suggestion.

"I guess you missed that part in the Marine Corp Manual, Switch" Chief stated. "Drinking urine is essentially drinking salt water; it's essentially the same composition and will dehydrate you even more, taking you out quicker."

"Yeah, I, uh, I knew that…I was just joking," Switch replied, attempting to cover his error, but not convincing anyone.

"The good news is that we've got two IV bags from our med kits that we can use as a last measure. I figure we can last another couple days, but I don't want to push it."

As they conversed, Chief broke apart an energy bar and gave everyone a small piece, except for Johnny who was still sleeping, but he kept his part for when he woke up.

"Chief, I think I'd like to try the rope…for real, I'm just so thirsty," Mike mentioned and then mumbled some incoherent words.

"It's all yours," Chief replied, removing the rope from the gear bag. "It's probably best to do this before nightfall fully sets in anyway—especially if we're right about those leviathans being more active at night."

"Good idea," Mike replied as he let the rope down into the swamp water.

"So, we're calling these creatures leviathan and not tanniyn?" Switch asked.

"Why not?" Chief replied. "With what Bling said, it seems fitting. I'm not really down to call it tanniyn; that's what the military calls it during their little worship ceremonies."

"Yeah, I like leviathan better," Sam entered the conversation as she sat next to the tree, her knees folded to her chest and arms wrapped around the sweatpants that Bling had given her.

"Speaking of the leviathan, Bling, I'd like to revisit what you were saying earlier," Chief indicated.

"Sure. I'd be glad to. That's why I'm here."

Chief looked baffled. "What did you say?"

"God told me dis da reason I'm on da team. Made it purdy clear actually. Said I'd have dis chance to speak to y'all."

"Wait, so you knew this was gonna happen? How long ago did you know it?"

"I ain't no psychic, if dat's what you axin'. It's a bit hard to explain, even harder to grasp, but sumtimes God speaks to me. I ain't know full details, but I knew when you invited me on dis team dat there's a bigger picture at play; it became clearer when you told us about dis here mission."

"So, there's a bigger picture here?"

"Oh, fo' sho'. Dis whole thing is to get yall's attention. God said I basically got released from prison and He put me in yo path for dis time right here."

"Well, did you hear if we're gonna make it out alive?"

"All He say is dat I would complete da task."

"Man, this is really disgusting," Mike complained as he placed his mouth under the end of the swamp-saturated rope, the cloudy water dripping onto his tongue. Sam stood next to him not necessarily anticipating her turn, but her pounding headache was screaming for some type of fluid.

As she took her turn with the rope, Johnny woke up, and he made sure everyone knew it. "Oh, hell, I'm still here! Man, that was a crazy dream!" he exclaimed, looking out into the clearing at the bloated dead bodies already attracting swarms of flies.

"What was your dream about, Johnny?" Switch asked curiously.

"I was lying on a plush bed next to a beach, sipping an *alcoholic* beverage, surrounded by beautiful Caribbean wom—"

"Hey, come on," Chief cut him off. There's a young lady here. If you wanna make your point to Bling, that's one thing, but let's keep it civil."

"My bad, boss." Johnny opened up a granola bar he had snuck into his pocket from one of the gear bags and Chief glared at him for a second, wondering where he had gotten the food.

"So, I guess you're gonna sit there and eat that in front of us, huh? We saved you a piece from the bar that we *shared*."

"You're not gonna make me feel bad about it, boss. After all, I'm the one who risked my life for it."

"Right. We remember. I guess one stupid turn deserves another. Hey, by the way, Bling is getting ready to teach us some more Bible," Chief smiled widely. "You wanna join in? You could use some with your attitude."

"Oh, Lord, please put me back in the dream!" Johnny slapped his forehead, embellishing his irritation, the stress and alcohol prompting his brashness.

"I didn't think you believed in the Lord, Johnny," Switch snickered, poking a little fun at him.

Johnny threw his hands up and reached for his flask to take another drink.

"Go ahead, Bling, tell us more how God chose you to tell us about Him," Chief nodded.

"Hold up," Johnny wobbled a bit as he stood to his feet. A bit of anger laced his slightly slurred words as he extended his hand and pointed at Bling. "So you think God chose you—a two-time ex-con—to share His message with us? And did God also choose Mack to be killed? Was that part of His grand plan? And you better think carefully before you speak."

"Like I told everyone when you was sleepin'…it's hard to grasp," Bling maintained. "But God redeems flawed people for His purposes. All them characters in da Bible was flawed. Noah, Abe, Mo, Rahab, Pete, da Samaritan lady…it's a mystery how He chooses to partner wit' us to share His truth…a miracle, really,"

"You only answered part of my question…In fact, I'll rephrase it better for you. I want to know why God didn't save Mack— especially since you Christians say He's all-powerful and all."

"Honestly, I could explain it to you, but in yo stupor, you ain't gonna get it…but there is a bigger plan at work here."

"Right, a big plan to kill Mack and all of us—some God!"

"Look, Johnny, there's something you should know about Mack. I've been holding off sharing this, but I think it would be good fo' you to know."

"Better not be more mumbo jumbo."

"Nah, man, afta da farm raid briefin' we had, Mack came to my room and shared sumtin' wit' me dat you should know. He confessed to me dat back in da day he lived a very wicked lifestyle, filled with women and booze. As a result of all his partyin', he contracted a disease. He shared wit' me dat he only had a few months to live. He knew dis was his last mission and he wanted me to share Jesus wit' him…he surrendered to Christ at da hotel dat very night."

"Bull—" Johnny cussed. "I don't believe you. I think you're making this up to go along with your crazy narrative."

"Johnny," Chief interjected. "Bling's telling the truth. I didn't know about the hotel part, but I knew he was dying; he told me. That's how I was able to process his death a little easier. He asked me not to share because he didn't want us to treat him differently. The doc told him he had less than a year left."

Johnny looked down, his hand pressed against his head.

Bling continued. "And that's why, if you remember, he ain't kill no one afta dat day at da hotel. He was slowly changin'. God always has a plan—it's just hard fo' us to see."

"Just…just leave me alone right now. I don't want to talk. My…my head hurts," he responded, confusion overtaking his mind as the darkness fully enveloped the swamp.

"I get it, Johnny. I ain't tryin' to upset you. I'll leave ya alone."

"Chief, it's 1930 hours," Switch reported, looking down at the glowing digits on his tactical watch, trying to change the subject. "Do you think we need a lookout tonight? The helo hasn't returned and we haven't seen any soldiers for hours."

"They probably think we were taken out by the leviathans, but we need to have our weapons ready."

"Roger that," Switch responded.

"Speaking of weapons, let's do a quick ammo check so we know where we stand," Chief instructed, removing his flashlight and clicking on the red light.

"Finally, something I can relate to," Johnny muttered, removing his MP5 magazine. "I've got…23 rounds for the MP and a full mag on my pistol."

"I've got one full mag left for each," Switch responded.

"Good. I've got 19 MP and half a mag on my 1911."

Johnny, Switch, and Chief loaded their mags back into their guns and Chief clicked off his light. When he did, it was like he turned off all the sound in the jungle. With little noise or light, their minds drifted into the unknown.

Several minutes later, Chief spoke up, breaking the silence. "How is everyone doing?" he asked, the darkness so thick no one could see one another, not even Mike and Sam who were basically leaning on each other.

"Arm is still throbbing like a mug," Switch indicated. "And I'm trying to stave off some grim thoughts."

"Same here," Johnny spoke flatly.

"Dark thoughts…yep," Mike replied.

Sam agreed with a nod, but no one could see her.

Chief felt it too. "I'm right there with y'all. I think it would be good to keep talking—we have to keep our minds right."

"The enemy is tryin' to attack yo mind," Bling interjected.

"The enemy?" Switch asked with confusion in his voice. "Like psychological warfare?"

"Yeah, I guess you could call it dat, but dis ain't comin' from da Burmese. Dis is from da invisible enemy we all face."

"Oh, now you've got me interested in this one," Switch responded. Bling paused for a few seconds waiting to see if he would need to contend with Johnny, but he didn't say anything, so he continued.

"There be lots of things we can't see, dark forces at work behind da scenes. Da Bible implies dat there's spiritual warfare in an unseen realm—and it manifests in da flesh. In fact, da story about da leviathan in Job is all about spiritual warfare."

"Can you explain that a little more?" Sam asked, her delicate voice a welcome sound amid the blackness of the swamp.

"Sure. There's a lot to da story, but basically, da Devil, who I like to call the Destroyer, he attacked Job by takin' out his kids, and even gave him a horrible disease. Then he used his friends to try and get him to give up on God. Dat's what spiritual warfare is. Da devil and his evil forces of darkness want to keep you from God any way they can. But if you make it through dat, then he try to murder your relationship with Him and yo' work for da kingdom…and he often uses suffering and other people to do it—just like he try to do with Job."

Mike spoke up. "A lot of people think there's no God because of the suffering in the world.

"You right," Bling replied and continued. "And, Johnny, dat's why you axed dat question about Mack. Da Destroyer puts them thoughts in our heads to get us offended at God. He wants us to turn on Him. If he can get you to think God is evil, you ain't never gonna trust Him."

For the first time, everyone was silent and listening intently.

"Same thing happened back in da garden wit' Adam and Eve. Da Destroyer tricked 'em by instillin' doubt in they mind 'bout who God is—made 'em think God was bad or holdin' sumptin' good back from 'em. All da while, God was tryin' to protect 'em from usherin' in sin and horrific sufferin' from they wrong choice. Da Destroyer and his dark forces been usin' dat same tactic forever. I can see it out here right now."

"Come on. I thought we were done with campfire stories, boss," Johnny had listened as long as he could before disagreeing.

"Bling, Johnny does have a point," Chief spoke up. "Probably not the best time to be sharing about the dark forces, but you could tell us more about the rainbow you were mentioning. I'm still a little curious about that."

"Me too," Sam indicated.

"Yeah, tell us about your mythical rainbows and unicorns, Bling," Johnny nearly hissed in sarcasm.

"Well, like I said," Bling began, "when the leviathan stepped out of da jungle into da light, its scales shined like a rainbow—and da rainbow represents God's kingdom. It's da mark of God."

"Hold up," Switch looked perplexed. "I might be leaning toward Johnny's side here. I thought rainbows meant something else—like gay pride or something."

"Nah, da rainbow is God's symbol. It first appears in da Bible as a sign of God's covenant wit' Noah—a promise dat He would never flood da whole earth again. Then it shows up wit' Joseph and his multi-colored robe; it's even in the last book of da Bible, where it says God's throne is encircled by a rainbow."

"That's interesting...I've not heard that one," Sam replied.

"Here's one more for you...and dis one will blow yo mind. Da Devil was once covered in a rainbow."

"Really?" Sam asked.

"Fo' sho'. A long time ago, he was covered in precious stones dat emitted a rainbow of color, but back then he worked for God and was called Lucifer. Da prophet Ezekiel mentioned it."

"So, you're saying that this leviathan beast has God's markings on it?" Sam asked, genuinely intrigued.

"Yeah, you right."

"But I don't understand, it's so ferocious and evil," she replied as everyone listened.

"Right, again. Da Devil got to it—just like he done to da rainbow and even to us humans. He twists things up, perverts 'em. In fact, da word leviathan means twisted. But don't get it twisted; leviathan is originally God's creation; it was meant to display God's might and wonder, but once da Devil got to it, the beast became an instrument of evil...killin' and destroyin'. He twists up humans to do his evil work in da same way."

Mike chimed in. "So, you're saying that the Devil is behind these beasts."

"I know dat's gonna sound strange, but it's da truth. He ain't just behind leviathan, he's behind all evil. Dis human traffickin' we dealin' wit'—da red haze as Johnny called it—dat's da Devil's work. Remember the rainbow of colorful lights we seen in Pattaya?"

"I certainly remember," Switch replied.

"Dat's only one example, but it goes further than dat. Child molesters, rapists, murderers...that's why we call 'em monsters. They unknowingly workin' for Da Devil—and it stems from when da first humans decided to heed da Devil's words instead of God's. Da prophet Joel say dat God desires to fill all peeps—boys and girls, mens and womens—wit' His Spirit, so He can know us personally. Da Devil wants da opposite, to fill us with wicked spirits to spread his evil on da earth. He wants anything but real love, joy, and peace—which is why he tricks peeps wit' counterfeits."

"Woah, that's kinda deep there, Bling," Switch replied. "But I got a question for you. Why did God create this evil Devil or Destroyer guy in the first place?"

"Yo, da Devil wasn't always tryin' to destroy stuff. Way back before da earth even exist, before Adam and Eve was in da garden, he was a type of archangel who lived in heaven. Some read da Bible and think he was some type of a heavenly worship leader, but dat's only part of it. Ezekiel say he was a type of military general—a defender of God's presence—and he had so much authority dat he convinced a third of da angels to join him in an attempt to overthrow God."

"What happened after that?" Sam innocently inquired—almost as though she were a child listening to a teacher share a story.

"God wasn't havin' it. He kicked him out of heaven and was cast to the earth, losing his position, his light, even his name. And dats where we humans come into da story."

"Bling, I don't think I've ever heard it taught like this," Chief mentioned. "You've honestly got me interested here. You're like a Bible scholar or something."

"Nope. Ain't no Bible scholar, but I am a Bible reader."

"You've certainly read more than us," Chief replied.

"I can keep sharin', if y'all want."

"I think that would do us all good, whether some of us want to admit it or not."

"A'ght, so yeah, when God created da earth, da crown of all of His creation was us humans. Humans are unique in dat they carry da image of God on 'em."

"Oh, I recently shared this with someon—" Sam excitedly interrupted and trailed off mid-sentence, her mind flooded with thoughts of Shein and her fateful demise.

"Yo, would you like to share wit' us 'bout God's image?"

"I...I don't know about that. I'm not all knowledgeable like you, Bling..."

"Why don't we give Bling a break?" Chief interjected. "I think it would do us good for you to share with us."

"Well, okay...I guess I can," she replied and continued. "Um...humans are...they're really special because, as Bling stated, they bear God's image. My mom, she, um, she always taught me that God gave both male and female a piece of Himself and that we're to be His reflection on the earth. She told me that His reflection is why we love and can know right from wrong and also why we seek justice and hold each other accountable and things like that. I hope that was right. I...I'm still learning."

"Dat was beautiful, Sam. Seriously. I couldn't have said it betta. Your mom did good sharin' dat wit' you," Bling replied as Sam smiled, but he couldn't see her through the intense darkness.

"What Sam say is truth. All humans have da image of God on 'em—which means we became an instant target for da Devil. He hates anything dat resembles God. Dat's why dis world be dealin' wit' murdahs and racism and such. It come from da Devil's hatred of God's image and da fact dat humans can have a relationship wit' God and communicate directly wit' Him, from our spirit to His. He also despises da dominion God gave to us. Ain't no other earthly creatures have these features 'bout 'em."

"So, let me get this right," Switch spoke up. "The Devil hates it because we can talk to God."

"Right. And our authority. But there's more. Our enemy also knows dat humans are da one thing dat God don't automatically possess. God owns everything in da earth, but He gave humans something else unique. He gave us choice. He ain't wanna force us to love Him; He wanted us to freely choose to have a relationship with Him…to ask Him for His Holy Spirit to live in us. Da Devil knows dat, so he used the same thing he got tripped up on—pride—to tempt da first humans to selfishly choose themselves over God—and in doing so, it damaged da image of God."

"Oh, I know this part," Switch boldly spoke up. "The Devil tempted them with an apple!"

"It was some kind of fruit fo' sho'," Bling responded, "But da Bible don't pacifically say what kind. But it wasn't really da fruit dat was da temptation, it was what da fruit signified—ultimate knowledge and God-likeness."

"Oh—"

"And because da Devil is an unseen spirit," Bling continued, "…he needed a host to communicate with da humans so he could tempt 'em."

"He took over a serpent," Mike interjected almost excitedly.

"Y'all know a little bit, I see. Dat's true. He entered da serpent, using its camouflage to lay low for da right moment to strike at

335

da first humans with his venomous, pride-filled fangs…he's da most cold-blooded eva!"

"Is this why what you read from Job calls leviathan the king of the children of pride?" Chief asked sincerely.

"You got it, Chief! Man, you was payin' attention. Pride is da Devil's main weapon. He knows da power of pride. Pride got him kicked out of God's presence and cast to da earth. He used pride on Adam and Eve and got them cast out of da perfect paradise of Eden."

"So, I'm guessing that pride keeps us from God as well," Sam suggested.

"Absolutely! Da pride of life makes us think we have all da answers and dat we know what's best fo' ourselves. Pride trys to speak to us dat we should live how we wanna live, love how we wanna love, but it's da one thang dat not only block's God's blessings, it actually turns us into an enemy of God."

"Whoa, an enemy of God?" Sam asked.

"Right. Chief, can I borrow yo' light for a sec? I wanna read sumthin'."

"Yeah, sure," Chief replied, clicking the red light on and handing it over to him.

Bling flipped through his Bible, turning the thin pages. "Here it is," he indicated. "Dis directly from da Bible. Da Apostle Peter, who walked with Jesus, said dat God is in opposition to the prideful, but He gives His favor to those who are humble."

"How would you define pride, Bling?" Sam inquired. "I want to make sure I understand as much as I can."

"Simple. Da word pride has sumtin' in da middle of it."

"The letter I, right?" Sam proposed.

"Exactly. Pride is doin' life yo way, not God's. It's self-centered. It only looks out fo' yo'self. Humility is da opposite of pride and have you livin' like Jesus who always did da Father's will. He always took others into consideration above Himself. Dat's love—and dat's how we should strive to live as well."

"I've got to be honest," Chief spoke quietly. "All of this is really heavy for me, but I think I'm getting some of it. What you said about the serpent and pride…hmm…I wonder if that's why humans are so fearful of reptiles. Maybe our fear is a result of Satan and pride…oh, and I think I remember too about how God took the serpent's legs—maybe that was because he wouldn't humble himself and God cut him down to the ground, as low as he could go."

"Chief, you're not buying into this stuff, are you?" Johnny asked, but Bling cut in before he could answer.

"Chief, what you just said is really good. I ain't even think of dat," Bling encouraged him. "But yeah, in da Bible, da Devil began as a serpent, but by da middle of da Bible, he's become so evil dat he resembles leviathan, a dinosaur-like creature. But check this out, at de end of the Bible, the camo comes completely off and he is revealed as a full-fledged dragon, full of chaos. Eventually, God gonna cut him down lower than da dirt and lock him up forever in da blackness and da flames of hell."

"Man, how did you learn all of this?" Switch asked.

"23-hour lockdown, just me and mines Bible."

"So, the Devil is leviathan?" Mike asked. "I'm not sure I'm following; it all seems sort of odd."

"It's not just odd, it's crazy," Johnny mumbled.

"No, da Devil ain't leviathan. Leviathan in his current state is just a symbol of him. Think 'bout them beasts. They kill just to kill. Da Devil has fill't up leviathans with evil, and these beasts unknowingly act as his pawns, much like humans do who kill, steal, and destroy on da earth. Anyone who doesn't live for God is a pawn of da Devil and contributes to dat red haze. It's a spiritual thing. Dat's why I call da Devil da Destroyer."

"It's obvious that you've studied your religion, Bling," Johnny snidely replied. "But I'm still having trouble with you thinking you're better than me…trying to tell me how to live and all. I don't appreciate you saying that I basically run with the Devil. Pretty hypocritical coming from an ex-con."

"Yo, is dat what you hearin'? I ain't tryin' to tell no one how to live. I'm just sayin' dat there's a mo' betta life available to you, an abundant life, where you can have a relationship wit' yo' Creator, yo. I'm made some huge mistakes in my past. I screwed up big time. You ain't even know da half of it. Alcohol, porn—which led to womanizin'—and all kinds of other stuff. How do you think I know so much about da Devil and his schemin'?"

As Bling spoke, Chief heard a sloshing sound in the water. He grabbed his night-vision and looked over the ledge.

"Y'all hold it down! The leviathan are coming back."

THIRTY-EIGHT
BLOOD SACRIFICES

C hief panned around the platform and saw the nervous tension in everyone except Bling. He was resting peacefully, his head propped up slightly on his makeshift pillow, gazing up at the stars.

Soon after, one of the leviathans circled the tree and then another joined in until all six of them riotously encircled it.

Slam! Slam! Slam! The leviathans again repeatedly beat their brawny tails against the ravished tree trunk, striking it every few seconds. The jarring jolts traced through everyone's body like jolts of electricity, continuing for several minutes.

Moments later, one of the beasts leapt from the water and gripped the tree's bark with its razor-sharp claws, attempting to climb high enough to destroy the platform with its mighty tail. It snarled aggressively as it tore into the bark, leaving deep, long streaks in the tree's flesh.

As the beast ascended a few feet up the tree, Chief looked down into its red eyes, seeing its violent and murderous intent. He aimed his MP5, targeting one of its crimson-colored eyeballs, but before he could fire it slipped back down into the water, tearing off a few of the steps and emitting a blaring shriek. Then, almost as quickly as their chaos began, the monsters disappeared beneath the shadowy swamp.

"Is it over?" Sam called out.

Everyone listened for them, but there was no sloshing or bubbling. Mike concentrated on his breathing, trying to calm himself, but it wasn't working. His heart was racing and he could feel his mind wandering to the brink of lunacy.

Achoo! Switch sucked in a whiff of the swamp's moldy dust and couldn't hold back his sneeze, the noise disturbing the leviathans, prompting a new assault.

Slam! Slam! Slam! The leviathans started in again. The beatings were so powerful that they vibrated the gear bag to the edge of the platform. Chief reached out and clutched the strap, drawing it back in before it fell over. When he did, Mike suddenly stood to his feet and looked up.

"Arghhhhhh!" He screamed in frustration, the panicked sound echoing throughout the swamp. "I can't take this anymore!" he shouted, grabbing the back of his head with both hands and yanking on his hair. He stepped to the edge of the platform as though he was about to jump off when Chief stood up behind up and wrapped his arm around his chest.

"Hey, you don't want to do that!" Chief whispered in his ear from behind, the beasts continuing to batter the tree.

"Why not!? We're gonna die anyway!" he responded, leaning forward and staring into the agitated waters, wondering how quickly the beasts would put him out of his misery.

"Yeah, why not, Chief?" Johnny suggested.

Seconds later the thrashing stopped and everything went silent again. Mike stood motionless, his eyes closed and his hair standing on end. He just wanted it all to be over.

Chief glanced into the swamp water, noticing the huge whirlpool had abruptly stopped and the swamp's stagnation was returning.

"They're still there," Chief remarked. "They're smart, like Bling said—lurking beneath the water for someone to step down like before. They're learning more about us than we are them."

"Mike, are you okay?" Sam asked, standing up and putting her arm around him.

"I'm…I'm just done with all of this," Mike spoke muffled words through gritted teeth. "These jolts…they remind me of that…that place when they locked…locked me up in the…" He trailed off, unable to finish his sentence. Sam felt his body's cold, rigidness and noted his wobbly knees as he struggled to remain standing.

"Do the jolts remind you of when the soldiers locked you in that metal box?" she asked compassionately. "It might be good to talk it out."

Mike nodded his head slowly, salty tears collecting at the top of his lower lip. No one dared speak up; they gave him time to process everything, not really knowing how to respond anyway.

"I don't know how long I was in that…that box, but it felt like an eternity. The heat. The darkness. The guards slamming the outside with their batons and the intense vibrations producing massive migraine headaches…it was like I was in a coffin, but worse…I was alive in it. I tried to get some sleep last night and every time I dozed off the nightmares came…it was like I was still in the box…happened at least three times."

"It's called post-traumatic stress, Mike," Chief explained. "Sam is right; it's good to talk it out. All of us have experienced some form of it. What these men did to you and Sam is unimaginable…I can only hope those evil men will get their day."

"God ain't gonna let dat slide," Bling inserted.

"Easy to say, Bling," Mike replied through his sniveling. "Who knows how long they've been doing this and how many young people they've tortured. I just don't get why God would allow that."

"There you have it, Bling," Johnny interjected. "That's why I can't believe in your God…and I wouldn't serve him even if he were real. Allowing innocents to be abused—psh! How could a good God allow something like that to happen?"

"You know what, Johnny," Sam curtly interrupted. "You've been nothing but unhelpful and rude. Why don't you just keep it to yourself."

"Well, okay there missy…" Johnny retorted.

"And I didn't appreciate you encouraging Mike to jump. That was a pretty low thing to do. If you want to be a jerk, go ahead, but stop involving me and Mike."

"Listen, everyone needs to calm down," Chief spoke up. "The stress is eating at us…and Johnny, that's enough, Sam is right," he finished, the quietness once again enveloping them.

"I have an answer for you, Johnny," Bling responded in a calm tone as everyone listened. "God will one day end all evil, but right now he's providin' time for peeps to turn to Him. There's a day of judgment coming for all wickedness, for all who don't know Him."

"You're full of it," Johnny snapped. "So, would I be part of that judgment?"

"There are only two kingdoms, Johnny. God's or da Devil's. God wants you in His family, but He ain't gonna force ya. We all have a choice. So, yeah, if you in da Devil's fam when da gavel come down, you'll be judged wit' him."

"This is stupid. I ain't bad. I've done a lot of good stuff in my life."

"Right, and many rapists have families at home and give they money to da church, but when they get caught, the good they done ain't on trial—only da bad they done. If you ain't wit' Jesus, you wit' the Devil. Dat's how it is."

Johnny sat quiet, clearly thinking about Bling's response.

"Yo, guys, while we have da time, I got one more thang I'd like to share wit' y'all."

"I don't know, I'm kinda late for my date," Switch tittered.

"I'd go on a date with the bearded lady if I didn't have to be stuck here listening to all of this bull," Johnny muttered.

"I told you, Johnny, dis is yo date. God put this together so you could hear about Him."

"Right. Whatever. I thought you said God doesn't force anyone."

"True. He ain't force you to be here. You made dozens of choices along da way to get to dis place. In fact, you still have a choice right now. You can jump down and swim outta here, but you may wanna think really hard 'bout dat choice."

"All your religious blabbing is making that choice a lot easier, I can tell you that much."

"Bling, what was it you wanted to share with us?" Chief asked, speaking up over Johnny's scorn.

"A'ight. Well, when you was axin' 'bout da rainbow, there's something from da Bible dat I ain't mention on purpose."

"Really? Why?"

"I wasn't sure y'all ready to go dis deep, but I think some of y'all can handle it."

"Too late now—you've got my attention. What is it?"

"Yeah, please share, Bling," Sam replied.

"Okay, well, remember how I was tellin' y'all about da Devil's rainbow coverin'?

"Yeah, how he was covered in precious gems in heaven," Chief responded.

"Right, well, dat same precious stone rainbow coverin' is found on da high priest."

"The high priest?" Chief questioned. "Like the guy who did mass every Sunday when I was a kid?"

"Nah, not yo Catholic priest—I'm talkin' 'bout da high priest back in da Bible times. He was responsible for representin' da people before God. Part of his ministry was takin' da blood of an innocent animal sacrifice and presentin' it before God for da people's sins. Dis shedding of innocent blood temporarily kept God's judgment from fallin' on 'em—and when he performed the sacrifice, he wore a rainbow of gems on his chest."

"I think I heard this before," Sam indicated.

"Sounds like savagery to me," Johnny piped up.

"Savagery?" Switch retorted. "Why? Because they were performing sacrifices? Are you sure that's savagery? Didn't your plan involve a sacrifice?" Switch let out a snarky laugh.

"Shut up, Switch," Johnny snapped back.

"What are you all talking about? What plan? What sacrifice?" Sam asked, seeking more information.

"It's nothing," Chief replied, protecting Johnny from his stupidity. "Just a really immature thought. Go ahead, Bling."

"So, like I was saying, da high priest and da blood sacrifice are both symbols of Jesus Christ. Jesus is God wit' skin on. He came down from heaven to give Himself as a sacrifice for sin by shedding His perfect blood and dying on da cross. But unlike da animal sacrifices, Jesus wasn't corrupted by sin and He rose back up alive three days later, proving His victory over sin and death, and providing us wit' an opportunity to know our Creator again."

"All this religious talk...giving me a headache," Johnny scowled. "This is impossible to understand anyway."

"I ain't understand it all at first either, but God will provide wisdom if you ask Him."

"Bling, forgive me," Chief replied, "I get the rainbow part, but I don't get the priest's connection to the leviathan. I think I missed something."

"I was gettin' to da good part. I meant to tell you da high priest was from da tribe and family of Levi," Bling paused, waiting to see if they would put it together, but there was only silence.

"Okay, look, Levi is da first four letters of leviathan and it has a deep meaning. In da ancient language, those four letters are a name and it means to join or cleave to...it's a marriage term."

"Interesting," Chief replied. "Like how the Bible says to cleave to your spouse."

"You gots it, yo! Da Bible gives us da model of marriage: one man and one woman who leave their family and cleave to each other forever. When a married couple do this, they become one flesh, but there's a lot mo' to it."

"It's spiritual isn't it?" Chief asked.

"Right. It's similar to how a wife takes a husband's last name and she becomes one with him in every regard."

"That's deep."

"It is. Bear wit' me and I'll try to explain it. So, because of sin, every person is born into da devil's kingdom, joined to his family, united with him in evil, but Jesus offers us a new life united wit'

Him in one flesh—He's basically offered to take us into His household that's full of love, joy, and peace."

"So Jesus gonna be our husband?...That's kinda weird," Switch laughed from the back of his throat.

"Not literally...you're still thinking fleshly; this is something that happens spiritually. Let me use an analogy y'all might get... Da Devil is like a pimp daddy and every human is part of his stable of ladies. They is coupled to him through all da temptations he offers—drugs, alcohol, sex, benjamins, power, you name it. Peeps be thinkin' they gettin' sumptin' good out da deal, but all da time, da Devil be consumin' 'em for his pleasure and his evil agenda. And the paycheck they gettin' from it is suffering and death."

"So, the spiritual battle you were referring to is the devil fighting to keep us joined to him and his clan so he can continue using people instead of them leaving him for Jesus and joining the household of God with a Heavenly Father that loves them?" Sam asked.

"Right! Da scales fallin' off yo eyes, girl. Da Devil is da biggest human trafficker ever, and he and his minions are battling in da spiritual realm, lobbin' out they fiery darts to keep peeps seduced."

"Now that you put it that way, I understand a little better myself," Switch replied.

"And dat ain't all. Da best part is dat just like a woman who gets married and is adopted into a new family, a believer in Christ gets a new name and a new purpose as well," Bling stated enthusiastically.

"A new purpose?" Mike asked.

"Sho' do. You get to help pull others out da Devil's darkness. It's called bearin' spiritual children for da Lort."

"I'm not sure I'm following. Can you explain a little more?" Chief asked.

"Sure. Just like da high priest mission was in da old days, those who have left da Devil and have become one flesh wit' Jesus are now joined with Him as mediators to help reconcile sinners back to God...to help raise spiritual children for God. "

As Sam listened it was like a light had turned on in her heart. "Ah, so just like how a woman leaves her family and hooks up with her husband to bear natural children, believers have a similar purpose, except in the spirit...they're to help get others adopted into the family of God," she replied.

"You could definitely say it like dat. Da ultimate goal is to bring peeps into God's family, yo."

"That's a powerful picture."

"Comes straight from the Bible...and it's also my personal story. I'm originally from da family of Levi, formerly joined to da Devil—the Great Leviathan—but I'm in God's family now, helpin' rescue those blinded by da Devil's schemes. Who best to take out da Great Leviathan than a Levi—da one who knows his ways best?"

"So you know how to take out the Devil?" Chief asked.

"Fo' sho! I take him out a little at a time by gettin' peeps outta his kingdom and gettin' them into God's. Da Devil and his principalities be workin' through personalities, but when they turn from him and get filled up wit' God, they stop destroyin' and start buildin'. And eventually, God will defeat da Devil once and fo' all at da end of da age."

"But do you know how to take out these leviathans?" Switch asked.

"Nothing can take 'em out except da sword of da Lort. Isaiah said dat. But I'm trustin' dat God will provide a way for us to escape."

"Great. Let's all hold hands and sing kumbaya to the Lord to get us out of this," Johnny countered.

"Glad to hear you is still listenin' over there, Johnny."

As they talked, Chief peered back down into the dark waters but the bubbles were gone. He inspected the area but didn't see anything but trees, ferns, and jungle vines as far as he could see. Moments later, he saw movement near the trail. He watched as two leviathans stepped into the clearing and roamed down the embankment, entering the brackish water. One waited close to the shore with its back exposed above the water and the other climbed on top of it, digging his sharp claws deep into his hide for a secure grip.

Screeeeeeeeech! The leviathan released an unsettling shriek as it floated into the water.

"Holy mother—" Chief exclaimed, fading off as he watched the leviathan's movements.

"What is it?" Switch asked, staring into the darkness, unable to see anything.

"These things are more intelligent than I thought. They're piggybacking on each other to make themselves bigger. It won't be long before they figure out how to get to us."

"Can't say I didn't warn you," Johnny snapped. "Told you they were relentless."

"What are we gonna do?" Sam asked, fear obvious in her voice.

"Switch, if we were to get to the gear bag with the drone, think there's any battery life left on it?" Chief asked.

"Maybe a minute or two. What's the plan?"

"Get those beast's attention somehow and see if they follow it."

"Won't work," Johnny replied.

"Why, because it's not a human?" Switch asked.

"No, because the gear bag it was in was smashed, dummy."

"Great," Chief frustratingly replied.

"Buuuut…there is still my plan," Johnny cautiously suggested.

"Forget it," Chief insisted. "They're heading back into the jungle now."

"Thank God," Sam mumbled, putting two and two together that Johnny was trying to use Mike to draw out the beasts, but remained quiet to keep the peace.

"Listen up, y'all," Chief instructed. "There's no way we can stay up here. The only option I can see is trying to outrun them down the trail. If anyone has any other ideas, now is the time to speak up. We're running out of time."

"I don't like it, but I can't see any other way," Switch spoke up.

"If we take off down the trail and can't get past them, direct fire to the eyes might work," Johnny indicated.

"Alright, here's what we're gonna do," Chief proposed. "I'm gonna hand out an energy bar to everyone and hook up the IV bags. We'll need as much food, fluids and rest as possible. We'll make our move at first light. The good thing is that the APC cleared out the trail for us…Oh, and when we leave, only take your primary weapon, nothing else. No scopes, no vests, no bags…and definitely no liquor flasks…we need to be as light as possible."

Johnny glared at Chief, but he understood the necessity of being lighter and mentally sharp.

"Roger that," Switch replied.

"Chief, If I don't make it, I want to say it's been a pleasure serving with you," Johnny stated a bit mockingly. "I mean, right now I could be sippin' a pina colada on a beach somewhere exotic."

"Yeah, or you could be kicking kids out of the local big box store for filling their water cups with soda pop at the cafe—isn't that where Chief met you?" Switch teased.

"Loss prevention patrol, Switch," Johnny replied brusquely. "We kept the prices lower."

"Okay there, buddy," Switch laughed as Chief passed out the energy bars and hooked Mike and Sam up to an IV bag.

"Everyone will get about a third of the bag and then we'll get a few hours rest."

THIRTY-NINE
CONDEMNED

O h, man, this is so good right now," Mike talked through the slow chew of his energy bar, relishing every bite. "I'm feeling better already."

Chief sat against the tree, his mind consumed with the responsibility of leading everyone out and hoping it wouldn't end in several grisly deaths.

"Bling, you know what? I'm glad you're here, brother," Chief stated to ease his stress. "I mean, I think it's good for us to cover all the bases, even spiritually."

"I still don't get why you picked him to be on the team, boss...needed a driver, I suppose."

"I chose Bling based on his character and morality. That's why he's on the team. He was workin' a dead-end job and we had an opening. I think he's fit in quite well."

"Yeah, he's like our chaplain," Switch suggested. "Even the military has chaplains."

"I'm glad to be on da team," Bling replied as everyone found a spot to get some rest.

"Even in our miserable situation?...you're still glad to be on the team?" Johnny asked.

"Sho' am."

"Listen, Bling, speaking of chaplains," Chief cut in, "You know what we're up against here and that there's a good chance we won't make it out—"

"Yo, if you wanna know more, all you gotsta do is ask," Bling interrupted before he could finish.

"Maybe one more question. I want to be ready, you know?"

"Axe away!"

"Well, you said there's a battle between God's kingdom and the Devil's. How does someone leave the Devil's kingdom and enter God's?"

"Ah, good question. I always like to use Jesus' words. He say you gotsta be born again."

"I'm pretty sure I've heard that term before."

"The pastor at the church I grew up in wore that word out," Sam indicated.

"I can imagine, but very few know da real meanin' of it."

"Born again?" Switch laughed as he looked at a few stars shining through the slivers of the treetops. "I don't mean to make light, but I have a strange picture goin' through my head right now."

"You ain't da only one. When Jesus said it, da guy he was speakin' to wondered how it was possible to go back inside his momma's belly to be born a second time."

Switch laughed. "I kinda had that same thought, but I didn't want to say it."

"Me, too," Chief agreed with a slight laugh.

"What does it mean then?" Mike asked sincerely.

"I want y'all to get a different picture. Think about da earth before God touched it wit' His Spirit. Da Bible say dat in da beginning, da earth was formless and void and covered in darkness. Basically, it was condemned…"

"Condemned? Like a dilapidated house or something?" Chief asked.

"Like a run-down house in da hood."

"Okay, I can see that."

"But when God poured His Spirit upon it, it became suitable fo' life. Da earth was literally born again—or born anew."

"Hmmm…interesting," Chief pondered aloud.

"If y'all think about it, every person who doesn't know Jesus as Savior is like da earth before God renewed it wit' His Spirit. I'll use my life as an example. Before I came to Jesus, my life was shapeless, empty and dark; I existed without purpose, but when I surrendered and invited God's Spirit to have His way wit' me, He breathed on me and removed da condemnation. I've been recreated by His light and love, and now I have a new mission to help restore others who are condemned."

"I think I understand what you're saying, but how does this happen?" Chief inquired.

"First, yo' prideful rebellion has to end. You gotsta leave da Devil and humbly turn to Christ, cleavin' to Him by faith, which means trustin' Him wit' every aspect of yo life."

"Faith?" Chief asked.

"Yeah, faith is another word for trust—and God's given every person a quantity of it. In fact, He lets you choose where you put yo faith. Some people put trust in themselves, some in science and education, some in money, some in religion, and some in Jesus."

"What do you mean by religion?" Switch asked. "Isn't Christianity a religion?"

Johnny cut in. "Sure it is—it's like all the other phony make-believe stuff out there."

"Many peeps define Christianity as a religion, but true Christianity is different; it's a relationship built on God's love, what He did to seek us out, not the traditions of men. Religion is man's methodical attempt to please God through works, traditions and external beautification, but all dat's just da Devil in a pretty dress. But like I mentioned earlier, a real Christian is becoming one flesh with Christ and allowing Him to live through you."

"So religion is bad?" Chief asked, slightly confused

"Ezekiel says da Devil became prideful of his own beauty. He was covered in precious gems, but his heart was corrupted. Religion is like dat. Religion will have you dressing up in your Sunday best, treating everyone at church kindly and even throwing money in da offerin' plate—everything appears great on da outside—but then a half-hour later you're at da restaurant cursin' out da wait staff because you got a smaller portion than normal. What's in yo' heart eventually comes out. Like da Devil, the camo eventually comes off and the real you is revealed."

"So true religion is living by faith from the heart, right?" Switch asked.

"I think you on to it, Switch. Someone once defined it like dis: Religion is sitting in church thinkin' 'bout huntin'. Relationship is goin' out huntin' and joyfully thinkin' 'bout Jesus. In other words, it's a heart thing that seeps into every aspect of life."

"I like that," Sam stated.

"What about people who put their faith in science?" Mike quietly asked. "I had faith in God up until high school, but I was turned off when my science teacher said there's no God and that we're all here by chance, a product of evolution."

"Dat's unfortunate, but it happens a lot, especially in high school and college, and it makes me mad."

"Woah, Bling, you get angry?" Johnny asked. "I thought you were perfect."

"I'm far from perfect, but in a world where children are looking for a place to fit in, where kids are gettin' addicted to drugs and alcohol and even takin' they own lives, we ain't need no one tellin' them dat they is an evolved animal a little higher up da food chain. Yeah, dat makes me angry, 'cuz kids deserve da truth about who they is and how they is pacifically made by God."

"That makes sense," Switch replied.

"This is another spiritual battle dat comes down to words. Either you put yo trust in man's word or God's. And there be a lot of men with a lot of words out there, but only God's Word is righteous and offers the promise of knowin' you Creator through Jesus Christ with da promise of eternal life."

"So, faith is thinking in our mind about God?" Switch asked. "Forgive me; I don't know if I'm following correctly or not."

"Faith certainly involves yo' mind, but it involves mo' than dat; it involves your whole being. It means every aspect of your life is surrendered and committed to lovin' God and people, as He's axed us to do. For example, some peeps pigeonhole dey faith to attendin' church and doing religious activities on a certain day, but dat ain't da full scope of faith. When you get married, every aspect of life changes, not just what happens on a Sunday. Ain't no man up here could get away wit' lovin' a woman only one day a week."

"I know I wouldn't put up with that," Sam replied, nudging Mike. "Hint for the future."

"Hmmm...those are really good points, Bling," Chief replied. "But speaking of church, don't you need an altar or a confession booth to—how do they say it—come to faith in Jesus?"

"I came to faith in Jesus Christ in a prison cell, Chief. If churches and altars is necessary to enter da kingdom, many ain't makin' it. Think about it—not only prisoners but those in nursing homes, hospitals, rehabs, shut-ins, da disabled—they ain't makin' it. Dat also goes for those locked up in brothels, peeps in remote villages and those who can't attend a church in persecuted countries. God's truth gotta be universal fo' all, not just some. If it ain't for everyone, it ain't for anyone."

"I can see that," Chief replied. "But how come pastors and such don't talk like you do?"

"Some do, but many don't. There are many blinded by money and power who want to build their own kingdoms—da same thangs dat got da Devil kicked outta heaven. Others are repeaters. They heard sumptin' taught and they repeat it wit'out checkin' da source. Da truth is dat God ain't tryin' to get you into a certain holy building. He's tryin' to make you His holy building—to get His Spirit in you so you can carry His presence to those who need Him."

"Now, I know I've never heard anything like that before."

"The Bible makes this very clear, but da Devil has tricked folk into suppressing da truth. God wants to work through you. Dat's how He does it. It's a beautiful story of redemption. Dat's why every mention of da church in da Bible refers to da entire body of believers who carry God's Holy Spirit, not a pacific buildin'. Ain't once where da Bible even mentions a church buildin'. In fact, da first church building wasn't even constructioned 'til 300 years after Jesus walked da earth."

"Hmmm…okay…so I guess I don't need a priest or a pastor then to do this," Chief suggested.

"To give your life to Christ? Not at all. Pastors are important to a believer's spiritual walk but consider Adam and Eve, Noah, Abe, Mo, Josh, and even Paul. They didn't have a pastor and there were no church buildin's. God communed directly wit' 'em and He wants to do da same wit' you. Too many peeps today only have a relationship wit' they church."

"You're losing me a little bit, here, Bling," Chief replied.

"Look, da main point is dat fellowshippin' wit' other believers is important, but we gotta focus on living as da church rather than only attendin' church. Christianity is mo' than a country club."

"This might be a dumb question, Bling," Sam replied timidly, "but how does someone live *as* the church?"

"Dat's a great question, young lady. Most believers ain't know how. They think dat means servin' in da buildin', 'cuz dat's all they know…plus, it's comfortable. But those things ain't what Jesus say to do. Peter and John both say dat all believers are royal priests unto God—dat is, they mission is like da high priest dat I told y'all about. Da high priest's mission was to help reconcile peeps back to God. Dat's who y'all destined to be as well."

"So, we're all destined to be preachers?" Chief asked.

"Nah, man. We're destined to be conformed to Jesus, which means we should follow after Him and da things He showed us to do. He ain't use crafty words from no pulpit; He came in da power of da Holy Spirit to deliver peeps from all forms of darkness. We're called to do the same—to allow da Holy Spirit to flow through us to touch others and reveal God to them. Not in word only, but also in action."

"So, it's not really about a church building at all," Sam suggested.

"Exactly," Bling nodded. "In fact, of da 37 miracles dat da Bible records Jesus as doing, only three were done inside a religious building—and in each of them accounts, Jesus healed a person of an evil spirit and battled men with religious spirits—that should tell us sumptin'."

"Religious spirits?" Switch asked.

"Yep, da same Spirit dat rose Jesus from da grave is alive and workin' through His believers today, but so is da same religious spirit dat killed Him. You can see dat spirit rise up any time someone attempts to replace a relationship with God wit' da traditions of man—very deceivin' stuff."

"I've seen that firsthand," Chief replied.

"I think we all done dealt wit' dat."

"Johnny, what do you think about all of this?" Chief asked. "I kind of miss your arguments—I think they bring the best out of Bling."

"Yeah, Johnny, you're really quiet over there," Switch stated.

"Honestly, I'm just chewing on what Bling's saying. I didn't think I would ever say this, but I'm a little curious. The stuff he's been saying is way different than what I've heard from any preacher."

"Well, now that's a change," Chief stated.

"It's weird…I sort of feel drawn to what you're saying, Bling. Now, I'm not saying I'm ready to be a holy roller like you; I'm just saying that everyone who ever spoke to me about faith invited me to their church and basically gave me a guilt trip if I didn't attend."

"I'm sorry peeps misrepresented God like dat, but dat drawin' you feel is from da Holy Spirit."

"Whatever you want to call it…But it's honestly refreshing. What I'm getting from it is that you're basically inviting us to the Creator who I can know personally without going through a religious guy—oh, and that we all have a part to play to rid evil. Is that right?"

"Johnny, did you just admit there's a Creator?" Switch interjected. "You've definitely come a long way in the last half hour."

"Look, I'm not saying I'm gonna become no fuddy duddy. I'm just saying that he made some good points. Besides, if I'm gonna be facin' death tomorrow, I may as well make sure I'm not an enemy of God. If you know of another religious person or scientific theory that has overcome death, please let me know. I'll consider that, too."

"Jesus is the only One, brother, and I'm glad you comin' around," Bling replied. "Death truly makes us consider Jesus because He's the only person in history who ever cheated it and offers us the same opportunity. But to answer yo question pacifically, yes, it's about knowing Jesus personally. Religious holy buildings are really man's idea, not God's. In fact, dat was da message of da first Christian martyr, Stephen, early on in da book of Acts. He told the religious rulers of his day dat God didn't desire a holy building...dat God didn't dwell in their revered religious temple...dat God wants to make us His temple with Jesus as da cornerstone. They took him out for dat message."

"They killed him for that? Man, that's brutal." Switch suggested.

"Yeah, dat's da religious spirit I was tellin' y'all about...and it's still doin' damage today. If I tried to talk like dis in most churches, I'd be hated. But da truth is dat God's never been down wit' da concept of designatin' certain buildings as holy and religious. His idea is to make what He created holy—to put His Holy Spirit in humankind to restore His image in da earth—and in dat way, wherever Spirit-filled believers go, dat place becomes holy—a kingdom outpost of light in da darkness if you will—all wit' da mission of rescuin' peeps from da Devil's corrupt kingdom and lovin' them into God's."

"So, God never wanted a physical temple?" Sam inquired. "That's contrary to what I was taught in church."

"God allowed it as an illustration, but dat wasn't His ultimate desire," Bling replied. "In fact, da very first mention of a permanent building in da Bible was da infamous tower of Babel, a type of religious temple—and God wasn't havin' it."

"The tower of Babel?" Sam asked. "Isn't that a story right after Noah and the flood in the Bible?"

"You got it! The humans of dat time spoke one language and they tried to build a big city wit' a huge tower. They was fill't up wit' a lot of pride, wantin' to make a great name for themselves."

"Sounds kinda like what the Devil did that got him cast to the earth," Sam proposed.

"Exactly. Good point, yo. But God saw they wicked intentions and brought their big tower to an end, scattering da peeps throughout da world."

"I remember that story," Mike replied. "I always thought dude's name was funny…Nimrod."

"Yep, he was da main guy behind da tower, but what most people don't know is dat there's another story like it in the Bible—and dat story is what gives us da full meaning of what was goin' on."

"Really?" Sam asked.

"Sho' is. Dat tower was about men buildin' they own kingdom. But thousands of years later, in da book of Acts, God found a people who would build His true temple and kingdom. Instead of using da spirit of pride and one earthly language to build a high temple, God released His Holy Spirit upon believers and established one heavenly language, uniting His people together to build them into one spiritual temple to reconcile all people to Him and declare His goodness in da earth. He ain't do it for them to make a name for themselves or to establish they own corrupt kingdom, but to establish His loving kingdom and true reputation in da earth. Once He poured out His Spirit, His peeps unified and then purposely scattered throughout the world to share da Good News of Jesus Christ so everyone could know about Him."

"I've never heard any of this before," Chief stated.

"Me neither," Sam replied.

"But it's all in da Bible," Bling replied and then continued. "Think about it. Every religion has holy buildings. Hindus and Buddhists gots temples. Muslims gots Mosques. Even da Jews and da Christians gots they synagogues and churches, but these are all buildings designed and built by men. All of them—even da Christian ones. But only one building is capable of holding sumtin' so special as God's Spirit—and dat's da human body, which is God's design, personally built by Him for da most special purpose of displayin' Him to da world."

"So, I want to be clear on something…are churches bad?" Sam asked.

"No, not at all, but many of them have overemphasized da religious buildin' and a religious personality over Jesus Christ. They relate to God through the brick and mortar buildin' and who they feel is a spiritual person without having a personal relationship with God. Not only dat, all they resources go into expensive buildin' funds and lavish decorations when da resources should go to expandin' God's kingdom."

"Yeah, but doesn't it take money to operate a church?" Sam asked.

"Fo' sho', but maybe dat's why da early church met in homes. It don't take nothin' to fellowship in someone's home—and it's more personable. But, again, I ain't cuttin' down churches. They lots of churches who pour they heart into ministerin' to peeps."

"And there's a lot of churches building their own personal kingdoms," Switch replied, unable to constrain his comment.

"Now, that's a true statement, Switch," Johnny agreed.

"You right, Switch. There have been many religious peeps who have done horrible damage in da name of God. Dat same word dat describes da Tower of Babel is da same word dat means elevated pulpit. Anytime we do a work for God, we gots to watch out for pride…everyone do…even if you is tellin' peeps 'bout Him on da street or wit' yo family at home. It's really easy to let yo heart get elevated and make you own stage like da Devil tried to do…but he lost his position, his jewels and his name…and dat's how he tempt peeps today…through power, money and fame…we all gots to watch out for it."

"I'm getting it, Bling," Chief responded. "Even though it doesn't all make sense to me, it's like my heart is on fire to hear more."

"I'm excited fo' you, Chief. Dat's God speakin' to you. Just surrender to Him and make Him Lort of yo life and He'll continue to show you great and mighty things like nevah before."

"I think I'm…I'm ready to surrender," Chief stuttered a bit. "But I do have one more question."

"Go for it, yo."

"If I put my faith in Jesus, does that mean I…that I have to give up my guns like you?" Chief asked hesitatingly, wondering how his question might be received. "I mean guns ain't no idol and they aren't necessarily bad. I could use 'em for target practice. There are even people who participate in skeet shooting in the Olympics," he reasoned, talking fast.

Bling chuckled. "Nah, man, ain't no Bible verses about givin' up guns, Chief, but I had to give 'em up because of my past gang life and what I did wit' 'em. Forgive da pun, but they is a trigger for me. When you in relationship wit' Jesus, He'll speak to you through da Holy Spirit about how you should live and He'll help remove things dat could harm yo relationship wit' Him. Remember, it's like marriage. You ain't gettin' divorced 'cuz you ain't take out da trash, but you might lose out on some intimate blessin's if ya don't listen to da wife—if ya catch my drift."

"Oh, yeah, I get ya."

"Chief, in all seriousness, you gots a special skill set. I ain't be surprised if God continues usin' dat for His glory and to help others. There is a Scripture dat say those who bear weapons are actin' as servants of God, avengers who carry out God's wrath upon evildoers. I believe you one of them avengers."

"Avengers? That's in the Bible?"

"Sho' is. And there's another verse dat talk about God trainin' hands fo' battle."

"I'll have to check those out."

"God not only works through us to show love to others, He also works through us to carry out justice. When you read da Bible, you'll find all kinds of interestin' things…there's battles and love stories and even a part where a righteous guy was fed to ferocious beasts but survived 'cuz God closed up they jaws. He had great faith."

"We could sure use some of that great faith right now," Chief suggested. "And with that said, I hear some snoring. I think everyone else dozed off…I guess we need to get some rest as well."

"I could use a little relaxin' fo' sho'. Big day tomorrow."

"Bling, I…umm…I believe everything you said. Is there something I have to do specifically?"

"Ain't nuthin' you need to do but to say 'I do' to da Lort—Da Bible say to believe in your heart and confess dat Jesus is Lort and dat He raised up alive da third day. Tell God in your own words how much He means to you and keep tellin' others about Him. Start livin' a life of confession and nevah stop. He makes it simple. Again, it's like marriage, but the 'I do' part is only da beginning. Once you make your pledge, it's a life-long commitment to honor and cherish da Lort above all else— through the rough times and the good."

"That's a perfect analogy. I get it. Thank you, Bling. I'll do that right now."

"Amen, Chief, amen!"

FORTY
SPIRITUAL WARFARE

A single droplet of water fell from the sky and landed on Sam's cheek. Then another and another, until the droplets joined hands in unending chains, further soaking the already stifling jungle. She slowly opened her eyes and looked out into the blue-tinted clearing as the morning light chased away the darkness for the beginning of a new day.

As the jungle woke up, the birds chirped and bugs buzzed, oblivious to the danger she and everyone else on the platform faced.

Johnny was the first of the team to wake up. He glanced across the platform and closed his eyes again, surprised that he had fallen asleep, knowing what lay ahead of them. A second later, he opened them fully. Something was off. He scanned the platform and noticed someone was missing. Bling was gone. He stood up, looking into the shadowy clearing and checking the waters below. There was no sign of him.

"Chief!" Johnny called out in a muffled yell.

Chief opened his eyes and jumped up. "Wha…what is it?!" he responded, reaching for the MP5.

"Where's Bling?" he asked.

Switch, Mike, and Sam heard the commotion and woke up soon after.

"What?" Chief wasn't sure if he was dreaming or awake. He shook his head and panned around the platform, checking for

Bling, but he was gone. He crawled to the edge of the platform and gazed into the water, hoping, praying that he hadn't fallen into the swamp in the middle of the night.

"There's no way he fell into the water," Chief spoke aloud, his voice stressed. "We would have heard it."

"Unless the leviathans somehow got to him—" Johnny trailed off, not really wanting to make the morbid suggestion.

"Guys, look!" Sam spoke up, rising to her knees and pointing past the hut's pile of debris.

Bling was standing in the clearing facing away from them with his hands raised to the sky as though in a worship posture, his matching, navy blue, basketball-style suit jacket and pants blending into the early morning haze.

"What's he doing?" Switch asked.

"I don't know," Chief whispered. "Everyone just stay calm. Don't call out to him. We'll pick him up on the way out. Make sure your radios are on. This is it. Johnny, you head out first and I'll bring up the rear."

"Roger that."

As they moved, Chief mumbled a quick prayer. "God, protect us as we leave this place, amen."

Johnny stepped to the edge of the platform with his gun slung over his shoulder and climbed down until there were no more steps. Mike and Sam followed after while Chief and Switch stood on the platform, their rifles pressed to their shoulder, closely examining the surface of the swamp.

"Go, go, go," Chief quietly urged.

Johnny released his grip, sliding down the tree into the water, trying not to make a splash, but making more noise than he wanted. Mike and Sam followed, cautiously swimming up to the embankment.

"You okay to do this with your arm?" Chief asked as Switch sat on the platform's ledge, his eyes still scouring the water.

"Yeah, I think so," he responded. Chief assisted him until his foot reached the first step. He tried not to make a large splash, but it was inevitable. He splashed into the water, the noise resounding through the jungle.

"Johnny," Chief spoke into the mic, "Get Bling. We gotta get out of here."

"Roger that."

Chief made his way down the tree, entering the water and catching up with Switch. He grabbed him by the back of his collar and assisted him to the shore.

"Chief, Bling's in some kind of a trance," Johnny stated. "His lips are moving like crazy, but I don't hear any words."

"Maybe he's praying. Grab him so we can go!"

As Chief led everyone to the trail, Sam saw something moving in the water out of her peripheral vision.

"Chief, look!" her voice shook as she the swamp's green water reflected off her bulging eyes. He turned and saw the top of the leviathans' scaly hide, their tails swishing through the water, propelling them forward at an incredible rate of speed.

"Move!" Chief yelled as they reached the disabled APC, hiding behind it.

"Johnny! We've gotta go now!" Chief nearly yelled into the mic, aiming his MP5 at the embankment, ready to fire on the swiftly swimming leviathans.

"He's not budging...what should I do?"

"Drag him if you have to! We'll meet up down the trail," Chief conveyed as he waved everyone down the trail, putting himself between them and the beasts.

With no options left, Johnny reached his arm around Bling's neck in a type of chokehold and pulled him backward, but he was like a dead weight.

"Bling, come on, man! Do you wanna die out here?"

The leviathans ascended up the embankment and their massive frame filled Johnny's eyes. There was no way he and Bling would make it out alive if he had to drag him. Seeing no other choice, he left Bling behind and scurried to the edge of the tree line a few yards away.

"Bling, come on!" Johnny shouted to him one last time from several feet away, but when he looked back he saw Bling had sat down and his body was slumped over like he had given up on life.

"Chief, I had to leave Bling. He wouldn't move."

"Copy that. You did everything you could. Meet us down the trail."

"Copy."

As Johnny continued to the trail, two leviathans reached the clearing and stopped, their eyes skimming the area and their nostrils flaring. Then two more sauntered up out of the water and ascended to the top, amassing together and considering their attack, their tongues flicking in and out. Two more followed, standing almost in rank, their bodies pulsating, ready for the assault.

Chief led his group along the trail, moving hurriedly, but as they progressed, Sam stepped on a tree limb and the snapping sound resonated through the jungle, giving away their position. The leviathans turned their monstrous faces toward the trail, their claws digging into the mud, ready to lunge toward it, but as they were about to make their move, a wondrous sound filled the air.

Johnny heard the sound and stepped behind some thick bushes, looking back at the clearing and listening as Bling belted out a song he wasn't familiar with.

"What are you doing, Bling," Johnny mumbled to himself.

Chief heard it, too, and nearly came to a stop, raising his chin and turning his head in the direction of the sound.

"Do you guys hear that?" Chief asked as Switch fell back behind a tree, struggling to point his rifle in the direction of the clearing.

"I hear it," Sam responded.

"Sounds like singing," Mike replied.

"Is that…Bling?" Switch asked. "What's he doing?"

"I don't know, but we have to keep going," Chief responded, pointing to everyone to keep moving down the trail.

The leviathans raised their gristly faces into the air and released their own sound, an earsplitting screech that drowned out Bling's song.

Johnny continued on to the trail and hurried behind the APC, hiding out and watching as the leviathans' gigantic feet pounded into the rain-soaked ground, sending tiny vibrations through his body as they moved.

The leviathans encircled Bling and snorting wildly, almost like bulls ready to charge. Their tails whipped violently and each opened their jaws, releasing a booming roar, their teeth only inches from his head. Johnny watched until the uneasiness crept up from his stomach into his mouth, initiating his gag reflex. Not wanting to see what was coming next, he sprinted down the trail and refused to look back.

As Chief led everyone down the trail, they were soon inundated by the inescapable, suffocating stench of death. Dozens of bloated soldiers were strewn about everywhere, most of them decapitated and missing limbs. Some of them were heaped up and swarms of flies buzzed around them, their guns close by, covered in blood.

"Chief, look!" Mike spotted the front of the military truck they had left behind days earlier, stuck in the vines.

Chief placed his finger vertically over his lips, indicating for everyone to stay quiet. He pointed at Switch and they took up a defensive position on both sides of the trail. Mike and Sam squatted behind them as they cautiously advanced to the truck, checking for movement, but before they could reach it they heard a muffled scream coming from the trail area, closer to the clearing.

"That...that sounds like Johnny," Switch indicated as he tried to shoulder his weapon through his pain.

Chief didn't reply; he turned and aimed his weapon as they slowly walked backward to the truck, anticipating the leviathans at any moment.

"Thud…thud…thud!" The leviathans charged after Johnny and the ground pulsated under everyone's feet.

"Everyone get in!" Chief yelled as they reached the truck. Mike helped Switch and Sam climb into the rear and Chief stepped inside the cab, removing the keys from his pants pocket.

"Vroom!" The truck started right up and Chief threw it in reverse, waiting for Johnny and hoping there would be enough time to get out before the beasts caught up to them.

He didn't have to wait long. Seconds later, Johnny appeared, scrambling down the trail as two leviathans pursued, only a few meters behind.

"C'mon, Johnny!" Sam screamed, encouraging him to run harder.

"Mike, take my gun!" Switch shouted, handing him his MP5. "Lay down some suppressing fire. Concentrate on their eyes."

"Okay!" Mike replied, fumbling the gun a bit, unsure if it was loaded and checking the safety.

"It's ready to go! Just aim it and press the trigger!"

"Right!" he replied, pointing it at the beast that was only a few feet from Johnny.

Phttt! Phttt! Phttt! He fired multiple times, striking the lead beast on its snout, but it didn't deter it at all.

He raised the gun slightly and fired again, hitting one directly in its eye. It instantly stopped it in its tracks and shook its head wildly.

"You got it, boy!" Switch shouted. "Good job! Run, Johnny!" he screamed as the other leviathan continued on, getting closer. Seconds later, Johnny reached the thick vines that had impeded the truck and pushed through them, but he stumbled on a root and fell down.

Come on, Johnny, get up, Chief muttered to himself as he held his foot over the gas pedal, ready to bolt off as soon as he reached to the truck.

Johnny stumbled forward, blind firing his gun at the beast, emptying his magazine. With one last effort, he leaped for the truck's bumper, grabbing ahold.

Chief stomped on the gas pedal as Mike fired at the beast, the bullets ricocheting off its armored scales, doing nothing to slow it down.

The beast reached the thick vines and bulldozed through them, shredding them like they were tissue paper. Chief drove backward as fast as the truck would drive, Johnny's feet dragging behind it, but the leviathan were moving faster and gaining on them.

"Lord, we need you help. Don't let Bling's sacrifice for us be in vain!" Chief prayed loudly as the beast pounded forward.

Johnny glanced behind him and his eyes were filled with reddish-green scales. He closed his eyes and clenched his jaw, waiting to be ripped away, but nothing happened. The beast suddenly stopped about three feet before it reached him.

Chief continued driving backward, getting about 50 meters distance from the beast, watching it closely. For reasons unknown to them, the leviathan was moving in circles and no longer pursuing them. Chief slowed to a stop, hoping Johnny could make it into the truck before it gave chase again.

Johnny reached the steps of the cab and the leviathan bowed its head, sneezing several times, the shockwave so powerful it pushed the truck backward a few inches.

Johnny climbed inside as Chief put the truck back into reverse again, everyone watching as the leviathan wandered over to the embankment and slipped back into the stagnant swamp water.

"Phew...that was too close," Johnny indicated, saturated in sweat, still catching his breath.

"Is Bling...is he...?" Chief couldn't finish the sentence.

Johnny nodded and Chief closed his eyes for a moment.

"He would want us to keep going," Chief surmised.

"How are we gonna get out of here?"

"There's no way we can just drive out...we don't have the manpower or firepower, but before we came in, I remember seeing a tiny village on the map at the opposite end of the island."

"So the plan is to get to the village—and then what?"

"Hopefully, they have a phone and we can call Randall for extraction."

"Who would live on this remote island—and how do we know they aren't military sympathizers?"

"Both legitimate questions…we'll have to keep our eyes open. The name of the town is called Sane, so maybe that's a good sign."

"Or maybe someone forgot to add the first two letters to the name."

"I see your point, but unless you have a better idea…"

As they were talking, Switch saw the top of the trees swaying and what sounded like a helicopter landing nearby.

Switch radioed in the report. "Chief, sounds like a helo just landed, but I can't see through the trees."

They were almost to the intersection with the main road when Chief stopped and jumped out of the truck. Johnny was close behind while Switch stood in the back of the truck, keeping an eye on the trail and the adjacent swamp.

Chief and Johnny stood behind a large tree and inspected the main road that led to the mainland. About 400 meters down, the Burmese Military blocked the road with some jeeps and a small olive drab green helicopter had landed nearby.

"What are the chances of that?" Chief mumbled.

"You thinking what I'm thinking?" Johnny asked. "You still know how to fly one of those things?"

"I think so…I mean, it's like riding a bike, right?"

"Guys, what's going on?" Switch shadowed behind them, interrupting their conversation.

"Look over there." Johnny stepped back and pointed down the road, a hint of excitement in his voice.

"Looks American," Switch suggested.

"It's an MD500," Chief relayed. "Aka Little Bird. We used them all the time for Delta operations. They're small and light enough to land into the bed of a pickup truck. The main issue is that it looks like it landed at the intersection with the lane that leads to the installation. It could be crawling with troops."

"How do they have an American chopper?" Switch wondered aloud.

"During the 80's war on drugs, we supplied the Burmese with a few helos…If we can get to that bird, it could be our ticket out of here," Chief speculated.

"But how do we get it started? We don't have the keys. Do we jump it or what?"

"No keys. Only a starting button, levers and pedals," Chief replied as Johnny surveyed the area around them, making sure the leviathans were still gone.

"Well, that's good."

"Yeah, well, it's still gonna be a huge challenge. I'm not seeing any troops, but we won't know for sure until we get down there. The one positive is that the compound is probably a half-klick from there, so that should give us enough time to start her up."

"Enough time to start her up?" Switch repeated. "How long do we need?"

"It's not a drone, Switch. In a perfect environment with a pilot who does this every day, about two mikes."

"Chief, two mikes? That's a long freakin' time."

"In a perfect environment…"

"Right, you said that. Are you sure there isn't a better plan?"

"It's our best option. Put it this way: we could be in a Thai hotel by nightfall."

"Forget the hotel. Just give me some ice-cold water," Johnny replied.

"Man, that sounds so go—," Switch half-smiled, but he quickly trailed off, hanging his head low.

"You alright?" Chief asked.

"I'll be alright…I just can't stop thinking about Bling and what he did for us…him and Mack."

"Honestly, I'm right there with you," Johnny replied. "I wasn't really serious about the boy sacrificing for us, but the fact that Bling gave up his life willingly…man, he certainly put his words to action, that's for sure. But what's eating at me most is that I never apologized to the guy. I treated him pretty badly."

"I'm feeling it too," Chief confirmed. "But right now we need to stay focused. What Bling and Mack did for us is deserving of the highest honor and soon we'll have all the time we need to grieve. They're gone, but we're still here and we have a mission to complete. They would want us to complete it."

"Roger that. I'm good to go," Switch replied.

"You know I'm ready, boss."

"Good. Switch, get the kids. Johnny and I will cross the road and provide cover."

"Roger that."

FORTY-ONE
HELO

Chief sprinted across the pot-holed road first, sliding down into the ravine and propping up his MP5 where the long grass met the concrete road, covering Johnny. Once Chief was in position, Johnny raced over, but when he reached the ravine, he stepped on a muddy section and slipped down to the swamp, landing face down and taking in a whiff of the moist, black mud. He shook his head, regaining his composure and pushed himself up on all fours, but when he turned to examine the swamp his eyes were filled with nothing but leathery, reptilian skin. He had landed only a few feet from the leviathan's cousins—three massive saltwater crocodiles, resting halfway out of the brackish water and basking in the shards of sunlight.

I haven't come this far to be eaten by no croc, he thought.

"Johnny, move slowly," Chief insisted, trying to keep from yelling. "I've got a bead on the closest one, but if I shoot it could give away our position."

Johnny closed his eyes and dug his boots into the mud for a sure grip, trying not to make any sudden movements.

Not wanting to take any more time, Chief motioned for Switch and the kids to cross over. Mike and Sam ran across first and Switch took up the rear.

"Oh my!" Sam muttered to herself as she saw Johnny lying next to the crocodiles. Seconds later, Johnny put all his energy into his legs and sprung up and crawled away. The croc swung its tail and snapped its jaws, but it wasn't interested in Johnny; it quickly quieted down, returning to its tranquil sunbath.

"Man, you have a knack for living on the edge, brother," Switch stated as Johnny met them at the top of the bank.

"Thank you, God, for answering my prayer," Sam mumbled as they trekked down the road, checking for anything that might want them dead.

"Did you...you prayed for me?" Johnny asked somewhat surprised.

"Yeah, I did," Sam responded as they moved along the top of the ravine to stay hidden.

"Thank...thank you," Johnny glanced at her, looking down, embarrassed at his earlier contentiousness with her.

"Don't mention it. You'd do the same for me, right?"

"Umm...I'd...I'd like to think so...maybe...I don't know."

"Well, you sacrificed your life to rescue me. Surely, you would pray for me, too."

"Yeah, you know what? You're right. I think I would."

"Good," she gave him an affirming smile. Johnny nodded, signifying that there was no offense between them and also to honor Bling—even though he didn't entirely agree with everything he shared.

"Alight, Johnny and Switch, y'all cover me while I go check out the bird. If it's unlocked, I'm gonna fire it up. Once you see the blades turning full speed, move out with the kids.

"We're ready," Mike suggested as he put his arm around Sam.

"Good. Now everyone pray. This is it."

Chief climbed up the ravine and stepped out behind one of the jeeps where he had a full view of the lane leading to the compound. He squinted to see better, but it was too dark to see more than a few meters. He rested against the jeep and reviewed the small helicopter about 15 meters away.

He took a deep breath and moved out from behind the jeep, sprinting toward the helo and keeping his finger on the trigger, ready to fire. He reached the chopper and tested the door, opening it on the first attempt.

Oh, thank God. Now, let's hope I remember how to fly this thing, Chief muttered as he took a seat inside. He reached up for a headset and slid the muffs over his ears, studying the controls.

Okay, collective, starter button, throttle, rotor, foot pedals. I've got this, he stated aloud, encouraging himself.

"What's taking him so long to start it?" Switch asked, the stress obvious in his words.

"It's harder than riding a bike," Johnny suggested. "He'll get it. Probably getting his bearings."

"Getting his bearings? Oh, man. I definitely need to start praying."

As soon as Switch replied, the rotor started up, spinning slowly.

Woosh, woosh, woosh...

Johnny scrutinized the lane leading to the compound, hoping they would meet no resistance. As the blades rotated faster, Chief motioned for everyone to move out.

Johnny reached the little bird first and laid down on his stomach, his gun pointed down the lane. Switch struggled to hold his rifle with one arm while Mike and Sam climbed into the back of the helo.

Ratatat...ratatat...ratatat...zip, zing, zoom! Two soldiers were sprinting down the dirt lane, firing their rifles at the chopper, but they were more than a hundred meters away and their Kalashnikov rifles lacked the accuracy and power to do any sizeable damage.

Johnny waited for the soldiers to get close enough, steadying his gun. Moments later they appeared and he pressed the trigger.

Phttt! Phttt! Phttt! Johnny struck one of the soldiers in the neck, dropping him instantly. The other soldier dove for a nearby tree as the bullets from Johnny's gun kicked up dirt at his heels.

The soldier hid behind a tree at the edge of the swamp and radioed in for reinforcements, but they were already on their way.

"Johnny...Switch, let's go!" Chief radioed loudly, raising his voice over the helo's loudly churning blades. Switch climbed inside and Johnny stepped onto the chopper's landing skid as two military jeeps drove up from the compound and stopped at the intersection, unloading several soldiers who fanned out across the lane, waiting for the order to fire.

Johnny cracked off several rounds as Chief aggressively pulled up on the collective, lifting the helicopter off the ground.

Seconds later, Chief watched as one of the jeep's passenger doors opened and the general appeared, giving the order to fire.

"Man, I'd like to take him out!" Chief fumed as Switch tried to get a view of what he was looking at.

Sing, ping, thunk! The soldiers emptied their rifles at the helo, the bullets ricocheting off the spinning blades, but one of them penetrated through the door, hitting Chief's right shoulder, causing him to let go of the throttle.

"Argh!" he cringed, trying to maintain control of the chopper.

Johnny held onto the helo's door frame with one hand and fired his gun until it was empty.

"I'm out," Johnny indicated, climbing inside.

"Chief's hit, Johnny," Switch spoke up, trying to hold pressure on the wound from behind him.

"Don't worry about me, drop the general!" Chief exclaimed.

"I'm out of bullets," Johnny indicated.

"Chief, RPG! Ten o'clock!" Switch shouted, spotting a soldier loading the grenade into the launcher.

"Hold tight!" Chief yelled, banking the helo hard to the right. As the helo rotated around, Johnny got a full view of the soldiers and the general.

"God, you're gonna have to take this guy out! We need your justice...and Your protection," Chief shouted.

"Amen!" Sam replied.

He hadn't even finished his prayer when Johnny watched two leviathans crawl out of the swamp near the soldiers. They raised their tails high into the air, slicing into the troops and battering them until they were unrecognizable.

"I think your prayer worked...look!" Johnny exclaimed, pointing to the leviathan as they shredded through the soldiers, scattering their body parts across the lane and surrounding the general, almost as if they knew he was their leader.

The massive creatures whipped their tails violently and opened their jaws wide as Johnny had seen them do with Bling. Seconds later they had clamped their teeth around the general's body, one on each side of him, tearing him apart until they each had a large piece hanging out of their jaws, his blood oozing to the ground.

"Let's get out of here," Chief suggested as Johnny helped him pull back on the chopper's controls, lifting up over the lush, green treetops and flying toward the mainland.

"Chief, when you find a safe spot, go ahead and land so I can dress your wound," Johnny spoke into the headset's microphone.

"No, I'm good. Have Mike hold the clotting agent on it. If I land, we won't have enough fuel to make it to the Thai border."

"Roger that, boss," Johnny replied as he removed his personal medical kit and handed it back to Mike. Mike pressed the clotting gauze against his wound and he winced in pain. He tried hard to stay focused, but he had lost quite a bit of blood.

As they flew over endless rows of rice and small mountains, Sam wondered if she and Mike were finally safe. Even though they weren't home yet, there was a peace she hadn't felt since arriving in Burma. Then she thought of her parents and how she would have to explain everything to them, but that would be a welcome relief compared to what she had already endured.

"Guys, low fuel light is on," Chief announced.

"We're landing then, right?" Switch asked nervously.

"No, we're only five nautical miles to the border. We're gonna try to make it."

"I was afraid of that," Switch replied unenthusiastically.

"Johnny, check the map for our coordinates and tune into the air distress frequency on the coms. Maybe we can hail someone."

"Copy, boss," Johnny replied, turning the dial to the correct frequency. "Mayday! Mayday! American rescue team needs emergency assistance. Multiple wounded at the…Salawin River, West End Zone. I repeat, multiple wounded needing assistance just inside the Thai border."

As Johnny called in their position, the engine sputtered and they quickly lost altitude.

"Guys, hang on, I'm setting her down hard in that clearing by the river…that should be the border."

Everyone clutched their seat tightly as Chief maneuvered the helo another 50 meters, eventually setting it down on the sandy riverbank, barely inside the Thailand.

Mike peered out his window at the river's semi-choppy, brown murky water and turned to the opposite window to see the uninterrupted clusters of pine trees. They were in the middle of nowhere.

Chief pulled off his headset and opened the helo's door, stepping onto the landing skid, removing his vest and exposing his blood-soaked shirt.

Johnny looked him over, noting his pale skin. "Chief, here, sit down. We need to patch you up before we move."

"Good…agh…idea," he replied as Johnny cut open his shirt and cleaned out the wound, plugging it with a new clotting gauze and taping him up.

"That should hold you for a while," Johnny indicated. "What's the plan?"

"From the old map I was looking at earlier, there's a Thai village a few klicks upriver to the east. We'll leave a note inside the bird and head that direction."

"Chief, what if the Burmese Military find the chopper? We'd be giving away our location?" Switch responded.

"I don't think they want to risk an international conflict by going after Americans inside the Thai border. We'll take our chances."

"Roger that."

Johnny scribbled a quick note and left it on the helo's seat and they all took off up the sandy shoreline, but they didn't even get a few feet before Chief collapsed under extreme pain.

"Chief, are you okay?" Sam asked, kneeling down to help him as everyone rushed to his aid.

"Guys, I'm not gonna make it to that village. Y'all let me rest. Just come back and get me."

"Not a chance, boss. We've come too far. We stay together," Johnny replied.

They rested for a short time when Sam's ears perked up.

"Do you guys hear that?" she asked, looking down the river.

"I hear it," Mike replied.

"Sounds like an outboard motor," Johnny suggested.

"It could be Burmese or Thai. Let's move back inside the tree line," Chief instructed.

"Right," Johnny replied. "Mike, give me a hand."

As they stood Chief up, a black Rigid Inflatable Boat rounded the river's bend from the south and was approaching at a high rate of speed. Johnny and Switch were still carrying their MP5s when a commanding voice boomed out of the boat's loudspeaker in a foreign language.

"Too late, we've been made," Johnny stated.

Everyone stood motionless, their backs to the boat, waiting for Chief's orders.

"Boss, what's your call here?"

"Throw your guns down and lay down on the sand, face first."

"You sure about—"

"Do it, Johnny," he interrupted. "We're in no shape to fight anyway."

Johnny reluctantly threw his weapon into the sand and bent down on his knees, eventually laying stomach first with Switch and the kids on the dry sand.

"I hope you're right about this, boss. I'm not gonna be tortured in a Burmese box."

Hearing Johnny's words, Mike grabbed Sam's hand and bolted for the trees.

Pow...pow...pow! One of the boat's crewmembers fired warning shots from his rifle and Mike and Sam abruptly stopped running, dropping face first into the sand, bracing for the worst.

As the boat roared out of the water onto the shoreline, Chief spotted an orange racing stripe on the side of the hull and the crew's yellow uniforms.

Almost instantly his tension lifted and he laughed.

"Chief?" Switch asked, confused by his unusual demeanor.

Seconds later, the boat's crew disembarked with their weapons drawn and Johnny turned to see what Chief was laughing at. When he saw the racing stripe, he joined in laughing, almost hysterically.

"Am I missing something here?" Switch asked as the crew put their knees in everyone's back, zip cuffing their hands together.

"Argh," Switch yelled as a sharp pain traveled from the middle of his back through his broken arm.

"Royal Thai Navy Coast Guard...they must have heard our distress," Johnny called out.

"What does this mean?" Sam asked.

Chief smiled at her. "It means we're going home."

FORTY-TWO
IMPRISONED

A short Thai nurse in an all-white uniform pushed Chief in his wheelchair down a long concrete corridor, his arm patched up in a sling. A guard followed them as they entered the brigade, rolling him into one of the eight cells and locking the barred doors behind them. Johnny was lying on a concrete bunk in one of the cells when he saw him roll in.

"Hey, boss, we thought you got a ride out to that Thai hotel you told us about...so much for that plan," he mumbled, his voice bouncing off the drab gray cinder blocks.

"Yeah, I can't believe they threw us in the brig," Switch spoke up as he stood at the cell door, his forehead pressed against the cold but humid steel bars, unable to see further than a few feet on each side of him.

"Can you blame them?" Chief responded. "They saw a downed Burmese Military helo and us with our military gear and guns. It's a wonder they didn't shoot us on sight."

"I suppose you're right," Switch replied, looking over the makeshift cast the nurse fixed him up with.

"I'd take this any day over leviathan," Sam spoke up from the end of the cell block, her soft soprano voice tempering the harshness of the brigade.

"Yeah, and no torture-happy Burmese Military," Mike replied from the next cell over.

"Randall is sorting it out now," Chief reported. "We should be out of here soon."

"What's next when we get back to the States?" Johnny asked sincerely.

"We get the kids back to their folks," Chief replied.

"I figured that much…but what about the bigger picture? It just feels like things are different now."

"You're right. They are different. There are a couple things on my agenda…things I need to do. What Bling said got to me. I'd like to shift focus and help a non-profit or something. Maybe I can provide security or assist with human trafficking operations—you know, on our downtime."

"I thought you'd be going to Russia to bust up the men behind the human trafficking ring we encountered…I'm sure there's more involved."

"Yeah, well, I'm also not stupid. Russians are a little too crazy for me, but I will be passing along what we know to Interpol."

"Boss, if you're serious about helping a nonprofit, I did some training with a faith-based group in Texas back when I was on the force. Ambassadors United in Houston. They offer a great certification course, but they also reach out to victims, johns and traffickers at massage brothels, shady motels, and truck stops— even the red light districts on the streets. That might be an option for you."

"Sounds perfect. I'll check them out when I get back."

"It's interesting that you say that, Chief," Sam interjected. "I'd like to do something along those lines as well. When I get back, I'm gonna make sure my mind is right and all that, but then I'd like to share my story with young people, maybe even hold events at middle and high schools to help kids see the dangers of human trafficking."

"That's awesome, Sam," Switch encouraged her. "There are so many young people who get caught up in human trafficking through someone they met online. Young people need someone like you to tell them the truth—and you have a great story to grab their attention."

"Thanks, Switch," she replied. "I would like to ask you a favor though since you're good at computers and all."

"Yeah, sure, anything I can do."

"Thanks. Well, when we first got to Burma, I met a girl at a brothel. She was trapped there...and she risked her life to help us escape. I don't know what happened to her, but the last thing she told me was that she wanted me to locate her parents so they would know she's alive."

Chief perked up. "Her name wouldn't be Kylee, would it?" he asked.

Sam jumped from the bunk and stood at the cell bars, clutching the smooth steel. "How...how do you know that, Chief?"

"She led us to you and Mike. She's not in the brothel anymore. She's safe. I'll fill you in on the long flight home."

"Oh, thank you...thank you, God!" she nearly yelled.

"She's strong, like you, Sam," he replied. "I believe God was working through every detail that y'all endured."

"I know He was," she replied, smiling wide, tears of joy creeping from her eyes.

"Mike, what about you?" Chief asked. "What will you do when you get back to the States? I'm curious."

"Me? I just want to see my family, grab a good burger and sleep in my own bed for about a month."

"I think we all have that as one of our goals," Johnny replied.

"Chief," Switch interjected somewhat somberly. "Are we going back for Mack...and maybe even Bling?"

"I don't like leaving them behind, but I can't put anyone's lives at risk," Chief spoke delicately. "I know this though, we need to notify next of kin and plan a celebration of life."

"Where are you gonna get a pastor to conduct the ceremony?" Switch asked.

"Honestly, I think I'll set it up and speak a little. I mean, why pay some religious guy who didn't know them? We knew them best. Besides, Bling said all believers are priests anyway. If you all want to help, let me know."

"You're really taking what he said to heart, huh…good for you, I guess."

"I'd love to help out," Sam replied.

"Count me in as well," Mike spoke up.

"Boss, you're organizing the ceremony?" Johnny asked. "So, what's the plan? Country line dancing and Budweiser for all?" he giggled.

"No, I've turned the page on all that. I'm not going to be living for only me anymore. I'm going to live for God. In honor of God and Bling, no alcohol."

"Man, what is the big deal with alcohol?" Johnny asked, shaking his head. "You're the only guy I know who could drink me under the table…you don't really want to lose that honor, do you?"

"There's no honor for me in that. I'm leaving that life behind. As Bling said, alcohol didn't give me anything but depression and drama anyway."

"Wow…I guess I never imagined I'd hear you say something like this," Johnny scratched his head.

"When we were on the platform, Bling and I had a deeper conversation about drinking after everyone went to sleep—and it made a lot of sense. I want to experience more of God…this life is too short."

"Great, so you're going the route of the typical Christian, eh? I guess that comes with the territory—you gotta hate beer, queers and baby killers," he laughed by himself.

"Come on, Johnny; it's not like that. Bling shared some stuff that opened my eyes…that's all."

"You've got me curious now," Switch asked, jumping into the conversation. "What was it that he said about drinking that changed your mind?"

"Well, for one, I've never had that joy he was talking about, and I want it. I want to be filled up with God's Spirit—and Bling said it starts with the tongue, like being filled up on liquor. He also said alcohol is associated with death, not life."

"What did mean by that?" Switch asked.

"He simply challenged me to consider the effects of alcohol and how it's connected to so many disastrous things, not just drunken driving accidents, but drownings, suicides, divorce, and even domestic violence. He also showed me in the Bible where God destroyed the earth through water because of man's corruption and how the drama started again when Noah planted a vineyard and got drunk. The same thing happened after God destroyed Sodom. Lot got drunk right afterward and his daughters laid down with him and they ended up having babies who became the fathers of the enemy tribes of Israel…that's not a coincidence if you ask me."

"I've got all the respect for Bling, but it wasn't right for him to force his convictions on you, boss," Johnny insisted.

"He wasn't forcing his convictions on me. I had some questions about it and he answered them. Honestly, it was me waking up to wisdom."

"I suppose what he said is true," Switch responded.

"Honestly," Sam interrupted, "If you think about it, what Johnny said about Christian supposedly hating certain things, all that has to do with death. Abortion certainly isn't about life…and we all know two of the same kind can't produce life."

"When you look at it that way…" Switch suggested.

"That's very true, Sam," Chief replied and continued. "Bling said the Devil has a lot of people all twisted up to where they think something is good for them when really it's evil. He also said it's the Devil's goal to get people locked up in things that cause death because he isn't all-knowing and he doesn't know who will wake up to their true identity and assault his dark forces to take back territory for God's kingdom. He said he's not a risk-taker because there's no faith in him. He would rather kill people from the start…and if he can't do that, he'll have them living under death, so they'll be stuck in darkness doing his bidding."

"Man, boss, you're really starting to talk like Bling," Johnny surmised.

"I think it's a good thing, Chief," Sam spoke up.

"Thanks. I know this isn't gonna be for everyone—and I'm not trying to force anyone to accept my new way of life."

"It makes perfect sense to me," Sam replied. "I'm making some changes as well. "Hey, Switch, you never said what your plans are after this. I'm just curious," Sam asked, wondering if he was having the same transformation.

"Are you kidding me," Johnny laughed. "He's a gamer. He's already fanaticizing about the next new game release."

"Actually, Johnny, I was thinking about writing a book."

"You…write a book?" Johnny snorted as he laughed.

"Seriously, what we've seen and lived through should be documented," Switch boldly maintained. "We all know it wasn't crocs that killed all those Japanese troops on Ramree; it was those leviathans."

"You're right about that," Johnny replied with a more serious tone. "But who is going to believe you? I'll be sure to pick up your book in the fiction section."

"He's got a point there, Switch," Chief suggested. "It's a nice idea, but I'm not sure who will believe it."

"Yeah, if we had some pictures…maybe," Mike submitted.

"In this day and age, people wouldn't believe that either," Sam suggested.

"It's probably best people don't know though, don't you think?" Chief asked. "I mean, people get crazy with these types of things. Scientists and journalists would want to visit and more people would die."

"You're probably right, Chief. Maybe fiction would be better."

FORTY-THREE
THE LETTER

One Month Later

A fter cleaning this place up, it actually resembles a church," Switch submitted as he looked at Sam. "And you, young lady, did an excellent job decorating for the ceremony. We needed a woman's touch around here."

"It was the least I could do for all Bling and Mack did for me and Mike."

"Chief, did you invite the new team members?" Johnny asked.

"Invite them to a celebration of life for our former brothers who died during an operation? Do you want them to get scared off?"

"I guess you have a point there."

"Besides, they both just left active duty combat and they're still trying to navigate through some PTSD like y'all were when I first found you guys. I wanted to give them a clean slate."

As they were talking, a loud knock came at the front door.

"It's a little too early for guests," Johnny surmised, checking the time displayed on his military watch.

"Switch, can you grab that?" Chief asked as he finished setting up the guest book on a small table.

"Sure," he replied. He opened the door and the sun's golden rays beamed into his face. He held his hand over his eyes and squinted to see through the blur of dust, catching a glimpse of a mail jeep as it sped back down the long driveway.

Hmm...must have left a package or something, he thought as he checked around the door, but there were no boxes. He turned to walk back in and saw a tan envelope stuck in between two of the church's old wooden slats. He pulled the envelope out and scanned the front, his face turning pale and eyes widening with wonder as he stumbled back inside.

"You okay, Switch?" Chief asked, staring at his dropped jaw.

"What's wrong with you, nerd? Looks like you just got a court order in the mail or something."

Switch didn't reply. His eyes were pinned open as he held the envelope out to Chief.

"What's this?" he asked, looking at the Asian writing on the stamps and checking the sender's information.

"William "Bling" Graham. Is this some type of joke?" he asked, looking everyone in their eyes.

"Don't look at me; I'm not that demented," Johnny insisted.

"Okay, this is really strange," Switch spoke up.

"Wait, is that a letter from Bling?" Sam asked quietly, stepping up to look at the envelope.

Mike was filling the punch bowl when he overheard and moved in to get a look.

"It's addressed to you, Chief, open it," Johnny suggested.

Chief was fixated on the envelope, still contemplating how it was possible that he was holding a letter from Bling. He rotated it in every direction, examining its thickness, bending it and holding it up to the light.

"Maybe he sent this before everything happened," Chief reasoned aloud.

"Boss, open it already," Johnny insisted, becoming impatient.

Chief slowly tore open the letter, unsure how to process what he was feeling. Inside the envelope were several handwritten letters. He unfolded them and silently read the first few words. As he read, his eyes burned, not wanting to blink for fear he was in a dream.

"Well, what's it say?" Johnny asked as everyone anxiously awaited his reply.

Chief hesitated for a moment and cleared his throat.

"It...it says Bling is ah...alive," Chief stood silent, his eyes locked onto the letter.

"What? That's impossible!" Johnny insisted, jerking the letter from his hands. "I saw the leviathan surround him..." Johnny paused. "They...they killed him!"

Johnny's eyes bulged as he read the first paragraph, his mouth falling agape and the papers falling out of his hand and floating to the ground. "I don't understand...how—"

Sam picked them up and read the first page aloud.

"Yo! Hey everyone," she began to read. "I know dis will come as a shock, but I made it out y'all; I'm alive. I sent dis here letter off as soon as I could. I've been stayin' at a small village not far from where we encountered da leviathan. Oddly, da name of da village is Sane. Da village is full of—"

"Boss...Sane...that's the same village we saw on the map," Johnny excitedly interrupted.

Chief remained quiet as he stared at Bling's bunk area and his footlocker that no one had the guts to remove.

Sam continued reading. "I ain't understand how dis happened, but them village peeps ain't Burmese, they is Chinese—and let me tell you, they is like sheeps wit'out a shepherd. No one has heard of da Lort here, and there's obviously a language barrier, but I'm workin' on sharin' Him through pictures."

"Chief, Chinese? That would explain the Chinese symbols we saw everywhere," Switch interjected. "When we got back I researched to see if anyone wrote about the leviathan and I came across some historical documents about the Chinese invading the Burmese lands centuries ago. Maybe those people are remnants of the invasion."

Chief didn't reply; he was still in shock about Bling. "Sam, keep reading," he asserted.

"Sure...He continues...Since I arrived here, the village peeps think I'm sumptin' special. For one, ever since I got here, they ain't heard from dat crazy Burmese general. They tell me dat every week he would raid da village for resources, especially they kids. When I first got here, all I seen was a bunch of old peeps, but I ain't realize da young peeps live mostly in hiding, but not anymore..."

"Wow, this is crazy," Switch interrupted. "Sorry, Sam, go ahead."

Sam nodded and kept reading. "These peep's ancestors have lived here a long time, and they even got old writin's about da leviathan. They too call it tanniyn, and they really scared of 'em. Another reason they took to me so well is dat I strolled in here in da middle of da night unharmed. They say dat don't happen. No one can go out at night—and a few times they have attacks durin' da day even. They lost six peeps in da last few months, but since I've been here, ain't nobody seen or even heard 'em. I believe it's a setup for me to share da Gospel wit' 'em."

"God is so amazing," Sam muttered under her breath, unable to restrain her comment. She looked up at the ceiling as though to acknowledge God and went back to reading, eager to finish the letter.

"I figure I'll stay here and share for another month or so, but after dat, I'm goin' back to dat Pattaya place. They is so many men locked up in darkness there and da Spirit of da Lort is upon me to preach da Good News to set 'em free. I got da liberty them guys desperately need and it would be criminal for me not to help rescue 'em. Chief, you knows what I'm talkin' 'bout. How's the Green Beret motto go? De Oppresso Liber...I ain't know Latin and all dat, but I know it means freedom for da oppressed...and I intend to introduce them boys to da Spirit of da Lort to get 'em truly free...dat's gonna be my new mission."

"Well, it sounds just like Bling," Johnny stated, "But I still don't understand how he made it out of that jungle."

"I'm just in awe right now," Switch commented. "I'm truly at a loss for words."

"We all are," Chief replied. "Keep reading, Sam."

Sam nodded.

"I'm guessin' y'all wonderin' how I got outta dat jam with them leviathan?"

Everyone nodded together, almost as though Bling was there with them, their emotions sending mixed signals.

"When y'all went to sleep dat last night, I was prayin' and God took me to Genesis and showed me how He originally gave mankind dominion over da serpents. Then He took me to da book of Luke where Jesus told His disciples dat they could cast out evil spirits 'cuz He gave 'em power over serpents and all the power of the enemy. I also read in Acts 'bout Jesus leavin' da Holy Spirit to restore our dominion to be powerful witnesses for Him. I 'bout shouted, y'all! Yo, I saw dat I had da power over them leviathans all along. At dat moment, I prayed to God and a wave of elation came on me and I felt da need to put myself to da side and take one for da team like Jesus did when He gave up His life for da whole world—I knew it was the only way y'all would live."

Sam paused, pondering what Bling had written, tears blurring her vision. She wiped her eyes and picked back up where she left off. "So, I got up and swam across the swamp to da clearing and started prayin' and singin'. Da more I sang, da more they looked almost hypnotized and it kept them from attackin' me. They was close, real close. Every few seconds they would stomp on the ground and them vibrations shot through my body. Then they opened they mouth. Da sound they made was raspy and they breath supa rank...like rotten eggs or sumthin'. One of them actually flicked its tongue against mines neck. Man, dat was nasty. Felt like slobbery sandpaper...and it was so rough it removed da flesh back there...I'm still healin' up from it. Probably have a scar from dat."

"This is just so surreal," Switch interjected. "I still can't believe Bling is probably still on that island...we need to go back for him!"

"Speak for yourself!" Johnny countered. "I'd be down to send someone to pick him up, but I'm not going anywhere near that cursed place."

"Let's hear everything he has to say first," Chief instructed. "Go ahead, Sam, keep reading."

"Okay," she replied, tracing her finger along Bling's sloppy handwriting to where she had left off.

"When the leviathans surrounded me, they snapped they chompers and let out a low rollin' growl, almost soundin' like thunder. They was so close I could feel they hot slobber splattering on my face. I ain't even gonna lie, at dat moment, when they dino teeth chompin' inches from mines head, fear slipped in. All I knew to do was worship. I sang dat ol' spiritual tune 'bout da blood of Jesus. I sang them words at da top of mines lungs. *What can wash away mines sin? Nothin' but da blood of Jesus? What can make me whole again? Nothin' but da blood of Jesus.* When I started singin' them lyrics, them beasts all of a sudden look confused and snotted and sneezed all over da place—almost like they got dat Coronavirus or sumptin'. It got so bad they had to take a dip in da swamp. It looked like da more I worshiped, da more it made they nostrils irritated."

"Chief, that's what we saw at the truck!" Switch exclaimed. "When that leviathan was about to attack Johnny, it stopped because it was sneezing. That was Bling's doing! He saved us!"

"It was either his worship or the fact that when he sang he sounded like a dying cat," Johnny snickered, but no one laughed.

"God was certainly working through Bling," Chief replied. "Keep reading, Sam."

"I closed my eyes and prayed and sang dat song for a while. Then I felt God's Spirit all ovah me. It wasn't long after dat I fell asleep. When I woke up, da sun was about to set and there was no sign of 'em, so I walked right out of there. I hiked down da trail, took a left at da road, and a few hours later I saw some lanterns on at a village, and I been here evah since."

"I...I don't know what to say right now...this is too surreal; he walked out of there like Daniel did in the lion's den," Sam commented, placing her hand over her mouth to keep from completely losing her emotions.

Chief did his best to keep a straight face as he was accustomed to doing. "I don't think any of us know what to say, but to just thank God that he's alive."

Unable to continue reading for her emotions, Sam handed the letter to Chief. He read silently until he got to where Sam left off and his eyebrows wrinkled as though something didn't make sense.

"What is it?" Switch asked.

"It looks like he wrote to each of us...some personal things...I guess I'll just pass the letters around for each of you to read."

"Nah, read my part out loud," Switch stated.

"Are you sure?"

"We all know each other anyway," Johnny replied.

"That is true. Okay, well, I've got your letter first, Switch."

"What did he write?"

"He begins...Yo Switch, when we was on da platform together, I could tell you interested every time I mentioned da end times stuff. I've always been interested, too—even before I was a believer. Deep down, I knew da truth, and what I really wanted to know was how much time I had to get right before I got left, if you know what I mean. Well, here's da truth about da end dat I want to share pacifically wit' you. I want you to know dat eventually God's gonna do away with them leviathans and everyone dat's an enemy of God, but He ain't gonna destroy da earth by water again like He done in Noah's time. Dis next time, He gonna baptize da world by fire."

Chief glanced at Switch and saw that he was deep in thought and continued reading. "Switch, when God baptized the world with water in Noah's judgment, none of da sea creatures were killed because they was in their own environment, which meant them leviathans and da Devil both escaped alive, but dis next time, God's goin' past da surface; He gonna baptize da world from da inside out in a baptism of fire. These are both powerful pictures in da Bible. When a Christian gets baptized in water, their skin gets clean on da outside. Dis is a symbol of their surrendering to Christ and being buried with Him in death and coming up into a new life, but there's an even more powerful baptism than dis; it's called da baptism in da Holy Spirit."

"That's deep right there," Sam indicated.

"He goes deeper," Chief relayed.

"Switch, da Holy Spirit's baptism ain't surface. Da Spirit's baptism gets on da inside and removes—or burns up—everything up dat ain't like Christ, slowly changin' everything about you, starting at da tongue and gettin' into da heart. Dat baptism releases yo tongue to boldly tell others about Him and it produces true love, joy, and peace in every area of yo life. If you wanna read about it, check out what happened in Acts in da Bible; it's a promise available to you…and to all who are afar off, as many as God will call. His Spirit is available to you, Switch. If you surrender to God's Spirit, you ain't gonna have to go through no fiery baptism of judgment, 'cuz God already burnt up da impurities in ya. But anyone not submitted to Him will go down wit' da leviathan and da Devil, and I would never wanna see dat happen to you man. You too valuable for dat. Please check out what I'm sayin'."

Switch's eyes were closed tight, contemplating Bling's words. Seconds later, he spoke up. "This is so crazy. Bling's absolutely right. I never knew much about the Bible, but I was always intrigued by Noah's flood and end times stuff—and here he's giving me details that I've never considered. I'm blown away."

"Johnny, he wrote to you next," Chief indicated.

"Well, we know how this will go. He's gonna rail me…but go ahead."

"Johnny, you remind me so much of me—I guess dat's why we bumped heads so much. I know dat when you lost your moms as a kid, you blamed God. I lost my pops at a young age too…made my life miserable…I thought God hated me. Dat's why I turned to gang life. I wanted a regular family so bad. Maybe dat's why you joined up wit' da military and why you still hangin' wit' Chief…for dat brotherhood."

392

"Johnny, I didn't know you lost your mom as a kid," Chief paused from reading, displaying a rare look of compassion.

"I...I never talked about it," Johnny revealed. "I don't know how Bling figured that out..."

"Well, hold on, because there's more," Chief replied, continuing to read the letter.

"Johnny, there's something else we have in common. We both have a past and we know we're sinners. In da Bible, Jesus picked a disciple who was known as a sinner to da whole community. His name was Levi. Maybe you can see where I'm goin' wit' dis. Levi was collectin' taxes from da people when Jesus came to him and told him just two words. He said, "Follow Me." After dat day, everyone called him Matthew, which means gift. Johnny, you a Levi like me. We're both from leviathan. We've both had our violent, aggressive tendencies, and everyone knows the monstrous things we've done. But we ain't try to hide nothin' neither. Jesus came for people like you and me...for those who know they ain't perfect and need a Savior. When you leave everythin' and follow Jesus, you'll get a new name, a new purpose, and a new family, just like Matthew. I pray you do dat, 'cuz you gonna be supa blessed...and you'll be a force to be reckoned wit' in da kingdom."

Johnny stood quiet, interlocking his hands on his head, thinking about Bling's words.

"A new name, a new purpose, and a new family..." Sam spoke aloud. "That's the opposite of what Bling said the Devil lost...his name, his purpose, and his family...that is so intriguing."

"Good thoughts, Sam," Chief proposed.

"Chief, did he write anything to me or Mike?" she asked.

"Actually, he did...to both of you," Chief indicated. "I've got Mike's letter next. Mike, do you want to read it for yourself?"

"No, go ahead and read it."

Chief nodded and read the letter aloud. "Mike, I know I ain't know y'all kids all dat well, but I know God's tryin' to get y'all attention. He was speaking to you from da beginnin', givin' you all them symbols, but you disregarded Him. He's givin' you

393

another chance, my friend, and He wants to show you amazin' things. Da truth you searchin' for ain't in science. Natural understanding and formulas can never explain supernatural designs. Only through faith in Jesus Christ can you understand who God is, who you is, and what your purpose is in life. Mike, I promise dat if you seek out Jesus, you'll find da way, da truth, and da life you seekin'. Draw near to Him and He will draw near to you."

Mike didn't say anything; he stared at the floor, knowing Bling had shared more truth with him in a few sentences than all his teachers had in more than a decade of schooling.

"What about me?" Sam asked excitedly as Chief skimmed the paper. He looked up at Sam and smiled.

"Sam," Chief began reading. "You an amazin' young lady. So strong. So gifted. You been through so much…what a testimony you have already. I feel God protected you so you could help rescue and give hope to others. Them men wanted to exploit you 'cuz they saw an attractive body, but you about to set people free 'cuz of what God's given you on da inside. You will be a modern day Harriet Tubman—rescuing souls and endin' human slavery."

"Sounds pretty accurate to me," Switch replied. "Isn't that what you told us you want to do with your life?"

"Yeah…yeah it is," Sam beamed as Chief continued reading. "Sam, there's a story in da Bible about a former harlot named Rahab dat I think will help you on your new mission. Rahab had only one encounter with God's people and she never returned to her old life of prostitutin'. Amazin'ly, she became part of Jesus' family tree. Sam, God has awakened you to da horrific crime of traffickin', and He's gonna use you to set girls free. When you go out, remembah dat God gave dominion to both man and woman over eve'ythin' dat creeps…over all them creeps! Make sure to listen to His voice. He'll help you conquer the creeps, lead you away from evil, and take you to where the Rahabs need His freeing touch."

Chief handed her the letter and she smiled, pressing it to her chest, a tear tracing down her cheek and cutting a line through her light makeup.

"What did he write to you, boss?" Johnny asked.

"Yeah, I'd like to know as well," Sam replied, figuring Bling had saved the best for last.

Chief remained quiet.

"You're gonna share with us, right?" Johnny pressed him a little more.

"He...umm...he only wrote a couple sentences. Nothing major."

"Okay, well, what did he write?"

"Well, he...umm...he wrote...Chief, You purchased what everyone considers a holy buildin' and transformed it into an office to help rescue and protect people, but now it's time to shift directions. Your main role is now to rescue people and help transform them into holy buildin's. Help da religious understand dat da goal is to raise up more holy people, not more holy buildings."

"That's what he wrote to you?" Johnny asked.

"That's all."

"I don't get it."

"You don't, but I do...I know what I need to do."

"Well, okay then," Johnny stated, not really sure what to make of Chief's statement. "I do have one question tough...what are we gonna tell these people showing up for his celebration of life—that this dude they thought was dead is really alive?"

"Right, this old church will be packed with people," Chief smiled. "It's all coming together."

"I'm not following."

"Not yet, but I am. There's another Guy who everyone thought was dead but is still very much alive. I know exactly what to do."

AFTERWORD

This book was based on a dream—a very odd dream. When I shared it with friends and family many were so fascinated by the details that they told me I should write it into a movie script, but there were a few problems. First, I'm no scriptwriter, but the main issue was that the dream was incomplete. I couldn't see the leviathan in my dream—only its back as it glided through the swamp water. I told the Lord that if He wanted me to do something more with the dream, He would need to provide all the details. Guess what? He did. The very next night I dreamed again, but this time I only saw exquisite details of the monstrous beast. That sealed it for me. I stepped out in faith and prayer to write my first fiction novel.

I pray you were encouraged by it in some way.

For God speaks once,
And *even* twice, yet no one notices it
In a dream, a vision of the night
When deep sleep falls on men
While slumbering upon the bed,
Then He opens the ears of men
And seals their instruction,
That He may turn man aside *from his* conduct,
And keep him from pride...

Job 33:14-17 AMP

SCRIPTURES MENTIONED

1. God doesn't dwell in buildings- Acts 7:48
2. Your body is God's building- 1 Corinthians 3:16; 6:19; 12:27
3. God is a God of Justice- Isaiah 30:18; Acts 17:31
4. You must replace the demons with the Holy Spirit- Matthew 12
5. Only God is good- Mark 10:18
6. The Holy Spirit provides freedom- 2 Corinthians 3:17
7. The Holy Spirit builds character- Galatians 5:22
8. You must renew your mind- Romans 12:2
9. All things work together for good for those who love God, to those called according to His purpose- Romans 8:28
10. People are made in God's image- Genesis 1:26; James 3:9
11. God has hidden eternity in our hearts-Ecclesiastes 3:11
12. Alcoholic drinks bite like a serpent- Proverbs 23:32
13. Jesus is peace- Romans 5:1; Isaiah 9:6
14. Do not be drunk on wine...but be filled with the Spirit- Ephesians 5:18
15. The Holy Spirit provides us with love, joy and peace- Galatians 5:22
16. It is God's good pleasure to give us the Holy Spirit- Luke 11:13
17. Unable to stand in the presence of God- Daniel 5:17; 10:15; John 5:14-15
18. God's Spirit fell on believers- Acts 2
19. If you're weighed down by this world, you will miss God's best- Luke 21:34
20. People in the Bible who got drunk and had problems because of it: Noah (Genesis 9:20-24), Lot (Genesis 19:33-38), Nadab and Abihu (Leviticus 10:1-9), Nabal (1 Samuel 25:2-3, 36-38). Samson's captors (Judges 16:25-30).
21. Wine is a mocker and strong drink is a brawler- Proverbs 20:1
22. Jesus turned the water into wine- John 2
23. Moses turned the water in blood- Exodus 7:14-25
24. Moses delivered the children of Israel through the blood of an innocent lamb- Exodus 12
25. Jesus is called the "Lamb of God who takes away the sin of the world"- John 1:29
26. Jesus shed His blood on the cross- Colossians 1:20; Hebrews 9:22
27. Jesus gives freedom over sin, through His blood- Ephesians 1:7
28. Yeast is a symbol of sin- 1 Corinthians 5:6-8
29. Decay is a symbol of sin- Psalm 16:10
30. Jesus saves His people from their sins- Matthew 1:21
31. The enemy attacks the mind- 1 Peter 5:8; 2 Corinthians 4:4

32. Spiritual warfare manifests in the flesh- Matthew 16:23; John 8:44-45
33. The Devil wants to keep you from God- 2 Corinthians 4:4
34. The Devil wants you to think that God isn't good, that He's holding out something good from you- Genesis 2
35. God made a covenant with Noah to never again flood the entire earth with water, and the sign of the covenant was a rainbow- Genesis 9
36. The Devil is behind all evil- Genesis 2; John 10:10
37. God wants all people, men and women, boys and girls, filled up with His Holy Spirit- Joel 2:28
38. The Devil was once a type of military general in heaven- Ezekiel 28:14-16
39. God kicked the Devil out of heaven- Ezekiel 28:16-17; Revelation 12:7-9
40. Humans can communicate directly with God- Genesis 3:8; Exodus 3:4-6; Acts 9:3-7
41. God doesn't automatically live in (or possess) humans- Exodus 19:5
42. God wants us to invite Him in- Revelation 3:20
43. The Devil succumbed to pride- Isaiah 14:12-14; Ezekiel 28:17
44. God gives us a choice to serve Him or not- Joshua 24:15; John 7:17
45. Leviathan is king over all the children of pride- Job 41:34
46. Pride turns us into an enemy of God- Proverbs 16:5, 6:16-17; 1 Peter 5:5-9
47. Adam and Eve succumbed to pride- Genesis 3:5-6
48. The Devil used a serpent to tempt Adam and Eve- Genesis 2-3
49. God is opposed to the proud, but He gives grace to the humble- 1 Peter 5:5-6; Isaiah 57:15
50. Jesus did the Father's will- Luke 22:42
51. Love God and love your neighbor- Matthew 22:36-40
52. God took away the Devil's legs- Genesis 3:13-15
53. The Devil is that Great Dragon- Revelation 12:9; 20:2
54. God will eventually lock up the Devil in hell- Revelation 20
55. Anyone who doesn't live for God is a pawn of the Devil- 1 John 3:1-10
56. There is a day of judgement coming- 2 Peter 3:9
57. There are only two kingdoms: God's or the Devil's- 1 Corinthians 6:9-10; Ephesians 2:2
58. The high priest wore a gemmed breastplate- Exodus 28:30
59. The high priest presented the blood of an innocent sacrifice on the Day of Atonement- Leviticus 16
60. Jesus is God with skin on- John 1:14
61. Jesus came and shed His blood on the cross as a sacrifice for sin- John 12:27
62. Jesus is sinless- 1 John 3:5; 1 Corinthians 5:21; Hebrews 4:15

63. Jesus defeated sin and death- 1 Corinthians 15:55-57
64. God gives understanding to those who ask- James 1:5
65. High priest from the tribe of Levi- Exodus 32:26-29
66. Biblical marriage is between one man and one woman- Genesis 2:24
67. Marriage is a mystery…it is spiritual- Ephesians 5
68. Every person is born into sin, and their father is the Devil- Romans 5:12; Psalm 51:5; John 8:44-45
69. Jesus offers us new life- Ephesians 2
70. Christ gives us a new name and purpose- Revelation 2:17; 3:12; Jeremiah 29:11
71. Believers are to help pull people out of the darkness- Acts 26:17-18
72. Believers are to be married to another to bear spiritual fruit for the Lord- Romans 7:4
73. Believers have a ministry of reconciliation- 2 Corinthians 5:18-21
74. God will defeat the Devil at the end of the age- Revelation 20:7-10
75. The Lord will defeat Leviathan with his sharp sword- Isaiah 27:1
76. To see the kingdom, you must be born again- John 3
77. The earth was once formless and void- Genesis 1
78. Anyone who doesn't believe in Christ is condemned- John 3:18
79. For a person to be saved, they must repent and believe- Mark 1:15
80. God has given everyone a measure of faith- Romans 12:3
81. Religion consists of attempting to please God through the traditions of men, works and external beautification. Mark 7:8; Ephesians 2:8-9; Luke 21:5-6
82. Relationship is knowing God and allow Him to live in and through you. Colossians 1:27; 2:9-10; John 1:10-13
83. God gives us a new heart and it affects everything- Ezekiel 36:26; Hebrews 8:10; 2 Corinthians 5:17
84. Only Jesus offers eternal life- Acts 4:12; John 14:6
85. Some ministers are blinded by money and power- 1 Timothy 6:10
86. God wants to make you His holy building- 1 Peter 2:5; Ephesians 2:19-22
87. The body of Christ is the church- Colossians 3:15; Romans 12:4-5; Ephesians 4:15; 1 Corinthians 3:9, 3:16, 12:13; Acts 12:5
88. We are priests unto God- 1 Peter 2:9; Revelation 1:6
89. We are destined to be conformed to Christ- Romans 8:29
90. The same Spirit that raised Christ is alive in believers- Romans 8:11
91. The same spirit that killed Christ is alive in the sons of disobedience- Ephesians 2:2
92. Stephen's address about the true church- Acts 7:37-60
93. Jesus is the believer's cornerstone- Ephesians 2:19-22
94. Let your light shine before men, that they may see your good works and glorify God- Matthew 5:16

95. The Tower of Babel compared to God's true Church- Genesis 11 & Acts 1-2
96. The early church met in homes- Acts 1:13
97. We must watch out for the lust of the eyes, lust of the flesh and the pride of life- 1 John 2:16
98. God will help remove anything that doesn't benefit your relationship with Him- John 15:1-27
99. Those who bear weapons act as God's servants, avengers of His justice on evildoers- Romans 13:4
100. Blessed be the God Most High, my Rock, who trains my hands for battle- Psalm 144:1
101. Bible battles- Joshua 6, 7-8; Judges 7-8:21; 1 Samuel 4:1-11; 15, 17; Revelation 19:11-21
102. Bible love stories- Genesis 17-18, 29; Ruth 4; Matthew 1
103. Daniel and the lion's den- Daniel 6
104. Say "I do!" to Christ by confessing with your mouth and believing in your heart that Jesus was raised from the dead- Romans 10:9-10
105. Noah Drunkenness- Genesis 9:21
106. Lots Drunkenness- Genesis 19:30-38
107. The Spirit of the Lord is upon Me to preach the Gospel- Isaiah 61:1; Luke 4:18
108. God originally gave man dominion. Man lost it, but Jesus restored it through the power of the Holy Spirit- Genesis 1:26; Luke 10:19; Acts 1:8
109. Take up your cross and follow Jesus- Matthew 16:24-26
110. Worship confuses the enemy- 2 Chronicles 20:22
111. God will baptize the world in fire- Matthew 3:11; Acts 2:2-3; 2 Peter 3
112. Water baptism- 1 Peter 3:21; Colossians 2:12
113. The Holy Spirit removes impurities- Ezekiel 36:25-26
114. The Holy Spirit is a promise to all who God calls- Acts 2:39
115. Jesus calls Matthew (Levi) to be His disciple- Luke 5:27-32
116. Jesus came for sinners- Luke 5:32
117. Jesus is the way, the truth, and the life. No one comes to the Father but by Him- John 14:6
118. Draw near to God and he will draw near to you- James 4:8
119. Rahab in the Bible- Joshua 2
120. Rahab in Jesus' family tree- Matthew 1:5